Jenny ~~Holmes~~ ... ...
and adults since her early twenties, having ..ad series
of children's books adapted for both the BBC and ITV.

Jenny was born and brought up in Yorkshire. After living in the Midlands and travelling widely in America,
she returned to Yorkshire and brought up her two
daughters with a spectacular view of the moors and a
sense of belonging to the special, still undiscovered
corners of the Yorkshire Dales.

One of three children brought up in Harrogate,
Jenny's links with Yorkshire stretch back through
many generations via a mother who served in the Land
Army during the Second World War and pharmacist
and shop-worker aunts, back to a maternal grand-
father who worked as a village blacksmith and pub
landlord. Her great-aunts worked in Edwardian times
as seamstresses, milliners and upholsterers. All told
stories of life lived with little material wealth but with
great spirit and independence, where a sense of community and family loyalty were fierce – sometimes uncomfortable but never to be ignored. Theirs are the
voices that echo down the years, and the author's hope
is that their strength is brought back to life in many of
the characters represented in these pages.

Also by Jenny Holmes

The Mill Girls of Albion Lane
The Shop Girls of Chapel Street
The Midwives of Raglan Road
The Telephone Girls

and published by Corgi Books

THE LAND GIRLS
AT CHRISTMAS

Jenny Holmes

CORGI BOOKS

TRANSWORLD PUBLISHERS
61–63 Uxbridge Road, London W5 5SA
www.penguin.co.uk

Transworld is part of the Penguin Random House group of companies
whose addresses can be found at global.penguinrandomhouse.com

Penguin
Random House
UK

First published in Great Britain in 2017 by Corgi Books
an imprint of Transworld Publishers

A CIP catalogue record for this book
is available from the British Library.

ISBN
9780552173667

Typeset in 11.5/14 pt New Baskerville ITC by Jouve (UK), Milton Keynes
Printed and bound in Great Britain by Clays Ltd, Bungay, Suffolk

Penguin Random House is committed to a sustainable
future for our business, our readers and our planet. This book is made
from Forest Stewardship Council® certified paper.

MIX
Paper from
responsible sources
FSC® C018179

1 3 5 7 9 10 8 6 4 2

In memory of my mother,
Barbara Holmes, 1923–2008;
a proud Yorkshire Land Girl

CAST OF CHARACTERS

LAND GIRLS

Brenda Appleby – worked at Maynard's butchers before she became a Land Girl

Dorothy Cook

Hilda Craven – warden at Fieldhead House hostel

Joyce Cutler – farmer's daughter from Warwickshire

Jean Fox – worked as a bank clerk before she joined the Land Girls

Kathleen Hirst – former hairdresser from Millwood

Grace Kershaw – daughter of Burnside's pub landlord and blacksmith

Ivy McNamara – former shorthand typist

Una Sharpe – former worker at Kingsley's Mill in Millwood

Elsie Walker – former groom from the Wolds

BURNSIDE VILLAGERS

Maurice Baxendale – owner of a car repair garage

Bob Baxendale – Maurice's brother and caretaker at the Institute

Lionel Foster – the local landed gentry, owner of Hawkshead Manor

Alice Foster – his wife

Shirley Foster – their daughter, in the WAF

Jack Hudson – Bill Mostyn's footballing pal

Cliff Kershaw – landlord of the Blacksmith's Arms and blacksmith

Edgar Kershaw – his son, an RAF gunner recently shot down over Germany

Thomas Lund – Bill Mostyn's footballing pal

Edith Mostyn – Land Girls representative

Vince Mostyn – her husband, owns a tractor repair company

Bill Mostyn – their son, works for his father and is thus exempt from call-up

Geoffrey Somers – Master of the Burnside hunt

BURNSIDE FARMERS

Joe Kellett – farmer at Home Farm

Emily Kellett – his wife

Frank Kellett – their son, village misfit

Henry Rowson – shepherd

Peggy Russell – widowed three years before, her farm is growing run down

Roland Thomson – farmer at Brigg Farm

Neville Thomson – his son

Horace Turnbull – farmer at Winsill Edge

Arnold White

ITALIAN PRISONERS OF WAR

Angelo Bachetti

Lorenzo

TOMMIES

Albert

Jack

CANADIAN AIR FORCE

Squadron Leader Jim Aldridge

Flight Lieutenant John Mackenzie

CHAPTER ONE

'Can you believe it? You need eighteen coupons for a decent winter coat.'

'And seven for a pair of shoes.'

'It'll get worse before it gets better. I hear they're thinking of cutting us back to forty-eight coupons for the whole year.'

'Blimey – we'll all be in rags by this time next year.'

The bus from Millwood rattled along country lanes, up hill and down dale, while Una Sharpe listened to the humdrum complaints of other passengers. She swayed in her seat and looked steadfastly out of the window at the dull brown moors rolling away into the distance, trying in vain to put to the back of her mind memories of busy, bustling streets lined with cinemas and shops, of smoking mill chimneys overlooking snaking canals. It was wartime and it was goodbye to all that. *Countryside, here we come*.

'Bye-bye, Una,' her brother Tom had called as he saw her off from the bus station. 'Be good!'

Dressed in her new uniform of brown corduroy breeches and green jumper under her short khaki overcoat, she'd waved and tried her best to look cheerful for his sake. Inwardly, she quaked in her stout lace-up shoes. *What have I done?* she'd wondered.

What had she done? The question still nagged at her as the bus trundled on. It gave way on a narrow, winding road to a lumbering tractor, paused to drop off passengers at the end of a farm lane and waited in a lay-by for a horse-drawn cart piled high with mud-encrusted turnips to pass. *I've answered the call – that's what I've done.*

'Calling all women!' On a stifling hot day in the August of 1941, words on a poster outside the Millwood town library had drawn Una in off the dusty street. It had been the middle of a heatwave. Headlines in the *Daily Mail* crowed over HMS *Severn's* sinking an Italian submarine in the Med. In smaller print, people were urged to dig for victory and not to mind about the shortage of razor blades, babies' feeding bottles and frying pans – not to mention clothes to keep you warm once winter came.

Why should it only be the Millwood men who join the war effort? she'd wondered. Why couldn't it be the women, too? Why not her – Una Sharpe, twenty years old and the youngest of five? Three of her brothers had already enlisted – two into the Merchant Navy and one into the army – with only Tom at home because of a bad accident at work in Kingsley's Mill that had left him with one arm paralysed. Apart from him, there was no one to object to her leaving home; no mother or father – they were both a long time dead – and no sweetheart either. In other words, she was fancy free . . .

In a spirit of derring-do she'd marched into the

library and asked to see the latest copy of *The Land Girl* magazine.

'Here you are, love.' The librarian had slid a copy of the magazine across the counter. 'Calling All Women!' shouted the front page. Inside there were photos of Land Girls in action – smiling girls picking apples and others atop hay wagons. The weather was sunny and everyone was smiling. 'Give me a job where you can see results!' was the clarion call. There were knitting patterns, too, a cake recipe using powdered egg, a short story and a crossword competition. It showed the enamelled Land Army badge with a wheat sheaf at its centre, inside a gold circle topped by a red and gold crown. Una remembered now that she'd been particularly smitten by that badge.

'Don't get too excited,' the middle-aged librarian had counselled, having taken a good look at the small, slight girl with dark-auburn hair and lively hazel eyes standing across the counter from her. 'It'll be a while before you're old enough to join up and do your bit.'

Una had taken offence. 'What do you mean? I was twenty in April just gone.'

'You don't look it,' had been the dubious response. 'More like fifteen, if you ask me.'

'Twenty,' Una had insisted before flouncing off. *That's it – I'll show them I can do any of the work the Land Army throws at me,* she'd decided then and there. *I can climb up haystacks and pick apples along with the best.*

It was hard now for her to recall that summertime

3

spirit. The good weather had broken and the air had turned crisp before Una had filled in her recruitment form and sent it off to Land Army HQ in West Sussex. Red tape delayed her acceptance until late October when she'd picked up the letter from the mat with trembling hands. She'd torn open the envelope and read its contents.

'Tom – I'm in!' she'd called up the stairs of the tiny terraced house that she'd shared with her brothers since the deaths of their parents from scarlet fever when Una had been just eight years old.

Tom came down and took the letter from her. He read it slowly then returned it without saying a word.

'See – the Land Army wants me.'

'Good for you,' he said with downcast eyes. 'That only leaves me not doing my bit.'

'Tom, no one expects . . .' She tailed off into an awkward silence. How could she explain without hurting his feelings that it felt like the right time for her to fly the nest? She took a deep breath then hurried on. 'I'm to be paid a weekly wage of thirty-two shillings, minus fourteen for board and lodgings . . .'

A week later, it was goodbye to 15 Wellington Street, goodbye to Douglas Fairbanks Jr and Bette Davis on the silver screen, goodbye to stone-flagged pavements and narrow alleyways. Hello, green grass and stunted hawthorn trees, black-and-white cows, grey sheep and dreary, rain-filled skies.

'A penny for them,' her neighbour commented as the bus plunged down a steep dip in the road. The woman who perched on the seat next to Una was not much bigger than her but her white hair was scraped back into a plaited bun and her thin face was lined. A wicker basket was balanced precariously on her knees, filled with a week's meagre rations of butter, sugar, meat, tea and jam.

Una pushed sad thoughts of home to the back of her mind. 'They're not worth it,' she said with a smile.

'Get along with you,' the woman persisted. 'I can tell by your uniform that you're doing your bit for King and country. That has to be worth crowing about.'

'I've just joined up, so there's not much to say yet,' Una explained.

'It'll get you out of munitions work, at least.' Her neighbour gave a knowing nod. 'Give me work on the land above standing in a freezing-cold factory making bombs to drop on Jerry any day. That's your only other option, unless you join the Wrens or the WAAF and that's not my idea of fun either. I'm Emily Kellett, by the way.'

'Una Sharpe.'

'Well now, Una Sharpe, who's meeting you off the bus when we get to Burnside?'

'I'm expecting a Mrs Mostyn to meet me outside the Blacksmith's Arms at four o'clock.' She trotted out the details that she'd rehearsed in her mind during the long journey.

'Ah yes, Lady Muck.' Emily leaned across the aisle to poke a fellow passenger in the arm. 'You hear that, Polly? Una Sharpe here has joined the Land Army and she's been thrown in at the deep end,

5

make no mistake. She's being met off the bus by Edith Mostyn, no less.'

'Good luck to her.' The stout woman named Polly stood up from her seat and rang the bell. 'This is where I get off,' she announced as they came to some crossroads. She delivered a parting shot as the bus juddered to a halt: 'Take it from me, lass – there will be far worse things than Edith Mostyn for you to worry about. Just ask Emily here – she knows what I'm talking about.'

'What do you mean?' Una felt a dart of apprehension that she quashed with a strong dose of common sense. It was obvious that these two old women were enjoying putting the wind up a raw recruit.

'Take no notice,' Emily said stiffly as she cast a daggers-drawn look at Polly's broad back view.

Two boys in school uniform ran, satchels flapping against their thighs, from the back seat of the bus down the central aisle. They hopped off behind Polly and landed with a triumphant splash in a muddy puddle. The bus pulled away again, turning left at the junction, following a sign that read: 'Burnside – 1 mile'.

One mile to go. Una took a deep breath and stared ahead to discourage Emily Kellett from pestering her. They sat in silence until they came to the first houses in the village where three more passengers alighted. As the bus eased forward again, Emily gathered her belongings and started to make her way to the front, stopping to talk to a young man in RAF uniform.

'Hello, Edgar, I wasn't expecting to see you back home this side of Christmas,' she said, loud enough for everyone to hear.

'Hello, Emily.' The two-word reply was delivered in a monotone – a clear message for the old woman to mind her own business. He kept his eyes fixed on the road ahead, fingers tapping the back of the empty seat in front.

Thick-skinned Emily ploughed on. 'I take it you're home on compassionate leave? Isn't that what they call it?'

He scowled then looked away without answering and by now the bus had pulled up under an inn sign saying: 'Blacksmith's Arms'. All the remaining passengers, including Una, stood up and filed towards the front, leaving Emily no option but to alight into the pub yard. The RAF man sat in surly silence until the bus was empty. Then he got off and lost no time in making his way towards the pub entrance. He walked with a limp and paid no attention to the goings-on around him.

A pale young woman appeared in the doorway to greet him. She was tall and her fair hair was swept clear of her face, kept in place by a green scarf tied turban-wise around her head. 'Edgar,' she said with a brief smile before taking his hand and ushering him inside.

Intrigued by the subdued greeting and wondering who they were, Una turned her attention to the other people in the yard. She watched Emily hook her shopping basket over the handlebars of an old bike before stepping up spryly into the saddle and pedalling off down the main street. A broad-shouldered, balding man wearing a leather apron came round from the back of the low stone building to speak with the bus driver who gestured towards the pub entrance. The man in the apron then disappeared inside. So far as Una could see, there was no sign of Mrs Mostyn, the Land Army representative she was due to meet.

She waited for five minutes, watching more comings and goings. A lad with a mop of floppy ginger hair led a shire horse up the street, the *clip-clop* of its hooves warning of their approach. Una had to step to one side as they crossed the yard and the boy tethered the grey horse to a post outside a wide entrance into what she guessed was the blacksmith's forge, which formed an L-shape with the main building. He glanced at Una in her too-large, brand-new uniform and gave a smirk. Then he turned his attention to the rider of a motor bike who had screeched to a halt outside the pub.

'Watch out, Malcolm Campbell!' the boy yelled, as the horse tried to shy away from the engine's throaty roar. 'You'll have Major yanking this post clean out of the ground if you're not careful.'

Una was surprised to see that the rider of the motor bike was a woman in faded overalls, mud-caked wellington boots and a black leather pilot's jacket. Catching sight of Una, she ignored the farm lad, set her bike on its stand, then made a beeline towards her.

'Una Sharpe?' she asked.

'That's me.'

'I'm Brenda Appleby. Mrs Mostyn says to tell you she's running late. You're to hang on here until she arrives.'

She rolled her eyes as she delivered her message,

as if to say sorry for the delay. 'I told Her Ladyship I could give you a ride out to Fieldhead on the back of the bike to save her the trouble, but she was having none of it.'

'Are you a Land Girl?' Una couldn't be sure, since Brenda wasn't in uniform. She looked a real tomboy, with the fleece collar of her jacket turned up. Her dark hair was cropped short and her face still tanned from the long, hot days of summer.

'I am,' Brenda confirmed. 'No need to look down your nose at me. I've been digging ditches out at Joe Kellett's place since six o'clock this morning – that's why I look such a sight.'

'I never said a word,' Una protested.

'You didn't have to – I saw your face. The Kelletts have never heard of the fifty-hour week and such like. They'll work your fingers to the bone doing mucky jobs they're too idle to do themselves.'

Una decided on the spot that she liked Brenda, who was as fresh and keen as the air out here, with a cheeky expression and a cheerful disrespect for her employers. 'I think I sat next to Mrs Kellett on the bus.'

'Talked the hind leg off a donkey, did she?'

Una nodded.

'That'll be Joe Kellett's wife, then.' At the sound of a car engine, Brenda glanced towards the crossroads. 'Here comes Mrs Mostyn now, if I'm not mistaken. I don't know why she bothered sending me on ahead, except she likes to dish out orders every chance she gets.'

The gleaming black car purred to a halt outside the pub and Edith Mostyn stepped out from behind the steering wheel – a trim, slim woman in a tweed jacket and matching skirt, well shod in soft leather shoes with small heels that clicked across the cobbles towards Una and Brenda. 'Thank you, Brenda, that will be all,' she said dismissively.

Brenda shrugged and sloped off to kick-start her bike before riding off in a cloud of petrol fumes and blue smoke.

'You must be Una.' Edith's tone was self-assured. Her arched eyebrows and high forehead gave her an aristocratic air. 'I was expecting someone a little more robust. And you're not very tall, are you?'

Una frowned. 'I passed my medical with flying colours – eyes, ears, heart – the lot.'

'Very well – beggars can't be choosers, I suppose.'

If this was meant to throw Una, it had the opposite effect. Her dander was up and she drew herself up to her full five feet one inch. 'I've worked on the looms for six years in Kingsley's Mill without any complaints. I've never had to take a single day off work except for the week four years ago this December when I stayed at home to nurse my brother after he came out of hospital.'

A frown creased Edith's powdered brow. 'As I say, I wish the recruitment criteria for the Land Army were a little more rigorous when it comes to physical aptitude, but sorry to say, these things are out of my hands.'

Recruitment criteria? Physical aptitude? What was the daft bat going on about? And what kind of welcome was this? Una's hands gripped her small brown suitcase more tightly and she clamped her lips firmly shut to stop a strongly worded retort from springing out.

'Anyway, ours is not to reason why. My job is to take you out to your billet, which as you know is to be the hostel at Fieldhead House. There are twenty girls there at present, including Brenda, whom you just met. You will be allocated a single bed with two blankets and a change of sheets every Monday morning. One bath per week is permitted, according to a strict rota. Meals will be served promptly at seven o'clock in the morning and six in the evening, unless you make prior arrangements with the warden. You will take sandwiches with you to eat in the middle of the day. Is that clear?'

As day, Una thought sulkily. 'Yes, Mrs Mostyn,' she replied.

'Very well. Get into the car.' Edith took Una's case and placed it in the boot while Una slid onto the brown leather passenger seat. 'You will be provided with a bicycle on which to ride out to the various farms in the locality. You do ride a bike, I suppose?'

'Yes,' Una fibbed. In fact, she'd never been on one in her life.

'The work will be varied.' Edith turned the car around in the yard, ignoring the red-haired lad's protests as she drove too close to jittery Major. 'It will include milking cows and cleaning out cowsheds, hen houses and stables. You will be expected to feed chickens, cows and sheep, dig ditches, thin turnips, bag potatoes, and so on. There will be no official training – you will have to learn on the job. Do you have any questions?'

Feeding, digging, thinning, bagging – the words didn't connect with any activity Una was familiar with so she quickly changed tack. 'Yes. How much time off do we get?' There must be some relief from farm work, surely.

By now they were on their way, past a row of stone cottages and a chapel, out into open countryside before Edith replied. 'Saturday afternoons and Sundays are free for girls to do laundry and catch up on letter writing, and so on.' Behind the wheel, she cut a slight but stylish figure, tilting her carefully coiffed head backwards to peer out through the windscreen and tooting her horn loudly at stray pheasants and cats. 'You will be homesick at first – that goes without saying. But bear in mind that this is your contribution to the war effort. We must all do our bit without complaining.'

Una couldn't argue with this so she let another silence develop, following the progress of a cloud of starlings as they rose from the ground and gusted overhead. She would be glad when they reached the hostel and she could meet the other girls. If they were all like Brenda, she felt sure she would like them and she would soon settle in. Meanwhile, she took in her surroundings.

The single-lane road beyond Burnside grew narrower and steeper and the signs of habitation more scattered. Drystone walls criss-crossed the hillsides, sometimes rising almost vertically to craggy ridges – dogged feats of back-breaking building work that beggared belief. Every now and then they came to a roadside barn and more rarely still to a ruggedly built farmhouse whose roofs were covered in moss and whose small windows let in little light. Their front gardens were black and bare. At one farm, a dog heard the approach of the car and ran out into the road, straining at his chain. The farmer's wife came to the door and called the dog's name, turning her back on the car as she sent him back into his kennel.

'That's Mrs Peggy Russell,' Edith informed Una. 'Her husband died of pneumonia three years ago so the farm is run-down. We'll help her with lambing when the time comes.'

How was it possible for an elderly woman to live so far out here by herself? Una wondered. Wasn't she frightened of having an accident, of falling down the stairs, say, and not being found for days afterwards? She was about to voice this thought when Edith slowed the car and turned in between tall stone gateposts then carried on along a straight, tree-lined drive towards an imposing house in the distance.

Una glimpsed the name, Fieldhead House, carved into each gatepost. The grandness of the house surprised her – it was three storeys high with tall pillars supporting a porticoed entrance and long windows down to the ground – the kind of dwelling where she could imagine ladies in crinolines and lace sweeping down long corridors and gentlemen in white breeches calling for their carriages to take them into town. As they drew closer, however, she saw that the stonework around the doorway was crumbling and the window frames starting to rot.

Weeds grew out of the high gutters, downpipes leaked and chimney stacks leaned.

'So this is the Land Army hostel?' Una turned to Edith with a questioning look. 'Or are there more modern buildings round the back?'

'This is it,' came the short answer. Edith stopped the car by the main door and got out to open the boot.

Una looked up at what she took to be the bedroom windows and spotted several faces staring down at her. The owners of the faces made no attempt to hide their curiosity or to step back out of sight. *Here goes!* Una thought as she took her suitcase and followed Edith up a set of wide stone steps and through the open door. *In for a penny, in for a pound.*

'There you are!' a voice cried and a figure flew down the stairs at the far side of the black-and-white tiled hallway. It was Brenda, still in overalls but minus her wellingtons and her airman's jacket. 'Girls, Una has arrived,' she called over her shoulder. 'Come and say hello.'

Several figures appeared on the landing that overlooked the hallway. They studied the newcomer but didn't hurry to follow Brenda's lead. They were a mixed bunch, Una thought – some tall, some small, some pretty, some not. Take the round-faced, dark-haired one who leaned her elbows on the banister and assessed Una from head to toe. She looked sturdy, with strength equal to any man's. By way of contrast, there was a tall, limp-looking girl whose breeches seemed to swamp her skinny thighs and who hung back in the shadows while the others slowly descended the stairs.

'Which room will she sleep in?' Brenda asked Edith.

'I'm afraid I'm not privy to that information. My job is simply to deliver new recruits safely to the door and make sure that they understand what's expected of them now that they've signed up.'

'Let me go and ask Mrs Craven.' A curly-haired girl jumped down the last three stairs and shot off through a side door.

'Thank you, Elsie.' Edith looked at her watch then decided to follow her. 'It's time for me to leave Una in your capable hands,' she told Brenda, who gave a mock curtsey behind her back.

'There's a spare bed in the room I share with Kathleen. You could have that,' Brenda suggested to Una. 'Ma C's a decent sort. I'm sure she won't mind us taking matters into our own hands. Kathleen, come and say hello.'

A strikingly pretty girl stepped forward. Her fair, wavy hair hung loose around her shoulders and she was already changed out of her uniform into a blue blouse with zig-zag patterns and a white collar, teamed with wide navy-blue slacks and white canvas shoes.

'Kathleen Hirst, meet Una ... Oh dear, I've forgotten.'

'Sharpe with an "e",' Una said. *Silly of me to bother about the 'e' at a time like this.* She blushed bright red.

'Una Sharpe with an "e" – that's the ticket. Kathleen, how do you feel about Una sharing our room? I think we'll get on like a house on fire, don't you?'

'I'm sure we will.' Despite her answer, a wary

Kathleen looked as though she would reserve judgement. 'Where are you from, Una?'

'From Millwood,' she replied with as much confidence as she could muster. The cool stares of her fellow Land Army girls were playing havoc with her nerves.

'Me too. I was a hairdresser on Union Street. Do you know it?'

Una shook her head. 'I was in the weaving shed at Kingsley's. They didn't want to let me go, what with the orders for cloth for army uniforms rolling in. My answer was that there were plenty of older, married women queuing up to fill my shoes, given half a chance. We young ones should put on uniform and do our bit.' *No need to go on about it,* she scolded herself. Nerves again – sometimes they turned her into a blabbermouth.

'Let me show you our room.' Brenda seized Una by the arm and led her up the curving staircase. 'It's number eight at the end of the corridor, overlooking the elm trees at the back of the house so it's nice and private. The bathroom is just here on our left – handy if you need to spend a penny in the middle of the night.'

Una hung back. 'Shouldn't we wait until we get the go-ahead?' There didn't seem to be any sense in jumping the gun, but Brenda was having none of it.

'Here – what do you think?' She flung open the door.

The bedroom was large and chilly. It contained a small fireplace, a large mahogany chest of drawers, a washstand and three single beds – one with a bare mattress and two neatly folded grey blankets. The bed nearest the window was badly made, with sheets and blankets askew and hair curlers scattered across the pillow.

'I know.' Brenda sighed when she saw Una's gaze fall on the untidy bed. 'Kathleen's the limit as far as tidiness goes. And would you believe it – she faints at the sight of blood and is scared of the dark.'

'La-la-la!' Kathleen had followed Una and Brenda into the room. 'Not true! You can't believe a word Brenda Appleby says.'

'All right then – she did pass out at her first sight of Emily Kellett wringing a chicken's neck but she hasn't done it since,' Brenda conceded. 'But I swear, hand on heart, that I found her in the yard of the Blacksmith's Arms one night last week, quivering like a jelly when she had to walk back home all on her ownio.'

'I can't say I blame her.' Una didn't fancy the long walk along unlit lanes either. She laid her case on the unmade bed, awash with anxiety as she thought of the days ahead. 'They won't make me wring chickens' necks, will they?'

'No, that's usually left to the farmer's wife.' Brenda winked at two girls who had drifted into the room after Kathleen. 'Anyway, it's nothing to fret about. Once the chicken's head is clean off, wifey puts it back down on the ground and watches it run around in circles for a minute or two until eventually it runs out of steam. That's it – one more poor chicken is bound for the pot.'

'No!' Una stared wide-eyed.

'Without a word of a lie,' Brenda said solemnly then burst out laughing. 'Now, pigs – they're a different matter. Nobody likes to hear a nice fat porker squealing while its throat is being cut, not even me. The sound carries from here to Timbuktu.'

Una put her hands over her ears. Volunteering for the Land Army had just become the worst mistake she'd ever made. Not only could she not ride a bike, but she'd never walked down an unlit road or been anywhere near a headless chicken, let alone a pig in its death throes.

Kathleen took pity on her. 'I told you – don't listen to Brenda,' she said as a matronly figure in a white apron came into the room. Kathleen turned to the newcomer with a winning smile. 'Mrs Craven, it's all right if Una takes Eunice's old bed, isn't it?'

'I don't see why not,' the warden readily agreed, taking in Una's small stature and pale face and judging how many bowls of porridge and fish-paste sandwiches it would take to build her up. The new girl's coat hung off her like a scarecrow's jacket and was six inches too long if it was an inch. Still, she seemed to have a bit of backbone about her and might do well enough in the end. 'Unpack your things and put them in the bottom drawer. You can hand over your coat to me, if you like – I'll see if I can unpick the shoulder seams and take them in for you. I might as well alter the hem while I'm at it.'

Una responded with a wan smile. 'Ta very much. This was the smallest size they had.'

Relieved of her coat, the other girls could see just how slight Una was.

'Goodness gracious, there's not an ounce of flesh on her,' the round-faced, sensible-looking one commented, sturdy arms folded across her chest as she leaned against the doorpost.

'That's Joyce Cutler giving you the once-over,' Brenda commented. 'Otherwise known as the Warwickshire Amazon.'

'Pleased to meet you,' Joyce said. 'I grew up on a farm outside Stratford-upon-Avon. We farmers' daughters can't afford to be weaklings.'

'They must put something in the water down there,' Brenda said with her customary wink as she dragged the lanky girl with straight, dark hair into the room. 'And this is Jean Fox. She's a town girl, like you and Kathleen. She worked in a bank, no less.'

Not like me, then. Una knew there was a world of difference between a mill girl and a bank clerk, and she immediately felt she had little in common with the sour-looking Jean. She watched the stocky, homely-looking warden leave the room carrying her coat over one arm then forced herself to engage in conversation. 'How long have you been a Land Girl, Jean?'

'Over a year.' The answer came slowly, unaccompanied by a smile.

'And how do you like it?'

'Not at all.' This reply was quick and emphatic. 'It's slave labour, if you ask me – scratting around in a turnip field on our hands and knees, tying sacks around our heads and shoulders to keep off the rain.'

Una's stomach tied itself into a knot but she did her best to sound upbeat. 'You know what they say – we all have to do our bit.'

Jean and Kathleen seemed unconvinced but Joyce and Brenda chorused their agreement.

'Come on, girls – let's leave Una to her unpacking.' Brenda took the lead as usual. 'It'll be supper time before we know it. Boiled beef and cabbage – six o'clock on the dot.'

To Una's surprise, Jean was the last to depart.

'It beats me why they gave you Eunice's bed,' she said with a grim shake of her head. 'Especially when she's not even cold in her grave.'

This was another shock to Una's system and she let it show. 'What do you mean?'

'She died, didn't she?'

Various images flashed into Una's mind of poor Eunice being caught up in the spikes of a giant threshing machine or else treading on an unexploded landmine in a farmer's field. 'Where did it happen?' she asked.

'Here in the hostel kitchen,' Jean explained in a voice that conveyed no emotion, though there was a dark glint in her eye that made Una dread what was to come. 'It was me who first smelled the gas.'

'Gas?' Una echoed.

'Yes, Eunice stuck her head in the oven while Mrs Craven was in town collecting the week's rations and we were all out at work. She'd timed it just right and given up the ghost long before we found her. Dead as a door nail.'

Una grimaced then shuddered.

'It turns out she was expecting,' Jean explained with unconcealed glee as she sauntered out of the room. 'Three months' gone and no one knows who the father was. Eunice made sure she took that little secret with her to her grave.'

CHAPTER TWO

Lying in a dead girl's bed, Una lay awake listening to the slow, regular breathing of Brenda and Kathleen and to the wind whistling through the trees in the copse of elms behind the house. The window frame rattled and the floorboards creaked whenever any of the girls in the rooms along the landing needed to use the toilet. She had kept her socks on in an attempt to keep warm and was glad she had brought her thick winter nightdress with her.

If it was as cold as this in early November, she dreaded to think what it would be like when the frost really took hold.

At four o'clock, just when Una was at last drifting off to sleep, Brenda sat up in bed with a start.

Una opened her eyes to see her throw back her blankets and creep over to the window. 'Blooming thing,' she muttered as she drew back the curtain and tried to wedge a rolled-up sock into the frame to stop the rattle. On her way back to bed, she noticed that Una was also awake. 'How are we meant to get any shut-eye with that racket going on?'

'I can't sleep either,' Una confessed.

'That's common when you first get here,' Brenda sympathized, reacting to the disgruntled moan from Kathleen's bed by beckoning to Una to get up and follow her out of the room. 'Your head's in a whirl, thinking about home and wondering why on earth you let yourself in for this in the first place.'

They were out in the dark corridor and creeping towards the stairs. 'Where are we going?' Una wanted to know.

'To the kitchen, for a cup of cocoa. Might as well, since neither of us is likely to get another wink of sleep before daybreak.'

Una followed obediently, down the stairs and into the hall where they went through the side door into a shabby corridor, dimly lit by a paraffin lamp at the far end. Yellow paint was flaking from the damp walls and there was a musty smell that made Una wrinkle her nose. But when Brenda opened the door onto a large kitchen lit by electric light bulbs and warmed by a wood stove set into an old inglenook fireplace, the smell disappeared.

'Hello, Elsie,' Brenda said to the girl who sat with her back turned, warming her hands at the stove. 'You must be on the early shift.'

Una noticed that the girl was already fully dressed and recognized her as the helpful one who had run off to find the warden soon after her arrival. She was small and wiry, with a healthy head of curly, light-brown hair and a face that seemed to be permanently smiling.

'Yes, worse luck,' Elsie said without letting the smile fade. 'Joyce and I are on milking duty at Home Farm.'

23

'Ugh. What did you two do to deserve that?' Brenda took a drum of cocoa from a shelf then poured milk from a jug into a small pan which she set on top of the stove.

'Don't ask me. All I know is we're due to be washing udders and putting on clamps half an hour from now. Oh, and by the way, take a look at today's rota – you and Una are listed to take over from us at one o'clock.' Elsie stood up and reached for her coat and hat, which she set on her head at a jaunty angle. She pulled knitted mittens out of her pocket and put them on. 'Don't be late,' she warned on her way out.

'Just our luck,' Brenda groaned. 'Still – at least we don't have to cycle out there in the dark.'

At the sound of the word 'cycle', Una frowned.

'What's the matter? Oh, don't tell me – you don't have a clue how to ride a bike?' Quick on the uptake, Brenda grinned broadly.

'I told a fib,' Una admitted. 'Anyway, what's to stop us from going to work on your motor bike?'

'Against the blessed rules, I'm afraid. It's either push bike or Shanks's pony. But don't worry, I can teach you the basics once it gets light.'

It would be the first of many lessons that Brenda had to teach her, Una was sure. 'Ta, you're a pal. How long have you been here, anyway?'

'This is the end of my third week. Before that, I was working behind the counter in Maynard's butchers in Commercial Street, Northgate.'

'Well, blow me down.' Una had assumed that Brenda was an old hand at the Land Army game. 'Were you here when Eunice . . . did what she did?'

'It happened the day after I arrived – here, in this very kitchen. It was a big shock, I can tell you.'

Una took in the orderly rows of green and cream canisters on the shelves and the spoons, knives and ladles hanging from hooks above the up-to-date gas stove. 'And no one knew she was expecting?'

'Not even the baby's father, if you ask me. Kathleen says Eunice Mason was a shy type who didn't join in much – she knew her a lot better than I did. Personally, I don't understand how anyone keeps a thing like that quiet – I'd explode if it was me and I had to keep it under my hat.'

The mystery and its tragic end kept Una guessing as Brenda served up the cocoa. 'How did her family take the news?'

'I've no idea. As I say, I didn't have a chance to find out much about her. Why are you so keen to know?'

'I'm sleeping in her bed for a start.'

'You're not expecting, though?' Bluntness was evidently Brenda's trademark.

Una gave an embarrassed laugh. 'Definitely not.' In fact, she'd never gone anywhere near that far with a man – not that she would admit this to the worldly-wise Brenda.

'Good. Because I like you, Una Sharpe with an "e", and I'd be sorry if you had to leave on account of being with child.'

'I like you too.' Una smiled back then changed the subject. 'Tell me about Mrs Mostyn. Is she as nasty as that with everyone?'

Brenda cocked her head to one side. 'Now that

you mention it – yes, she is. They say it's because she married beneath her and she's regretted it ever since.'

'Married beneath her?' There'd been nothing to suggest this. In fact, the Land Army representative had been exceptionally well dressed and spoke as if she'd been born with a silver spoon in her mouth.

'She grew up here at Fieldhead House, don't you know?' Brenda tipped the end of her nose with her forefinger. 'It was a private boys' school before the government requisitioned it as a hostel – no hoi-polloi allowed through the hallowed gates. Edith Mostyn's father was headmaster here.'

'And now?'

'Edith has been married to Vince Mostyn for thirty years. They have a grown-up son, Bill. Bill isn't half bad, actually.'

Una noted the twinkle in Brenda's eyes. 'A bit of a catch?' she guessed.

'Yes, and not likely to be called up in the near future because he helps his father to mend Ferguson tractors belonging to farmers all over Yorkshire, according to Grace. Mr Churchill needs men like Bill Mostyn to keep things running smoothly on the Home Front.' Brenda took her empty cup to the tap and rinsed it.

'Grace?' Una prompted.

'Grace Kershaw. She lives at the Blacksmith's Arms with her father, but she's one of us.'

'A Land Girl?'

Brenda nodded. 'She's on the rota to cycle out to Home Farm with us later today. We'll stop by to pick her up on our way there. Grace is a decent sort. You'll like her.'

'If I learn to ride a bike before then, I'm sure I will.' Una wondered if Grace Kershaw was the tall, fair-haired woman she'd seen at the pub door, greeting the RAF man. There was so much to learn in such a short time and she felt briefly overwhelmed.

'You will,' Brenda assured her brightly. 'And it's true what they say – once you learn you never forget.'

It was all to do with balance. Una looked straight ahead at a row of semi-derelict stables in the yard behind Fieldhead House while Brenda stood astride the back wheel holding onto her saddle.

'Ready?' Brenda asked as she shoved hard and set Una in motion. 'Pedal!' she instructed.

Una wobbled slowly across the cobbled, leaf-strewn yard. *Concentrate. Don't look down. Press forward and down onto the pedals.* 'Whoa!' she cried as she leaned like the Tower of Pisa, first this way and then that. She put her foot down just in time to stop herself from toppling to the ground.

'Try again,' Brenda insisted.

Una glanced back at the house to see Jean and Kathleen at an upstairs window. The wind whipped her hair from her face and tore straight through her woollen jumper, but as soon as she realized she had an audience she grew determined to get the hang of it. 'It's all right, I can manage,' she told Brenda, who was standing by. She set off by herself, her hands gripping the handlebars, her feet pedalling slowly. *So far, so good.* She was halfway across the yard, ignoring the raucous call of the rooks circling overhead, eyes fixed firmly on the stable at the far end of the row.

'Use your brakes!' Brenda yelled as a dog burst out of one of the stables in hot pursuit of a squawking red hen.

Too late. Una swerved to avoid the dog and sailed straight into the stable. Luckily a heap of old straw provided her with a soft landing. She got up and brushed herself down.

'Try again?' Brenda enquired from the doorway, the corners of her mouth twitching.

'Yes, stand back – let the dog see the rabbit.' Una picked up the bike and wheeled it back out. She had straw in her hair and the dust had brought on a fit of sneezing, but she would not give in.

'You stick at a job once you've started – I'll say that for you.' Brenda cycled behind Una along the road leading to Burnside.

It had taken most of the morning for Una to master the art of riding a bike but by dinner time she could balance, pedal, change gear and apply the brakes with aplomb. She'd been able to look Jean in the eye as she'd sat opposite her at a long trestle table in what had once been a grand dining room, now pared back to barracks-like efficiency.

'You've got straw in your hair,' Jean had taken pains to point out, her spoon poised over a bowl of beef and vegetable broth.

'Ta for letting me know,' Una had replied, running

28

a hand through her hair and taking quiet satisfaction in watching bits of straw drift across the table and into Jean's bowl.

Now, with her hastily altered coat buttoned tightly across her chest and her hat pulled well down, she braved the wind ahead of Brenda, wobbling every now and then but mostly keeping a steady course until they reached the village.

'Hold on here for a tick,' Brenda shouted outside the Blacksmith's Arms. She asked Una to hold her bike while she went to fetch Grace, who came around the side of the forge wheeling her own bike.

'Tally ho!' Brenda's cry got them moving three abreast, past the terraced cottages and taking the left fork in the road when they came to the chapel. 'Not far now. Home Farm is over the brow of the next hill,' she told Una.

'I wouldn't be in any big hurry to get there if I were you,' Grace warned.

She was dressed today in worn dungarees and wellingtons, with the same green scarf tied around her head. In spite of this, she somehow managed to look graceful, Una thought. She was nothing like Brenda – in fact, the exact opposite, with her fair colouring and serious face, high cheekbones and clear grey eyes.

'Why's that?' Una asked.

'Old Joe Kellett is a hard taskmaster, that's why. He'll throw you in at the deep end, you'll see.'

'He's one of the worst for taking advantage,' Brenda agreed. 'But don't worry, Grace and I will look after you.'

Una's legs ached as they changed into a low gear and pedalled more slowly. The road was bordered by bare hawthorn hedges beyond which lay freshly ploughed, late-autumn fields that had attracted a whirling flock of white gulls.

'Nearly there,' Grace promised as they crested the brow of the hill and Una took in the new vista. 'The farm is nestled in that dip to our left.'

On they rode, buffeted by the wind, until they came to the rough lane leading to Home Farm where they got off and walked, crossing paths with Elsie and Joyce who wheeled their bikes towards them.

'He's in the kitchen with Frank and Mrs K,' Joyce reported without bothering to mention the old farmer by name, her cheeks flushed with the effort of the morning's work.

'What sort of mood is he in?' Brenda asked.

'The usual,' Elsie reported. Her breeches and boots were caked in mud, her curls plastered flat to her forehead.

'He'll have you digging ditches all afternoon, if I know him.'

'Oh no, not again.' Brenda sighed.

So Una was prepared as they arrived in the farm-yard and leaned their bikes against a cowshed wall. She heard the muffled sound of cows mooing and shuffling through their beds of straw and she got a strong, sweet whiff of them as she, Grace and Brenda headed for the porch at the front of the house.

'About time too,' was Joe Kellett's churlish greeting when he opened the door to Grace's knock.

Una had a glimpse of a dark kitchen with low

beams from which hung two sides of bacon and some large cast-iron cooking pots. A small fire struggled to keep going inside a large fireplace, fed only with a heap of coal slacking that sent blue smoke billowing into the room.

'Shut that door after you.' Emily's irritable voice cut through an awkward silence as the old man stuffed his feet into a pair of hobnailed boots. She came forward to make sure he did as he was told, recognized Una and tutted.

Her husband – a thin, stooping man with a shock of white hair – tutted back at her. Over his blue overalls he wore a threadbare overcoat tied at the waist with string. 'What's up with you?'

'They've only gone and sent us their newest recruit,' Emily muttered. 'A fat lot of good she'll be.'

Joe grunted then shuffled off out of sight.

'Muddy boots!' Emily croaked after him. 'I've just got Joyce to scrub that floor.'

Joe came back with a younger version of himself – a skinny man of around thirty whose thick hair was almost black, and whose features were long and pinched, with eyes that were close together and a chin that hadn't seen a razor since the start of the week.

'Frank here will lend a hand with the digging,' Joe told his small team of Land Girls. 'Don't bother talking to him, though – he's deaf as a post. That's right, isn't it, Grace?'

Grace nodded while Brenda raised her eyebrows at Una then each of the girls took a spade from Joe and followed him across the yard. Frank stayed behind to put on his boots and took his time to join them at the edge of the ploughed field behind the cowshed.

'I want all these old twigs and weeds pulled out before you start digging,' Joe instructed. 'You can pile them up to make a bonfire in that top corner. After that, I want you to dig down two spits from end to end, which is fifty yards, give or take.'

Una pulled a face. 'What's a spit?' she whispered to Grace.

'A spade's depth. We'll never get it all done before dark, with or without Frank's help.'

Brenda set to straight away, dragging small branches out of the clogged channel and making a pile for Una to carry up the slope to the corner of the field. All three were hard at work when Frank finally appeared. His father signalled with his hands to show him where to start digging. 'No slacking,' he warned the girls as he left them to it.

Brenda nudged Grace with her elbow and pointed at Frank, who had rammed his spade into the ground and pulled a cigarette from the packet in his shirt pocket the moment his father had gone. 'It's not us who'll be slacking, if the old man did but know it.'

Grace put a finger to her lips. For as long as she could remember, Frank Kellett had been an odd presence in the village, turning up when least expected – at whist drives in the Village Institute, for example, or at Whit Monday processions from the chapel to the cricket field near the junction. He was always on the edge of things, staring and hovering without saying a word. Some put his eccentric behaviour down to his deafness, others to the suspicion that he wasn't quite right in the head. Once in a while there were reports that he'd gone missing for a few days, or else had been responsible for the mysterious disappearance of a child's pet cat or rabbit. No one knew where he went on these silent furloughs or whether the rumours about missing animals were true, but they crystallized over the years and people now preferred to give Frank Kellett a wide berth, whether or not he deserved it.

He smoked his cigarette and watched Una pick up a bundle of wet branches and carry them up the field while Brenda cleared the ditch and Grace started to dig.

'Oh no, this is all we need,' Brenda sighed, ankle deep in mud as she held out her hand and felt the first cold spots of rain.

Grace looked up at the sky. 'It won't be much,' she predicted. 'The wind will soon clear those clouds away.'

They worked on, lifting and carrying, thrusting their spades into the mud to clear the ditch one yard at a time. After an hour their backs ached and red blisters had begun to form on the palms of their hands. Frank, meanwhile, had found a tree to lean against and carried on watching silently.

'Wouldn't you like to box his ears?' Brenda said in a burst of frustration as he took out yet another cigarette. 'He's a lazy so-and-so. Don't Mr and Mrs Kellett realize that their precious son never lifts a finger?'

'If they do, they don't do anything about it,' Grace replied. 'Emily especially won't hear a word said against him. And she's glad for once that he's stone deaf – it means he won't be called up. In any case, he's probably too old.'

Brenda sighed loudly. 'That's enough about Frank Kellett. How's your brother?'

'He's doing as well as can be expected.' Grace's reply gave little away. She knew that the last thing Edgar wanted was to be the subject of gossip. Of course, she was worried about him – partly because the break in his leg had been slow to heal, but also because the doctors were concerned that he wouldn't cope with being sent back into action. 'The mind is an unknown quantity,' they'd told her when she'd visited Edgar in his convalescent home near York. 'We can see quite well when the body is mended but we can't be so sure about what happens to a man's mental state after his plane is brought down by enemy fire. Onlookers on the ground were afraid that your brother wouldn't come out of it alive, so of course, he's extremely lucky. But then there's the psychological damage.'

They'd sent him home to complete his recovery and here he was – here but not here, with a vacancy behind his eyes, saying hardly anything and refusing to eat; nothing like the eager young recruit who had gone willingly to war two years before.

'As well as can be expected, eh? That's good to hear.' For once Brenda tapped into a vein of tact and instead of pressing the point she got back to her digging. When she looked up again, she found that Frank had disappeared. 'Where did he slink off to?' she wondered out loud.

It wasn't long before they found out, because Una came running from the top of the field. 'Did you see that?' she cried. 'Frank Kellett crept up on me when I wasn't looking and scared the life out of me.'

'Why, what did he do?' Grace put down her spade and climbed out of the ditch.

'He didn't *do* anything. I was piling wood onto the bonfire and when I turned round he was just standing there, about three feet away from me, staring right at me.'

'What did *you* do?' Looking up the field, Brenda saw that there was now no sign of Frank.

'Nothing. But the way he looked at me gave me the shivers. So I ran down here.'

'Not me. I'd have soon set him straight,' Brenda declared.

Grace spoke more slowly. 'How,' she asked, 'when Frank can't hear a word you say? And you can't box a man's ears, as you put it, just for staring.'

'It was silly of me to run away, though.' Una regretted not standing her ground. 'He caught me off guard, that's all.'

'So let's forget about him, shall we?' Grace thrust her spade into the mud and carried on digging. 'It'll be dark before we know it and we haven't got through half of what Joe wants us to do.'

CHAPTER THREE

'The trick is not to let anything get you down,' Brenda told Una later that evening. She'd offered her a lift into Burnside on the back of her motor bike and here they were, ensconced in a quiet corner of the Blacksmith's Arms, sipping cider as they sat on a wooden settle close to a roaring fire. The pub was packed, with customers queuing up at the bar.

'I learned that lesson after my first week,' she went on. 'You have to do as you're told and not ask questions. Even though Joe Kellett is a mean old sod, you can't complain. You just have to get on with it.'

Una wasn't sure that Brenda always followed her own advice. 'So we've to put up with Frank trailing round after us all afternoon without doing a stroke of work?'

Brenda nodded. 'Yes, and with Peggy Russell getting us to clear nettles from her vegetable patch without offering us any gloves, or being blinded and choked by smoke from Arnold White's dratted threshing machine. I'm told that's one of the worst jobs you'll get around here – feeding the metal monster with sheaves of corn then carting away the chaff.

You'll be coughing up dust for a week.' She paused to take a long drink from her glass and scan the room. 'That must be Grace's brother sitting in the corner all on his ownio.' She pointed to Edgar Kershaw who was still in his RAF uniform, staring into space and surrounded by a gloomy cloud that seemed to keep everyone at a safe distance.

'I suppose so,' Una agreed. Wondering about the reason for his return home, she directed her attention towards the thick-set, balding man serving behind the bar. 'Is that their dad?'

'Yes, that's Cliff Kershaw.' Brenda paid scant attention. She was on the lookout for someone interesting to talk to but meanwhile she didn't mind filling Una in on the locals. 'He's Burnside's blacksmith and publican rolled into one. You'll see him hammering away in the forge most days.'

Una watched Cliff call abruptly for Edgar before disappearing down some steps. Edgar took his time to respond.

'I expect they have to change the barrel,' Brenda commented before catching sight of three young men standing at the bar. 'Now, Una Sharpe, which of those three would you most like to pass the time of day with?'

'It's hard to say. I can only see their back view.' It was true, but even so she quickly chose the tallest of the three. He was the best dressed, in a navy-blue suit, with smooth, dark hair and a sportsman's physique.

'The one in the middle?' Brenda prompted.

Una nodded.

'That's Bill Mostyn,' Brenda said with a coquettish

tilt of her head as the three men picked up their glasses and turned around.

'Ssh! He'll guess we're talking about him.'

Brenda smiled winningly at Bill. She knew she cut a dash in her dark slacks and white silk blouse, nipped in at the waist by a shiny black belt.

Bill had spotted her and he smiled back but then went off with his pals in another direction.

'Where's Grace, I wonder?' Having spent a long afternoon with her out at Home Farm, Una was eager to get to know her better.

'Sitting with her feet up, if she's got any sense.' Brenda was in two minds whether to risk crossing the room to join Bill's little threesome but decided against it. *Maybe later,* she thought. *Best not to look too eager.* Then again, a good-looking man like Bill Mostyn could be snapped up for the evening by any of the Land Girls arriving in twos and threes, dressed up to the nines in their best frocks and high heels.

'I wish Grace was billeted at Fieldhead with us,' Una went on, glancing down at her sore palms where the evidence of their afternoon's hard labour was plain to see. 'But I suppose the local girls live at home.'

'Unlike us town girls, eh?' Brenda fidgeted in her seat. 'Someone like me sticks out like a sore thumb in this countrified neck of the woods.'

'What do you mean?'

'Riding a motor bike, for a start. Everyone stares.'

Una laughed. 'It's not something you see every day back in Millwood either, to tell the truth.'

'No?' Brenda seemed surprised. 'I don't see why a girl shouldn't – it's not hard to learn. I've been doing it since I was sixteen and I was twenty-one last August. I bought my first bike off Teddy Garside, the young man I was walking out with at the time.'

'And where's Teddy now?'

'Long gone,' Brenda said with a hint of regret. 'The last I heard he was braving the Atlantic in the Merchant Navy. Lord knows if he's still in the land of the living.'

Una frowned. Who would have thought two years earlier that young men's lives would be so quickly and commonly snuffed out – not in ones or twos but in their hundreds and thousands? It was normal now to wonder about the fate of the boy who'd lived at the end of the street and for mothers, wives and sweethearts to dread the arrival of the telegram that would shatter their lives for good. 'I have three brothers in uniform,' she told Brenda quietly.

'All still in one piece?'

'Yes, touch wood.'

'There's just me in my family. Dad wanted a boy – can't you tell?'

Brenda's open way of talking made Una smile. 'No ribbons and bows for you, then, when you were little?'

'No, he was only happy if I was kicking a football or climbing trees, bless him. Not like Grace over there. I'll bet she's always been polite and ladylike.'

Una saw that Grace had joined her father behind the bar. She and Brenda waved at her and Grace waved back. 'I know what you mean,' Una agreed. 'Never a hair out of place. But she's friendly and helpful enough – I like her.'

'Hard to get to know her, though.'

Una disagreed. 'My first impression is that she's someone you can rely on.'

'But a bit too serious?'

'No,' Una insisted. 'Straightforward and reliable – that's how I see her.'

'Too clever?' Brenda wouldn't let it drop. 'The type who always has her head in the clouds?'

'Clever, yes. But not too clever. And not at all stuck up.'

'All right, you win. Grace Kershaw is an angel in disguise.' Brenda gave up and called across the room to three newcomers. 'Kathleen, Ivy, Jean – I'm over here. Una, this is Ivy McNamara.'

'Hello, Ivy.' Una greeted a thin girl with a long, serious face who nodded briefly back at her.

'Shift over – there's plenty of room for three littl'uns . . .'

Two ciders later, Brenda had plucked up the courage to approach Bill Mostyn.

'Wish me luck,' she told the other girls before she sashayed across the room.

'She's not backwards in coming forward, I'll give her that.' Kathleen's faint disapproval hung in the air.

'Just because he's the one you've had your eye on for the last six months,' Jean muttered. 'Anyway, you can relax – Brenda's not his type.'

'What is his type?' Una asked, trying hard not to get caught in the crossfire. Feelings between the girls at the hostel ran beneath the surface and she was only just beginning to work them out. It was clear that Ivy was jealous of Brenda, for a start. And Jean – well, Jean enjoyed upsetting people and never cracked a smile. She and Ivy could definitely make more of themselves, Una decided, if only they would do their hair and use a bit of make-up.

Jean shrugged. 'To tell the truth, I've never seen Bill walking out with anyone. He's always too busy messing about with tractors and when he's not working he's playing football. They've made him captain of the local team, a real man's man.'

'Jean's right,' Kathleen agreed. 'Tractor engines and football mean more to Bill Mostyn than anything else. I tried to get to know him a bit better at the last dance they held at Penny Lane—'

'She means the Canadian Air Force quarters in the old isolation hospital,' Jean informed Una without being asked. 'It was requisitioned by the War Office soon after war was declared.'

'As I say, Bill was there with some of his footballing pals. The night was young and the band was playing, so I went right up and asked him to dance the foxtrot with me, because what does a girl have to lose?'

'Her good name?' Jean suggested under her breath. 'Oh no, I forgot; this is wartime. Everything's different.'

'Sourpuss.' Kathleen scowled at her. 'Let me finish my story. I said, "Hello, Bill. Would you like this dance?" "I'm sorry, I have two left feet," he snapped right back. *Then why did you come?* I might have said, but I bit my tongue. I soon found myself a handsome Canadian airman instead.'

So Una feared the worst for Brenda who had

broken into the conversation Bill was having with his two pals. She was experiencing no more luck than Kathleen, to judge by Bill's stiff responses.

Brenda's opening gambit had been one that she thought would appeal. 'I hear you're good with tractor engines. You must know all about spark plugs and head gaskets, and so on.'

Frown lines appeared between Bill's eyebrows. 'I work on them, if that's what you mean.'

She smiled brightly back. 'I happen to have a BSA single-cylinder Sloper with an oil leak. Do you know someone who would take a look at it for me?' *Meaning you,* she thought, looking him in the eye. 'It might be nothing much, but I'd like to have it checked.'

'Good idea.' He nodded slowly, ignoring the sly glances that were being exchanged by Thomas Lund and Jack Hudson and providing a literal answer. 'Have you topped up the oil recently? If there's a leak you mustn't let it drop down below the minimum level.'

'Rightio, I'll do that first thing in the morning. Tomorrow's Saturday. I'll be free in the afternoon. Perhaps I could call in at your workshop to let one of your mechanics give it a quick once-over?'

More looks were exchanged and there was the suggestion of a snigger from Thomas. Bill's frown deepened. 'I'm not really your man,' he told Brenda. 'Maurice Baxendale runs a little car repair garage tucked away behind the Village Institute. He's a better bet.'

'Oh.' Brenda returned the frown. Bill Mostyn was

proving to be as stand-offish as his mother. Yes, he was devilishly handsome but he seemed to lack what she called vim and vigour. There was no sparkle in his brown eyes. In fact, his face conveyed barely any expression at all. 'Ta,' she said lamely.

'I know for a fact Maurice won't be open tomorrow afternoon, though,' Thomas pointed out obligingly. 'He'll be playing in goal for us against Thornley.'

'Fair enough.' She realized she'd been sent packing with her tail between her legs.

'Well?' Kathleen asked when a disgruntled Brenda plonked herself back down on the fireside settle.

'Well, nothing.' She sniffed and ran a hand through her cropped hair.

'That's a pity.' Jean feigned sympathy by putting her hand on Brenda's arm. 'She doesn't want to talk about it, do you, Brenda?'

'What makes you think that?' Brenda pursed her lips and kept Bill within her sights. 'If at first you don't succeed . . .' she muttered.

'That's the ticket.' Una grinned at her. 'Would you like another drink?'

'No, ta.' She gave a loud yawn. 'I'm ready for my bed. Do you want a lift back?'

'Yes, please.' Una jumped up and fastened her coat.

Brenda shook off her bad mood and turned to Jean and Ivy with a well-meaning word of advice. 'Remember – don't let Kathleen walk home by herself.'

Ivy glanced at Kathleen who seemed suddenly nervous. 'Rightio.'

'Good, that's settled.' Brenda was satisfied. 'Come on, Una. It's time for beddy-byes.'

At eight o'clock next morning, Grace and Una were back digging ditches at Home Farm while Brenda was kept busy in the dairy. She eventually emerged at half past nine, having lugged heavy metal churns across the floor and taken a whack in the face from more than one swishing tail.

'Ouch, that last one hurt,' she grumbled when she joined the others, her cheek still stinging. 'I was in there with Frank, worse luck.'

Grace noticed the red mark. 'He didn't clout you, did he?'

'No, a cow did this to me.' Brenda rubbed her cheek.

'Where is he now?' Una asked as she handed her a spade.

'Having his breakfast.' Brenda started digging vigorously to work off her frustration. 'Don't worry – he'll soon be out here getting under our feet as per usual.'

They worked in silence for a while, heads down. The sticking plasters that Una had wrapped around her fingers had soon come off and exposed her blisters to more chafing. Her feet got tangled in brambles and at one point the oozing mud in the bottom of the ditch claimed one of her wellingtons and she was left hopping on one leg while Grace retrieved it.

'Give me a munitions factory any day,' she sighed, remembering her conversation with Emily Kellett on the bus. To cap it all, the rain came back and this time it set in for good. By the end of the morning all three looked like drowned rats.

'Is that as far as you've got?' Joe grumbled when he came out to the field at one o'clock. He wore a sack around his shoulders and his cap was pulled well down.

Grace climbed out of the ditch, smiling in spite of her aching back. 'We've done our best, Mr Kellett. It's heavy work, especially when it's raining.'

'We've done our best, Mr Kellett,' he mimicked meanly. 'If it was up to me, I'd make you stay until it was finished.'

'Luckily, it's not up to you.' Brenda handed him her spade. Grace might choose to be polite to the old so-and-so but she'd be blowed if she followed suit. 'So, if you don't mind we'll down tools and be on our way.'

Whether he minded or not, off they trudged up the field to collect their bikes, running slap-bang into Frank as he came out of the dairy where he'd skulked all morning. Scowling, he brushed Grace and Brenda aside and took hold of Una's wrist.

'What do you think you're doing?' She tried to pull free but found he was stronger than he looked.

He would have dragged her out of sight round the back of the dairy in full view of the others if Emily hadn't spotted him from the farmhouse porch.

She ran across the yard to stand in his way. 'Let her go, Frank,' she said slowly and deliberately so that he could read her lips.

He hesitated, giving Una the chance to escape his

grasp. She rubbed her wrist and rejoined Brenda and Grace.

'Well!' Disgust rendered Brenda speechless.

'Good boy,' Emily said. 'I've told you over and over – you have to learn not to lay hold of people like that.'

Frank shook his head in puzzlement then disappeared behind the shed.

'Don't take the hump. You'll get used to him,' Emily told Una. 'She will, won't she, Grace? Everyone in the village knows that Frank wouldn't harm a fly.'

'Where did he want me to go?' Una demanded.

There was no time for Emily to answer because Frank quickly reappeared holding three hen's eggs in the palm of his hand. He held them out to Una and waited for her to take them from him.

'You see,' his mother said soothingly. 'He only wanted to give you a little present.'

The eggs were warm and the small act of generosity confused Una. 'Ta,' she told Frank as she slipped the eggs into the top pocket of her dungarees.

'That's one each.' Brenda broke through the awkwardness with a chirpy smile. 'Ta, Frank. Ta, Mrs K. Come along, girls. Our work here is done.'

Una lay in the bath looking out at the elm trees behind the house. She'd bartered with Kathleen for this bathroom slot – one newly laid egg for ten minutes of peace and quiet soaking her aching limbs and going over recent events. It was three o'clock in the afternoon and the daylight was already starting to fade.

The bath was one of the big Victorian ones with claw-feet. The gas boiler on the wall had only provided three or four inches of hot water before it ran cold. There were bottle-green tiles on the bathroom walls with a frieze of pink and white lilies forming a waist-high dado rail – yet more reminders of Field-head's more illustrious past.

As Una sank low in the water to ease her aching back, she felt tears form in her eyes. Was every day going to be this bad? she wondered. Was there nothing but endless digging, scratched arms, aches and pains and blisters ahead of her?

The tears dribbled down her cheeks and blurred her view of the bare elms swaying in the wind. What would Tom be up to, right now, this minute? He would probably be sitting by the wireless listening to the Home Service, leaning forward to tap his pipe against the fire grate to empty its contents. Then he would take his pouch and with his one good hand he would pack the bowl with fresh tobacco that always smelled so sweet and aromatic. He would light it with a long spill and suck in the first breath. The smoke would emerge from his lips with a popping sound. Dear Tom – back in Wellington Street all on his own.

She would write a letter to him after she'd had her bath, she decided. She would choose to tell him only the good things – how nice and lively Brenda was and how much she liked the way Grace dressed and did her hair. There would be no mention of blisters or mud, nothing about Eunice Mason's sad end. She was dwelling on this when there was a sharp rap on the door.

'Get a move on in there,' Jean said. 'Your time was up five minutes ago. I'm next in the queue.'

'Sorry, I didn't realize.' Una stood up and reached for her towel, hurriedly drying herself before slipping on her dressing-gown. She opened the door to find Jean standing there, towel and washbag in hand. Her lank hair was pinned behind her ears and her thin lips were pressed together.

'It's blinking freezing out here,' Jean complained. She was about to squeeze past Una but changed her mind. 'By the way, Brenda told me what Frank Kellett got up to.'

'Oh yes, he gave us some eggs.' As usual with Jean, Una suspected there was something unpleasant coming.

'What did he want for them, that's the question.'

'Nothing. It was a present.' The hairs at the back of Una's neck prickled as she remembered the look on Frank's face – his eyes narrowed, his jaw clenched tight shut.

Jean arched her eyebrows. 'If you believe that, you'll believe anything.'

'Why? What do you mean?'

'Nothing. My lips are sealed.' She made as if to close the door on Una, who stopped her by putting her foot in the way.

'That's not fair. Say what you have to say.'

Jean sighed. 'Very well. Kathleen made me promise to keep this under my hat but since you insist – Frank Kellett is the reason she won't walk home alone at night.' She held up her hand to stop Una from interrupting, colour rising in her pale

48

cheeks as she rushed to share Kathleen's secret. 'She's scared stiff of him after what happened outside the Blacksmith's Arms and I don't blame her – him lurking behind the forge like that and jumping out at her when she went to fetch her bike. It was pitch dark. Frank started to drag her into the field behind the pub. She bit his hand – that's how she got away, but Lord knows what he'd have done given the chance.'

'All right, stop now,' Una pleaded to no avail.

'Kathleen wasn't the first and she won't be the last. So from now on, you'll know to keep out of Frank's way and not take any more presents from him.'

Una took a deep breath and tried to collect her thoughts. 'But Emily swears he's harmless.'

'Harmless, my backside!' Jean looked at Una as if she was still wet behind the ears. 'She's bound to stick up for him, isn't she? She's his mother.'

Unsurprised by what she'd heard, Una decided she would definitely be on her guard from now on.

Still Jean wasn't finished. 'Mind you, I suppose you should be flattered.'

Yet again the sly remark irritated Una. Though she only came up to Jean's shoulder, she kept her foot jammed against the door. 'What do you mean by that?'

Jean pulled hard on the door handle until Una was forced to remove her foot. 'Frank only goes after the pretty ones,' she declared then slammed the door in her face.

*

Brenda made the most of her afternoon off. First she rode her motor bike into the village and found Maurice Baxendale's workshop, slipping a note under his door to ask him if he would be good enough to take a look at her oil leak the following Monday. Then she dropped in at the pub for a chat with Grace. She found her tucked away in a kitchen overlooking a neat vegetable patch, paintbrush and a set of watercolours to hand.

'I didn't realize you were an artist on the side.' Brenda unzipped her jacket and looked over Grace's shoulder at a lifelike study of a sprig of holly complete with bright red berries.

'I'm not.' Grace rinsed her brush in a jar of water then laid it down. 'It keeps me out of mischief, that's all.'

'Don't be so modest – this is very good.' Brenda took up the small picture and studied it. 'Will you frame it when it's finished?'

'Either that or I'll make it into a Christmas card. There's only just over a month to go, you know.'

'Talking of which – we Land Girls ought to do something to celebrate, don't you think?'

Grace nodded and led Brenda into the family kitchen where she set the kettle on the hob. 'Last year we put on a song and dance show for the prisoners of war at Beckwith Camp. We held it at the Institute, two days before Christmas. It went down jolly well, actually.'

'I'll bet it did.' Brenda pictured the rows of prisoners lapping up the sight of twirling skirts and neat ankles.

'We finished off with our Land Army song – "Back

to the land, we must all lend a hand . . ." You know the one.'

'"To the farms and the fields we must go . . ."' Brenda swung her arms and marched on the spot. 'Who are these prisoners when they're at home?'

'Italians. They're not a bad lot. We got a bunch of new ones in March, straight off an armed raider that went down off the Maldives. I suppose we could put on a repeat performance for them.'

Brenda swiftly changed her stance, then, hand on chest, broke into operatic song. '"O sole mio . . ." Definitely, we should!' she declared. 'But we'd better get a move on. Christmas will be here before we know it.'

'Then let's mention it to Joyce. Last time she played the piano for us – she's very good. And Elsie did a tap dance.'

'What did you do?' Brenda asked, taking a cup of tea and warming her back against the iron range.

'A group of us sang old music hall songs then I recited a Stanley Holloway poem about a boy's visit to the zoo. You know the one – in the end Albert gets eaten by the lion.'

'How did that go down?'

'Not very well,' Grace admitted with a blush. 'The audience didn't see the funny side.'

Brenda laughed out loud. 'That settles it. Let me talk to Joyce and see if we can come up with something more up to the minute. But before that, I've set my mind on paying Edith Mostyn a visit. I dropped by partly to ask if you know where she lives.'

Grace seemed taken aback but quickly adjusted her expression. 'She's in the house next to the chapel, set back from the road with a monkey puzzle tree in front. Why do you want to call in on her?'

'I'm on the war path, that's why. I want her to change the rota. Honestly, Grace, I've been sent to dig ditches for the Kelletts three days on the trot and that's slave labour – it's not fair. They have to send someone else and give me a break.'

'I see. Try not to charge at it like a bull in a china shop, though. You know what Edith is like.'

'I'll put it to her nicely, don't worry.' Brenda had placed her teacup in the sink and was already on her way. 'The house with the monkey puzzle tree – ta very much.'

'Good luck,' Grace called after her. 'Let me know how you get on.'

CHAPTER FOUR

Brenda discovered that Edith's desire to keep up appearances extended to her newly built house and orderly garden. The peculiar spiky tree stood to attention at the gate and what had once been lawn had been dug up for victory and transformed into soldierly rows of leeks and Brussels sprouts. The lion's head knocker on the green front door was polished and the downstairs windows to each side were spotlessly clean.

'Yes?' Edith enquired as she opened the door. 'Oh hello, Brenda – what can I do for you?'

A tall, grey-haired, sickly-looking man hovered in the background. He carried a rolled-up newspaper under one arm, was thin as a rake and dressed in a russet-coloured cardigan, white shirt and yellow cravat.

'I'm sorry to bother you,' Brenda began, 'but it's about next week's rota.'

'What about it?' Edith stepped outside and closed the door behind her. Her navy-blue twin set was nicely complemented by a string of pearls with a matching brooch.

'I was wondering – have you got a copy I could

see?' Brenda felt the contrast between them. Her Land Army hat was pulled over her forehead at a rakish angle, her jacket hung open and her cheeks were flushed after her fireside chat with Grace.

Edith nodded slowly. 'I do, as a matter of fact.'

'Have you had a chance to look at it yourself?'

A shake of the head was accompanied by an irritated frown.

This was like getting blood out of a stone. 'I'd like to know – am I being sent back to Home Farm? Because, if I am, I want to put in a request to go somewhere different.' No-frills Brenda forgot Grace's good advice and forged ahead. 'It's slave labour out there. Mr Kellett takes advantage and gets us to do the worst possible jobs in all weathers. It's only fair that some of the other girls take their turn.'

'In principle, yes; I agree.' Edith took her responsibility as the local WLA representative seriously and so she conceded the point. 'However, it's a little late in the day to be changing next week's rota.'

'Couldn't you make a telephone call to Head Office?'

'Not until Monday, I'm afraid. But come in, Brenda, and let me check to see where you're being sent.' She opened the door onto a well-presented hallway decorated in an expensive, modern style. On the wall above the fireplace there was a gold clock in the shape of a sunburst; there was a metal umbrella stand to one side and a yellow-and-green striped rug covered a parquet floor. Edith asked Brenda to wait while she went to fetch the rota.

Meanwhile, her husband made a point of introducing himself.

'Vincent Mostyn,' he said in a gruff voice. He took in Brenda's windswept appearance and the non-regulation angle of her felt hat.

She shook his hand. 'Pleased to meet you, Mr Mostyn.'

He regarded her warily and pushed the conversation towards the war effort in order to gauge her response. 'I see in today's paper that Stalin is claiming that the Soviets are on the verge of victory. He says their scorched-earth policy is working a treat.'

'I didn't know that. That's good news.'

'I wouldn't bank on it, though. In my opinion, Hitler's not going to give in that easily.'

'I suppose not.' Though Vincent Mostyn was frail, he exerted his authority through a deep voice and a military manner, enhanced by a neatly clipped moustache and upright bearing. Brenda snatched her hat from her head and held it in front of her, feeling like a schoolchild called before the headmaster.

'Here it is.' Edith came back brandishing a sheet of paper. 'And I'm afraid to say that your name is down for Home Farm on Monday, Tuesday and Wednesday of next week, along with Grace Kershaw and Una Sharpe.'

'I knew it.' Brenda bit her bottom lip and tried to work out her next move. 'Joe Kellett made us dig ditches in the driving rain this morning. It's a wonder we didn't catch our deaths.' She decided to put the responsibility squarely on Edith's shoulders.

'We're relying on you, Mrs Mostyn. As our rep, it's up to you to take my complaint further if you see fit.'

Vincent stepped in before his wife could answer. 'There are no easy jobs on farms,' he pointed out. 'Digging ditches is no worse than thinning turnips or mucking out stables.'

Brenda disagreed. 'A lot of the girls are given indoor jobs,' she pointed out, so intent on making her case that she didn't hear the front door open or see Bill Mostyn come in and put his sports hold-all down on the polished floor. 'Elsie Walker and Jean Fox have just spent a few days on the trot collecting eggs in Horace Turnbull's hen huts at Winsill Edge. It's only fair that Grace, Una and I should have a break from digging ditches and take our turn at that.'

'What's this?' Bill broke in. 'Is there a mutiny among the ranks?'

His unexpected arrival further energized Brenda, but before she could continue his mother showered him with anxious questions.

'Bill, what are you doing home so early? Why aren't you playing football? Have you hurt yourself?'

'The Thornley pitch was waterlogged when we got there so the match was called off,' he replied with a casual shrug, all the time looking at Brenda. 'I saw your Sloper at the gate. Is it still leaking oil?'

She nodded. 'I left a note at Baxendale's. I'll get it seen to on Monday after work.'

'And are you making headway with my mother?' He gave a genial smile, sidled towards Edith and put his arm around her waist. 'Be a sport and alter the rota, Mum. Brenda and her pals deserve a break.'

Edith pulled away. 'It's all very well you trying to get around me, Bill, but you know I can't do that off my own bat.'

'For good reason,' Vincent pointed out. 'If your mother did it for one person, word would get round and there'd be no end of girls knocking at our door.'

Bill shook his head and sighed. 'I'm sorry, Brenda. It looks as if you'll have to go through official channels.'

'That's all right.' The way he looked at her with a half-smile unsettled her. 'It was worth a try.'

'Why don't I take a quick look at that oil leak while you're here?' Bill opened the door and waited for her to follow. 'If it's something that I can fix here and now, then at least your time won't have been entirely wasted.'

She answered with unconcealed surprise. 'Ta very much. That's very nice of you.' It was as if she was speaking to a different person to the man she'd approached in the pub. Instead of a stiff rebuff and a blank expression, he was obliging and relaxed. The effect was heightened by his weekend attire of sports jacket and open-necked shirt and as he crouched beside her bike to discover the source of the leak, she stood back and admired the view.

Cinema-buff Brenda knew that there were many different types of handsome men, from the suave, smooth charm of a Clark Gable to the aristocratic elegance of Leslie Howard, from the smouldering, romantic allure of Robert Donat to the sensitive, self-effacing attraction of James Stewart. She'd stud-ied them all on the silver screen and to her mind it was James Stewart that Bill Mostyn most resembled. He spoke quietly and unassumingly and what she'd mistaken at first as a lack of expression and energy now came across as genuine shyness. He had the tall, loose-limbed build of her favourite film star and the same, unselfconscious habit of quietly concentrating on the task in hand.

'I think I've spotted the problem.' He pointed to a drip of oil under the petrol tank. 'Hang on a minute while I fetch a spanner.'

She waited beneath the monkey puzzle tree, trying to ignore the flutter in her stomach while Bill fetched his bag of tools.

'If I tighten this nut it should do the trick.' No sooner said than he fixed the fault with a deft twist of the spanner. 'There; it shouldn't give you any more trouble,' he said as he stood back from the bike. 'I'm sorry I couldn't get you out of more visits to the Kelletts' farm, though.'

She gave a small tut and a smile. 'Never mind – we'll live.' The fluttering couldn't be ignored. Something about Bill Mostyn drew her in – his deep, quiet voice, perhaps, or the suggestion of amusement in his brown eyes.

'I agree that the other girls should be made to pull their weight. I'll have another go at Mother for you when I go back in.' The tools in his bag clinked as he stooped to pick it up. 'Anyway, no need to worry about your leak, so that's one good thing.'

'I feel a bit of a fool for not mending it myself.' Brenda admitted a weakness in order to keep Bill talking a while longer. 'I love riding the darned thing but I'm not so hot at tinkering with engines, et cetera.'

'You can't be expected to know everything.' His smile broadened. He liked the look of this dark, slim girl who blushed easily and came straight out with what she was thinking. She made a change to the sometimes dour, stolid types who were billeted at Fieldhead.

'In any case, let me buy you a drink,' she offered. Her insides were playing havoc with her; her heart raced and her stomach churned as she waited for his reply.

Bill shifted his weight from one foot to the other, gave her a keen look then suddenly turned away. 'No. There's no need for that,' he said shortly as he swung through the gate and set off up the path.

She breathed out. *Good Lord, what happened there?* Taken aback by the swift change of mood, she sat astride her bike and kick-started it. The engine growled as she steered away from the kerb. *I was only talking about a harmless little drink,* she said to herself as she roared off up the main street. *What could possibly be wrong with that?*

Painting with watercolours was the hobby Grace loved the most. An accomplished embroiderer and an avid reader, she still found most contentment in watching the paint flow over a wet surface – cobalt blue for the sky on a rare sunny day, cadmium yellow mixed with umber for cornfields in August, vermilion for holly berries as Christmas approached. Time was precious, though; she had to snatch spare

59

minutes for her painting between farm work and serving behind the bar. That was why she was up early on Sunday morning, before her father was awake, sitting near the kitchen window where the light was best, dipping her brush into water and making a quick study of a robin redbreast perched on top of a spade out in the garden, chest puffed out and head cocked to one side.

The silence in the house was broken by the sound of uneven footsteps on the stairs and soon Edgar appeared in a collarless shirt, his braces dangling from his waist and his trousers creased as if he'd slept in them. He hadn't shaved or combed his fair hair and he was looking the worse for wear in other ways, with red-rimmed eyes and a grey pallor to his skin.

'You're up nice and early,' she remarked. It wouldn't do to comment on the details of her brother's appearance, she decided.

'I couldn't sleep.' He went to the sink and filled a glass with water but put it aside before drinking it. Instead, he stared blankly out of the window.

'You're in my light,' Grace pointed out after a long silence.

He grunted and stepped aside, only to flop down in their father's rocking chair to one side of the polished black range.

She went on painting the robin. 'How's your leg this morning?'

'The same.'

'Did the doctors say how long it would be before you were back to normal?'

'In what way?' he shot back.

'Your leg,' she insisted. His hypersensitivity upset her but she did her best to soothe him. 'I didn't mean anything else.'

'They didn't say,' he grunted. In fact, the fracture had healed well. He knew he would always walk with a limp but it didn't bother him. After all, he'd got off lightly compared ... 'What you really want to know is how much extra leave they gave me and why.'

Grace put down her brush. 'Only if you want to tell me,' she said quietly. So far Edgar had said nothing about being shot down during a mission over France and she understood why. Some things that happened in war were too terrible to describe.

He sat by the empty grate, head hanging. When he spoke it was without conviction. 'I'll be ready for action within the week, don't you worry.'

'That's good,' she murmured then changed the subject. 'Did you notice that we've got a new recruit? Una Sharpe. She's so small and slim she had to have her uniform altered – really tiny. And Brenda Appleby had to teach her how to ride a bike. But you should see Una get stuck in, Edgar. She's a little dynamo when she gets cracking.'

'Good for her,' he said, again without meaning it.

'She was working at Home Farm with me and Brenda. You might have spotted her here in the bar on Friday – her auburn hair is what makes her stand out. And she's pretty, too.'

'Honestly, Grace, I couldn't care less.' He stood up abruptly and went out to the porch to put on his boots. 'I'm only interested in keeping out of Father's way and minding my own business.'

'Why? What's he said?' Overcoming her own hurt feelings, she joined him in the porch. 'Has he been having a go at you?'

'What do you think?' The old man had been on at him since the moment he walked through the door – fetch this, carry that, pull yourself together. 'He's downright ashamed of me – anyone can see that.'

'No, he's worried about you, that's all.'

'He's got a funny way of showing it.'

Well aware of the increasingly bad atmosphere between Edgar and their father, Grace sought for a way forward. 'I'll ask him to stop nagging you. He might listen to me.'

'And pigs might fly.' Edgar let his resentment show. As far as he was concerned, the old man was an overbearing bully. Not that his customers saw that side of him when he was behind the bar, where he was cheerful and easy-going enough to serve drinks well after closing time and to turn a blind eye to strict measures. An extra tot or two of rum would be repaid by a rabbit, skinned and ready for the pot, or else half a dozen eggs and a quarter of tea delivered anonymously to the back doorstep.

'I'll try, anyway.' Over the last few days, Grace had found herself growing desperate to ease Edgar's suffering. There was obviously something terrible on his mind that made him shut her out so completely. At this moment, he seemed to hate her, along with their father and the whole world.

'I'm not a child. You don't have to look after me.'

He took his RAF greatcoat from the peg and stormed off, making the robin fly away.

The gulf yawned between them – a silence as thick and solid as the stone walls of this house where they'd grown up together. Frustration brought tears to Grace's eyes. *He hasn't taken any interest in home news since he got back – none whatsoever.* Grace gave a regretful sigh. Lots had happened since Edgar had been away. She had so much to tell him – so many hopes and fears. And one big secret that she hadn't yet shared with a single soul.'

'Guess who drew the short straw.' It was seven o'clock on Monday morning and Joyce was setting off by bike from Fieldhead with Una, Brenda, Elsie and Jean. She led the way along the frosty lane, laughing as she lodged her complaint. 'Me and Jean – that's who. We've been sent in your place to Home Farm, worse luck.'

Una felt a twinge of guilt but kept quiet while Jean moaned away behind her.

'If Joe Kellett thinks I'm going to dig ditches, he's got another think coming. It's bad enough keeping his cows fed and watered now that he's brought them inside. The stink is enough to put you off your food for a week.'

Brenda was silent too as she contemplated something of a pyrrhic victory. It seemed that Bill Mostyn had kept his promise and succeeded in persuading Edith to alter the rota. But she, Grace and Una found they'd been sent to bag potatoes at a farm she didn't know. The wind was keen and the weather forecast predicted that the cold spell was set to continue, so they were being sent from one form of outdoor drudgery to another. Still, a change was as good as a rest.

Joyce let Jean's complaints wash over her. 'Not to worry; your job will be to look after the bonfire. I've brought a kettle in my saddlebag to make us gypsy tea for our elevenses. I'll get Frank to do the digging with me. It's about time he pulled his weight.'

'If anyone can get him to do a decent day's work, you can.' Brenda reached the crossroads leading to Burnside and pulled in at the side of the road.

'You leave Frank Kellett to me,' Joyce said with a wink.

'Oh and by the way, if you run into Grace, tell her we've gone on ahead. We'll see her at Brigg Farm,' Brenda told Joyce and Jean.

'No need – here she is now.' Joyce saw Grace cycling up the road. 'Come on, Jean, the sooner we get this dratted ditch dug, the better.'

Brenda intervened quickly. 'Before you go – I haven't had a chance to ask you if you'll play the piano for us at the Christmas show.'

'What's that you say? I didn't even know we were doing another show,' Jean muttered.

'We're not, unless Joyce agrees to tinkle the ivories for us,' Brenda went blithely on. 'What do you say, maestro?'

'Count me in,' Joyce agreed. 'Make a list of the tunes you want me to play and I'll practise them on the piano at the hostel.'

'We haven't decided on the songs yet.' Brenda realized there was a lot of preparation to be done in a short time. 'We want them to be bright and breezy, though. Nothing too highbrow. What did you do for last year's show, Jean?'

Jean was still in a huff. 'I served tea and biscuits during the interval. You wouldn't get me up on stage in a month of Sundays.'

'What about you, Una? Do you fancy doing a charleston for us?'

Una shook her head. 'I don't know if I'll be here over Christmas. I might want to apply for leave and spend it with Tom at Wellington Street.'

'Oh no, don't do that!' Brenda brooked no argument. 'Your duty is to stay here and serve King and country.'

Yes, by prancing about on a stage. Una didn't voice her doubts. 'Maybe. But charleston's old hat these days.'

'But you will do something? It's for the Italian POWs – a captive audience, you might say.'

Una said she would think about it as Grace joined them and Jean and Joyce carried on towards the village. Grace greeted them cheerily and their mood stayed buoyant despite the prospect of unearthing potatoes from their winter clamps and putting them into one-hundredweight sacks.

'What did you do at the weekend?' Grace asked Una as they pedalled slowly uphill. 'Did you have a good rest?'

'I slept in until nine o'clock yesterday morning then I cycled into the village to post a letter to my brother.'

'You should have dropped in at the pub,' Grace told her. 'I was doing nothing all morning.'

In fact, she'd been worrying about Edgar, trying in vain to talk to her father about the state he was in. Her father had brushed aside her concerns. 'That lad needs to get back in harness double quick,' he'd retorted. 'He can't sit here twiddling his thumbs.'

'Next time I will,' Una promised. Grace gave off a warmth that was irresistible. If Una had had an older sister, she would have wished her to be exactly like her, she realized.

'Over there – that's our farm for today.' Grace's heart sank as she saw that a thin layer of snow covered the high ground surrounding Brigg Farm, but it rose again when she realized that they weren't the only ones who had been sent to work for Roland Thomson. There was a large green lorry parked outside the farmhouse, currently disgorging a dozen or so men in grey uniforms under the watchful eye of two soldiers bearing rifles. The uniforms were marked by large red circles sewn onto the back.

'It seems we've got some help,' she pointed out to Una and Brenda. 'They've brought the Italians in from Beckwith Camp.'

It was the first time either of the new girls had encountered prisoners of war and both felt nervous as they left the lane and cycled up the rutted, frozen track. By the time they arrived at the farm, the Italians had been shepherded over the snowy ridge, out of sight.

'Leave your bikes in the barn and be quick about it.' Roland Thomson didn't bother with greetings. Like most of the farmers, he was still sceptical of how much use the Land Army girls could be and he had a small man's belligerence in his dealings with the world. 'You three can work on the clamp furthest away from the house. Grace, I take it you know what you're doing? You can show the other two.'

So they followed instructions and made their way over the hilltop to find the prisoners already at work lifting the top layers of straw from five separate clamps set against the sheltered side of the hill. Each clamp was between twenty-five and thirty feet long and about three feet high, made up of nine-inch layers of straw, then potatoes, then straw again. The two Tommies leaned against a gnarled tree trunk smoking and keeping watch, occasionally shouting an order at one of the Italians.

'The straw is to keep out the frost,' Grace explained to Una and Brenda, keeping her mind on the job in hand. 'If the frost gets to the potatoes they go rotten and have to be thrown away.'

The four Italians working at the nearest clamp stopped work and watched the girls walk by. They smiled and called hello in English then lapsed into rapid Italian. The second group picked up on the arrival of female reinforcements and also stopped work, as did the third.

One of the Tommies grinned at the girls. 'Hello, ladies. You've got plenty of admirers today, eh?'

'Yes, and don't we look the bees' knees?' Brenda pulled a face as she glanced down at her muddy breeches and wellingtons. There seemed to be no need to keep a close watch on the prisoners since their two guards had turned their backs on them and decided to walk with her, Una and Grace to the last clamp in the row.

'Do they speak much English, or is it just "hello"?' Una wanted to know. She felt dozens of eyes following them and was still not sure how to react. One of the Italians had stepped forward to speak to them as they passed – he had the darkest hair she'd ever seen, so dark it was almost black, and he was clean shaven with a wide, friendly smile.

'My name is Angelo,' he told them in a lilting voice. 'I am pleased to meet you.'

'Likewise.' Brenda was the first to respond by shaking his hand. 'I'm Brenda Appleby and this is Una Sharpe and Grace Kershaw.'

After this there was much eager hand shaking and smiling and very little potato lifting for five or ten minutes until one of the Tommies broke up the party and the girls were encouraged to continue on their way.

'Don't worry; this lot won't bother you,' the soldier who said his name was Jack told them. 'They're all right, on the whole. Friendly but lazy just about sums them up.'

'But there are only two of you.' Brenda was intrigued. 'Don't they ever try to run away?'

'Where would they run to?' Jack gestured towards the frozen slopes stretching into the far distance. 'And I've got this, remember.' He tapped the butt of his rifle.

Albert, the second guard, nodded his agreement. 'Anyway, life's not too bad for them. They can get hold of better coffee and cigarettes than we can, for a start. Plus, they're fed and watered so they might as well sit it out here and let their Jerry pals do all the hard work.'

Listening in, Una felt she was learning a lot, and not just about bagging potatoes.

'Una,' Angelo called to her as she began to lift the first layer of straw. 'I have gloves – you want?'

'No, ta,' she called back shyly.

Brenda, however, quickly saw the advantage of protecting her hands and she accepted the same offer from Angelo's taller, even better-looking friend.

'I am Lorenzo,' the other man said in a deep voice as he handed over his gloves. He smiled less than Angelo but he was polite and attentive, warning her about a hidden dip in the ground and the dangers of slipping on the snowy surface. 'Later I make fire and we bake potatoes, drink coffee – OK?'

'Make a fire where? What with?' The day was turning out surprisingly well and Brenda was in no hurry to get back to her own clamp.

'Here. With wood from hedge. You like potatoes?'

She gave a raucous laugh. 'Lorenzo, I love them!'

'This is true?'

'No!' She laughed again and her smile lit up her whole face. 'We've brought sandwiches. But coffee – yes, please.'

'Then we will meet at noon,' he promised as she walked away.

CHAPTER FIVE

The Italians sang as they worked – sad, lilting songs from operas that were unfamiliar to Una, Brenda and Grace – in voices that soared as high as the rooks circling overhead. They picked potatoes from the clamps and dropped them into hessian sacks, ignoring their frost-pinched fingers and stopping from time to time to add hedge clippings to the bonfire that they'd started on the brow of the hill. By mid-morning the sacks were full and Angelo ran to fetch Roland's son with his horse-drawn cart.

Una recognized the cart's driver and the grey shire horse she'd seen in the pub yard on the day she'd arrived. The carroty-red hair was unmistakeable, along with the big-toothed, cheeky grin. Major plodded towards them, breathing clouds of steam into the cold air.

'Whoa!' the boy cried as they reached the first clamp. He watched as the prisoners hoisted the full sacks onto the cart then gave a click of his tongue for the horse to move on. When he reached the final clamp he jumped down from the cart. 'Now then, how are you three getting on with the enemy?' he asked the girls with a wink and a glance over his shoulder. 'Not too friendly, I hope.'

'Fat chance,' Brenda replied. 'We've done nothing but pick blooming potatoes since we got here. What's your name, by the way?'

'Neville Thomson. You can call me Nev.'

'Well, Nev, are you going to give us a hand loading these sacks?' Dwarfed by the carthorse, Brenda took care to stand well clear of his enormous hooves.

Angelo appeared out of nowhere. 'This I do,' he said, picking up the nearest sack and slinging it onto the cart. Soon Lorenzo and two other prisoners had joined in the task and within minutes the sacks were loaded without Neville or the girls lifting a finger.

'Ta, that's good of you,' Grace told the prisoners with genuine gratitude. She didn't think her aching back would have taken the weight of the heavy sacks.

Lorenzo gave a formal bow then took hold of Major's harness while Neville climbed back onto the cart. He helped him steer it in a wide circle to face the way they'd come, led the horse a few steps along the ridge then let go.

'Giddy up.' Neville clicked his tongue and shook the reins and, with a creak of straining leather, Major pulled away.

'What was that last song you were singing?' Una asked Angelo as the cart rattled over the frozen ground.

'From *Tosca*,' he replied with a warm smile. 'The song of the shepherd boy; "Io de' sospiri".'

'And what does that mean?'

'It means: "I give you sighs".' He stayed after the others had returned to their clamps.

Una got the gist of what he was saying and smiled back. 'I didn't understand the words but I liked the sound of it. Will you sing some more?'

Angelo nodded. 'You drink coffee?'

'We will, won't we?' Una appealed to Brenda and Grace, already hard at work.

Grace lifted the next layer of straw while Brenda opened the necks of the empty sacks. Grace followed Brenda in agreeing to join the Italians around the bonfire and Angelo went away happy.

'My, my,' Brenda commented on Una's flushed cheeks. 'That's made your day.'

Una ignored her and held a sack open while Brenda threw potatoes into it. 'Angelo invited all three of us, not just me.' One of the potatoes missed the sack and she stooped to pick it up to hide her blushes.

'Take no notice,' Grace said. 'I learned early on that Brenda likes to tease.'

They worked on, getting into the rhythm of lifting and picking, soothed by the repetitive regularity of the work and by the sound of mellifluous voices raised to sing again. As they filled each sack to the brim they saw the clear results of their labour. Then, when at noon the sun broke briefly through the clouds and slanting rays fell across the snowy hillside, they felt warmth on their faces and satisfaction in their hearts.

They were almost sorry when the private they knew as Albert left his post by the solitary tree and came to tell them it was dinner time. 'There's coffee on the go,' he promised them, gesturing towards the circle of prisoners already gathered round the bonfire. 'And baked potatoes, if you want them.'

'No, ta.' Brenda stood up straight to ease her back. 'To be honest with you, I'd be quite happy if I never saw another potato ever again.'

'Please yourself.' Albert shrugged and led the way to the fire. 'I'm only the messenger.'

'Drat – I've left my sandwiches in my saddlebag,' Brenda remembered, cutting off across the hillside towards the farm buildings to fetch them. 'Don't do anything I wouldn't do,' she warned Una and Grace as Angelo, Lorenzo and the other prisoners welcomed them into the group.

Lorenzo handed them enamelled tin mugs full of steaming black coffee. 'Drink,' he encouraged.

Grace stood by the crackling heat of the fire, sipping slowly. The coffee was good and strong and she felt revived.

'You like?' Angelo asked Una, holding up a blue paper bag. When she nodded he tilted the bag carefully and poured a trickle of sugar into her drink, offering to stir it with a stick.

His concentration amused her – the way he knitted his smooth brows only made him more handsome, she thought. 'Enough,' she said and he looked at her with those smiling, dark-brown eyes. He'd managed to add style to his grey prisoner's jacket by turning up the collar and winding a white scarf around his neck. His olive skin and black hair made a strong contrast. The small fact that his nails were bitten back and his fingers stained by nicotine didn't bother her. In her eyes, he was perfect.

'I show you something,' he told her confidentially as if there was no one else around. He drew a small wooden whistle from his top pocket and handed it to her. 'I make for my sister's son in Pisa where I live.'

The whistle was skilfully made. It had a pattern of leaves and flowers carved into it. 'Pisa,' she repeated. 'You're a long way from home.'

'Yes.' Angelo took the child's instrument and placed it back in his pocket. 'I come here from far away when ship sink. Many dead. I live.'

'You were lucky,' Una said quietly. It struck her that this was the first time she'd spoken to anyone on the enemy side and that it was the same as talking to Albert – apart from the language, of course. They were both just young men, called up to do their bit. 'I have three brothers – two in the Merchant Navy, one in the army.'

'They are safe?'

'So far,' she replied, fingers crossed.

A prisoner came up to her and held out a baked potato. She took it and he moved on to Grace.

'Thank you.' Grace took one for politeness's sake. Flames from the bonfire flickered across her face until Lorenzo came and stood between her and the fire. 'I have seen you before,' he reminded her. 'Last year at Christmas. You read a poem about a boy and a lion.'

'Oh, that!' She was embarrassed by the memory. 'You've been at Beckwith Camp all this time?'

'Just over a year,' he said solemnly. His voice was

less heavily accented than Angelo's and his air more sophisticated. 'Rome is not my home now.'

'Oh, but really it is. You'll go back there after the war, I'm sure.'

'I hope.' Lorenzo was a head taller than her and completely self-assured. Most women fell for him at first glance. He had them swooning at his feet the moment he turned on his charm. Not this one, though – a fair-haired English rose with serious, clear grey eyes.

'We've decided to put on another show at the Institute this Christmas.' Grace filled the awkward gap. 'It's not official yet but you're welcome to come and see it.'

He nodded and stared thoughtfully at her.

'No more poems,' she promised. 'This time it'll be just singing and dancing.'

Another nod, followed by a long pause, followed by a question that took Grace by surprise. 'Eunice is your friend?'

'Yes, that is . . .'

'She is my friend too. But I have not seen her for a few weeks. She wasn't at Home Farm or at Winsill Edge.'

'The hen farm – yes.' Grace stalled for time. She remembered seeing Eunice Mason having a long conversation with Lorenzo after the show last year. They'd made a striking couple – he handsome but vain and rather louche, she blonde and vivacious for once and obviously under his spell.

'Where does she work now?' Lorenzo asked. 'Has she gone away from Fieldhead?'

Grace sighed and shook her head. There was no avoiding it; she had to tell him the truth. 'I'm sorry, Eunice has passed away.'

'She's dead?' Lorenzo's face changed suddenly. He took a sharp intake of breath then closed his eyes, crossed himself and uttered a rapid prayer. 'This is true?' he asked Grace.

'I'm afraid it is.' She judged that the gruesome details of Eunice's suicide were too private to share. 'It happened last month.'

Again a sharp breath before he stepped away. He had no more questions but his distress was clear.

'What's wrong with Lorenzo?' Brenda asked as she rejoined the group, a half-eaten sandwich in her hand.

'I told him about Eunice. He took it badly,' Grace reported.

They looked at each other, perhaps thinking along the same lines but saying nothing as Lorenzo walked away from the fire, up onto the ridge.

Work continued all afternoon. Neville came and went with his horse and cart. The two soldiers smoked and chatted while Una, Grace and Brenda bagged potatoes alongside the prisoners of war. The job was shared but their thoughts were their own.

Brenda spent a long time mulling over her latest conversation with Bill Mostyn – how surprised she'd been when he'd taken her side in the tussle over the rota, how relaxed he'd seemed as he'd volunteered to take a look at her bike. She'd seen a new, nicer side to him than she'd expected. She'd always found him attractive, though, ever since she'd first come across him in the Blacksmith's Arms soon after she'd arrived at Fieldhead.

'Who's that?' she'd asked Grace, pointing to where Bill stood and joked with a gang of pals. 'The man in the thick of things, in the tweed sports jacket.'

Grace had told her his name and a bit about him.

'He's been working in the family firm since he left school,' she'd reported. 'He's an only child, so Edith smothers him rather and his father puts too much responsibility onto his shoulders.'

'Which are broad enough to bear the weight, I should think.' Brenda's first impression had been favourable – Bill was strong and tall, with a casual ease in his movements, not at all a namby-pamby mother's boy. She would have asked more about him if Grace hadn't had to rush off to serve new customers.

Which brought her to the moment on Saturday afternoon when he'd stood up from mending the bike and a look had been exchanged. A thrill like a small electric shock had run through her and she'd seized the moment to offer to buy him a drink. She'd been sure he would say yes.

'There's no need,' he'd said, shutting down the look and spoiling the moment.

His abruptness had puzzled her and the hurt had lingered.

'You're quiet.' Grace interrupted Brenda's train of thought. The sky was beginning to darken and the two Tommies were rounding up prisoners ready to march them back to the lorry parked in the farmyard. In the far distance they heard the low rumble of plane engines, gradually growing louder.

'Are you all right?'

'Yes, right as rain,' Brenda assured her. Remembering the borrowed gloves, she ran after Lorenzo to hand them back.

When she returned to Una and Grace they were looking up at the sky, watching an arrow-shaped formation of planes appear on the horizon. The Lancasters – twelve in all – flew low and level along the line of the valley, propellers churning.

'Heading for Germany,' Grace surmised. She saw light snowflakes drift down and felt them melt on her cheeks.

Una, Brenda and Grace followed the progress of the bombers for a long time, until they rose higher and disappeared behind a bank of clouds.

'That was the type of plane Edgar was in when he was shot down.' Grace's quiet voice claimed their attention. 'He was in the gun turret at the back. Somehow he came out of it alive.'

'Thank goodness,' Una and Brenda murmured. The day had ended on a sad note that no one could shift as they collected their bikes from Roland Thomson's barn and cycled home in silence.

Three days later, Jean was the first to comment on how eagerly Brenda and Una set off for work each morning.

'You see that, Elsie? Last week they were moaning and groaning about digging ditches. Now wild horses wouldn't stop them from getting out to Brigg

Farm. What's the attraction out there, I wonder?' Of course, word had got around about the prisoners of war and Jean had seized on it and gnawed away at it every chance she got.

Elsie stood with her at an upstairs window, hearing laughter as the duo crossed the yard. She'd come to Fieldhead straight from a stable yard on the Wolds where she'd worked as a groom. She had a reputation for having an old head on her young shoulders, for letting nothing bother her or send her into a spin – in fact, she was the ideal Land Army girl. 'Come off it, Jean. We know perfectly well what the attraction is. And I don't blame them.'

'You say that.' Jean's look was narrow and spiteful. 'But some people don't have the common sense that you do – mentioning no names. Their heads can be turned as easily as anything.'

Elsie smiled to herself. 'Don't be such an old misery. Anyway, you're jealous; there's no chance of you having your head turned by Horace Turnbull and his toothless old dad.' A day at Winsill Edge beckoned, collecting eggs, feeding the hens with a grain mixture, cleaning out the huts and laying fresh straw.

Meanwhile, Brenda and Una met up with Grace and were well on their way to work for their last day of bagging potatoes. They were overtaken at the bottom of Brigg Hill by the familiar green lorry carrying the Italians to work. The men leaned out of the back, waving and cheering, their faces wreathed in smiles.

'I don't care what anyone says, I'm going to miss

our Italian friends after we've finished at Brigg Farm,' Brenda confessed. 'But we'll see them again at the Christmas show.' She and Grace had done a lot of organizing during the last few days to make sure that it took place. They'd asked for volunteers and discussed ideas for songs, dances and costumes then got together with Joyce at the piano for a first rehearsal. 'A shambles,' had been the general verdict. The piano was out of tune, Elsie's tap dance needed a lot of work and Una's attempt to find a song from a recent musical had ended in failure. But it was a start, Grace had insisted, determined not to let the prisoners down and settling on Friday evening for the next proper rehearsal.

They pedalled hard up the hill in the wake of the lorry. After only a week of farm work, Una felt fitter, stronger and less clueless – more on a par with the other girls. Though she was still bothered by homesickness, especially first thing in the morning, she now plunged into each fresh challenge with gusto.

'We'll see Angelo again, won't we?' She made no bones about picking out the prisoner who had made the strongest impression on her. 'I don't mean in the audience for the Christmas show – I mean at farms round and about.'

'Cue violins!' Brenda called over her shoulder to Grace. 'Una is in love!'

'I know what you're going to say – "Take no notice!"' Una pre-empted Grace's advice, but her heart fluttered all the same.

'Watch where you're going,' Grace warned Brenda. 'Pothole ahead!'

The last layer of straw was lifted and the last potato safely bagged. The bonfire on the hill was allowed to die.

'*Ciao*,' the prisoners said to Brenda, Una and Grace as they waited in single file to climb into the lorry.

'*Ciao*,' they said back to each in turn. 'Good luck. We hope we'll see you again.'

Lorenzo took Grace to one side. 'I am sad about Eunice,' he told her. 'I wish to know how she died.'

Grace shook her head. 'It wouldn't be right,' she began.

'It was not an illness?'

'No.'

'An accident?'

'No.'

He understood what this must mean and looked stricken all over again.

Lorenzo loved her, Grace thought. *Lorenzo was in love with Eunice Mason.* The truth stunned her into silence. Who would have thought that this suave, over-confident ladies' man would have given his heart to a Land Girl?

He backed off and pushed his way to the front of the queue, then he climbed up into the lorry and sat down out of sight.

'*Ciao.*' It was Angelo's turn to say goodbye to Una. He took her hand and pressed it, thought about leaning in to kiss her cheek then resisted.

'Goodbye,' she whispered back. When she looked down at her palm she saw a small piece of paper with words written in capital letters. She closed her fingers over the note then quickly slid it into the pocket of her overcoat.

The prisoners were safely counted in so Albert and Jack raised the back ramp. They bolted it in place then took their seats in the front cab. Una could see Angelo leaning out to wave along with a dozen others.

She waved back. The unread note seemed to burn a hole in the cloth.

'*Ciao, ciao!*' Brenda called.

Grace looked in vain for a last sight of Lorenzo.

The lorry drove away and the girls went to fetch their bikes. Roland and Neville shook them by the hand.

'You put your backs into your work,' Roland acknowledged grudgingly, while Neville seemed to single out Una and wink at her. 'You three can come back and help with the grain threshing if you like.'

'No ta!' Brenda was the first to move off. 'Sugar beet, turnips – anything but that!'

Angelo's note was written on a sheet of toilet paper. Una's first reaction when she took it out of her pocket in the privacy of her bedroom was to screw it up in disgust and throw it away. But she thought again – this must have been the only paper he could get his hands on without the two guards noticing. Besides, it showed how determined he'd been to write her a message. So she laid the note on her bed, smoothed the creases and read what he had written.

DEAR OONA
YOU ARE SO BEAUTIFUL. MY HEART ACHES.
COME TO CAMP AT NIGHT. MEET ME IN
TREES. GIVE NOTE TO NEV. I LONG FOR YOU.
SAY YES.

That was all. The writing was neat and clear and its contents sent her head spinning. When eventually she took her thoughts in hand, she made herself concentrate on the facts. Angelo must mean Beckwith Camp and there must be a copse behind it, as there was here at Fieldhead. He'd spelt her name wrong. And what had Neville Thomson got to do with it?

There was no time to work out the answers to these questions or how she was feeling because Kathleen burst into the room and flung herself down on her bed.

'That's the limit!' she exclaimed. 'If I'm sent to catch rats one more time, I'm going to do what Brenda did and put in a complaint.'

'Where did you have to go?' Una's hand was over Angelo's note. Her head was in a whirl.

'To Peggy Russell's sheep farm then out to the Kelletts' place. Don't they know there's a whole pest control section to deal with vermin? We're farm workers – we shouldn't have to do it.' Kathleen sat up to untie the two pieces of sacking that she'd wrapped around her legs to stop the rats from scurrying up

83

her dungarees. 'I wish I'd worn my breeches. Honestly, Una, I'm sick of it.'

Kathleen was the most unlikely rat-catcher. The pretty hairdresser belonged to the world of tea dances and ballrooms, not cowsheds and hen huts. 'You're right – you should complain,' Una agreed.

'I was by myself for the whole day, coping with Emily Kellett and that son of hers breathing down my neck all over again. According to her, I couldn't do anything right. I said she should keep all food out of harm's way – hang it from the ceiling beams, if necessary. Otherwise, she'd keep on being overrun.'

'Especially at this time of year.' When would Kathleen run out of breath? Una was dying to reread Angelo's message.

Rid of her improvised gaiters, Kathleen kicked off her shoes then took off her jumper and dungarees and picked up her towel. 'I'm going to see if the bathroom's free. I need to scrub myself from head to toe.'

Una waited for the door to close behind her disgruntled room-mate then lifted her hand to reveal the crumpled note. The words 'AT NIGHT' jumped out as she read it again then she moved on to wonder once more about Neville's role. She remembered the wink that the farmer's son had given her on parting. Perhaps Angelo had already arranged for him to be their go-between.

She was so deep in thought that she didn't react quickly enough to Brenda's sudden entrance into the room.

'What's this?' Brenda tried to seize the paper but

Una snatched it away. 'Don't tell me; it's a *billet-doux*!' She guessed everything in an instant from the deep blush on Una's face. 'It is, isn't it?' she said more gently as she sat down on the bed. 'It's from Angelo. He says he wants you to meet him.'

Una nodded. 'What should I do?'

Brenda noticed that her hands were trembling. 'You're in a quandary, I can see that. So the first question is: do you like him?'

'Yes.'

'How much?'

'A lot,' Una confessed. Her heart had melted the moment he showed her the carved whistle, and again as she'd listened to the rolling 'o's, 'l's and 'r's of his deep voice. 'I know it sounds daft.'

'You like him a lot,' Brenda echoed as she took up the note. 'And it's obvious from this that he likes you. So you're asking yourself, how do you go on from here?'

'I don't even know if I should send him an answer. What would people think if they found out?'

'Because he's a POW, you mean?' Though there was less than a year between them, Brenda was by far the worldlier of the two. It was her nature to be breezy and outgoing and she'd always been the ringleader in seeking out any fun there was to be had, from riding her Sloper to unselfconsciously going up to boys at the local dance hall and asking them to dance. Now she smiled and patted Una's hand. 'You're not the first girl to fraternize with the enemy, you know. And you won't be the last.'

'But is it right?' Una's sigh filled the room.

Outside, the night had already drawn in and the only sounds were the echoing sighs of the wind blowing through the elms.

Brenda raised her shoulders in an exaggerated shrug. 'Who knows what's right and what's wrong these days? Everything has been turned on its head. We were watching those Lancasters fly out earlier and I found myself wondering, *How many of those brave boys will fly back again?* Then I had to stop myself from imagining where they will drop their bombs. Will it be over Berlin, or closer to home in northern France? And who will be on the receiving end?'

'Hush.' Una didn't want to follow this line of thinking any further.

'You see?' Brenda said quietly. 'It's all topsy-turvy. Why shouldn't you meet up with an Italian POW if he's kind and handsome?'

'He says it has to be at night. I'd have to ride my bike in the dark.'

'Unless I drove you there on Old Sloper.'

Brenda's impetuousness was infectious and Una nodded eagerly. 'Would you?'

'Why not?' It was decided in a flash. 'You write a reply to Angelo arranging a time to meet. Give the note to Neville then light the blue touch paper and stand well back.'

CHAPTER SIX

The next day was set to be the second rehearsal for the Christmas show until Joyce lifted the dusty lid of the piano in what had once been the school's music room and declared that she wouldn't play an instrument that was so completely out of tune.

'I can't play on that old thing again,' she told Brenda and Jean at Friday breakfast time. She used the top of the long trestle table to mime running her fingers up and down musical scales. 'Plinkety-plonk, plinkety-plonk.'

'Tell everyone – the rehearsal's off.' Jean sounded relieved as she passed the word around. However, she reckoned without Brenda's commitment to the cause.

'Wait, I have an idea.' She stood up to make an announcement. 'Listen, everyone. What do you say to shifting tonight's rehearsal to the Blacksmith's Arms? I'm sure they've got a piano tucked away somewhere.'

Several voices confirmed that Cliff Kershaw encouraged weekend singalongs and kept an upright piano for the purpose.

'No doubt it draws more customers in if they can tap their feet and have a sing-song while they're downing their pints.' Joyce backed the idea. 'Don't forget, girls, write down the titles of the songs you'd like to sing before you leave for work today. That'll give me enough time to flick through my book of Broadway hits.'

So it was agreed – rehearsal for the Christmas show, tonight at seven o'clock at the Blacksmith's Arms.

The arrangement made, the girls arrived that evening in dribs and drabs. All were dressed to impress in pastel-coloured frocks with shoulder pads and nipped-in waists, their hair carefully curled, winter coats slung casually around their shoulders. They went straight to the bar to order their drinks and if they were lucky a gallant young man from the village would step in and pay. There were smiles and laughter, the sound of pints being pulled, glasses chinking and jokes being told.

'Good evening, Cliff.' Bill Mostyn presented himself at the bar and took a quick look around. 'Are you on your own tonight?'

The landlord grunted his reply. 'It looks like it. Grace is busy with her Land Army pals over there in the corner. And don't ask me where Edgar has got to.' His protruding bottom lip stuck out further than ever to show his displeasure. His bald head shone in the gaslight glare from the sconces on the wall behind him.

'I'll have two pints of best bitter and a Guinness, please.' Bill took in the busy scene and saw that the

Land Girls were already bunched around the piano, chattering ten to the dozen. 'What are they up to?'

'They're rehearsing another Christmas show. Don't worry about not being able to hear yourself speak above the cats' chorus – they've promised to keep the noise down.'

'I'm not worried.' Bill was used to Cliff's curmudgeonly mutterings. He made out Joyce at the piano and Brenda and Grace amongst the excited group.

'Cole Porter's "Anything Goes".' Joyce flicked through her book of popular songs. 'Yes, Kathleen – here it is, after "I Get a Kick out of You". Hmm, that's an Ethel Merman song. Would you like to try that one, Elsie? It would suit you down to the ground.'

'We could sing it as a duet,' Elsie said to Una. The one-time stable girl was transformed into a vision of loveliness in a light wool dress of palest blue with a sparkling brooch in the shape of a bouquet on her breast and a touch of rose-pink lipstick on her full lips. 'What do you think? Una, did you hear me?'

'What? Yes, I'm sorry. I wasn't concentrating.' Not to be outdone, Una too had worn her best outfit. Her dress was jade green to set off the reddish tone of her hair and it was cut in a wrap-over style that made the most of her slim waist.

'"I Get a Kick out of You" – shall we give it a go?'

'If you like.' Her gaze flicked over the crowd at the bar. The reply to Angelo that she'd penned the night before was in her pocket but so far there was no sign of Neville Thomson. She'd half expected him not to be here, it was true. He looked too young to drink and probably wouldn't get served even if he tried. Yet she'd still hoped to see her go-between.

Dear Angelo
   Thank you for your note. It would be nice to meet up. How does this coming Sunday evening sound? I can be there by six o'clock. I hope you get this message in time. Love from Una

The words were etched on her brain.

'That would be two Cole Porter songs in the programme,' Joyce went on. 'Now, who would like to sing something from *The Wizard of Oz*?'

Brenda took up the suggestion. '"Over the Rainbow" would go down well,' she decided. 'It's about dreams coming true and we could all do with a bit of that in our lives.' A switch from monochrome reality to full Technicolor in the whoosh of a good witch's wand.

'Very well. Kathleen, your turn first,' Joyce ordered.

The young hairdresser sang 'Anything Goes' with gusto. Her choice was lively and the lyrics risqué, with references to a glimpse of stockings and fast cars drawing wolf whistles and whoops from the men by the bar. Towards the end she stumbled over the words and apologized.

Brenda put an arm around her waist. 'Don't worry, we don't expect you to be word perfect at this point. Wait until we get to my turn.'

Now Una and Elsie were due to sing along but this time it was Joyce who had difficulty finding the right notes. 'Let's leave that for now,' she decided as her fingers faltered and she closed the song book. Her civilian garb consisted of sensible blouse and skirt, brightened by a yellow silk scarf. She'd pinned up her dark-brown hair in a fancy French pleat and wore pearl earrings to add another feminine touch. Taking a fresh sheet of music from the pile on top of the piano, she turned to talk to Brenda.

'Phew!' Elsie let Una know that she was relieved to be let off the hook then went to join two fellow horse enthusiasts on the settle next to the inglenook – Alice Foster from Hawkshead Manor and Geoffrey Somers, Master of the Burnside hunt. She left Una still looking for Neville and hoping against hope.

Over by the piano, Brenda and Joyce tried the first few bars of the Judy Garland song, but Brenda soon lost her way. '. . . Way up high, there's a land . . . once in a lullaby.' Her rhythm was wrong and she struggled to remember all the words. She laughed and turned her failure into a joke.

'Maybe I should have picked the Scarecrow's song.'

'"If I Only Had a Brain",' Jean cut in sharply, giving Brenda a significant look.

'Tut-tut.' Joyce grimaced then compared Jean to the Tin Man. 'He doesn't have a heart,' she said pointedly.

Una stood a little distance away. It struck her that Brenda rarely took things seriously and suddenly this bothered her. What if her advice about Angelo was as shallow and mischievous as many other things about her? Should she have followed it and written the reply or was it all foolishness? Well, as things had turned out, she still had time to change her mind. *Dear Angelo, Thank you for your note. It would be nice to meet up . . .* She recited the words over and over inside her head. *To send or not to send?* If it came to it and she decided to go ahead, she could probably cycle out to Brigg Farm to find Neville tomorrow afternoon. *Or then again, perhaps not.*

'They're putting on another show.' Bill stood with his usual group of friends close to the door, explaining to a newcomer the reason behind the noisy gaggle of Land Girls gathered around the piano. He noticed that Grace had left the group to lend her father a hand and was responding as quickly as she could to Cliff's gruff orders. Feeling irritated, he put down his glass and walked outside to the gents' toilet. He didn't get far across the yard, however, before he saw Edgar lurching in the dark towards him.

Edgar stumbled and dropped his cigarette. 'Watch where you're going,' he told Bill, his voice slurred and accusatory, his gaze unfocused as he stooped to pick up the glowing cigarette. He swore as he took it by the wrong end and burned his finger.

In fact, Bill had only reached out to steady the other man. He caught the stale alcohol on Edgar's breath as he stood up straight. 'Steady on,' he advised in a friendly manner.

Edgar shoved him away, swayed backwards then took an unsteady step towards the pub door. Thomas Lund had followed Bill's lead and only just got out of Edgar's way as he blundered on. 'Someone's had a skinful,' he remarked before accompanying Bill to the gents'.

Bill thought no more of the incident when he went back to the bar. His pals had moved in on the Land Girls as soon as their rehearsal had finished and Brenda Appleby was heading his way.

'I just wanted to say ta for persuading your mother to rearrange this week's rota after all,' she began breezily. 'I don't think I could have stood many more days at Home Farm.'

Bill looked mystified. 'It was nothing to do with me. It's Mother you have to thank; she must have had a change of heart.'

'Well, tell her thanks from me.' She raised her glass and was pleased that he responded with a chink of his own glass. 'Chin-chin,' she added with a smile.

Thomas swung through the door and noticed the spark between them. On the spur of the moment he decided to play Cupid. 'It's my round,' he announced. 'Brenda, what'll you have? Bill – another pint of bitter?' This left Bill alone with Brenda again while he went to the bar.

She plunged in with the first topic of conversation that came into her head. 'How do you think our rehearsal went?'

'So-so.' His answer was honest. 'When do you have to be ready by?'

'The twenty-third. It's for the prisoners at Beckwith Camp, like last year.' She rolled her eyes in dismay. 'I know for a fact that they can out-sing us any day of the week.'

'It won't be the singing they're interested in.' In spite of himself, Brenda's infectious good humour steered his response. 'They'll be chuffed to be let out of their barracks to get an eyeful of you lot.'

Brenda pretended to huff and puff. 'You can't say that! Your answer should be something like, "You have the voice of an angel, Miss Appleby, and so does the rest of your merry band."'

'You have the voice of an angel,' he concurred. 'An angel who forgets the words to her song.'

She laughed. 'It's from *The Wizard of Oz*. Do you know it?'

'No, musicals aren't really my cup of tea.' Standing close beside her in the increasingly crowded bar, Bill could smell Brenda's flowery perfume and almost feel the warmth of her skin, which was smooth and creamy. She had long, thick lashes and a smile that would light up the darkest day.

'Judy Garland is marvellous in it. And you should see the little Munchkins – they're a scream.' *Gabble-gabble*. She opened her mouth and words tumbled out willy-nilly. One day she would learn not to do this, but for now she let her tongue run on. She told Bill about the brainless scarecrow and the cowardly lion. 'Do you like dogs?' she asked him. 'Dorothy has a little pet dog called Toto, who gets transported with her into the World of Oz.'

Her radiant face fascinated him, her eyes especially. Her dark lashes were complemented by finely arched eyebrows and a high forehead, half covered by a sweep of dark, glossy hair. He frowned and pulled himself up short for staring at her.

'Sorry,' she said with a low, breathy laugh, 'I'm going on a bit.'

'I do like dogs,' he admitted. 'We never had one, though. They bring Mum out in a rash, the same as horses.'

Too quickly for her liking, Thomas came back with the drinks and the chat turned to the football match that the Burnside eleven were due to play the next day. 'It's at home,' Thomas explained to Brenda. 'Why not come along and watch?'

'Perhaps I will.' Taking a sip from her glass of sweet martini, she tuned out of the conversation about team tactics and gave herself time to plan ahead. She would stay with Bill and Thomas for as long as her drink lasted, keeping in the background for once, chipping in every now and then but mainly listening and smiling, as women did when men talked football. It wouldn't come naturally to her but she would try.

It worked well for a while. '. . . Tall centre forward . . . keep the ball out on the right wing . . . hope that the pitch thaws out—' There was a sudden interruption.

'Bill, can you come please?' It was Grace. She was obviously distressed as she tugged at his sleeve. 'I'm sorry – it's Edgar. Can you come?'

He went with her straight away, behind the bar then down some worn steps to the cellar where he found Edgar slumped across a barrel with Cliff trying to pull him upright.

'He's too heavy for us to manage,' Grace told Bill. 'It was Dad who found him when he came down to tap a new barrel.'

The cellar was small and damp, with a vaulted ceiling. A row of full barrels was lined up down one side and a stack of empties on the other. There was no light except for a paraffin lamp hanging from an overhead hook.

Bill quickly assessed the situation. From what he'd seen of Edgar half an hour earlier and from the way he was bunching his fists and flailing his arms now, he decided there was no hope of getting him to stand on his own two feet. 'Where do you want to take him?' he asked Grace, whose face was pale and strained.

'Upstairs, to the back bedroom.'

Cliff abandoned his efforts and stood back to draw breath. His watch had slipped out of his waistcoat pocket and hung down on its silver chain. His face was shiny with sweat. 'Don't bother. Leave him where he is,' he told Bill. 'Let him sleep it off.'

'We can't do that,' Grace argued. 'It's damp down here. He'll catch his death.'

'A fat lot I care.' Disgust marked Cliff's features and he couldn't resist giving Edgar a nudge with the toe of his boot. 'Bloody idiot.'

Edgar's eyes were closed. He struck out with his fists but only succeeded in slumping further onto the floor where he sprawled face-down.

'Idiot,' Cliff repeated as he gave up on his son and left.

Bill went across to Edgar, turned him over and propped him up against the wall. 'Listen to me. I'm going to take one arm and Grace here is going to take the other. We'll stand you up then get you up the stairs to bed.' There was no response so he spoke to Grace. 'It's no good – he's a dead weight. We'll need Thomas to lend a hand.'

'I've never seen him as bad as this,' she said. Edgar's face and neck were a mottled red and saliva slid out of one corner of his mouth.

'I know. But fetch Thomas, there's a good girl.' Bill squatted beside Edgar while Grace went for extra help. Edgar's head lolled forward, his legs splayed wide. *Edgar Kershaw has broken more than his leg* was the alarming thought that passed through Bill's mind.

Within a minute Grace was back with Thomas. The two men hauled the drunk man to his feet and took his weight. They began to drag him to the bottom of the cellar steps. Thomas's head caught on the paraffin lamp and it swung precariously on its hook. 'Steady,' Bill cautioned.

Grace held her breath. They had to negotiate the stone steps. Would there be enough space for three men abreast? She felt sick as she went ahead. What in God's name had happened to Edgar to make him like this?

Bill and Thomas struggled but at last they got him to the cellar head where Joyce had come to Grace's aid.

'You looked upset so I guessed something was wrong,' she explained as she stepped in to steady Edgar while Thomas and Bill had a breather. She made no fuss as she took his weight, merely waited to see what would happen next.

Eager to get Edgar out of sight of customers and to keep him out of their father's clutches, Grace held open a door that led into the kitchen at the back of the house. The hum of voices made her brother open his eyes and groan. 'In here, quick,' Grace said.

Joyce straightened Edgar's jacket as she handed him back to the two men. 'Poor blighter,' she murmured.

They got him across the kitchen and up another flight of stairs, along the corridor and into a small room with a patchwork quilt across a single bed underneath a cross-stitch picture saying, *Home Sweet Home*.

'Bloody hell.' An exhausted Thomas stood back as Bill eased Edgar onto the bed.

Grace gave a sound between a sigh and a sob. She unlaced Edgar's shoes and loosened the top button of his stained and crumpled shirt.

'Lay him on his side,' Thomas suggested and Bill followed his advice.

'Keep an eye on him,' Joyce told Grace as she and Thomas backed out of the room. No fuss, no judgement.

'Ta – I will.' Grace had to blink back tears. She felt helpless and desperate.

Edgar lay on the bed breathing heavily now. He drew his knees to his chest and curled into a ball. Grace and Bill retreated to the door then turned to take one last look.

'You did the right thing,' Bill reassured her. He took her hands between his. Hot tears brimmed and trickled down her cold cheeks. He brushed them away with his thumbs. 'Edgar will be all right in the morning; you'll see.'

'I'm on tenterhooks to see if I get a reply,' Una confessed to Grace. It was a bright, cold Sunday morning. After the fog of the night before, rime frost lay thick on the wall tops and shrouded the bare trees as she'd cycled into Burnside. 'Do you think I will?'

Grace had put aside the painting of a Christmas tree that she'd been working on and sat her down with a cup of tea. 'Let me get this straight. One of the Italian prisoners—'

'Angelo. His name is Angelo.'

'Yes, I know who you mean. Angelo is sweet on you. He wrote you a note and you've written back.'

Una nodded. 'Neville Thomson is in on it. He's promised to take letters back and forth.'

'That's the bit I'm not sure about.' Grace felt a sharp pang of sympathy for her visitor. 'Is Neville reliable?'

'I'm not sure either.' After she'd finally overcome her doubts about Angelo, she'd cycled up Brigg Hill, her heart in her mouth.

She'd arrived at the farm and Roland Thomson had given her short shrift. 'Neville's playing football. What do you want him for?'

'Nothing,' she'd replied, kicking herself for not thinking of this. After all, she'd heard the raucous yells and shouts coming from the playing field behind the Institute as she'd cycled by. Of course Neville would be playing for the Burnside team – he was one of the few remaining fit young men around. She'd cycled away from the farm on the hill, back down to the village, then hung around in the Institute porch until the whistle had blown to end the match and Neville had at last got changed and sauntered up the yard.

'Heck,' he'd said when he spotted her, his wet hair sticking to his scalp after a quick cold shower. 'Don't tell me, let me guess – you want me to play postman for you.'

His mockery had galvanized her into action and she'd quickly handed over the note. 'Don't sound so surprised.'

'I am. In fact, I'd have laid money against it happening.'

'Then you would have lost your bet,' she'd retorted, taking her bike from its stand. Neville reminded her of her youngest brother Geoffrey who had joined the army and she hoped that, just as with him, there was no malice beneath the cheeky persona.

Neville had put the note into his jacket pocket. 'Your secret's safe with me,' he'd said with a wink.

'I think it'll be all right, though,' she told Grace now, her mittened hands wrapped around a mug of hot tea. 'I gave Neville sixpence for his trouble.'

Grace said nothing except, 'Let's wait and see.'

'This is nice and cosy,' Una said, looking around the room at the hand-made rag rug and the old pewter plates lined up along the high mantelpiece. The fire burned brightly in the kitchen grate. She heard movement in one of the upstairs rooms and looked enquiringly at Grace.

'That's Father. He went upstairs to wake Edgar just before you arrived.' A troubled expression flitted across her face and she tried to smooth it away by drawing her fingers across her forehead.

'How is Edgar?' Una didn't pretend not to know

what had happened on Friday night. 'Was he badly hungover?'

'Yes, as bad as can be. He was good for nothing all day yesterday.'

The floorboards above their heads went on creaking then a door closed firmly and there were footsteps on the stairs. The kitchen door opened and Cliff glared in at Grace and Una.

'Well?' Grace asked. 'Is he awake?'

'He's not there. And his bed hasn't been slept in either.' Cliff's accusing look made it seem as if Grace had known this all along but Grace jumped up in alarm. If Una hadn't been there, she would have run upstairs to check for herself. As it was, she tried to keep her worries in check. 'What do you mean?'

'What I say. He must have stopped out all night.'

'Where?' The last time Grace had seen Edgar had been yesterday teatime when he'd finally emerged from his room. Unshaven and bleary eyed, he'd come into the kitchen as dusk fell, put on his overcoat and gone out without saying a word. 'Where would he go?'

Cliff shook his head and closed the door. 'I don't know and I don't care.'

Una and Grace looked at each other in alarm, each thinking of the freezing fog that had cloaked the hillsides all night long.

'Could he have stayed at a friend's house?' Una asked.

'I don't think so. Edgar hasn't been in touch with any of his old pals since he came back. Anyway, most have been called up.'

'Could he have caught the bus into Northgate to see a film, perhaps?'

'And missed the last bus back? Yes, that's possible.' But the more Grace thought about it, the less likely it seemed. 'We have a telephone here. Edgar would have rung us if that had been the case.' She frowned then spoke in an undertone. 'The truth is, I'm worried that Dad might have driven Edgar away.'

'By something he said?'

'Exactly. He seems not to care about what Edgar's been through. You see, he came through the First War when the attitude was you have to grin and bear it, no matter what. He was blacksmith for a cavalry regiment in Belgium, which kept him away from the front line.'

Una understood what she was getting at. 'He doesn't see that everything is different this time around.' Machines were the killers now – not men on horseback.

'With Dad everything is black and white. Edgar has no business being at home. His duty is to serve his country, full stop.'

'Has he said as much?'

'To Edgar? I'm not sure. What I do know is that Edgar is in a poor way and if Dad has spoken his mind, he'll have taken it badly.'

Kind-hearted Una cast around for ways to help. 'Just suppose that the two of them did have an argument that made Edgar storm off. I'm trying to think what I would do next if I was him. It's getting foggy and dusk is falling. I know the countryside well because I grew up here so it's not too hard to make my way to the nearest barn and climb up into the hayloft for the night. Yes – something like that, don't you think?'

Grace nodded. 'You're right. I have to remember that Edgar is his own man. If he chooses to keep out of Dad's way for a while, it's up to him.' But still she couldn't get rid of the pathetic sight of him lying dead drunk in the cellar, and being dragged upstairs to bed by Bill and Thomas.

'I'll tell you what,' Una said as she prepared to take her leave, 'I'll keep a lookout for him on my way back to the hostel. I could get the other girls to do the same while they're out and about.'

'No, you've got much nicer things to think about.' Grace gave herself a shake. 'Good luck tonight with your handsome Italian. I'll be thinking of you.'

'If it ever comes off.'

'It will.'

Una buttoned her coat and tied a scarf around her head then she held up two sets of crossed fingers. 'Ta for the tea, Grace. If we hear any news of Edgar, I'll give you a call.'

'These days we have to think the unthinkable.' Vince Mostyn was in a gloomy mood on the way back from Hawkshead Manor where he'd spent the morning bemoaning the state of the world over a glass of sherry with Alice and Lionel Foster. Bill had picked him up at noon and now they were speeding back over the moors in his Austin 7. 'Did you know that the *Ark Royal* went down off Gibraltar?'

'Yes, I heard it on the wireless.' Bill kept his eyes

on the icy road ahead. 'She was under tow at the time.'

'A U-boat got her.' Vince spoke with a tone of disbelief. 'If they can sink her, they can sink anything. We've already lost HMS *Hood*, and she was the pride of the Royal Navy.'

'It's not all bad news, though. Mr Churchill's doing his best to persuade Roosevelt to declare his hand and come in with us. It'll happen if the trouble that's brewing over Pearl Harbor comes to a head. That'll turn things around, you'll see.'

'The Yanks should have been in before now,' Vince pointed out. 'Hitler needed stopping long before he got a grip on Yugoslavia and Greece, let alone Poland and France.'

Bill couldn't disagree, though his father's belligerent patriotism disturbed him. He didn't like to discuss the war with him because deep down he had a certain amount of sympathy for conscientious objectors, although he kept that well hidden. In any case, he probably wouldn't have the courage to voice his convictions if his call-up papers ever landed on the mat. He would take up arms like everyone else. 'How were the Fosters?' he asked.

'Worried. With their two boys in the RAF as well as Shirley in the WAF, you can understand it.'

The conversation was like every other between Bill and his pessimistic father. If it wasn't war casualties, it was the German Chancellor's iniquitous treatment of the Jews, if not food shortages then the shameless black marketeers. 'Cheer up, Dad,' he said as he put on the brakes to avoid a rabbit sitting bang in the middle of the road. The car hit a patch of ice and the back end swung round, sending them up onto the grass verge. 'Sorry about that.'

'You should have run it over,' Vince commented as Bill steered them back onto the road.

'Why – did you want it for your supper?'

Unexpectedly, the near miss and his son's joke jolted Vince out of his cloud of gloom. 'I can't see your mother skinning a rabbit and putting it in the pot, can you?'

Bill laughed and looked in the mirror to check that the rabbit hadn't been harmed. The road was clear but a movement off to the side caught his eye. He looked harder. A figure had stood up from behind one of the stone hides built for the 'guns', marksmen who came up onto the moors in August to shoot pheasants. 'What the heck?' he muttered as he slammed on the brakes a second time.

The man left the hide and limped away from the road through the dead heather towards the crest of the exposed hillside, his coat flapping open.

Something told Bill that he should investigate so he pulled over to the side of the road. 'There's a chap up there heading off into the middle of nowhere,' he told his father. 'Wait here – I won't be long.'

Bracing himself against the bitter wind, Bill climbed the low drystone wall and went after the figure on the hill. He quickly gained on him. 'Are you lost? Can I help you find your way?' he yelled, cupping his hands around his mouth.

The man ignored him and stumbled on.

He looks familiar, even from the back, Bill thought.

105

I'm sure that's Edgar Kershaw. Bloody hell, what's he up to? 'Edgar, it's me – Bill Mostyn! Hold on a minute, I want to have a word.'

Edgar recognized Bill's voice and picked up his pace. The frost-covered heather tugged at his feet and he staggered sideways as a strong gust of wind almost tore the coat from his back. 'Get stuffed,' he muttered to his pursuer. After a night of misery spent huddling in the lee of the gamekeeper's hide, he was hell-bent on heading for wilderness and oblivion.

Bill broke into a run but the closer he got, the more determined Edgar was to ignore him. 'Hang on. I just want to see that you're OK. Slow down, hang on—'

Edgar whirled around and held up his fists, ready to fight.

Bill stopped and kept his distance. 'Whoa. It's all right; I'll stay where I am.' *My God, he looks awful,* he thought. Edgar's face was blue with cold. There were dark circles under his eyes, which were sunk far back in his head. *What the hell is he up to?*

'Fuck off, Bill. I said, fuck off!'

'All right, all right.' He made a conciliatory gesture. 'Listen, I'm not going to make you do anything you don't want to do.'

Edgar let his fists drop to his side. The wind gusted so strongly that he lost his balance again and went down onto one knee. Placing his palm flat on the ground, he leaned sideways, feeling the cold pierce his entire body. Then suddenly his arm was too weak to bear his weight and he found himself falling flat on his face and rolling down the cold, cold slope towards Bill.

Bill stooped to pull him up. 'Let me help, there's a good chap. That's right – I'm hooking your arm around my shoulder. There, that's better.'

Edgar felt the huge sky press down on him. He saw the yellow, snow-laden clouds through half-closed eyes, felt the black earth spin. He had no strength to resist.

'Now then, we'll walk back down to the road together. You see my car down there? That's where we're heading.' Slowly Bill led Edgar down the steep moor side. He saw his father get out of the car, cross the road and wait by the wall. 'There's a blanket in the boot,' he called down to him.

Vince went to fetch it. He handed it over as Bill helped Edgar over the wall. 'Good Lord, I thought it was a tramp but it's Cliff Kershaw's lad. What's wrong with him? What's he doing all the way out here?'

Bill shook his head. 'Wait till we get him home. We'll leave it to Grace to try to get some answers.' Easier said than done; Edgar was heavier than he looked and his body was rigid with cold. At last, however, they managed to sit him on the back seat and close the door. Fifteen minutes later they arrived at the Blacksmith's Arms.

Grace had been on the lookout for Edgar all morning and at the sound of Bill's car she dashed outside. She saw Edgar wrapped in a blanket, hunched forward on the back seat, and Bill opening the door to let him out. Bill's father sat in the front passenger seat.

'Oh, Edgar, thank heavens!' she cried. 'I've been worried sick about you.'

Bill held up a warning finger. 'Stand back, Grace – don't crowd him. Come on, Edgar – you're home now. Grace will look after you.'

Edgar sat with his head hanging, showing no sign of getting out of the car, and Grace felt her heart skip a beat and then quicken. 'What's wrong with him?' she begged.

'We found him up on Swinsty Edge – just in time, by the look of it. I think he's been out there all night.'

Suppressing a groan, she stepped forward, crouched to Edgar's level then took his hand. 'It's me – Grace,' she whispered gently.

Edgar turned his head towards her with a dark, empty gaze then glanced down at her hand clasped over his. He looked up again with dead eyes.

'You're home,' she murmured, willing him to respond. 'Can you walk across the yard?'

'I don't think he can answer you.' Bill ushered her to one side and leaned inside the car. 'Go around the other side and sit beside him,' he told Grace. 'A little push from you might galvanize him into action. I'll be ready here to fish him out.'

The plan worked and Bill supported Edgar as he stepped shakily out of the car. 'Easy does it,' he cajoled before asking his father to go ahead and warn Cliff of Edgar's imminent arrival.

'Oh, Edgar,' Grace said, sorrowfully brushing aside the idea that her brother might have lost his way in the fog. No – his decision to stay out all night had been premeditated. 'Things can't be that bad, surely.'

Bill said nothing until they'd got him into the house and sat him down at the kitchen table.

Vince stayed with Cliff in the doorway, advising him not to say too much. 'Better to let Edgar thaw out by the fire before you start firing questions at him.'

'You're right. But I'm not expecting to get any sense out of him, even then.' His son looked like the living dead, so gaunt and vacant that Cliff was shaken to his core. 'He's not right in the head, is he?'

'He's not,' Vince agreed. He'd seen enough cases of shell shock as a stretcher bearer in the First War to recognize it in Edgar. 'Give him time to come to his senses, there's a good chap.'

'Is that why the doctors sent him home?' Cliff was stricken by sudden guilt. 'Why the heck didn't he say something?'

'I expect he felt he couldn't.' Vince led his old friend down a corridor into the deserted forge. 'Don't be too hard on the lad.' His voice echoed in the barn-like space. Old horseshoes lay in a pile under the window, two pairs of bellows leaned against the wall and Cliff's blacksmith's hammers and tongs hung in a tidy row next to the unlit furnace. 'Time will be the healer here, and plenty of it.'

By late afternoon, Bill and Grace had at last managed to get Edgar to bed. They stood outside in the quiet pub yard, looking up at light clouds scudding across the big moon.

'What would have happened if you hadn't found him?' she said with a shudder and a glance up at the light glimmering in Edgar's window. 'Do you think he would have made his own way home eventually?'

'There's no point wondering.'

'Anyway, thank you.' Her plain words fell far short of expressing the gratitude she felt.

'Shall we walk a little way?' He put his arm around her shoulder, led her behind the forge and over the stile into the field.

They fell into step in the moonlight and soon left the lights of the village behind.

'This is the first bit of time we've spent together for more than a week.' He'd missed the sway of her body against him as they walked and the light feel of her arm around his waist. 'How did we let that happen?'

She smiled but didn't reply as she leaned in closer.

'We won't do it again,' he assured her.

They'd reached another stile. He stepped to one side and watched her climb over it. Her hair looked fairer in this light, her face paler. She was a slender woodland creature surrounded by silvery branches, turning to wait for him. He jumped down and wrapped his arms around her, drawing her close. 'This is what I've missed the most,' he whispered as he kissed her lips.

CHAPTER SEVEN

Out at Fieldhead, Una waited an age for darkness to fall. Time dragged as she methodically polished her shoes and folded her laundry then reluctantly went to rehearse her duet in Elsie's room.

'You're a bag of nerves,' Elsie chided as Una dropped her sheet music for the third time. 'What's wrong with you?'

'Nothing. I'm tired, that's all.' It was a decent excuse after her first solid week of working on the land. 'Nine hours at a loom was nothing compared to this.'

'You should try being the only lass on a stable yard full of lads,' Elsie pointed out. 'They're scrawny but strong – ex-jockeys most of them. I had to work twice as hard to prove my worth.'

Una liked Elsie but she was scarcely listening. 'What time is it?' she interrupted.

'Half past four. Why?'

Suddenly it was time to leave and Una thrust the music into Elsie's hands. 'Sorry, I have to go. Brenda's promised me a ride on her motor bike.'

She shot down the corridor into her own room

where she found Brenda and Kathleen lounging on their beds. 'Ready?' she asked Brenda who carried on flicking through her copy of *The Land Girl* magazine.

'It says here that Lady Denman is pleased with her appeal to bring in new volunteers. It's paid off, apparently.'

'That's because they put our wages up to thirty-two shillings.' Kathleen was waiting for her hair to set before she took out her curlers. 'I'll bet that's why you joined up, Una – because you're earning more than you did as a mill girl.'

'And aren't you glad you did!' Brenda leaped up then searched in her drawer for her pair of goggles and leather gloves. 'Think of all the fun you'd have missed if you hadn't.'

Kathleen raised a sarcastic eyebrow. 'All the cowsheds and hen huts you wouldn't have had to clean, all the ditches you wouldn't have had to dig . . .'

'Shut up, Kathleen!' Brenda waltzed Una out of the room then hustled her down the stairs, along the damp corridor into the kitchen. 'Did Nev deliver your note?' she hissed in her ear.

'I'm not sure. I hope so.' At around midday, shortly after her visit to the Blacksmith's Arms, Una's stomach had tied itself into a knot that had twisted tighter as the afternoon had worn on. What if Neville had just pocketed her sixpence and was laughing up his sleeve?

'Ah, little chicken,' Brenda cooed. She found a pencil and paper on a shelf and scribbled a note for the warden:

Ma C,

Please keep our cottage pie warm in the oven. Back around nine. Ta.

Love from Brenda and Una

This done, she used the servants' door to slip away. 'There's no point drawing attention to ourselves,' she explained as they crossed the yard to the old stable where she kept her bike.

'How far is it to Beckwith Camp?' Una asked once they were on their way, roaring past Peggy Russell's farm with its noisy dog.

'It's eight miles to the north, so no more than fifteen minutes on Old Sloper here. It'll be almost dark by the time we get there. I'll drop you off at the junction of Penny Lane and wait for you there.'

Una crouched behind Brenda to stay out of the wind. She felt as if she was stepping into the unknown, with no clue about what she would find at the camp, but visualizing barbed-wire fences and armed guards at the very least.

'Or else I can take you as close to the woods as we can get.' Brenda sensed a growing nervousness in Una's silence. 'Then I'll be within shouting distance if you need me.'

'Don't worry, I won't.' *This will go well*, she told herself firmly. Angelo had come across as gentle and sincere. They would meet and talk as they walked, exchanging facts about their families, taking things one slow step at a time.

At the crossroads into Burnside, Brenda turned right along the road leading towards Swinsty Edge then, after a mile along this road, she turned away from the ridge down a more sheltered lane that came out onto a long lane that ran as straight as a die with a large, brick-built building in the distance.

'This is Penny Lane and that's the old isolation hospital,' Brenda said over her shoulder. 'They've turned it into officers' quarters for the Canadian Air Force now. Beckwith Camp is half a mile beyond that.'

In the dim dusk light Una could just make out the outline of the old hospital, with its ornate gables and arched windows. There was a sentry box at the gates and two servicemen leaning out of a Land Rover to talk to the armed occupant.

'Perhaps we'll invite the Canadians to our Christmas show as well as the prisoners.' This new idea appealed to Brenda and she resolved to talk to Edith Mostyn about it the first chance she got. 'After all, why shouldn't they join in the fun?'

'Where's the prisoners' camp?' Una clung tight as Brenda braked suddenly, came to a halt and pointed. 'Oh, I see.' She took in orderly rows of Nissen huts laid out in a flat field in front of some tall conifers. There were no high fences or guards, only the usual low stone walls and a five-barred gate across the narrow driveway.

'Is this close enough?'

Una nodded then dismounted. She took off her hat and patted her hair. 'How do I look?'

'Adorable, baby.'

Una smiled at Brenda's American drawl. 'All right, I'm ready. Wish me luck.'

'Good luck, Una.' Straddling her bike with her

arms folded, Brenda followed Una's progress with interest. Would she march straight up to the gate and risk being turned back, or would she work her way around the side of the Nissen huts and enter the wood from behind? Brenda thought that the cloak-and-dagger style would produce better results.

The approach to Beckwith Camp was bare of trees and, sure enough, Una quickly realized that the only way to reach the meeting place without being spotted was to climb a stile and follow a cart track to one side of the open field. Luckily for her, centuries of use had created a rutted dip between two stone walls so that her head barely came up to the wall tops and she could easily make her way to the wood unseen. *As long as I don't trip and fall, I should get there safely enough,* she thought. She stopped and took a deep breath, looked up at the darkening sky then walked on.

Sounds from the camp reached her as she drew near. A car engine started up, followed by a shout of *'grazie'* and doors slamming shut. Someone whistled a tune then there was laughter, footsteps on gravel, more doors slamming.

Una paused again before entering the wood. She tried not to think of how silly she would feel if Angelo didn't turn up; she would just have to swallow the bitter pill of disappointment and make Brenda promise not to tell a living soul.

New sounds drifted through the calm, moonlit air. She heard more men's voices, this time from among the trees. Then she made out two figures stooped over a pile of logs that had been neatly stacked between two tree trunks. One was Angelo, the other Lorenzo. Her heart jumped and she suppressed an urge to hurry towards them.

Lorenzo stood up straight to let Angelo load pine logs into his outstretched arms. Both men were looking keenly around them, anticipating her arrival, and it wasn't long before Angelo spotted Una waiting silently at the edge of the wood. He spoke rapidly to Lorenzo then came to meet her.

Una held her breath. Here he was, striding towards her, his hand raised in glad greeting. The white scarf at his throat stood out in the gathering darkness.

'You are here,' he began, taking her by the hand. His smile was broad as he linked arms and walked her into the wood to join his friend.

'He hoped but he didn't believe,' Lorenzo told her with an amused grin. 'I said yes, this one, she will keep her promise.'

'Neville gave you my note?' she asked Angelo, who kept tight hold of her arm. Her heart soared and sang, her body tingled with excitement.

He nodded and patted her hand.

'I take wood for the fire.' Lorenzo glanced in the direction of the camp. 'I tell the guard, ten minutes then Angelo will come with more.'

She understood the plan. 'Thank you,' she whispered, her voice seeming to float away from her into the gathering darkness.

Then she and Angelo were alone. She breathed in the strong, sweet smell of pine resin.

'*Bene*,' he murmured and smiled. Their footfall was silent as they trod over a thick bed of pine needles towards a fast-running beck at the far side of the wood. 'Good, good, you are here. How are you? You are well?'

Una smiled at the formality of the phrases. 'Very well, thank you. How do you say "thank you" in Italian?'

'*Grazie*,' he said with a roll of the 'r'. He found a flat rock by the side of the stream and they sat side by side. 'Sorry . . . my English.'

'No, don't apologize – my Italian is worse.'

'You are Una. I am Angelo. My home is Pisa in Italy. Your home?'

'Millwood,' she told him. 'It has mills, making cloth – the name tells you that. I worked as a weaver.' She made an undulating movement with her arm to mime the action of a shuttle darting across a loom. 'You understand?'

He nodded. 'Family?' he asked.

'Four brothers – Tom, Douglas, Ernest and Geoffrey.'

'Mother, father?'

'They died when I was young. Yours?'

'They live,' he replied, moving closer. 'In Pisa I work for them as cook.'

'In a restaurant?'

'In hotel. Why you smile?'

'You make me smile, that's why.' She felt his arm slide around her waist and let her body lean against his.

'You are happy?'

She nodded. His voice was warm and tender, his gaze clear. Water rushed over rocks, moonlight filtered through the pine canopy and she was falling, falling . . .

'You are here,' he murmured again as he brushed her cheek with his fingertips. Then he put his hand to his chest and tapped it rapidly. 'My heart.'

'Mine too,' she confessed.

They kissed. Falling and melting, giving way to a feeling that was too strong to resist, here on their first meeting, lips touching, hands caressing, hearts beating fast. They embraced in that moment and let go of the world.

The second half of November brought some good news for a country already wearied by war. In North Africa the British 8th Army began an operation to relieve Tobruk and HMS *Devonshire* sank the German cruiser *Atlantis*. Better still, Stalin had stood firm and kept the enemy out of Moscow, where the cold forced them into an ignominious retreat. However, the Americans still teetered on the brink of declaring war against Japan and German air raids continued over Britain's major cities and sea ports. Rationing was extended to include eggs, lard and milk.

'It's the price we have to pay,' Vince Mostyn insisted whenever Edith grumbled about an almost empty larder. 'If Adolf thinks he can starve us into surrender, he has another think coming.'

This was the widely held opinion amongst Burnside residents. Horace Turnbull out at Winsill Edge and Roland Thomson from Brigg Farm had their regular get-togethers in the Blacksmith's Arms with Maurice Baxendale and Joe Kellett when they pored over the latest newspaper reports. Churchill was the man to carry on leading the charge against Herr

Hitler – no one better. And Jerry was on the verge of being frozen out of their approach to Moscow. On the last Saturday in November, the pub was busier than usual and Grace and Cliff worked hard to slake their customers' thirst.

'Did you hear on the wireless that Jerry dropped his bombs over Thornley Reservoir earlier this week?' Maurice kept the closest eye on local events. 'He intended to destroy the dam and cut off our water supply.'

'Did he do any damage?' Roland was keen to find out. He conjured up the low rumble of enemy engines over the moors, the whir of propellers, the thud of bombs on the ground, the ear-splitting explosion.

'No, he missed his target by a mile.'

'But he'll be back,' Joe predicted.

Drinking beer next to a warm fire was the best way to end a hard working week. You could sit here and have a natter, watch the Land Girls gather around the piano and listen to them warble. Yes, war would get you down if you let it, but you were better off than the poor buggers in the cities being bombed to smithereens, and you must always look on the bright side.

'I haven't seen anything of Edgar lately,' Bill mentioned to Cliff while he waited his turn at the bar. 'How's he getting on?'

'Don't ask me. Grace took him to the quack's yesterday to see if there was a medicine to help steady his nerves.'

'And was there?' Bill was surprised she hadn't

mentioned it to him beforehand. He leaned forward to catch her attention. 'What did the doctor say about Edgar? Was he any help?'

Grace slid two glasses of cider towards Brenda.

'Ta very much.' Brenda took them and seized her chance to chat with Bill about the day's football result. 'I hear your team won. What was the score?'

'Two – nil. It was a scrappy match, though.'

'Never mind, the result is what matters.' She smiled brightly to hide a small stab of disappointment that he'd turned his back on her, then she carried the drinks to the piano – one for her and one for Joyce.

'Sorry about that,' Bill told Grace. 'Carry on.'

'The doctor listened to Edgar's heart, took his blood pressure, and so on. He could tell he was far from right, but he admitted there wasn't much he could do except write to the RAF base to recommend keeping him at home for a few more weeks.'

'Until after Christmas, then?' Bill considered this for a while. 'Do you think that's the answer? Mightn't it be better for him to get back to flying before then or at least to being with his pals?'

Grace shook her head. 'You haven't seen him lately.'

'No, not since the day we found him on Swinsty Edge.'

'He's worse, if anything.' She sighed deeply. 'He won't eat. I try to stop him drinking whisky, but the moment my back is turned . . .'

Bill saw her shoulders sag. 'Where is he now? I could have a word with him if you like.'

'He's in bed.'

'With a bottle for company?' It wasn't fair of Edgar to pile more worry onto Grace's shoulders – he might at least see that. Bill frowned at the hopelessness of the situation.

'That'll be one and threepence, please.' She took money from Maurice and put it in the till.

'Meet me outside.' Bill decided on the spur of the moment that he and Grace needed to talk. 'After you've finished here. I'll wait in the car.'

Across the room, Brenda leaned against the piano and considered the latest snub from Bill. She confessed to Joyce that she found him hard to weigh up. 'He blows hot and cold,' she confided. 'Sometimes he's nice as pie, all smiles and offering to mend my bike.'

'But not tonight?' Joyce was accustomed to the other girls using her as a sounding board. She was a few years older and seemingly wiser, preferring to listen as a way of keeping attention away from herself. No one here knew about her life in Warwickshire, how her father had gone wrong in business in the build-up to war and the farm had been sold to pay his debts, or how her fiancé's ship, the HMS *Southampton*, had been sunk off Malta in January this year and he was missing presumed dead.

Brenda ran her fingernail along the top of the piano. 'No, not tonight. Still, I'm glad Una is having better luck with her Italian.'

'Yes, he sounds nice.'

'She can't stop babbling on about him. It's Angelo this, Angelo that. Apparently he's shown her a photograph of himself and his sister standing in front of the Leaning Tower. He's teaching her the different words for "love", "dear" and "darling". *Amore, amore!*'

'Sweet nothings,' Joyce murmured.

'Una was over the moon on Thursday when she and Kathleen were sent back to Home Farm and he and a bunch of his friends happened to be hedge cutting there. That was their third meeting in the space of two weeks and every time she sees him she falls more and more in love.'

'She does look happy.' Joyce felt a painful tug at her heartstrings as she recalled the early days of her romance with Walter Johnson. They'd met in Stratford when he was on leave from the Royal Navy and she'd been there for the day, selling off farm machinery at an auction. Afterwards she'd gone with her sister Patricia to drown their sorrows in a pub overlooking the Avon and Walter had arrived in uniform with two of his pals. 'Look out; here comes the Navy,' Patricia had said with a nudge and a wink.

It had been love at first sight on both sides and a whirlwind romance. Joyce had loved Walter with a hot flame of passion that she hadn't known existed. Bright and dangerous, short lived and fragile – now it was nothing but ashes and memories.

'Lucky her,' Brenda said with a sigh as she watched Una and Elsie practise a few bars of the song they were working on for the show. They went wrong and giggled then tried again.

Joyce closed her book of sheet music. She was slowly starting to accept that though Walter was gone, life went on. 'Yes, good luck to her, I say.'

*

Later that night, Bill drove Grace out of Burnside towards Swinsty Edge. It was gone midnight when he parked the car under Kelsey Crag, a remote beauty spot famed for its overhanging cliff and fast-running trout stream. Out here, in the dead of night, not a creature stirred.

'I'm glad you managed to slip away,' he told her.

'I had to wait until Dad had called last orders. He went straight up to bed afterwards and that was my chance.'

'I'm sorry.'

'What for?'

'You must be tired, for a start.' He studied her face. 'Yes, you are – I can see that.'

'Tomorrow's Sunday. I'll have a lie-in.' There were few stars. Clouds scudded across the face of the moon but the massive shadow cast by the crag was impenetrable. 'Is everything all right, Bill? Has something happened?'

'No, nothing,' he assured her. He turned on the interior light then rested his arm along the back of Grace's seat. 'I'm worried about you, that's all. You've got too much on your plate.'

'I can cope. As long as Edgar doesn't do anything silly, I'll be fine.'

'I don't help either, do I?'

'Don't say that.' She looked away and saw their reflections in the side window – two pale, unsmiling faces.

'I don't, though,' he said glumly. 'I just make things more complicated, that's all.'

Grace glanced down at her lap. She saw that her

hands were trembling. '*Everything* is complicated these days. It's not just us.'

'You mean the war? Yes, I suppose so. No one knows what's going to happen from one day to the next.' Only this week, Thomas Lund had received his call-up papers because the rules had been changed again and his clerical job with the civil service was no longer protected. As the feeling of uncertainty built, so Bill grew less sure of his own footing and place in the world. 'But look, Grace, if you wanted to break off, I'd understand. Honestly, I would.'

She took a sharp, short breath and an ice-cold chill ran through her. 'Why would I want that?'

'Because we can't be open and above board about it. We have to keep it a secret in case people gossip. And that's my fault.'

'No, it's not. I agreed to it, remember.' Somewhere she found the strength to stop shaking and her voice grew calm. 'I understand the reasons.'

Plagued by guilt, Bill plunged into a sea of self-justification. 'It's a combination of things. First off, there's Mother to consider. You know what a fusspot she is and she doesn't seem to see that it's high time for me to lead my own life.'

'And you haven't the heart to tell her.' Bill's kind-heartedness was a double-edged sword in Grace's eyes. It was why she'd fallen in love with him in the first place, but it was also what held them back.

'It's Dad as well. He's more and more set on me stepping into his shoes as far as the business goes. In his eyes, I don't have time for anything else – it's all work, work, work. And back to Mother; she's scared to death to upset Dad in case it sets off another heart attack. I tell you, between the pair of them, I can hardly find room to breathe in that house.'

'Stop, Bill – don't go on.' Grace had long held a suspicion that there was a darker reason that hadn't yet seen the light of day. It was rooted in Edith Mostyn's snobbish resentment at having 'married beneath herself', as the saying went. The marriage to Vincent had dragged her out of a world of books and scholarship into one where Ferguson tractor engines and Shell motor oil reigned supreme. Now she wanted better for her son and had persuaded her husband to set their sights on Alice and Lionel Foster's daughter Shirley, who was due home on leave from the WAF at Christmas. The Fosters were well off and had the status in the neighbourhood that Bill's parents craved. Whereas what was she, Grace Kershaw? The daughter of the village blacksmith and publican, that's what.

'I *will* tell them,' Bill vowed. He felt diminished by his own weakness but circumstance trapped him, like a fly set in gleaming amber. 'When the time is right.'

Grace turned in her seat and faced him fair and square. She spoke without blame. 'We both know I'll never match up to Shirley in their eyes. No, let me say what needs to be said. It's her they want you to marry.'

'This isn't the Dark Ages. It's not up to them.' He took her hand and squeezed it. 'I don't have any feelings for Shirley – you know that. It's you I dream about, you I want to marry.'

She sighed and leaned her head back against the seat, staring out into the darkness.

'Do you hear me? This Shirley business doesn't change the way I feel. I love *you*.'

'And I love you,' she murmured, taking his hands and pressing them to her cheeks.

'Grace, you mean the world to me. I'd do anything not to hurt you.'

His hands were cold. 'I believe you, Bill. And I do understand. You're their only child; your future's important to them.'

'Yes. I don't want to upset them, especially now that Dad's poorly.'

Though it made sense, Grace's heart felt squeezed by constantly having to keep disappointment at bay. At the same time, she couldn't muster enough confidence to override Bill's fears, to hold him in her arms and to convince him that love would conquer all. 'It's not your fault,' she murmured. 'And I am willing to stick to our agreement. We'll keep things quiet until the time is right.'

'And I *will* tell them,' he insisted again, but each time he said it he felt his courage slip away. 'Once Dad has been to the doctor's for his check-up, I'll tell them we're engaged and you can start wearing your ring. I'll do it at Christmas. We'll have a party. What do you say to that?'

'Is this supposed to be his sister?' Elsie studied the sunny photograph of Angelo and a young woman with long, black hair wearing a sleeveless summer dress, standing in front of the famous tower. The two people in the picture had their arms around each other's waists and smiled for the camera.

'Yes, her name is Maria. She works in the family's hotel as a chamber maid.' Una wished she hadn't broken off from scrubbing the collar of her shirt to show Elsie the picture that she carried with her everywhere she went. 'Why are you staring at me like that?'

'She doesn't look much like him.' The woman was in her late twenties, much smaller than Angelo, with rounder features. 'She's pretty, though.'

Una snatched back the photo. 'Maria is Angelo's older sister,' she insisted. 'Why would he show it to me otherwise?'

'True,' Elsie conceded. 'But it pays to be careful. You shouldn't take everything he says at face value.'

'Why not?' Until this moment Una hadn't had a single doubt. She'd been floating, flying, soaring from one day to the next. Mud and scratches, aching back and fingers stiff from frostbite meant nothing because she was in love with Angelo. 'Honestly, I might have expected this from Jean or Ivy, but not from you.'

In the laundry room next to the kitchen, Elsie carried on ironing her dungarees. She slapped the iron down hard onto the coarse cotton fabric. 'What else has he told you? That he's the bambino of his family, that his mamma adores him and he has a little dog called Mimi who loves ice cream?'

'Oh, I'm not listening to you any more.' Una was ready to storm off. 'You're jealous, that's your trouble. You just want to spoil everything for me.'

'Yes, all right; I'm only teasing.' Elsie relented and put down her iron for a second time. 'You may be lucky and find out that your Angelo lives up to his name. Angelo for Angel, don't you know.'

'He is very nice.' Una kicked herself for sounding so prim and faint hearted. 'No, that's the wrong word. He's sincere. What he says comes from his heart.'

'Not like our home-grown boys, then?' Elsie had been out with plenty of reticent stable lads in her time – the type who kept their feelings so well hidden beneath their flat caps that she sometimes wondered if they had any to speak of. 'It's like getting blood out of a stone trying to find out what goes on in their hearts. But Italians are different, I grant you.'

'So you do like him?'

Elsie shrugged. 'He has a nice smile. No, listen – I'm serious,' she said, tugging Una's sleeve as she frowned once more. 'You can tell more from a smile than from a hundred words. That's what I told Eunice, but she wouldn't listen.'

Again, that name! 'What has Eunice Mason got to do with this? Come on, Elsie, spit it out.'

'You don't want to know.' Giving a regretful shake of her head, she started ironing again, this time with renewed vigour until her face grew flushed and her forehead damp.

'Yes, I do. Are you trying to tell me that Eunice fell for one of the Italian prisoners too?'

'Yes, but not Angelo.'

'Who then?' A relieved Una pestered to get at the truth and rid herself of the feeling that she was forever in Eunice's unhappy shadow.

'Lorenzo, that's who. And I had an uneasy feeling about him from the start. That's what I mean about a smile that's not from the heart.'

'He's not so bad,' Una objected. True, Lorenzo seemed a touch vain and he had a superior air. But he'd played a big part in organizing her first meeting with Angelo and for that she was grateful.

'Wait until you hear the rest.' Now that she'd started, Elsie was eager to press her point home. 'Yes, Lorenzo is charming and of course, with looks like his, he can sweet talk any girl he likes, including Eunice. She would come back to Fieldhead after a day's haymaking with the Beckwith Camp prisoners and she would sing his praises all night long. Ask Jean and Kathleen – ask anyone. It was high summer and Eunice lived, breathed and ate Lorenzo.'

Am I like that with Angelo? Una forced herself to ask the difficult question. So far they'd engineered four meetings in all – the first one at the Camp with Lorenzo and Brenda's help then one close to home while working together at Peggy Russell's farm. The next had been on Thursday when she'd run into him again at Home Farm and their snatched dinner-time conversation had been rudely interrupted by Frank. The latest was yesterday afternoon when Angelo and a large group of prisoners had been given permission to come to Burnside to watch the football match. Giving the unwary guard the slip had proved easy and they'd spent an hour together inside the unheated Institute building. They'd sat on a bench and kissed and hugged each other for warmth then kissed again. *Yes, I am exactly the same,* she thought with a sigh. *Even when I'm not seeing Angelo, I think about him morning, noon and night.*

'There was only one problem.' Elsie closed her eyes for a moment then opened them and looked steadily at Una. 'Eventually Eunice found out that Lorenzo was married with a wife and three children back home in Rome. She was heartbroken of course.'

'Who told her?' Una saw it all in a flash – the love, the desire and the sudden, crushing fall into black despair.

'He did. He told the truth to put an end to it. Ask Kathleen how she had to listen to her crying all night long.'

No one's slate was clean. Every soldier, sailor or airman on every side – English, German, French, Russian and Italian – had come into the war with a history, a job, a family. A handsome POW might pass his spare time writing love letters to half a dozen local girls while his *Fräulein* or *mademoiselle* waited patiently for him to return home. Una visualized all too clearly Lorenzo's cruel deceit and fear formed like icicles in her heart.

CHAPTER EIGHT

'Tell me – what would you do without me?' Neville waylaid Una in the stable at Brigg Farm just as she was finishing mucking out Major's box. He teased her by waving a small sheet of paper under her nose then wafting it out of reach. Then he scrambled up the stone steps into the hayloft and grinned down at her. 'Guess what this is!'

She leaned her fork against the wall and stood, hands on hips, glaring up at him. 'I know what it is. Just give it to me, please.'

A weak afternoon sun slanted into the loft. Outside in the yard, the big grey horse munched oats from his bucket, occasionally shifting his weight and blowing softly through his nose. 'What's it worth?'

'Stop mucking around, Nev. You'll have your sixpence as soon as you've handed it over.'

'"Romeo, Romeo!"' He brandished Angelo's note and gave a croaky guffaw. '"Wherefore art thou?"'

'You're the limit,' she fumed as she set foot on the bottom step. 'I'm coming up there and when I get hold of you, you'll wish I hadn't.'

He waited until she reached the top step and made a lunge towards him. '"A rose by any other name . . ."' He dodged sideways out of her grasp then jumped the full set of steps onto the ground below, taking with him a shower of loose hay. He made a soft landing in a barrel full of fresh straw.

There was nothing for it but to go back down. 'Please, Neville. I don't have time for this.'

'Ah, but you've got all the time in the world for our Italian friend.' In his role as go-between, he'd kept track of Una and Angelo's budding romance. 'Anyone would think there wasn't a war on, the way you two bill and coo. Oh yes, you find time for him all right.'

Una knitted her brows. 'That's not fair. I work as hard as anyone else around here – harder than some I could mention.'

Seeing that she was growing truly angry, Neville resisted the temptation to prolong the suspense. 'I know you do. Don't get upset.'

'I'm not upset.' She held out her hand and waited.

He kept the note just out of reach. 'Do I get extra pay for first-class delivery?'

'Neville!' She darted forward and snatched it from him, delving into the pocket of her corduroy breeches for the sixpence she owed him. 'Thank you. Now, scram!'

'Amore mio.'

She waited until Neville's footsteps had faded before sitting on the bottom step to read the famil-iar handwriting.

I miss you *molto, molto*. I think of you always. I wait tonight in our wood. Please be here.

    With love in my heart from your Angelo.

A rush of emotion filled her chest. First there was relief that he had written after twenty-four hours of waiting and wondering. Then there was a longing to see him and feel his kisses on her cheeks and lips, then worry that there was no time to send a message back saying yes, of course she would come – unless she were to chase after Neville and ask him if he would cycle over to Beckwith Camp with a reply. She dashed across the yard, almost bumping into Major's hefty hind quarters and only narrowly avoiding a swift kick from his back leg.

'Oi, what's your hurry?' Roland Thomson called from the back of his cart where he stood with his pitchfork, ready to unload sugar beet.

Just then Brenda rode into the yard on her motor bike. 'Ah, there you are,' she said to Una as she came to a halt and cut the engine. 'I've been looking for you all over the place. I thought you were with Joyce and Jean, digging on the top field.'

'We finished the beet early,' Una explained. 'They went back to the hostel. I had to stay behind to muck out.'

Brenda turned to Roland. 'Is she free to go now, please?'

With a swift nod, he released Una. 'Are you back here tomorrow?'

'What's tomorrow? Saturday.' Una ran through the week's rota in her head. 'No, I'll be working at

Home Farm with Grace.' She could hardly leave fast enough, flinging her answer over her shoulder as she mounted the pillion seat and set off with Brenda down the farm track towards the road. 'Why did you want me?' she asked Brenda.

'Because I've got permission from Her Ladyship to deliver the invitations for the Christmas show, that's why. It's taken this long for her to talk to HQ about it. Then she had to ask if the Canadian officers could come too. Red tape – you know how it is.'

'So that's where we're going now?' The lucky coincidence made Una laugh. 'To Beckwith Camp?'

Brenda eased out onto the tarmac road then opened the throttle and sped down into the valley. 'Yes. I thought that would cheer you up and it did, didn't it? We have to call at the old hospital first but that shouldn't take long.'

It must be fate, Una decided, holding tight to the luggage rack behind her as they sped along the twisting lanes until they arrived at Penny Lane.

'Do you know why this road is so straight?' Brenda asked, closing down the throttle to take the corner. 'It's because it was a Roman road between two hill forts, that's why.'

At that moment Una couldn't have cared less. Her mind was working out the details of how she would let Angelo know that she was here so that he could arrange to slip away and meet her. Would she have to wait until it was dark? she wondered. Might Brenda be able to distract the guard while she went looking for him?

'Here we are at our first stop.' Brenda slowed

down again at the gates of the gloomy building that had been commandeered by the Canadian Air Force then she parked the bike by the sentry box. 'Come on, Una – best foot forward.'

The sentry came out to meet them. He was small and clean shaven, sporting an American-style crew cut and a broad, welcoming smile. 'Hi there, ladies. How can I help?'

Brenda took out a manila envelope from the satchel slung across her shoulder. 'Could we deliver this to the officer in charge, please?'

While the guard enquired about its contents then went on to make a telephone call from inside his sentry box, Una let her attention wander to the isolated building at the end of the short drive. It was built on three storeys, with narrow, arched windows and ornate chimney stacks. The gabled main entrance was in deep shadow but she was soon able to see the door open and two uniformed men emerge. They came quickly towards them.

'Hey, girls!' The taller of the two opened up the conversation. He clicked his heels and gave a casual salute. 'Jim Aldridge, Squadron Leader. This is my second in command, Flight Lieutenant John Mackenzie – Mac for short. To what do we owe the pleasure?'

Encouraged by the friendly greeting, Brenda showed him the envelope. 'This is an invitation for you all to join us in Burnside for our Land Army Christmas show. There'll be singing and dancing, including an interval with tea and sandwiches. We're even getting a Christmas tree. We hope you'll allow your men to come.'

Food at the interval? Una thought. *A Christmas tree?* This was the first she'd heard of either.

The squadron leader took the envelope. 'You bet,' he said eagerly. 'The men get lonesome so far away from home, especially at this time of year. This will put mighty big smiles on their faces.'

'Champion. The letter tells you the time and the place, et cetera. How many seats shall we put out for you?'

'How many, Mac?'

Mackenzie did a quick count in his head. 'Fifteen. Unless it turns out that the Luftwaffe has other plans for us that evening.'

This reminder of the RCAF pilots' role in resisting the enemy created an awkward pause. Beyond the house Una could see an open area with a basketball net where four men were practising in the fading light. They passed the ball between them until one aimed then gave a triumphant shout when it dropped through the net. 'Let's hope not,' she said quietly.

'Fifteen,' Brenda repeated with a firm nod of her head. 'We'll see you on the twenty-third, Squadron Leader Aldridge.'

'You sure will,' he agreed. 'You Land Girls are flavour of the month with our guys. Ain't that so, Mac?'

'Yessir!' Mackenzie winked at Una while Brenda kick-started her bike. Like the sentry on duty, he wore his hair very short. He pushed his shoulders back, feet together, hands by his sides as if standing to attention though his handsome face expressed wry amusement.

Una returned his smile. At that moment she felt immensely proud of her Land Army hat with its shiny badge, of her smart, double-breasted coat, shiny shoes and tailored breeches.

'We'll be there,' Mackenzie promised as he and his superior officer turned to walk back up the drive.

The sentry leaned close to whisper in her ear. 'You hit it off with the flight lieutenant,' he confided with a cheeky grin. 'You're Mac's kind of girl – small and neat.'

The compliment embarrassed her and she felt her cheeks go red.

'No offence,' the sentry added.

'None taken,' she replied as she hurried to join Brenda.

'Mission accomplished,' Brenda said brightly as she pulled away. 'Beckwith Camp, here we come.'

'I hear motor bike,' Angelo told Una, taking her hand as they walked through the quiet, secret wood. 'I look out and see.'

She and Brenda had arrived at the camp gates at the same time as a covered lorry delivering boxes of butter, sacks of flour and potatoes – kitchen provisions for the week ahead. They'd been waved through the gate and crawled after the truck between rows of Nissen huts until they'd been flagged down by a corporal.

'Come into the office,' he'd told Brenda when she explained their business. 'Let me make a quick telephone call.'

'You can put the kettle on while you're at it.' She'd

given Una a shove in the direction of the copse of pine trees then followed quickly. 'I haven't wet my whistle all afternoon. I'm parched.'

Una had taken the hint and now here she was hand in hand with the man who'd captured her heart. 'I got your note,' she explained.

'*Bene*. You are happy?' He clasped her hand tightly and led her onwards to their spot by the stream.

'Of course. I'm here, aren't I?' Happy, bowled over, head over heels – there were never the right words to describe this unexpected, heady feeling that hit her every time she set eyes on this beautiful man.

'As well, I am happy.' He sat her down and gazed at her. He wore a grey shirt, open at the neck to show his throat, and the small gold cross hanging from a chain. 'I hope to see you every day.'

Una heard him struggle to express his feelings. Her heart opened out like blossom and her smile was soft and tender.

'I sleep and I dream only of you.'

She put her finger to his lips. 'I have lovely dreams too.'

He kissed her fingers and then her mouth. Water eddied and gurgled at their feet. Trees rose high and straight into the dusk sky.

After a while, she drew back and asked him a question that she'd framed carefully in advance. 'Angelo, do you ever talk about me?'

He gave her a puzzled look. 'Talk?'

'Yes – about you and me. To Lorenzo or to any of the others?'

'Ah. To Lorenzo only.'

'What does he say?'

'Why you want to know?' Brushing her hair back from her face, he cradled the back of her head.

'Does he – I don't know – does he approve?'

'He like you, yes.' Angelo smiled as if that settled the matter.

Una didn't smile back. She went on shaping the words so that he would understand. 'But he says be careful?'

'Careful?'

'Not to make promises,' she explained. 'Not to get carried away.'

Angelo shook his head. 'Carried?'

Una needed to be more direct to arrive at the point she wanted to make. 'I know about Lorenzo and Eunice. Do you remember Eunice?'

He nodded cautiously.

'They were in love, weren't they? But I'm afraid Lorenzo made promises that he couldn't keep. He warns you not to make the same mistake?'

The light dawned. He stood up suddenly in protest and pulled her to her feet.

'I am not Lorenzo!'

'Don't be angry. I have to ask you, Angelo – do you have a girl back in Pisa? If you have, please tell me then I'll know where I stand.' She held her breath in an agony of suspense and waited for his answer.

He kept her at arm's length but his expression softened. 'I am not Lorenzo,' he repeated more tenderly. 'There is no other girl. I am free.'

It was what she longed to hear and she let out a long sigh of relief. 'Oh, that's marvellous.'

'You believe?'

'Yes, I believe you,' she whispered.

He drew her to him and held her fast. She leaned her head against his chest and felt the cold metal of his crucifix against her cheek.

'I am for you, Una. Now and tomorrow and for always.'

'So now we have to give the Italians a slap-up sandwich supper as well as a show?' Jean, backed by Ivy McNamara and her best friend Dorothy Cook, quizzed Brenda over breakfast next morning. Her spoon hovered over her porridge bowl and she spoke loudly so that everyone could hear. 'Tea and biscuits isn't good enough this time around.'

'And the Canadian pilots as well.' Jean's criticism didn't dent Brenda's enthusiasm. 'They're coming too. That'll be fifteen extra – which makes fifty-odd in total. Don't worry, we can fit them all in.'

'What kind of supper?' Kathleen wanted to know. She sat in her curlers, with a checked scarf tied around her head.

Brenda had already worked out the details. 'I say we get Ma C to bake us some cakes here at Fieldhead.'

'With nice fresh scones,' Elsie suggested as she reached over the table for the milk.

'Good idea. Then we can take them down to the Institute and plate them up in their kitchen.' Joyce had just sat down beside Una and she joined in enthusiastically. 'Somehow we'll have to get hold of extra flour and egg rations that week. Or no – wait. We can ask the Italian and Canadian cooks to contribute their share as well.'

'You see, Jean – where there's a will there's a way.' With Una, Elsie and Joyce definitely on board, Brenda was satisfied. 'We want it to be a really special occasion. That's why I thought we should have a nice big tree as well. Even though it's not strictly within rules.'

There were cries of agreement and increasingly far-fetched suggestions from further down the table.

'Rules be blowed; let's have a tree with glass baubles . . .'

'Plenty of tinsel and a fairy on the top.'

'What about a Christmas cake with sugar icing?'

'Who'll be Father Christmas?'

'Steady on.' Hilda Craven came along the row with a ladle and a heavy pan. The hostel warden doled out common sense along with extra helpings of porridge. 'There's a war on, remember.'

'As if we could forget.' Elsie reminded everyone that one of the unexploded bombs intended for Thornley Reservoir had recently blown up in a farmer's field. 'I was talking to Bill Mostyn in the pub last night. He said the poor old chap drove right over the darned thing in his tractor. He was blown to smithereens.'

The table fell quiet at this, except for the scraping of spoons in bowls, until Joyce brought the conversation back round to preparations for the show. 'If it's a Christmas tree we want, I've spotted a nice specimen growing in the wood at the back of us,' she told Una, who had finished breakfast and was about to set off on her bike. 'You can't miss it among all the elms. Take a look and see what you think.'

'Some other time,' Una told her on her way out. 'I have to meet Grace and go on to Home Farm. I don't want to keep her waiting.'

'Very good – one home-grown Christmas tree, waiting for the axe to fall.' Brenda scraped back her chair and stood up with a smile. 'Now all we have to do is learn the steps to The Skaters' Waltz and not trip over our two left feet, eh, Jean?'

Grace put her back into ditch-digging for four hours straight, jamming her spade into the mud and hearing the satisfying squelch as she lifted it and heaved the load onto the bank. The work punished her body but eased her aching soul.

'Have a rest,' Una suggested. She stood by the hawthorn hedge, blowing into her hands to warm them and looking over her shoulder towards the farmhouse. 'Joe and Frank are still in the dairy so they won't notice.'

'No, I'd rather keep busy.' In went the spade and out again, in deep and out with a regular, unbroken rhythm.

If only Edgar would open up about what had happened. Grace was sure that keeping everything bottled up was making him worse and worse. He was like a ghost in the house, silent and gaunt, jumping out of his skin at the least little sound. In and out, lift, twist and dump the mud under the hedgerow. 'You have three brothers, don't you, Una?'

Una gave a hollow clap then blew again. 'Four. There's only Tom left at home. The rest are in uniform.'

'Are any of them in the RAF?'

'No, thank goodness.' She realized as soon as she said this that she'd been tactless. 'I'm sorry, Grace. I wasn't thinking.'

'No, you're right. We all know that flying a Lancaster over Berlin or Dresden is risky, to say the least.'

'Still, I didn't mean to upset you. Here, let me lift this out of your way.' Una knelt then leaned forward to drag a waterlogged branch out of the ditch. 'How is Edgar, by the way?'

'Honestly, I'm worried sick about him.' Grace talked as she worked on. 'I heard him last night, shouting out in his sleep. When I went in to see him, I found him curled up in a corner of the room, eyes wide open but not really awake, shaking from head to toe. He wouldn't let me anywhere near him, just kept pushing me away and screaming. I'm sorry; I shouldn't be telling you this.'

'Why ever not?'

'For a start, Edgar wouldn't like it if he knew we were talking about him. Besides, we all have relatives who've rallied to Mr Churchill's call and put themselves in harm's way. I'm sure my family is no worse off than anyone else's.'

'That's not the point, though. You have to cope with seeing what the war has done to your brother day in, day out.' Una lifted more dead branches out of the ditch, grunting as she did so.

'Ta, Una.' Grace took a deep breath then leaned on her spade. 'To be honest, I don't know what I'd do without my Land Army pals. You're what keeps me going.'

Deep in conversation, neither Grace nor Una noticed Joe leave the dairy and go into the house, followed soon after by Frank who stood in the yard watching them as usual.

'That's nice to know.' Grace's confession led Una into a more cheerful confidence of her own. 'Don't tell anyone, but I saw Angelo yesterday and for the first time he told me he loves me. How about that?'

'Did he now? And have you fallen in love with him?'

'I suppose so. I didn't expect to, but yes, I have!' If falling in love meant thinking about someone every minute of every day, revelling in his touch and longing for him whenever you were apart.

Grace saw the dreamy look in her new friend's eyes and easily pictured what she was feeling because it had been like this for her and Bill during their first heady days together. 'That's good, then.'

'Even if we're on opposite sides?' Una queried.

'Yes. Being in love should never be anything to be ashamed of.' If only this could apply to her, she thought. To wear Bill's ring, to celebrate their love out in the open, would be a glorious thing when it finally happened. 'The war won't go on for ever and afterwards you two will be free to live where you want – here in England or in Italy if that's what you decide.'

'And Angelo did promise that he would love me tomorrow and always. That's what he said. And he doesn't have a fiancé or a wife.'

Una's solemn expression brought a smile to Grace's lips, which she failed to hide.

'He doesn't!' Una protested. 'I asked him straight out. He's not like Lorenzo.'

Grace nodded. 'I agree with you, he's not.'

The conversation fell away and they got back to work. Then Grace spoke again. 'To give Lorenzo his due, he was upset when I told him about Eunice. I think he worked out that it wasn't an accident.'

'Did he know about the baby?'

'No. At least, I didn't tell him.'

'Why not?'

'It wasn't my place. Besides, it might have had nothing to do with him.'

'Really?' The implications shocked Una and she didn't stop turning them over in her mind until Emily came out of the house into the yard, cupped her hands around her mouth and called to them.

'What did she say?' Una asked.

'Saturday's our half day. It's time to clock off.' Grace clambered out of the ditch and shouldered her spade. 'Come on – before Joe sticks his oar in and makes us stay.'

The wind gusted across the hillside, bringing sleet with it, so that by the time they'd scraped mud off their boots and reclaimed their bikes from the shed, it was almost impossible to see where they were going. It bounced onto the stone flags and stung their faces as they set off along the rutted lane. They leaned into the wind and pedalled hard, eyes half shut, frozen fingers gripping the handlebars.

Frank followed them on foot. He stuck close to the hedgerows and matched his pace with theirs, running to keep up as they free-wheeled downhill then dodging behind walls as they slowly climbed the hills. He stood in the chapel porch to watch Una say goodbye to Grace outside the Blacksmith's Arms. Grace wheeled her bike round the side of the forge and disappeared. Una cycled on towards the crossroads and Frank turned up his jacket collar, pulled his cap down over his forehead, stepped out into the frozen rain and followed her.

CHAPTER NINE

The short, dark days of winter spread extra gloom throughout the war-torn land. All talk at home was of shortages and blockades. Abroad, the Japanese attack on Pearl Harbor brought Roosevelt to a declaration of war at last.

'As if it wasn't bad enough for the Japs to sink half the American fleet, they've gone and attacked Hong Kong as well.' Cliff brought Grace up to date with the most recent threat to the British Crown colony as she sat at the kitchen table writing her Christmas cards before she set off for work.

'Yes, I heard it on the wireless.' She blotted the ink dry then slotted the last card into its envelope. 'It's not looking good. The Canadians have had to send troops out there to back us up.'

'And the very latest is that the Japanese have sunk two of our battleships in the South China Sea. HMS *Prince of Wales* and HMS *Repulse* both went down off Singapore.'

The feeling of helplessness that had threatened to engulf Grace before she switched off the morning news bulletin returned with a vengeance. Everywhere you turned there was terrifying talk of horrid Herr Hitler's blitzkrieg. She looked at her small pile of sealed envelopes and thought how useless this tiny gesture of good cheer was, set against world-wide chaos. *How can we bear to celebrate Christmas with all this going on?* she wondered with a sinking heart.

Her father sat on a stool to lace up his boots. Bending over brought a rush of blood to his cheeks and he grunted in discomfort. 'Have you clapped eyes on your brother yet?'

'I heard him get up a while ago.' The sound of Edgar shuffling along the landing had woken her and she'd lain in the dark listening to him descend the stairs and move about the kitchen, turning on the tap and rattling the kettle down on the grate. By the time she was up and dressed, his coat was missing from its hook and he was gone from the house.

'If you see him, tell him I'll need a hand to shift barrels before opening time,' Cliff mumbled as he tied on his apron and left for the forge.

Grace pursed her lips. *How am I supposed to do that when I'm out at work all day?* she wanted to retort. Instead, she checked the hand-written rota pinned to the back of the door, put on her coat and hat and set out for Horace Turnbull's hen farm on Winsill Edge.

Brenda, Una and Joyce spent that Wednesday with Henry Rowson, who was the fifth generation of his family to have kept sheep on the fells above Kelsey Crag. Henry was seventy-two years young, hale and hearty, and determined to carry on farming until he dropped. His call for Land Army help to bring his sheep down to lower ground ready for lambing in January was one of his few concessions to the advancing years.

It was the first day that Una and Brenda had spent herding sheep high above Burnside and they loved every minute.

'I feel as if I'm on top of the world,' Una exclaimed, standing next to Brenda on a limestone ledge overlooking an immense sweep of open country. Sheep were scattered across the hillside and Jess, Henry's black-and-white dog, was out on a fetch, approaching a huddle of sheep then crouching low to wait for the next whistled command. Once given the signal, she would dart forward again to snap at their heels, worrying at them and herding them down the slope into the valley below.

'Hey, you two, there's no time to admire the view!' Joyce called. She'd borrowed Henry's other dog, Ben, for the day and had been working with him on the far side of the fell. Now she appeared on the ridge with Ben at her heels. 'I've got two dozen pregnant ewes up here. One of you needs to come and lend a hand.'

Una volunteered and set off up the steep, rock-strewn hillside.

'Brenda, you go down and help Henry,' Joyce yelled above the blustering wind. 'Tell him Una and I will bring the rest of the flock down to the fold.'

It sounded simple enough, but Una found that there was a lot of hard work still to be done. Joyce's sheep were a scraggy, miserable-looking bunch whose mission seemed to be to defeat the dog's efforts to bring them down off the fell. Every time Ben darted then crouched then darted again, they scattered in all directions. 'Sprint down to that big rock and head them off.' Joyce issued orders and Una obeyed, arms flailing in an attempt to redirect the runaways. 'Left, left – turn them to your left!' Then, two minutes later, 'Down in the dip – get after those three strays, bring them back up!'

The relentless wind buffeted them, Joyce blew the whistle that she'd borrowed from the farmer, the ewes bleated until, as dusk drew in and a pale moon appeared in the clear sky, they came to the start of a green lane long used by shepherds to bring sheep off the hills into the lee of Kelsey Crag. 'Close that gate behind us.' Joyce's final order came as the last of the flock entered the lane. All that remained was to chivvy them forward the few hundred yards into the fold where they found Henry and Brenda waiting for them.

'You took your time,' Henry grumbled as he slammed the fold gate on the last of his flock. 'Thank you' and 'Goodbye' were not in the old man's vocabulary, it seemed. He called Ben and Jess to heel then set off for his farmhouse, which lay across the trout stream at the far side of an ancient stone bridge.

Brenda grinned as she gave a mock curtsey behind his back. 'Ta, girls. I'm much obliged.' Looking at her watch, she saw that she had time to cycle to Fieldhead and fit in her bath before dinner. 'I'll race you back,' she challenged the others.

It was only when they were half a mile down the road that Joyce remembered the borrowed whistle in her coat pocket. 'Uh-oh, I'd better go back,' she decided.

'It'll be dark before you reach home if you do,' Brenda warned.

'I don't mind. You two go ahead without me.' Joyce turned around and headed back towards the overhanging crag. Though she was level headed and practical, she found there was something primitive about Kelsey and its surroundings that made the hairs at the nape of her neck prickle – a vastness and an unchanging nature that highlighted her own insignificance. The sky darkened as she cycled towards it. The thin bleat of Henry Rowson's sheep was the only sound to break the silence.

This won't take long, Joyce told herself as she neared the old footbridge. There was a light on in the nearby farmhouse. Two large birds flew out from under the stone arch, quacking excitedly as they kept low and followed the course of the fast-flowing stream.

Something had disturbed the ducks, but what? Perhaps the sound of her bicycle wheels rattling over the rocky path, though she wasn't aware of having made much noise. Something else, then? She glanced over the waist-high parapet and saw a man crouched on his haunches, leaning forward to dip his hands into the water.

'Edgar?'

He was startled but he didn't look round. Instead, he stood up and stumbled along the bank, one foot slipping and splashing into the stream. He overbalanced and crashed headlong onto the rocks. The sound of his fall set Henry's dogs barking.

Joyce abandoned her bike and ran to help. 'Here, take hold of my hand. The rocks are slippery. That's right, easy does it.'

Instead of righting himself, Edgar pulled free and fell a second time. The hem of his overcoat dragged in the water so he shrugged it off and left it behind as he crawled away.

'Wait,' Joyce implored. She knew she couldn't let this desperate man run off into the night but she needed help to stop him. Luckily the dogs' barking had brought old Henry to his front door so she shouted for him to come quick.

By now Edgar was back on his feet and scrambling up the muddy bank, still intent on getting away.

Taking in the scene without recognizing the fugitive, the farmer cut him off and forced him to turn back the way he'd come. 'Now then, my lad – I'll let the dogs loose if you go on like this,' he warned.

Edgar stopped dead about ten paces from where Joyce stood. The urge to flee vanished as suddenly as it had come and he dropped to his knees. Everything was dark, he had no strength, no will to go on – only a hollow in the very centre of his being.

Henry kept a wary distance while Joyce stepped towards Edgar. She took off her coat and wrapped it around his shoulders. 'Come with me,' she murmured. 'That's right, I'll look after you. Come with me.'

Henry Rowson had no telephone and he didn't drive a car. He lived as his forefathers had lived, without electricity, getting about by bicycle or by thumbing a lift into Burnside with his nearest neighbour, three miles down the road.

'Tell him he can stay there in the barn for the night if he likes,' he said to Joyce. 'He can't sleep in the house with me – there's only the one bedroom.'

'I'll stay there with him then,' she decided. 'You've seen the state he's in. It wouldn't be right to leave him by himself.'

'Whatever you think's best.' Henry had done his bit and was ready to close his door. 'As long as you don't mind tongues wagging.'

'I don't care about that.' What she did care about was getting word back to Fieldhead to tell them why she'd been held up but even this she would have to give up on, she decided. 'I'd better go and make sure he hasn't run off again.'

She carried the heel of a loaf and small wedge of cheese that Henry had been able to spare back to the barn and found Edgar exactly where she'd left him: in the corner of an empty stall, hugging his knees to his chest and staring straight ahead. He didn't react as she crouched beside him. 'I've brought you something to eat,' she said quietly.

His eyes flickered shut then open again.

'Bread and cheese, if you're hungry. And Mr Rowson is happy for you to bed down here.' As her eyes grew used to the dark interior, she could make out pitchforks and spades stacked against a wall and a hayloft over their heads with a ladder leading up. She climbed it and brought down an armful of dry straw – the beginnings of a bed for Edgar to stretch out on. 'In case you want to sleep,' she explained.

She might as well have been talking to an empty shell, a husk of a man instead of the man himself.

'You don't have to,' she went on cautiously, as if the breath from her words might blow the husk away. 'Sleep might be the last thing you want to do. That's how I was at the start of this year, after my fiancé's ship sank. I didn't want to fall asleep in case I had nightmares.'

Edgar turned his head away and then back again. He unclasped his hands.

'I'm not saying it's the same thing as what you're going through. It wasn't me in that water when the ship went down, it was Walter.' *Surrounded by drowning sailors and their cries, lungs filling with water, hands reaching upwards towards the moon and stars.*

He felt the *thud-thud-thud* of enemy fire as it raked through the Lancaster's cockpit, heard the engines cut out, saw Billy slump forward.

'Walter couldn't swim. It's a strange thing – a lot of sailors don't bother to learn.' *A direct hit in the thick of night. Oily black water, the suck and pull as she sank.*

The silent spiral downwards, blood seeping through Billy's shrapnel-torn jacket, the motionless propellers. Their plane had hit the tree canopy and come to an uneasy rest supported by branches, twenty feet above the ground. Edgar took a shuddering breath then spoke. 'Why?'

She rested her hand on his arm and waited.

'Why Billy and not me?'

Why Walter? Why anyone?

The inside of the barn was pitch black. Memories

154

drifted upwards and were caught in cobwebs. Silence comforted them even though sleep refused to come.

At dawn, Brenda rode out on her motor bike to find out what had happened to Joyce. She went back to the village and informed Edith Mostyn, who sent Bill out in the car to bring Edgar home.

'Again, please!' Kathleen clapped her hands to draw everyone's attention. She looked stylish and up to date in her navy-blue slacks and cream sweater, with not a blonde hair out of place. 'Jean and Elsie, put down your magazines. We have to go through the whole routine one more time.'

'Slave driver,' Jean grumbled. She regretted sacrificing the whole of her Saturday afternoon to attend a rehearsal less than two weeks before Christmas. 'I wish I'd never agreed to do this in the first place.'

Elsie pulled her to her feet then dragged her towards the low stage at the far end of the Institute hall. 'Stop moaning, for once in your life.'

Joyce called out to Kathleen from behind the piano. It was their first time in the actual venue and the acoustics were far from perfect. 'Do you want it from the very top?'

'Yes, please.' Kathleen was in her element and enjoying every moment. 'Una, I want you to be Elsie's partner from now on – you're around the same height. Brenda, come further forward and centre stage for your solo spot. Jean, you're an inch taller than Ivy. Switch places with her and take the man's part. You'll have to alter your hold.' She went up onto the stage to demonstrate. 'There, that's better. The rest of you are fine as you are.'

There was a buzz of chatter and a jockeying for position as Joyce prepared to play again.

'Remember, nice and smooth. Pretend you're gliding over the ice.' Kathleen issued her final instructions. 'One-two-three, one-two-three, slide your leading foot along the boards with no rise and fall. This isn't called The Skaters' Waltz for nothing.'

'Blimey, Kathleen has turned into Busby Berkeley all of a sudden,' Brenda joked with the girl nearest to her. 'Next we'll be wearing ostrich feathers and fishnet tights.'

'Yes, you'd better get your solo right, or else,' came the reply.

There were eighteen dancers on the small stage, with hardly enough room to swing a cat, as Jean grumbled from her place on the back row. 'And it's freezing in here,' she complained. 'Has anyone besides me felt the radiator pipes? They're stone cold.'

'Hush! Is everybody ready? Play us in please, Joyce.'

Piano notes tinkled and the Land Girls glided in pairs, weaving in and out, one-two-three, turning and twirling in time to the music. Dust rose from the rough boards beneath their feet. There was a small mistake here, a faltering step there.

'Still not right,' Kathleen said with a frown when the music stopped. 'Brenda, raise your leg higher in the arabesque and try not to wobble. Elsie, don't use so much force to swing Una around. And smile, please – everybody smile!'

'Is it time to call a halt?' Joyce asked from her

156

piano stool. There were some disgruntled faces up there and she could understand why. Who would have thought that Kathleen would turn into such a martinet? 'It's half past four already.'

'All right,' Kathleen agreed. 'I'll ask the caretaker if he can open the hall for us again tomorrow afternoon. What time would suit everyone?'

Two o'clock was agreed upon and the girls began to disperse.

Grace came down from the stage to speak with Joyce. 'I haven't said a proper thank-you for last Wednesday,' she began hesitantly.

'There's no need.'

'Yes,' she insisted, 'there is. When Edgar takes it into his head to wander off, he seems to forget the time of day and where he is. If he stays out all night at this time of year, he'll freeze to death.'

Joyce stopped tidying her sheets of music and looked up at her. 'It was pure luck that made me cycle back to the farm. And after I stumbled across him, it was clear he couldn't be left.'

'It must have been a long, cold night for you too.' Since Edgar's return two days earlier Grace and her father had been treading on eggshells, praying that he didn't go off again. 'Why do you think he does it?' she asked Joyce. 'What drives him away from us?'

Joyce smoothed the pages flat. 'We didn't talk much but he did mention the name Billy.'

'Who's Billy?'

'He was the pilot in his plane when they were shot down. He asked why Billy died and not him. To my mind, guilt is what bothers him.'

157

Grace gave a small nod. 'For still being alive.' *Oh, Edgar!* Her heart was pressed tight by the thought of him walking and walking into the wilderness. Always in vain, because he would never leave behind the crushing sense that he'd cheated death while his comrade had been taken.

She was jolted back into the present by a request from Brenda. 'Joyce, do you mind handing over a copy of the words and music for "Over the Rainbow"? I'd like to stay behind for half an hour and practise.'

Joyce did as she asked and Grace waited for her while she found the sheet and handed it over. Then they walked out together behind Kathleen and Una. It was already dark and the lights of the Blacksmith's Arms beckoned.

Elsie had crossed the road ahead of the others. 'There's just time for a quick half of cider before supper,' she said as she swung through the door.

Soon Brenda was left alone. She picked out the notes on the piano in a half-hearted attempt to get the melody into her head before she broke into song. The Victorian hall was drab and cold, with high, exposed eaves and a door close to the stage leading into an old-fashioned kitchen. There was a brass plaque on the wall acknowledging an endowment in 1872 by Mr Josiah Foster of Hawkshead Manor. Next to it was a faded sepia photograph of the man himself in a stiff, high collar and tweed waistcoat, with a heavy moustache and round spectacles.

Brenda found that it was hard to concentrate. Her mind wandered to what might be for supper and what she would do with her Sunday morning off work. Absent-mindedly she hummed the 'Rainbow' tune until she heard peculiar noises in the heating pipes that ran the length of the room – loud gurgles and knocking sounds that deserved investigation. She closed the piano lid and went outside to the small stone lean-to where the boiler was housed. Here she found Bill Mostyn with his back turned and his bag of tools open on the floor.

He heard her footsteps and shone his torch in her direction. 'Oh hello, Brenda. This boiler's sprung a leak. I've had to turn the stop tap off while I work on it.'

'Oh dear.' She shielded her eyes from the torch beam. 'Do you think you can mend it?'

'I'm not sure what's wrong yet. I might have to drain the water from the whole system.' As luck would have it, Bob Baxendale, the caretaker, had collared Bill on the coach during the drive back from their team's away match and asked him to take a quick look.

'I'd get our Maurice to do it but he's laid up with the flu,' Bob had explained. 'There's no heating in the place until the boiler's fixed and there's a whist drive on in the hall tonight.'

Promising to see what he could do, Bill had stopped off at home to pick up his tools and come straight here.

'Where's the leak?' Brenda wondered. The coal-fired boiler looked rusty and antiquated and the cramped boiler room was permeated by a smell of smoke and damp coke.

'It could be coming from the pump. I'll have to unscrew this casing and take a closer look.'

'Here, let me hold the torch for you.' She squeezed into the small space, aware of how little room there was. He'd taken off his jacket and rolled up his sleeves and now he worked deftly with the screwdriver until the metal plate came away.

'No, that's not where the problem lies,' he decided after a quick inspection. 'Everything here is in working order.' He knocked his elbow against her arm as he fitted the plate back into position. The torch fell from her hand and they both bent down to pick it up, their hands closing over it at the same time.

'Sorry,' they both said.

Surprised by the thrilling tingle of excitement that had passed between them, Bill kept his hand over hers for a moment longer than was necessary. A tremor ran through her too as she slipped her hand free and left him to pick up the torch.

He felt thrown. What was this connection between them? Every time he came across Brenda he felt a renewed interest, which he immediately pushed to one side. It was partly the way she looked, of course, but more what she said and did. He was attracted by her quick, bright way of speaking and the fearless habit of riding her motor bike up and down the dale that flashed into his mind during quiet moments. He tried to pin it down to one word and eventually came up with 'rebel'. That must be it – Brenda Appleby was the rebel he could never be.

She took the torch from him and directed the beam towards the boiler. There it was again – that spark between them. She'd felt it and so had he.

This time she would hang fire, wait for him to make the next move.

'Do you see this hose?' He squatted down and pointed to a tube connected to a tap on the wall. 'The rubber's perished so there's no proper water flow into the boiler. I think that's what's wrong.'

She gave a tut and a nod. *I'll wait forever at this rate.* Could Bill really be this slow to pick up a signal and respond?

'There's a spare piece of hose in the boot of my car. Can you hang on here a minute?' Without waiting for an answer he ran up the yard and came back with the hose. 'I always keep some handy,' he explained as he squeezed in beside her. He tilted the torch so that the beam shone in the right place then used a penknife to cut the new tubing to the right length. 'It's a lifesaver when you're working on tractor engines and such like.'

Engines, for goodness' sake! The moment of hands touching had come and gone and here they were tinkering about with lengths of rubber hose – very romantic!

He picked up on her impatience and misread it. 'Do you have to be somewhere else?' he asked as he eased one end of the new tube onto a brass spigot. 'If you do, I'm sure I can manage.'

'It's all right. I'm not in a rush.' She was squashed in a corner and one leg had gone to sleep so she shifted her weight and lost her balance, making the torch beam shoot up towards the sloping roof.

He put out a hand to stop her from falling. She

grabbed it and pulled herself upright. He kept his hand on the small of her back. They were so close that their features blurred. This was it – it was now or never. Brenda leaned in and kissed him gently on the lips.

Their fingers were still interlocked when Grace discovered them.

'I've brought the Institute key.' She looked in cool astonishment from Brenda to Bill and back again.

He let go of Brenda's hand and stepped out of the boiler house without saying a word.

Grace held up the key and stared at him. 'Kathleen took it with her by mistake. I offered to bring it across for Brenda to lock the door after her.'

'Yes, the key!' Brenda grabbed it and made herself scarce. There was something going on here that she didn't understand but she definitely knew when she wasn't wanted.

Grace watched her disappear through the side door. 'What were you and Brenda up to?'

'Nothing. She was lending a hand, that's all.' A flat denial emerged through clenched teeth.

'That didn't look like nothing.' It looked like betrayal from where she stood. 'You were holding hands.'

'She fell over. I helped her up.'

'Bill!'

'It's true, hand on heart.' His weak defence fell flat and he knew it.

Cold shock was replaced by a flare of anger from deep within. It blazed into Grace's eyes. 'How could you?'

'How could I what?'

'I don't know – lead Brenda on like that. Let her think she has a chance.' Their hands had been locked together and there was a second before they'd noticed her when she'd seen the look they'd exchanged. *It was definitely not nothing*, she told herself firmly.

'It wasn't me, it was her.' He knew the moment he said this that he'd made things ten times worse. How had that slipped out? He realized that he'd stooped low and in an instant he'd lost Grace's respect.

'Really and truly?' She walked away from him towards the road then stopped at the gate. 'Even if it was that way round – and I'm not saying I believe you – it was still up to you to put her right.'

'I know and I'm sorry.'

She laid her hand on his chest to keep him at arm's length. 'Brenda has no idea that we're engaged. No one does.'

He shook his head. There was no point telling her that his father had just received more bad news from the doctor. There would have to be an operation before Christmas. Everything had landed on Bill's shoulders with a vengeance and he had to bear it in silence for his mother's sake.

'Even I don't really know where I stand.' For once Grace didn't spare his feelings. 'You say you love me but you don't always act as if you do. It's actions I want, Bill, not words.'

'I know.' He was shame faced at having been caught out, stumbling over his words.

Anger pushed her on. 'Besides, I'm in an awkward

position as far as being honest with my friends goes. You can see that, can't you?'

'You said you didn't mind.' He panicked as he felt her all at once slipping away, shutting him out and disappearing from his future.

'I didn't, not at first. It was exciting for a while, living like Romeo and Juliet. Except this is England, Bill. It's Yorkshire, not Verona, and it's real life.'

'I know that.' Damn it, now he sounded sullen without meaning to.

She pushed him away then took a step back. 'You see, when it comes to it, I find that secrets don't suit me.'

'Wait. What are you saying? Are you breaking off our engagement?'

She sighed then nodded. 'I'm sorry,' she murmured as she crossed the street and left him standing in the gateway. Noise from the pub drifted out through the open door. She spotted Neville in the yard, deep in conversation with Una, and then Frank sitting by himself on the stile at the back of the forge. Kathleen came out arm in arm with Jack Hudson. The door closed behind them, sounds faded. Grace thought of the sparkling ruby and emerald ring that Bill had given her, tucked away in her dressing-table drawer. *I'll have to give it back*, she thought with the deepest of sighs. *It will be as if we were never engaged.*

CHAPTER TEN

Dear Tom, Una wrote. Sitting cross-legged on her bed, she leaned over to switch off the latest wireless report about Allied losses in the Med. This was her chance to snatch a few minutes of peace and quiet after the hurly-burly of supper time in the hostel dining room. She felt sorry for not having written to her brother for so long and was determined to make amends.

> How time flies. I've been at Fieldhead for just over a month and already it feels like a lifetime. Mind you, it means that I'm a dab hand with a pitchfork and hedge clippers now. Earlier this week we were out on the fell rounding up sheep and before that I was digging up beet for a farmer called Roland Thomson. Yes, that's right; your little sister doesn't go to the flicks and look at fashion magazines any more. No, I pull my weight by milking cows and mucking out stables. I haven't plucked a chicken yet, but I've had a go at most other things.

She paused for a while and wondered whether or not she should mention the Italian prisoners and her tender feelings for Angelo. It was best to be careful on that front, she decided.

She began a new paragraph.

The girls and I are putting on a Christmas show. We'll be singing and dancing for the lads in the Canadian Royal Air Force stationed nearby. Some POWs from Beckwith Camp have been invited too. It turns out that the two girls I share a room with are leading lights in amateur theatricals. Brenda, who I've mentioned before, is performing a musical number from *The Wizard of Oz*. Kathleen is knocking us all into shape for The Skaters' Waltz. She's worse than any sergeant major for dishing out the orders. (Ha-ha.)

Una was running out of space so her writing grew more cramped.

And now, Tom, how are you getting along by yourself on Wellington Street? Have you any news about Douglas, Ernest and Geoff? Write to me soon, please, and be sure to send me a Christmas card in good time so as not to miss the last Christmas post. From your loving sister, Una.

Putting a row of kisses under her name, she folded the sheet of paper and slipped it into an envelope then sighed without knowing why.

'What's this?' Brenda wanted to know as she breezed into the room, followed by Kathleen. Both were dressed in pyjamas and dressing-gowns with toothbrushes in hand. 'Why so sad? Wait, let me guess. You haven't heard from Angelo for at least twenty-four hours so you've written him a lovelorn note telling him how much you miss him and how you long to see him again.'

'Oh, very funny.' Una licked then sealed the envelope. She wrote her brother's name and address on the front then held it up to show Brenda.

Kathleen took off her dressing-gown and got into bed, talking to Brenda as if Una wasn't in the room. 'Someone we know would love to hear what a little bird told me as we were leaving the pub earlier.'

'Which little bird was this? Could it be Jack Hudson, by any chance?'

'As a matter of fact, no. I was talking to Bob Baxendale before Jack offered to give me a lift home. Bob happened to mention that a group of prisoners has been press ganged into giving the hall at the Institute a quick lick of paint in time for our Christmas show.'

Una pricked up her ears for more.

'It could certainly do with it,' Brenda commented. 'It doesn't look as if it's been done for donkey's years.'

'Starting tomorrow morning.' Kathleen gave Una a significant look. 'They've promised to be packed up and gone by one o'clock so that we can go ahead with our rehearsal. Of course, there's nothing to stop any of us from turning up early to practise our dance steps.'

Grateful for the tip-off, Una decided it was time to turn the tables on Kathleen. 'So Jack Hudson thought it was worthwhile to use up half his week's petrol ration on you, did he?'

'Yes, Kathleen.' Brenda joined in the fun. 'You could have let Una and me hop in the back of the car with you to save us the walk.'

'What for? You had your Old Sloper.'

'It would have been warmer in Jack's Baby Austin, though.'

Kathleen shook her head. 'Stop it, you two. There's nothing going on between Jack and me. And all joking apart, I only went with Jack to keep out of Frank Kellett's way.'

'Ah yes, I did see him hanging around outside the pub.' Brenda frowned at the memory. 'He's definitely an odd-bod.'

'Then I don't blame you for accepting the lift,' Una agreed.

'I get the shivers every time I see him.' Once started on the subject of Frank, Kathleen couldn't stop. 'He used to follow me everywhere when I first came here. He'd stand in my way and refuse to budge. And he'd watch me all day long if I had to work at Home Farm.'

'See, Una; you're not the only one,' Brenda remarked.

'You'd have hoped he'd have learned his lesson by now.' Sitting up in bed, Kathleen leaned forward and hugged her knees. 'Listen, girls, I'd rather you didn't spread this around, but after Frank laid in wait for me outside the pub and, you know . . .'

'After he attacked you and you managed to fight him off.' Brenda supplied the next part of her sentence.

'Yes. Well, after that, I had half a mind to report

168

Frank to the police so I went to see Mrs Mostyn to ask her advice and she said not to take it any further. She would talk to Frank's mother and make sure it didn't happen again.'

'That's not right.' Una was adamant. 'Under the law, a woman has the right to come and go as she pleases without running that kind of risk.'

'But this was Frank,' Kathleen tried to explain. 'Mrs Mostyn told me that everyone in the village knows he's a bit simple so they make allowances.'

'It's still not right,' Brenda agreed. 'And whatever Emily Kellett said to Frank, it didn't work because now he's pestering Una.'

Kathleen rested her head on her knees. 'First me, then Eunice, now you,' she said to Una in a pained voice.

Una gasped and looked at Brenda who slipped out of bed to put her arm around Kathleen's shoulder. 'Are you sure about Eunice?' she asked quietly.

Kathleen answered without raising her head. 'Yes – she told me about it the day after he made his move. It was the end of July, during the heatwave. She'd been hay making at Home Farm. I only found out because I caught her crying in one of the out-houses and it all came pouring out.'

'But she didn't want anyone else to know?' Una saw how it must have been.

'No. She wouldn't let me tell a soul. And I didn't hear the full story, I know that now.'

Like Una, Brenda was quick to put two and two together. 'Are you saying that Frank forced himself on her? That he was responsible?'

169

When Kathleen looked up there were tears trickling down her face. 'He must have been, mustn't he?'

'You mean Lorenzo wasn't the father?'

'No. Eunice liked him but she would never have . . . not willingly. She was brought up not to . . .'

'Oh, the poor thing.' Brenda sat down on the edge of Kathleen's bed and stared hopelessly at the floor.

Una felt her skin crawl. 'We should warn people about Frank. We should tell Mrs Mostyn.'

'Tell her what?' Kathleen took a hankie from under her pillow and blew her nose. 'We don't have any proof that what I've said is true.'

'So we just go on as normal? Poor Eunice is dead but nothing happens?' Una was reluctant to accept that life could be so unfair.

'Hush.' It was Brenda who saw that there was little point in going on because Kathleen was on the verge of bursting into tears again. 'Let's keep this under our hats for now. We'll get some sleep and think about it again tomorrow.'

A big bucket of whitewash blocked the entrance to the hall. Lorenzo was giving it a good stir when Una arrived and he greeted her with a conspiratorial smile. '*Buon giorno, Una.*'

She nodded expectantly.

'It's a happy day for you – Angelo is here.'

'In the hall?'

Lorenzo nodded. 'But wait. I will bring him.'

He picked up the heavy bucket and carried it inside. A few seconds later, Angelo appeared, smiling broadly.

Without saying a word, he led her around the back of the building then embraced her.

'I hope with my heart, and now you are here,' he began.

'Look at your face.' She used her thumb to wipe away small specks of white paint then she kissed his cheek.

He delved into his pocket. 'This is for you. I make.'

She took a small wooden box from him and read the interlinked initials on the lid: 'A' and 'U'. The carving into the beech wood was delicate. On the underside there was a butterfly, and on the sides a pattern of leaves. She clasped the box to her chest then kissed him again. 'This is lovely.'

They were standing out of the wind in a bicycle shed at the back of the Institute, looking out over the football pitch to farmland beyond. Four crows rose from a sycamore tree and sailed on air currents, followed by a clumsier grey wood pigeon and its mate. In the distance, a dog barked.

Una turned the box over and over. She imagined the hours of work that had gone into it. 'I mean it. This is the best present I've ever had.'

'I am happy you like.' He had to say with a gift what he wished he could say in words – that though the war had taken him from his sun-filled home and revealed to him the brutality that lurked in men's hearts, though it had imprisoned him in this grey, cold country and locked him into endless winter, still there was love.

He kissed her and held her. She was small like a bird. She made his heart soar.

*

171

'A word of warning,' Elsie said to Una after the prisoners had left and the Land Girls gathered for their rehearsal. Though Una had barely had time to catch her breath since Angelo had been driven away with his fellow prisoners, Elsie took her to one side and spoke seriously. 'Jean and a couple of the others got here early. I overheard them saying that they spied you round the back of the building with your Italian friend.'

A flicker of alarm passed across Una's features. 'What did they say?'

'They weren't best pleased.' Elsie didn't sugar the pill. 'Ivy's brother was on HMS *Fearless* when the Italian fleet crippled her, that's why. Dorothy backs up whatever Ivy says. And Jean's just Jean.'

'Did they call me nasty names?'

'The word "collaborator" was mentioned.' Elsie gave Una's arm a friendly pat. 'Between you and me, I don't have any time for that sort of name-calling. I think we're all in the same boat – English, French, Italians, even Jerry. We're all doing our best to get through this mess in one piece.'

Una glanced at Jean sitting on the edge of the stage with Ivy on one side and Dorothy on the other. They made a formidable trio – Jean with her permanent frown and the equally dour-looking Ivy and Dorothy in their dungarees and stout brogues – and she felt her heart begin to beat faster as they glowered back at her. 'What if they send me to Coventry? What then?'

'Try not to take it to heart.' Elsie did her best to reassure her. 'Those three will soon find someone else to be catty about. And if they don't, look on the bright side. Being ignored by Jean and her moaning-Minnie pals isn't the worst thing that could happen.'

Una wanted to follow Elsie's friendly advice but, as the afternoon progressed, it was hard to shake off a feeling of mounting apprehension. Ivy, for instance, made a point of standing in her way when she tried to take her position onstage for the waltz number and sneered unpleasantly when Una knocked down one of the flimsy side flats. Dorothy too made clear her antagonism by complaining to Kathleen that Una had bumped into her and sent her flying. They were small things in themselves but Una felt intimidated and couldn't brush them to one side.

'Are they ganging up on you?' Elsie asked her during a break in the rehearsal.

She was overheard by Joyce, who managed to glean from Elsie something of what was going on. 'Take no notice.' Joyce's advice mirrored Elsie's as she drew them both to the piano for a quick run-through of their duet. 'They're jealous, that's all.' She struck up the melody with extra gusto to take Una's mind off Jean, Ivy and Dorothy gossiping in a corner.

'Mind that wet paint.' Across the room, Brenda saw that Kathleen was about to lean against a section of wall that had been redecorated. She was carrying two cups of tea from the kitchen, one for her and one for Grace, who looked tired and hadn't seemed herself all afternoon. 'Here, take this,' she said when she spotted her sitting on a bench next to the piano.

173

Grace took the cup with a formal thank-you.

'There's no sugar, I'm afraid. Anyway, you're sweet enough.' There was still no smile so Brenda fell silent.

'Have you posted your Christmas cards yet?' Grace made a half-hearted attempt to fill the awkward gap.

'It's nice and warm in here today,' Brenda said at the same time.

Grace took a sip of tea. Brenda tapped her fingers against the side of her cup.

'I must remember to buy stamps from the post office next time I'm in town.'

'It's a good job Bill managed to mend the boiler otherwise we'd be freezing.'

Grace blinked hard but said nothing.

'He's a handy chap to have around when something needs fixing. He's a bit touchy, though.' Brenda had been genuinely puzzled by the episode with the key yesterday evening and now she was eager to clear the air with Grace. 'You've known him a lot longer than I have. Don't you agree that it's sometimes hard to work him out?'

'I'm sorry, I'd rather not—' Grace blushed bright red and stopped mid sentence.

Brenda frowned. 'Look, I didn't mean . . .'

'I know you didn't.'

'Oh, but . . . Oh yes, I see.' What an idiot she'd been not to pick it up before now. Grace and Bill had grown up in Burnside together and sensitive young Grace had most likely suffered the painful pangs of unrequited love over him. A shy, beautiful girl is bound to fall for the best-looking boy in the dale – it was obvious when she thought about it. There again, surely Grace would have got over it by now.

Grace stood up from the bench. 'I'm sorry, I have to go. I'm not feeling well.'

Brenda took the half-empty cup from her trembling hand. 'Will you be all right?'

'Yes, I'll be fine, ta.' The colour that had mounted to her cheeks had faded and left her skin as pale as porcelain. 'Will you tell Kathleen that I had to leave early, please?'

Brenda accompanied her to the door. 'I will, don't worry. Shall I pop in and see how you are after we've finished here?'

'No, don't do that. But thank you anyway.' Cold fresh air sent a shudder through her. 'I'm due at the Kelletts' place with you and Una tomorrow morning. I'll see you both there.'

'Eight o'clock sharp,' Brenda promised, standing at the door and questioning her own judgement as Grace hurried away.

'Heigh-ho, heigh-ho, di-di-diddle-dum.' Joyce hummed the tune to Walt Disney's Seven Dwarfs song as she and Jean searched for pine cones under the trees close to Beckwith Camp. It was Monday morning and they were delivering Horace Turnbull's eggs to both the POW camp and the Canadian barracks. 'It's off to work we go!' Jean's company was hard going at the best of times but this last hour or so had been worse than usual.

'It's not on,' Jean had grumbled on the cycle ride

175

across the frost-covered moor. 'Una ought to know better.'

Joyce had known what she was referring to but had pretended to ignore her. She'd blocked that line of conversation and talked instead about the week-end rehearsals, chilblains, chapped lips and how far she'd got with knitting a jacket for her sister Patricia's baby – anything to stop Jean's moaning.

Jean, however, was not to be thrown off track. 'I've read that in France women like her have their hair shaved off,' she'd snipped. 'They deserve it too for collaborating with the Nazis.'

There was no arguing with her so Joyce had chosen the hunt for pine cones as a last effort to wander off and escape her company, filling her empty egg basket with dry, undamaged ones that could be painted silver and used as decorations for the Christmas tree.

The plan had not worked. 'I would never do anything like that, would you?' Jean stood and watched from the edge of the wood. She cast suspicious glances at the roofs of the nearby Nissen huts. 'I don't care how handsome and charming they are with their "*ciao*s" and their "*bella, bella*s", I wouldn't go near them with a barge pole.'

Joyce sighed, put down her basket and walked towards the other woman. When she spoke it was with slow, heavy emphasis. 'For heaven's sake, Jean, will you please shut up?'

A strangled cry of protest escaped Jean's lips.

'I mean it. I've had enough. Now, are you going to collect pine cones with me or not?'

'I was only saying—'

'Are you?'

'No.' Jean stalked off, promising herself that Joyce Cutler wouldn't get away with treating her like this. Who did she think she was? She would have a word with Dorothy and Ivy when they got back from work. 'Be careful what you say to Joyce,' she would warn them. 'She's taken Una's side over the affair with the POW, and we all know from Eunice's experience how that's bound to end.'

Home Farm was the last place Una, Grace and Brenda wanted to be on a Monday morning ten days before Christmas. To make matters worse, they found that their job was to feed wheat into Arnold White's threshing machine, which Joe Kellett had hired for the day. This meant they had to start by setting up sacks to collect the grain out of one outlet pipe then lay out hessian sheets over the cobbles to gather the chaff that the giant machine would spew out at the far end.

'Have you got any goggles for us?' Grace asked the old farmer as he stoked up the steam engine in the yard. Without protection, clouds of dust and fluff would make their eyes itchy and sore. The engine chugged into life and drowned her out. 'Did you hear me, Joe?'

'I wouldn't bother if I were you.' Knowing that the answer would be no, Brenda got ready to feed wheat into the machine. It had been stored since harvest time in a barn beyond the dairy building, and carting it into the yard had brought a dozen or more hens out into the open to peck at the spilt ears.

Joe closed the door on the roaring furnace and gave orders for Grace to start stuffing wheat into the maw of the metal monster where it would be churned inside a huge drum. He gave Una a pitchfork and told her to stand by at the chute where the straw came out. Brenda got landed with the worst job of gathering up the chaff. He watched them until he was sure they'd got the hang of things – grains into sacks, straw pitched onto the nearby cart, chaff piled onto the sheets then gathered up for disposal. After ten minutes he was satisfied. 'I'll leave you to it,' he told Brenda as he made his way towards the dairy. 'I'll send Frank out in half an hour to stoke the fire.'

As if things aren't bad enough without him getting under our feet. Brenda's mouth and nostrils were already choked by dust and the engine was so loud that she could hardly hear herself think. Kathleen's account of what had happened to Eunice was still at the forefront of her mind and she knew that both she and Una would find it hard to work with him after what they'd heard. She coughed as she bent over to pull at the drawstrings that would shape the hessian into a large bag.

Clouds of steam billowed out of the funnel and the engine chugged relentlessly. Thirty minutes of back-breaking work passed but there was no sign of Frank.

'We're running out of steam. Shall I chuck more coal in?' Brenda yelled above the slowing churn of the machine.

'No. Let me go and tell Frank.' Grace left her post and rushed off in search of the farmer's son. She knew that feeding the furnace was his job, not theirs, but when she went into the dairy she found that the morning milking had been done and the metal churns taken away. The floors were scrubbed and hosed, the building empty. She sighed and went from there into the cowshed where a dozen black-and-white Friesians swished their tails as they stared out from their straw-lined stalls. There was still no sign of Frank.

'Hurry up, Grace,' Brenda called as she emerged from the shed. 'Trust Mr Kellett Junior not to be on hand on the one occasion when you actually need him. We're grinding to a halt here.'

So Grace hurried on towards the farmhouse and was about to knock on the door when she heard angry voices from inside the kitchen.

'Where's Frank?' Joe hectored. 'He's not in the cow-shed and he's not in the dairy, so where's he got to?'

'Don't ask me,' Emily fired back.

Grace stayed her hand, uncertain whether or not to interrupt the row that was building between man and wife.

'Come off it – you always know where he is. You never let him out of your sight if you can help it.'

'Because someone has to keep an eye on him, that's why. Anyway, you're not listening to me. I haven't clapped eyes on Frank since before breakfast.'

'That's typical – him buggering off for the day. One look at the threshing machine coming up the lane and he's off.'

'Yes, and who can blame him? You work everyone to death when that machine arrives.'

'Oh yes, stick up for him as usual, why don't you?'

Grace heard Joe swear then there was the sound of a door slamming. She knocked timidly and peered into the kitchen to see Emily lowering herself into a chair and rubbing her forehead. Steam rose from a copper tub in one corner in readiness for the weekly wash. A pile of dirty laundry lay in a heap on the wooden draining board.

'Excuse me, Emily,' Grace began.

The older woman looked up wearily. Wisps of white hair had escaped from the bun at the nape of her neck and she looked worn down. 'Yes, what is it?'

'I'm sorry to bother you but the furnace in the threshing machine is running low on coal.' A closer look around the kitchen told Grace that Emily wasn't keeping up with the housework. There was a layer of dust on the mantelpiece and holes in the net curtain strung haphazardly across the window. 'Shall we wait for someone to come or shall we see to it ourselves?'

Joe stamped back into the room before Emily had a chance to answer. His face was red and the veins on his forehead stood out. 'Didn't you hear what she said just now? The useless bugger has left us in the lurch yet again.'

'You listen to me, Joe Kellett.' Emily raised herself to her feet in fresh fury. 'I don't blame Frank for making himself scarce after the thrashing you gave him last night. And why? All because he wouldn't tell you where he'd been.'

Joe growled his sardonic reply. 'We already knew where he'd been – that was the trouble.'

180

Emily shot a wary glance at Grace before she went on. 'And was that any reason to beat the boy black and blue? He had bruises all down his arm from your belt buckle after you'd finished with him.'

Grace winced and took a step backwards.

Joe gathered phlegm in his throat then spat into the hearth. 'He had it coming.'

'No, he didn't. All he did was to sit on a bench in the village.'

'In the middle of winter.'

'What's wrong with that? And because of that you've flogged him and driven him away.'

Grace gave a small cough. 'It's all right; I expect we can keep the furnace going by ourselves,' she said as she backed out into the porch.

'He's a bloody useless sod!' The old man's voice followed her as she retreated. 'Always was, always will be!'

'You're the limit, Joe.' Emily's voice rose to a high-pitched wail. 'You treat that boy worse than the beasts in your cowshed and this time you've gone a step too far.'

CHAPTER ELEVEN

In the small community of Burnside, news of Frank Kellett's disappearance spread fast. The farmers in the neighbourhood gave vague promises to search their barns and outhouses in case he took refuge there. Cliff Kershaw mentioned it to his regulars when they called in on their way home from work. In truth, no one was particularly bothered or looked as if they would go out of their way to find him.

'Surely he can't have gone far,' Edith Mostyn said when she heard the news from Hilda Craven during a routine visit to Fieldhead that afternoon. 'Not if he's on foot.'

Hilda had supplied Edith with up-to-date details for the girls' medical cards then asked for help in folding clean sheets ready for ironing. 'Frank hasn't gone AWOL recently. In fact, the last time was over two years back and it wasn't the middle of winter, it was July.'

Edith held one end of a sheet and matched up the corners. 'Do we know what made him run off?'

'I did hear rumours from one of the girls. According to Brenda, who heard it from Grace—'

'You can't always rely on their word,' Edith interrupted.

'Yes. Anyway, according to Brenda there was a bad falling-out on Sunday night between Frank and his father.' Hilda pressed her lips together then gave her end of the sheet a sharp tug to make it hang straight before they folded it again. 'Need I say more?'

'No, indeed.' As lifelong residents in the village, though at different ends of the social scale, Edith and Hilda both knew Joe's cruel reputation for beating sense into his hapless son. They'd watched it from afar, since the days when young Frank used to skip school and roam the moor looking for birds' eggs or baby rabbits. His father would stand at the gate waiting for him to return, leather belt in hand. As the deaf boy had grown up and it had become obvious that there were other reasons he would never be able to fend for himself, Joe's treatment had if anything grown worse.

'It's Emily Kellett I feel sorry for,' Hilda went on. 'It's not always been easy but she's done her best with Frank. It's not her fault that he'll never amount to much.'

As Edith handed over the sheet, she decided to draw a line under the gossip. 'We have no idea what it must be like for the Kelletts,' she said with a sigh. 'In any case, let's hope that one night sleeping out in the open is enough for him.'

'For Emily's sake, if no one else's,' Hilda agreed.

Edith left the warden to her laundry and went upstairs to make a list of items needing repair or replacement. There was a broken light shade in

Jean, Ivy and Dorothy's room, a moth-eaten net curtain in the window at the end of the landing, a cracked pane of glass in the bathroom door. Fieldhead was growing shabbier by the week and though she put in regular requests to the County Office, there was rarely any money forthcoming for repairs. She noticed that the rubber sole of someone's shoe had scuffed the skirting board at the head of the stairs and that a brass stair rod had been kicked loose halfway down. Such carelessness offended her. When she had lived here, every inch of oak panelling had been bees-waxed and every brass doorknob given a daily polish. Times tables had been recited in a well-regulated chorus; globes of the world had displayed the glories of the British Empire.

On her way out to her car, Edith saw Elsie about to lean her bike against the front steps. 'Please don't leave it there!' she called out in a shrill voice. 'Take it round to the back of the building, out of sight.'

'Right you are,' Elsie replied obligingly. She glanced up at a solitary Lancaster bomber leaving a trail of vapour across the clear dusk sky. 'By the way, Mrs Mostyn, did you hear the latest? Ivy and Dorothy spotted Frank Kellett all by himself out at Kelsey Tarn.'

'When was this?'

'It must have been an hour and a half ago, at about three o'clock. They didn't talk to him, though – he was too far away.'

'So they just left him there?'

Elsie nodded. 'What else could they do? They were busy bringing more sheep down off the fell.'

Edith frowned and got into her car. She pulled on

her gloves then turned on the ignition, ready to drive straight to Home Farm. If there was any chance that Frank was still out by the isolated lake, then Emily and Joe needed to know.

'Eight days to go and we're nowhere near ready.' Joyce placed a shoebox filled with silvered pine cones on Grace's kitchen table. 'Elsie and Una can't seem to get the hang of "I Get a Kick out of You" and Brenda is still struggling with Dorothy's song from *The Wizard of Oz*. I've told them to rehearse without me tonight.'

Grace took off her coat and hung it on its hook. She picked up one of the cones and turned it between her slim fingers. 'These will do nicely as tree decorations.'

'Oh yes – the blessed tree! I've been badgering Brenda to flout the rules and help me to chop it down. It was her idea, after all.' Joyce sat heavily then leaned her elbows on the table. 'Honestly, Grace, sometimes I don't know why I bother. I still can't get a decent note out of the Fieldhead piano and no one else seems to be bothered about how little time we have left.'

Grace sat down beside her. 'I'll come over and give you a hand with the tree on Saturday afternoon. We'll cut it down, tie it to my bike and then I can wheel it back to the Institute.'

Joyce nodded and looked absent-mindedly out of the window, taking pins out of her hair and slipping them between her lips while she rearranged her French pleat.

'What's up, Joyce? This isn't like you. You're usually so full of beans.'

'I know and I'm sorry. I'll be all right once I've had a good night's sleep.'

'Are you sure nothing's bothering you?' Grace too was feeling heartsore and desperately confused over Bill, but she managed to put aside her own worries.

'I'm fine, thanks.'

'Really and truly? You know what they say about a problem shared.'

Joyce gave in to Grace's gentle insistence. 'Well, if you must know, I've had to work with Jean today and she's spent the whole time pulling poor Una to pieces, harping on about her friendship with Angelo and issuing dire warnings about fraternizing with the enemy. In the end I had to tell her to shut up.'

'Good for you!' Grace smiled warmly. 'I'm sure you're not the only one who's been tempted.'

'What makes Jean so permanently down in the mouth?'

'I did hear that she was poorly with scarlet fever when she was little. She missed a lot of school and had to stay back a year while her friends went on to the grammar school. I expect that made her feel left out.'

'Yes, that might account for it.' Joyce resolved to try to be more patient with Jean in future. 'I'm still worried about Una, though. Did you see how Jean, Ivy and Dorothy ganged up on her at Sunday's rehearsal?'

'I didn't notice. But then, I wasn't feeling very well.' Settling in for a chat with Joyce was doing

Grace good. They were on the same wavelength about most things and she always felt relaxed in her company.

'What was it – a gippy tummy?' Joyce took the silver cones from the box and lined them up in a row – fifteen in all. They would look just right hanging from the Christmas tree.

If only it was as simple as that, Grace thought. An image of Bill's face popped into her head – the look of alarm in his eyes when she'd caught him hand in hand with Brenda and the blow it had dealt. The wound hadn't healed; rather it had festered as she went over Bill's poor excuses time after time. 'Yes, it must have been something I'd eaten,' she said quietly.

Joyce gave her a quizzical glance and saw from Grace's downcast eyes that there was more to it. Her thoughts flew to her friend's worries about her brother. 'A problem shared . . . ?' she reminded her.

Grace sighed and carefully rearranged the cones into a circle. 'I'd had an argument,' she confessed. 'I won't say who with but it upset me a great deal.'

'I can see that. And bridges can't be built?' Joyce asked hopefully. She was convinced that there was a way back from every argument – where there's life, there's hope was her hard-earned motto.

'No.' *A look of alarm swiftly followed by guilt on Bill's face as Brenda had taken the key and hurried off. His desperately disappointing excuses. A shared secret that had cracked open, the sparkle of rubies and emeralds still in the box in her bedroom.* 'I'm afraid not.'

*

The forge at night was the place where Edgar felt safest. He sat in the dark and listened to the glowing embers settle, surrounded by the tools of his father's trade – hammers of all sizes, callipers, tongs, boxes of nails, metal rods stacked against the wall, cast-off horseshoes, bellows made of wood and leather, secured by brass studs. There were echoes of his childhood here. His own footsteps ran in from the sunny yard, his boyish voice demanded to know when his father would come in for his tea. Endless tapping and hammering, a blast of air from the bellows, the flare of flames in the red-hot furnace. His father would look up, his face red and shiny, his strong, bare arm wielding his hammer high above his head. 'Tell your mother I'll be finished in half an hour.' Edgar remembered how he'd run back into the house. His mum would be in the kitchen, boiling a ham hock in a big pan perhaps. Grace would be drawing flowers at the kitchen table. Daisies in a jam jar, picked from the field behind the forge. Bare legs tickled by long grass in the still heat of midsummer. And always the sound of the hammer in the background to his boyhood days.

'Hello, Edgar.' Joyce had said goodbye to Grace in the kitchen then taken a short cut through the forge to collect her bike. She'd been startled to see him sitting on the anvil, staring into space. 'I didn't see you there.'

Her voice rang out in the cavernous space but there was no reply.

She walked on towards the side door, opened it, then paused. 'Do you hear that?' She meant the low rumble of planes flying overhead. 'Are they Spitfires or Lancasters?'

'Heinkels. No – two Heinkels and a Dornier.'

'You can tell that without seeing them?'

'Every plane has a different sound – that's two night fighters and a bomber, heading north-east towards the RAF base up there on the coast. With luck, our chaps will intercept them.'

'What about the Canadian training centre on Penny Lane – does Jerry know about that?'

Edgar's voice was expressionless. 'He knows everything. He was there on the ground waiting for Billy and me in Brittany. It was as if they'd been expecting us.'

'But you managed to get away?' Joyce had retraced her steps to where he sat. The question hung in the air.

'I was jammed in the gun turret, twenty feet up,' he said at last. 'We landed in some trees and the plane was left hanging there. Billy had been shot in the chest. There was blood and bits of him everywhere. A dozen of them came swarming towards us when the whole thing went up in flames. I had to climb over Billy to smash my way out. Their lot stood back and watched it burn – no survivors is what they reckoned. They turned back the way they'd come.'

'Leaving you with a broken leg and lucky to be alive.'

He shook his head and lapsed into silence. His face was drained of emotion in the dim light and his mind was hundreds of miles away, smashing its way out of a burning cockpit after a failed night-time mission over northern France.

*

189

In Burnside the build-up to Christmas continued even as enemy bombers flew overhead with increasing regularity. Further afield, the Pact of Steel was strengthened between Hitler and Mussolini. The Italians threatened the British fleet off the coast of Egypt and Churchill made yet another inspiring speech in the House of Commons, broadcast on the Home Service and listened to by millions.

'It does make you wonder if we're right to carry on as usual.' Elsie voiced what many of the Land Girls at Fieldhead were secretly feeling. It was eight days before Christmas and they'd got together in the middle of the week for an extra rehearsal at the Blacksmith's Arms. 'I probably shouldn't say it, but with the Japs and the Yanks at each other's throats in Hong Kong, besides everything that's going on in Europe and North Africa, there might be something to be said for having a quiet Christmas this year, without too much fuss.'

'What, and let Jerry think that he's got the better of us?' Brenda's was the first voice to object. 'Personally, I'm for keeping calm and carrying on like those poor blighters in London did in the early days of the Blitz.'

There was a slow murmur of agreement from those around the piano.

'Yes, if Londoners can cope with kipping all night in Underground stations and come up in the morning to find their homes blown to smithereens, I'm sure we can deal with a Messerschmitt dropping the odd bomb over Thornley Dam.' Kathleen's steely determination to go on with preparations for the show wasn't to be shaken. In fact, she'd decided to take it easy at work so that she would have spare energy to put into rehearsals in the evenings. Tonight they were to learn a new song for the finale – Vera Lynn's 'We'll Meet Again', which was guaranteed to bring tears to everyone's eyes.

'These may be dark days,' Una agreed with her usual sincerity, 'but I do believe Mr Churchill's bright light will soon be seen shining over all the land and sea.'

'Yes, and our job is to bring a bit of that light to Burnside.' Joyce was at the piano, tentatively running through the melody of the new song. She looked up to see a contingent of three Canadian Air Force men come into the mostly empty pub.

'Hello there, girls.' Flight Lieutenant Mackenzie immediately broke away from the trio and treated them to his broad, confident grin. 'What's this – a run-through for next week's Christmas spectacular?'

Brenda mirrored his smile as she came forward to meet him. 'Yes, but we'll be forced to call a halt while you're here, won't we, girls?'

Kathleen joined her, sheet music in hand. 'Definitely. We need to keep a few surprises up our sleeve – otherwise the evening will fall flat.'

Mac sandwiched himself between them and shook his head. 'There's no chance of that,' he assured them. 'Our guys can't wait for Tuesday. In fact, I'm struggling to find volunteers to man the base while the rest of us come to see the show.'

'You hear that, girls?' Brenda called for the others

to gather round. 'Mac is promising us a nice, friendly audience so it won't matter if we make fools of ourselves by tripping and falling off the stage into their laps.'

Una dragged Joyce and Grace across the room to enjoy the glamorous interruption. Mac smiled at her and said hi and she felt flattered that he remembered her.

'It's the girl on the back of the motor bike, isn't it? What's your name?'

'Una. And this is Joyce.'

'Hi, Joyce.'

'And Grace.'

'Hi, Grace. I've seen you working behind the bar.'

'That's right. I live here.' Grace knew how popular the Canadian servicemen were and she shared the enthusiasm of the local women. Their smart uniforms, well-groomed hair and the relaxed openness of their smiles caused a flutter of excitement whenever they walked in.

'Well, ladies, I have some good news.' Mac enjoyed the attention. 'Not only are we nice and friendly, as you put it, but I can guarantee you a total of thirty eager airmen.'

Brenda couldn't help raising a doubtful eyebrow. 'But you said fifteen.'

'Yeah, but we got a batch of fresh recruits on account of recent events in the Far East. Is thirty a problem?'

'Not at all.' Kathleen swept aside any complications – such as space and the number of chairs available. 'The more the merrier.'

'We'll check with the caretaker.' Brenda felt a twinge of resentment against Kathleen. Since when had she taken over the role of impresario? 'But don't worry – I'm sure we'll be able to squeeze you in at the back.'

'That sounds good to me, Miss Motor-bike-rider.'

'Brenda.' She gave him her brightest smile. As far as she was concerned, you could keep Italians with their romantic, rolling *arrivederci*s and their *donna bella*s. For her, this cool, up-front Canadian charm did it every time.

'Well, Brenda, you can squeeze me in at the back any time,' he assured her with a wink. 'Hey, Brenda and Una, why not come and talk numbers with my squadron leader?' Mac took each of them by the elbow and clicked his heels smartly at the rest of the group. 'Excuse us, ladies. And please, don't hold up your rehearsal on our account. We're like the three monkeys – we promise not to look, listen or speak a word.'

Brenda and Una felt themselves being ushered towards the bar. They soon had drinks in their hands and while Jim Aldridge introduced Una to his companion, Mac commandeered Brenda all to himself.

'So, Brenda, how do you like the Land Army?'

'I like it a lot. It beats working in a butcher's shop.'

'The outdoor life must suit a girl like you. It does wonders for the figure, for a start. And yeah – that's a compliment.'

'Thank you.' Unabashed, Brenda sipped her cider and enjoyed his admiring glances. There were none

193

of the complications here that she'd encountered with Bill Mostyn – it was out and out flattery.

'And is there a guy tucked away back home?' he wanted to know. 'I guess there must be, for a good-looking gal like you.'

'No guy,' she insisted.

'How come?' Mac leaned one elbow on the bar and gave her his full attention.

'Because I choose not to toe the line. I mean, I don't take any of the usual clap-trap – hearts and flowers, and such like. I prefer people to be straight with me.'

Mac gave a hearty laugh. '*Clap-trap!* Is that even a word?'

'It is where I come from. Anyway, what about you? Are you engaged to a "gee-whiz" girl in Toronto?'

'Vancouver,' he corrected. 'No fiancée, gee-whiz or otherwise.' He turned to tap Jim Aldridge on the arm. 'Vouch for me, sir – tell Brenda I'm single and fancy free.'

Brenda leaned behind the two men and spoke to Una in a stage whisper. 'Take my advice – do *not* believe a word they say!'

'Hey, that's not very nice.' Mac played Brenda's game and pretended to take offence. 'We're Canadians, not Italians, remember. Talking of which, did you hear that they're thinking of closing down Beckwith Camp?'

It was as if a bolt from a crossbow had thudded into Una's ribcage. She felt all the blood drain from her face and had to hold onto the bar to stay upright.

'Come again!' Brenda too was startled.

'Don't worry – it's not happening until after Christmas so you won't be playing to a half-empty house.'

'But what do you mean?' Brenda tried to frame a sensible question. 'If they close the camp, where will the prisoners go?'

It can't be true, Una thought. *He's made a mistake.*

'According to what I heard, they're moving them further north, to the west coast of Scotland.' Puzzled by the impact his snippet of information seemed to have made, Mac shrugged and tried to move the subject on. 'The plan is for us to expand our base and use the Beckwith Camp huts for new trainees.'

'Wait a second – why Scotland, for heaven's sake?' Brenda asked.

It was Aldridge's turn to fend off questions. 'I guess that information is classified.' He spoke with authority, making it clear that such talk was off limits.

'What will you Land Army girls do without the POWs working with you?' Mac wondered in the same amused tone as before. 'Who'll do the heavy work?'

'*We* will.' An arch look from Brenda made it clear that his last remark had caused offence. Then a quick glance in Una's direction told her that she had to get her friend out of the smoky pub into the fresh air. She put down her glass and grabbed her by the arm. 'Now if you'll excuse us, Una and I have to go and powder our noses then get back to rehearsal.'

'It's not definite. Mac only said they're thinking of closing the camp.' Brenda leaned Una against the forge door and fanned her face with the copy of the

195

Vera Lynn song that she had in her pocket. 'He didn't say that they actually will.'

'How will I cope?' The bolt had struck and Una was struggling to breathe. 'I'll be lost without him. I won't be able to stand it.'

'Stop. Listen to me. You've only known Angelo for five minutes. It won't be the end of the world, I promise.'

Una grasped her wrist. 'Brenda, he can't go to Scotland. He can't.'

'You'll be able to write to him. He can write to you.'

There was a terrible pain in her chest. 'No, it's not the same – words on a page. His English is . . .' She trailed off into a dry sob.

'Listen, it might never happen. Take a deep breath, try to calm down.'

'I need to see him face to face,' Una pleaded.

'When? Uh-oh, you mean now, don't you?'

'Yes.'

Una's stricken look quickly convinced Brenda. She glanced at her watch to see that it was ten to seven. Fifteen minutes on the bike would get them to Penny Lane. 'All right, I'll drive you over there. Wait here. I'll fetch our jackets and tell Grace and the others where we're going.'

Without wasting any time, she kept her promise and five minutes later they were on their way, travelling at high speed and meeting no traffic. 'Hold tight,' she warned Una as she leaned the Sloper into a sharp bend. Luckily there was no ice or fog and only the lightest of drizzles in the air.

Una's heart was thumping, her mouth dry. She didn't notice the road or anything about her surroundings. Brenda was taking her to see Angelo – that was all that mattered.

They turned into Penny Lane and Brenda eased off the throttle. 'Be prepared – they might not let us in,' she warned as the bike slowed down. 'I'll think up some excuse about preparations for the show, but it depends who's on sentry duty.'

I have to see him. I have to talk to him.

'Do you hear me?' Brenda prompted.

'Yes.'

'I'll do my best. Here we go.' She revved again, passing the Canadian base and arriving at the sentry box outside Beckwith Camp with a roar of her engine. 'Angelo would have to be deaf not to hear that,' she said to Una as they got off the bike. 'Keep your eyes peeled.'

They walked the twenty yards from the lane to the gate where the sentry stepped out, his rifle at the ready. Beyond the gate, there were lights on in the huts and the usual sounds of doors opening and closing, men's voices calling in Italian and footsteps coming and going.

Neither Brenda nor Una recognized the private who barred their way. He wore steel-rimmed glasses and his face was broad and smooth, his hair clipped in army-style short back and sides. 'Yes?' he asked.

'We've come about the Christmas show at Burnside,' Brenda began in her most perky manner. Una stayed tucked in behind her to hide her pale face and shaking hands. 'It's on Tuesday of next week.

197

We'd like to talk to your sergeant to finalize numbers.'

There were more voices. One was Angelo's, Una was sure.

The dark pine trees behind the camp swayed in a wind that blew gusts of cold mist against their faces. Voices were raised. A door slammed shut.

'The sergeant is busy. Come back tomorrow in the daylight,' the sentry told Brenda.

'We can't – we'll be busy working.'

'Then make a phone call if you can't come in person.'

'Listen – all we need is the number of prisoners so we can set out enough seats.' Brenda could see from the sentry's blank expression that she wasn't getting anywhere. 'You ought to make sure that your name is on the list too,' she said with her most winning smile. 'And Albert and Jack – tell them that it's going to be a jolly good show. They should try to come.'

'Miss, I haven't got time to listen to this.' Eyeing Brenda's thrown-together outfit of breeches, airman's jacket and felt hat, he sniffed and shook his head. 'There are reports of an intruder. A man was seen in the vicinity.'

Una peered over his shoulder and saw a figure she was sure was Angelo being marched by an armed guard towards the single brick-built building in the camp. The door was opened by someone inside then closed firmly behind them.

'Just five minutes with your sergeant,' Brenda implored, though by now she knew it was useless.

'Did you hear me, miss? An intruder.' The sentry

tapped his rifle butt. 'Step back. Go straight home if you know what's good for you.'

With despair in her heart, Una pulled Brenda away. The entrance was barred. Angelo was in trouble with the guards and it was her fault. They walked back to the bike and Brenda started the engine.

'Just our luck to come up against a stickler for the rules,' she muttered.

Una felt the Sloper kick into life. *I'll write,* she thought as she gripped the cold metal of the narrow luggage rack behind the pillion seat. *I'll tell Angelo how much I love him and I always will . . .*

CHAPTER TWELVE

Friday morning saw Grace, Brenda and Una working together at Brigg Farm. Roland set them to work on a new set of potato clamps in a field furthest from the farmhouse where they were exposed to a bitterly cold wind. It blew the thin covering of powdery snow into their faces and froze their fingers. Today there was to be no comforting bonfire and no help from the team of POWs, the dour farmer warned them as he left.

'You're out of luck,' Neville remarked to Una when he arrived with the horse and cart two hours later to collect the full sacks. A knitted balaclava protected his head from the worst of the cold and he wore a threadbare jacket over two jumpers and a set of his father's combinations. He jumped down clumsily from the driver's seat and set to work lifting the sacks.

'What do you mean by that?' she retorted as she stood up straight to ease her aching back.

'Your Angelo is filling in for Frank Kellett over at Home Farm, so there'll be no lovey-dovey chats for you today.'

While Grace and Brenda worked on, Una took

Neville to one side and felt in her pocket. With numb, mud-encrusted fingers she drew out the letter she'd written the night before. 'Can you make sure he gets this?'

He took it and tucked it into his inside pocket then held his hand out for payment.

Again she fumbled until she found a sixpence and gave it to him. Then she picked his brains. 'Nev, have you heard any rumours about them closing the camp?'

'No. That's news to me.'

'Are you sure? Nothing about the Canadians taking it over?'

'Not a dicky bird,' he assured her. He frowned when he realized that this would put an end to his source of extra income then considered putting up his charges for as long as it lasted before taking pity on a miserable Una. 'Leave it with me. I'll find out for you.'

'And you'll deliver the letter today?' In it she'd poured out her heart, telling Angelo that her feelings for him were true and they would never change, that she kept the little box he'd made for her under her pillow and it was where she stored his precious letters tied with a red satin ribbon. There was much more – a promise that she would go on loving him even if the war were to force them apart, the hope that he felt as she did and would not forget her. The war would end eventually. Their countries would make peace and after that they could be together.

'I'll get it to him if I can.' Neville was making no promises. His dad had given him a list of jobs as long as his arm – take Major down to the smithy for a full set of new shoes, replace the washer on the yard tap, collect a dozen eggs from Winsill Edge.

'Please.'

'I said I'll try.' This go-between lark wasn't easy. His best bet was to track Angelo down before he finished work at Home Farm, which would mean making a detour on the way to Horace Turnbull's hen farm. He could do that before he took Major to the forge.

Una mouthed a thank-you and went to rejoin Grace and Brenda while Neville loaded the sacks.

'Chin up,' Grace murmured as an anxious Una watched him drive the cart away. 'Did I hear him say that Angelo is filling in for Frank?'

'Yes.' Una made a reckoning of the number of days that the Kelletts' son had been missing. 'It's Friday today and he vanished on Monday morning. That's five whole days. Emily must be worried sick.'

Brenda started on a fresh layer of straw, unearthing yet more potatoes. If anything, the weather was turning even colder and frost nipped at her fingers and turned them red-raw. 'Do you remember the intruder we heard about on Wednesday night?' she began as Una got back to work. 'I was wondering if it might have been him, by any chance.'

'The sentry at the camp warned us about it,' Una explained to Grace. 'But what would Frank have been doing there?'

'Maybe he was on the lookout for something to eat?' Grace suggested.

'Or for a place to keep warm.' Brenda could see

why Beckwith Camp's kitchen storeroom and wood fires might lure Frank in.

'He must be at his wits' end.' Grace imagined him roaming far and wide, from Kelsey Tarn right down to Beckwith Camp in the valley bottom. 'So yes, it would make sense for him to scavenge and creep around in the dark, trying to keep body and soul together.'

'Creep around is right.' Brenda's frozen fingers fumbled to pick potatoes out of the straw. 'Remember – we all need to be on our guard against Frank Kellett.'

Hard work and harsh conditions kept them quiet for a while, until Grace started to hum quietly. Brenda and Una soon picked up the tune to 'We'll Meet Again' and joined in with the sweetly sad words. They began softly but then raised their voices until they rang out across the fields, switching from Vera Lynn to Judy Garland and another song of longing, this time for a land over the rainbow where the grey skies turned blue amid a Technicolor riot of yellows, reds and blues.

The song ended and Brenda looked from Una and Grace's pinched faces to their sacks of potatoes and on across the snow-covered fields then back again. She burst out laughing at Una. 'Look at us. We're a right set of scarecrows – me with sacking tied around my legs, poor little you shivering from head to toe, Grace with mud and straw in her hair!'

'Me – a scarecrow?' Una giggled as she squared her shoulders, swung her arms and marched on the spot. 'I'm off to find the wizard!'

'Wait for us!' Grace cried as Una set off around the clamp, closely followed by Brenda.

The sky was heavy with snow and the frozen ground crunched under their feet. But the three women marched up and down the field as if there really was a rainbow with a pot of gold at its end, as if a wand could be waved and magic would solve their heartache and grant them all a happy-ever-after.

'Remind Joyce that I'll be over tomorrow afternoon to help cut down the Christmas tree,' Grace told Una and Brenda as they parted outside the Blacksmith's Arms.

'We'll be back here later for a rehearsal so you can tell her yourself,' Una pointed out. 'Kathleen wants us to run through all our songs in their proper order. On top of which, she's booked the Institute for Sunday afternoon for a full dress rehearsal.'

'Then we'd better dig out our Sunday best,' Brenda added with a wink as she cycled on.

Grace stood in the yard and watched the pair of dim beams from their bike lamps wobble on up the street. She heard a hum of voices from the bar and took her time to wheel her bike around the side of the forge. Deciding to take the short cut through the forge to the house, she came across her brother sitting in the dark by the still-warm furnace.

'Edgar, you made me jump. What are you doing here?' Her voice sounded hollow in the barn-like space.

'Staying out of harm's way.' He jerked his thumb towards the pub. His gaunt face was lit by flickering embers and his eyes gleamed as he looked at her.

'How come?'

'I've signed the pledge, haven't I? Gone teetotal.'

'Since when?'

'Since yesterday.'

'That's marvellous, Edgar.' Her voice was tinged with disbelief and caution kept her from giving him a hug. 'What made you decide?'

'I realized that the booze wasn't doing me any good, that's all.'

'Well, it wasn't – that's true. Honestly, it's wonderful – I mean it.'

'But you don't believe I can do it?'

'I didn't say that.' She stood in the warm, flickering light, taking off her hat and unbuttoning her coat. 'Go on – tell me more.'

'There is no more. I'll stay here in the peace and quiet for a while then I'm going to have an early night.'

Grace saw that this was all she would get out of him. 'Have you had something to eat? Would you like me to bring you a sandwich and a cup of tea?'

'Nothing,' he replied, putting his hands over his ears to cut out the sounds of customers arriving and car doors slamming. His hands shook and he hung his head so that she couldn't see his face.

'All right. I'll leave you to it.' Resolving to keep an eye on him during the evening, she went out into the yard to see Bill's car pulling in. He wound down his window as he drove slowly towards her.

'Hop in?' he asked tentatively.

Her heart suffered a small shock at the sight of his worried face and she shook her head. 'I'm sorry – I'm busy.'

'Please, Grace.' He leaned over and opened the passenger door. 'I have to talk to you.'

She stayed where she was. 'There's nothing to talk about.' There was the engagement ring, of course. She ought to tell him to wait there while she went to fetch it but her courage failed her.

'Please,' he said again.

She shook her head a second time so he turned off the engine and got out of the car. He caught hold of her hand before she could walk away. 'It won't take long.'

'You're right – it won't.' She had to stand firm, even though her feelings ran wild as she saw him close to. His physical presence always set off a longing in her – an ache to have his arms around her and to feel his lips on hers. And it was still here, in spite of recent events.

'Walk with me.' He put his arm around her waist and in that moment of weakness she didn't resist. They walked out of the yard towards the chapel, past Maurice and Bob Baxendale who hid their surprise at them walking down the street as a couple.

'Now then, Bill,' Maurice said, ignoring Grace completely.

Once they were out of earshot, Grace pulled away in confusion and confronted him. 'What do you want?'

'I have something to tell you.'

'What, Bill – what? I heard everything I needed to hear and saw everything I needed to see last Saturday – you and Brenda together, your miserable, feeble excuses.'

'I know and it's been hell ever since. I'm serious – I've been kicking myself for being such an idiot. Brenda doesn't mean anything to me. Nothing happened between us and nothing ever will – you've got to believe me.'

'That's not the point. She's my friend. I work with her and Una day in, day out. But I could never break my promise and tell them about us. *That's* the point!' She looked up at him with the same anger she'd felt a week before. 'Do I have to spell it out any more?'

Bill shook his head slowly. They'd reached his house and stood in the shade of the tall monkey puzzle tree.

Grace went on anyway. 'If Brenda had known about our engagement, she would have stayed well away from you. As it was, she saw you as fair game, just like a lot of the other girls.'

Gradually he took in what she was saying. 'Who?'

'Kathleen, for a start. And half a dozen others, I shouldn't wonder. Do you know what the girls in the hostel say about you, Bill? They say you're a good catch. And on top of that, there are the Fosters and your parents. They can't wait for Shirley to get home on Christmas leave so they can pick up their matchmaking plans where they left off.'

Mention of his mother and father made him wince then he forged ahead with what he had come to tell her. 'I've just brought Mum back from the hospital. Dad's had another heart attack.'

'Oh no!' The news pushed Grace's emotions in a new direction. She gasped and clutched at his sleeve. 'How is he? Is he all right?'

'It's touch and go. The doctors say they'll know more in the morning.'

'And your mother?'

'She's holding up; you know how she is. Luckily she was there when it happened – she was on the phone to County Office, sorting out an overtime problem for Dorothy Cook. When she finished the call, she found Dad lying on the lounge floor.'

'And was he conscious?'

'Barely. She phoned the ambulance and they took him straight to the Queen Victoria. I got there as quick as I could.'

'What a terrible shock,' Grace murmured as she slid her hand down his sleeve and grasped his hand.

'Not really. We knew his heart was bad and that he needed the operation as soon as possible.' Bill looked down at her pale hand. The effort of delivering the bad news had made him feel impossibly weary and sick at heart. 'I can't leave Mum for very long, but I just had to come and tell you.'

She opened the gate then stood to one side. 'You go in. Tell her I – we – all the girls will be thinking of her and hoping for the best.'

He glanced back up the road towards the pub. 'What about my car?'

'Leave it there overnight. It won't come to any harm.'

'I'm sorry, Grace.' His voice broke as he said her name then he paused to take a deep breath. 'I shouldn't have . . .'

'Don't say sorry,' she murmured, not knowing how far the apology stretched – for seeking her out tonight, for the episode with Brenda, for wrapping their love affair in a shroud of secrecy? 'And if you or your mother need me for anything . . .'

He swayed then leaned in towards her. For a moment he rested his cheek against the top of her head.

She stepped back, wishing with all her heart that things could be as they had been but fearing they could never be ever again. He looked dreadful in the half-light cast by a gas lamp outside the chapel – weighed down by the events of the day, almost unable to put one foot in front of the other – so she led him two or three steps up the path towards the door then slipped her hand from his grasp. She thought she saw a slight movement of the curtains in the front lounge but perhaps it was her imagination. 'Remember, I'm just up the road,' she whispered, leaving him to go into the house alone.

The Christmas tree was taller than Grace had expected. She stood with Una, Brenda and Joyce in the copse behind Fieldhead.

'Blimey, that's a belter!' Brenda stood, hands on hips, looking up at the eight-foot monster. 'I was imagining a titchy little thing.'

'It's a good shape, though.' Una circled it appreciatively. Its branches were evenly spread and it would look well in a tub wrapped around with a red-and-green crêpe paper bow.

'We'll have to work out a different way of carrying it to the village. It's far too big for my push bike.' Grace was the practical one as usual.

Joyce took the saw that Grace had brought, knelt down and set to work on the trunk. 'If it comes to it, we can lug it across country, taking turns to carry it, one at either end.'

All around them the elm trees stood tall and straight, their bare branches providing little shelter from the flakes of snow that drifted down from a leaden sky. Underfoot the ground was spongy with moss and to the back of them the high stone wall of the vegetable garden hid them from view of the house.

'We won't be lugging it anywhere if this snow sets in,' Brenda predicted. She was in high spirits as she watched Joyce saw away. '"Back to the land, we must all lend a hand,"' she sang. '"To the farms and the fields we must go. There's a job to be done."'

'"Though we can't fire a gun we can still do our bit with a hoe."' Una and Joyce joined in with gusto while Grace took a back seat.

'They go on about farms and fields and country life,' Joyce commented as she took a few moments' break. 'And barley and wheat and potatoes to eat – tra-la-la – but what they don't mention is the frostbite and chilblains that come with it.'

They all laughed as Brenda pushed her to one side. 'Let the dog see the rabbit,' she chided as she began to saw vigorously. Within a couple of minutes there was a small heap of sawdust on the frosty ground and a cry of 'Timber!' from Grace, Una and Joyce.

'We have our tree!' Brenda stood up while Una and Joyce manhandled their prize and the snow-flakes whirled down in earnest.

Grace bit her lip, looked up at the clouds, but said nothing.

'Is it too heavy?' Brenda offered to take over from Una, who had lifted the thick end of the trunk and was taking her lead from Joyce at the top end. Joyce manoeuvred them between the elms for the trudge towards the house.

'No, ta, I can manage.' *Just because I'm little,* she thought, *it doesn't mean I can't pull my weight.* Anyway, she preferred to concentrate on the task because it took her mind off Angelo and her as yet unanswered letter.

'Watch out for that big tree root,' Grace warned. It seemed there was going to be a blizzard and she started to wonder how she would get back home in time to make tea for her father and Edgar. On top of that, though she hadn't heard from Bill all morning and had been at work when he came to collect his car, she had promised she would be on hand if he needed her.

Brenda's chatter kept Joyce and Una going until they reached the wall of the vegetable garden where they laid the tree on the ground then shook snow from their hats. 'Did anyone hear the latest news about Her Ladyship? Well, not Mrs M exactly, but her old man. Dorothy stopped off at the house to find out if she'd sorted out her overtime but it was Bill who came to the door. He told her that Mr M has been carted off to hospital with a heart attack and for her to come back another time.'

Grace's heart thudded while Una and Joyce expressed their surprise.

'That'll put a stop to their Christmas celebrations,' Brenda rattled on. 'Anyway, the weather's too bad for us to take this tree down to the village this afternoon. We'll have to store it in one of the stables for now.'

'How are you going to get home?' Joyce asked Grace with an anxious look at the sky. The snow was already lying an inch thick on the ground and didn't look like stopping for the rest of the afternoon.

'I don't know but I'll have to try.' Grace opened the tall gate that led into the walled garden while Una and Joyce picked up the tree. She led the way down the central path with sprouts and leeks growing to one side and rows of cabbages to the other. 'The sooner I set off, the better.'

The others were quick to advise her against it. 'Why not wait until it eases off?' Brenda asked.

'Yes, stay here,' Una agreed. 'I don't like the idea of you setting off in a snow storm – you could lose your way as easy as anything.'

'Even if you think you know this area like the back of your hand.' Joyce was adamant – they would not let her go.

Reluctantly Grace gave in. She used the warden's telephone to call home and tell her father that she'd been delayed. 'Make sure that Edgar has something to eat,' she told him. 'I'll set off once the snow's stopped.' She was about to ring off but held back while her father complained about his tools being disturbed.

'Someone's been in there during the night,' he said angrily. 'My bellows have been moved. They weren't where I left them.'

212

'Are you sure it wasn't Edgar?' she asked.

'What would Edgar be doing in my forge?' he demanded. 'Anyway, a knife's gone missing as well – the sharp one I use to cut strips of leather with.'

Grace was only half listening. 'Never mind, Dad, I'm sure it'll turn up.'

They said goodbye then Grace left the warden's office and set off to rejoin the others who were warming their cold hands and feet by the fire in the common room leading off from the entrance hall. Hearing a conversation through the half-open door and seeing a recent trail of snowy footprints, she hesitated.

'Wait here, Bill, while I go and fetch Grace,' Brenda volunteered from inside the room. She'd been the first to get over their surprise at finding him at the front door, dressed in a trench coat and brown trilby, his face drawn and fearful as if about to face a firing squad. She had ushered him in and tried to sit him down in one of the easy chairs close to the fire, and she had reacted quickly when he'd mentioned Grace's name.

Grace heard Brenda say his name and took a sharp intake of breath. She glanced out of the tall hall window and saw Bill's Austin 7 parked outside.

'No, don't do that,' he countered. 'I said I'd come to talk to you *about* Grace, not *to* her.'

'Are you sure?' Una voiced the general confusion. 'As it happens, Grace is right here in the hostel. Anyway, we wouldn't want to talk about her behind her back.'

'Quite right,' Joyce added.

Bill paced the room, turning the brim of his hat

in his hands. He'd taken his mother to the hospital and they'd talked to the doctors who explained that Vince had had a decent night and that they wished to keep him in and perform his heart operation on the Monday. Bill had left her there at his father's bedside then driven straight out to Fieldhead. But now that he was here, awkwardness took hold of him. 'I don't know how to put this,' he stuttered, 'but, Brenda, it's most definitely you that I wanted to have a word with.'

Outside in the hallway, Grace's mouth went dry as she held her breath and went on listening. This was the last thing she'd been expecting.

Joyce sensed that it might be time for her and Una to make themselves scarce. 'Come on, Una – we know when we're not wanted.'

Bill walked quickly to the door and blocked their way. 'No – stay. It'd be better for you all to hear this.' He batted his hat against his thigh in an effort to pull himself together. 'I don't want you to take offence, Brenda. I'd like to say sorry if I've ever given you the wrong idea.'

Brenda fought against the increasing seriousness in his voice. She felt a flutter in her stomach as she chipped in with a typically flippant remark. 'What's this, Mr M, are you giving me the brush-off in front of my pals?'

'Hush, Brenda,' Joyce cautioned.

'If I have given you the wrong idea, I'm very sorry,' he said again. 'I shouldn't have let it happen.'

'Apology accepted, I'm sure,' Joyce interrupted. 'But what has Grace got to do with any of this?'

Grace breathed out slowly then in again – long and deep. She felt dizzy and leaned against the nearby newel post. Outside, snowflakes fell thick and fast onto the roof and bonnet of Bill's black car.

'She's the reason I'm here,' he explained. 'I'm making a hash of this, I know, so I'll just come out with it. Grace and I are – that is, we were – engaged to be married.'

'Goodness gracious,' Joyce said softly.

Una was too startled to say anything, while Brenda walked swiftly to the window, folded her arms across her chest and stared out at the snow-covered elms.

'I asked Grace to keep it a secret until I was ready to tell my parents,' Bill confessed. 'That was wrong of me and I regret it. It was the worst mistake of my life.'

'You say you two *were* engaged. Does that mean you're not any more?' Una asked after a while.

Grace closed her eyes in an effort to steady herself. She could picture his face, the frown lines between his eyebrows, the clench of his jaw and the narrowing of his dark-brown eyes.

He sighed. 'Grace saw Brenda and me in the boiler room at the Institute – you remember, Brenda?' There was a stony silence so he carried on. 'I won't go into details but I shouldn't have kissed you. It was wrong.'

Joyce walked to the window and waited for a reaction. 'Brenda?'

'It was my fault,' Bill insisted. 'I let everyone in the village think I was single. I didn't ... I shouldn't have ...'

215

'Brenda?' Joyce said again.

Brenda turned towards Bill and spoke in a voice that was unlike her own – slow and hesitant, accompanied by a look of dawning realization. 'Grace broke off your engagement because of me?'

'Not you – me!' he insisted. 'This is my fault. It might be too late to change things but I've come here to set the record straight.'

'Which you've done, and now you should go,' Joyce told him calmly as she pushed the door open and spied Grace at the bottom of the stairs. She could see from her face that she'd overheard every word. She went over to her and spoke earnestly. 'Is that what you want? Would you like Bill to leave?'

He followed Joyce into the black-and-white tiled hallway. When he saw Grace, he rushed towards her but Joyce stood in his way.

Grace took a deep breath and stepped out from behind her. 'Yes, go,' she echoed. 'The snow's already deep. If you don't leave now, the roads to the hospital will be blocked.'

'Come with me,' he pleaded, reaching out for her to take his hand. 'Say you forgive me and let me drive you home.'

'No.' She steadied herself against the wave of emotions breaking over her head, holding Bill's gaze for what seemed like an age. 'I'll stay here.'

Snow lay six inches deep. Gazing out of her bedroom window later that night, Una absorbed its pure, unmarked beauty – deep and crisp and even, as the Wenceslas carol had it. The clouds had lifted

216

and the moon shone brightly while in the bed behind her, Kathleen slept soundly. Brenda's bed was still empty.

The last time Una had seen her, Brenda had retired to the sick bay pleading a bad headache.

'I'm sorry, girls,' she'd announced before dinner as Mrs Craven had been sorting out the bedding for Grace's overnight stay, 'I've got a stinker. I might even throw up, it hurts so much.' She'd given a wan smile, collected her pyjamas and toothbrush from their room then disappeared.

No one had commented but it surely hadn't been Una alone who'd put down the source of Brenda's headache to the aftermath of Bill Mostyn's visit. Brenda had been speechless for an hour afterwards and she'd gone out of her way to avoid Grace during an impromptu rehearsal of 'Back to the Land' – a last-minute addition to the Christmas show.

'As long as we can keep our faces straight while we sing it,' Kathleen had insisted. 'No larking about like last year.'

'Why not?' Elsie had favoured a spoof version of the Land Army song. 'We can all wink at the audience and mime different actions – firing a gun, bang-bang, speeding the plough, showing our strong biceps, and so on. We'll do it with military precision, like the Busby Berkeley girls.'

'Yes, that would go down a treat with the powers that be,' Jean had noted sardonically. 'They'd love it if we made fun of being a Land Girl.'

'We don't care, do we, Brenda?' Elsie had expected support but that was just before Brenda had backed out of the group. She did look pale, they'd all agreed. It definitely wasn't like her to take to her bed.

Grace had been quiet too, but that was to be expected after Bill Mostyn's unexpected visit. Joyce had been gently sympathetic, suggesting to Mrs Craven that Grace could have the spare bed in her room then taking her upstairs to sort out the bed-clothes. 'I won't ask you anything about what Bill said earlier unless you want me to,' she'd told her as they smoothed the sheets. 'I'll take my lead from you.'

'No, I don't want to talk about it, ta – except to say that I only saw Bill and Brenda holding hands at the Institute. It came as a bit of a bombshell to hear that they'd actually kissed.' She had a new image to come to terms with now – Brenda and Bill with their arms around each other, lips touching then pressing hard, bodies clinging, passions roused.

'Take your time to think things through,' Joyce had said, patting the pillow case and turning back the sheets. 'You won't do anything hasty, I know.'

But jealousy had wormed its way into Grace's heart and it bore a strong, unfamiliar poison. Who knew how many times Bill had kissed Brenda? He'd admitted to the one occasion because he'd been caught red handed, but what was to stop it from being more? Or to prevent it happening again and him swearing that it wasn't so? He was good at keeping secrets, as she knew to her cost. Oh, how she wished that she no longer worried about anything that Bill said or did! But there was no getting away from it – she did still care – and cared deeply.

So the rehearsal had ended and everyone had gone their separate ways up to their rooms. The snow had stopped falling and a restless Una stood at the window, looking out. Her gaze raked across the silhouetted trees beyond the wall then across the vegetable garden, unrecognizable under a blanket of snow. It lay thick and smooth on the roofs of the stables and on the cobbles of the yard, except for a single, clear set of footprints between the back of the house and the gate leading into the vegetable patch. Who would venture outside on a night like this? she wondered. She looked again and found it even more peculiar – the footprints showed that someone had approached the house from the direction of the wood, not the other way around.

Una glanced round at Kathleen fast asleep. She looked again at the footprints and let a thrilling idea take shape. What if these were Angelo's tracks?

No – how can they be?

What if they are his? What if he knows for certain that he's being shipped off to Scotland and is desperate to see me?

Even so – only a madman would risk sneaking out of the camp tonight of all nights.

What if he loves me and would do anything in the world to prove it?

The dialogue galloped on inside her head, unsettling her so much that she slid her feet into her slippers and softly left the room. She crept downstairs and into the silent hallway then along the dimly lit passage that led to the kitchen and the back door.

A noise came from inside the kitchen. She hesitated. It happened again – a chair being scraped across the floor then the sound of a tap running. Disappointment reared its head – of course, it was just one of the girls unable to sleep who had come down here for a glass of water. Accepting this logic, Una forgot about the footsteps in the snow and opened the kitchen door.

Frank Kellett stood at the far end of the dark room. He let go of the cup in his hand, letting it smash in the brown earthenware sink. On the shelves to one side there were tins of flour with their lids off while other canisters spilled their contents onto the floor.

She gasped and started to back out of the room.

He took a step towards her, holding out his hand.

'No – stay where you are.' She shook her head as she took another step backwards.

Before Una could gather her wits, Frank lunged towards her. He took hold of her by the shoulders and pushed her off balance so that she fell backwards, knocking her head on the edge of the open door and landing in a pile on the floor.

Frank closed the door then stood over her, his face blurring, his stale breath on her face as he crouched forward and hooked his hands under her armpits. Then he hauled her into a sitting position and leaned her against the wall. Breathing hard, she pulled down her nightdress to cover her legs then drew her knees towards her chest. She couldn't fend him off, even though she hit out at him and tried to pummel his chest with her fists.

By now her eyes had got used to the darkness and there was just enough moonlight to see his narrow, wolf-like face and his too-close-together, glinting eyes, his matted hair and the jump of the Adam's apple in his scrawny neck.

Terror paralysed her from head to toe. She froze and lost the ability to speak, even to cry out for help.

Frank's face was close. He smelled of earth and dampness, of cold and sour hunger. She shuddered and groaned at the inevitability of what would happen next.

Putting one hand to her throat, he touched her cheek with his fingertips.

She shuddered again at the dry, rough feel of his fingers. He was shaking, she realized. He was staring at her, touching her hair, her collarbone, her chest. And oh, the animal smell of an outcast – the sweat and stench of neglect, the hotness of his breath. His hand pressed at her throat, her head was forced back against the damp, cold plaster.

Then the door into the passage opened and the beam of a torchlight raked across table and sink, shelves and chairs until it came to rest on Frank crouching over Una to one side of the door.

Kathleen screamed in horror. She saw a knife on the table at the moment that Frank sprang away from Una. She screamed again, loud enough to wake the whole house. He overbalanced, saved himself and jumped back up, scrabbling to reach the knife before Kathleen did. He grabbed the handle and jabbed the blade towards her.

Una took a deep, shuddering breath and got to her feet. Kathleen kept the torch beam on Frank's face. As he raised a hand to shield his eyes from the light, he hunched his shoulders forward, moving like a cornered animal sideways towards the unbolted door that led out into the yard.

'It's all right, Kathleen,' Una gasped, one hand to her throat where Frank had pressed so hard. 'He didn't hurt me.'

Kathleen's screams became calls for help as they heard footsteps clatter downstairs. 'Here – we're in the kitchen! It's Frank Kellett. He's got a knife!'

Frank saw her open her mouth but heard no sounds. He saw Una in her white nightdress with her hand protecting her throat.

'It's all right, Frank,' she repeated – words that came from nowhere and made no sense, even to her.

He watched her lips move. She was speaking to him but he didn't understand. The other girl dazzled him with her torch. Two others entered the room. They opened their mouths and shouted, advancing towards him. He held out the knife to make them stop.

Joyce advanced ahead of Grace. She took in the scene and fearlessly seized the nearest chair to act as a shield. Frank thrust the knife at her. It thudded into the wooden seat. He tried to wrest it out but it was stuck solid. Joyce lifted the chair, knife and all, intending to bring it smashing down on his head. He dodged sideways and it caught his right shoulder. There was a door behind him. It was off the latch. He flung it open and as Joyce raised the chair a second time, he escaped into the night.

CHAPTER THIRTEEN

The whole house was awake. Though it was past midnight, every light was switched on, every Land Girl out of bed and standing in her dressing-gown outside Mrs Craven's office as the police were called.

'Hello? This is Hilda Craven at Fieldhead House. We've had an intruder. One of our girls has been attacked.'

Grace held Una's trembling hand while Kathleen shoved her way into the office to supply more information if needed. Elsie and Joyce tried to keep everyone quiet while the phone call proceeded.

'Her name is Una Sharpe,' the warden went on in a slow, deliberate tone. 'She's twenty years old. The name of her attacker is Frank Kellett.'

'Frank pinned her against the wall and tried to throttle her,' Kathleen hissed in her ear. 'He had a knife.'

The crowd of girls at the door heard the warden repeat these facts into the phone. There was a fresh buzz of outrage on Una's behalf.

'I'm all right.' Una repeated the same phrases as before in a hardly audible voice. 'He didn't hurt me.'

'Hush,' Grace said, holding her hand tightly.

'There's blood in your hair,' Elsie whispered over her shoulder. 'Did he thump you on the back of the head?'

'No, he pushed me and I fell. I hit it on the edge of the door.'

'I understand.' Mrs Craven had listened to what the policeman had told her. 'We're not to clear up the mess in the kitchen or to touch anything whatsoever. We're to wait for a constable to arrive first thing in the morning. The snow's too bad for anyone to get to us before then . . . yes, thank you, Sergeant, I do understand.'

There was a murmur of disgruntled protests at the delay. 'Frank Kellett will have got clean away by then,' Ivy pointed out, while Brenda took it upon herself to race upstairs and look through the landing window for his escape route.

She came back down and reported that there were two sets of footprints in the snow – one leading towards the house and another trail from the kitchen door, curving around the side of the main house towards the road. 'The second lot are scuffed, as if he was slipping and sliding in his rush to get away,' she reported.

By this time the warden had almost finished her conversation with the desk sergeant. 'Yes – Frank Kellett of Home Farm, Cragg Lane, Burnside. He's been missing from his home since Monday. He's small and weedy-looking, with jet-black hair. Oh, and he's stone deaf. He won't be able to hear a word you say.'

225

The tight knot of listeners heard the click of the phone into its cradle. They dispersed slowly into different corners – some to the common room, others to the dining room – to talk through what had happened. This left Kathleen and Grace to take Una to the sick room to bathe the cut on her head. They found that Brenda had got there ahead of them and had already run warm water into a small enamel basin and found a wad of cotton wool and some iodine with which to clean the wound.

The girls crowded into the small, antiseptic room. It contained a narrow bed and a folding screen on castors, a sink, a medicine cupboard and a weighing scale tucked away in the corner. On the wall there were two framed prints of landscapes painted by a local artist.

'I *am* all right,' Una kept on insisting. She managed not to wince as Brenda parted her hair to dab the cut and she felt the first sting of the iodine. 'I swear he was as frightened as I was when I opened the door on him – I could see it in his eyes.'

Kathleen disagreed. 'Good Lord, Una – he had you pinned against the wall. I saw it for myself.'

'There's not too much blood.' Brenda examined the wound. 'It's more of a graze than a cut. Sorry if this hurts – I just want to make sure it's properly clean.'

'That doesn't mean he wasn't frightened,' Una reasoned. 'I think he was in a panic – he didn't know what he was doing.'

'Why are you sticking up for him?' Kathleen demanded. She ignored Grace's attempt to quieten

226

her. 'Frank Kellett is well known for following us girls around then pouncing on us. He'd do God knows what to us if he got the chance.'

Una breathed in through her nose. Perhaps Kathleen was right.

Her next remark was conclusive. 'I haven't forgotten about Eunice, even if the rest of you have.'

The implications of Kathleen's words hung heavily in the air as Brenda cleared away the basin and the stained swabs of cotton wool. Grace paid silent respect to the memory of the shy Land Girl with a winning smile who had chosen a tragic way out of an impossible situation. She recalled with a sharp stab of loss her discussion of the day's events at the dinner table and the trouble she had getting up in the morning for the early shifts, the way she swore by Pond's cold cream for face and hands.

Kathleen felt that she had proved her point. 'You see – that ne'er-do-well is a danger to us all. I hope the police find him and lock him up for good.'

Opinions were exchanged and details of the attack combed through. Squares of precious chocolate were shared and words of consolation showered upon Una's throbbing head. By three o'clock, everyone was back in bed and the hostel fell quiet.

Una lay in the darkness. It was the dead of night when lives ebbed away to the *tick-tick-tick* of the clock. This was the hour when fragile links with the living were broken and souls departed. She felt the strong presence of death. An unexplained creak of a floorboard conjured up ghostly occupants of the old house, as did the rattle of a window pane and scratching sounds behind the oak panelling on the landing. It was only the house settling on its ancient foundations, she told herself – only the wind outside and rats scuttling along their night-time runs.

She stared up at the ceiling, using the moonlight to trace cracks in the plaster. She could make out the profile of a human face – a prominent forehead and a hooked nose, a receding chin – and less distinctly the shape of a butterfly with its wings spread wide. Minutes crawled by. She went on staring and thought of Frank, of how he'd taken her by the arm the first time she'd been sent to work at Home Farm and had been going to make off with her around the back of the barn until Emily had stepped in. *He brought me some eggs,* she remembered.

It was his stare that upset people. His intense, slack-jawed, unblinking stare. And his sudden movements, the clutch of his fingers as he took hold of you, as if he couldn't judge his own strength. The unchanging, unbroken silence of his world. The lash of his father's belt, the escape onto bleak hillsides and always the silence. A life that was cold and dark, utterly without joy.

Una made herself stay in bed until the house started to awake. A light went on and she heard voices along the landing. Creeping to the door, she opened it and saw Joyce and Grace going down the stairs. 'Wait for me,' she whispered as she reached for her dressing-gown and followed them.

'The kitchen is out of bounds until after the police have been,' Joyce reminded Grace as Una joined them in the common room. 'Otherwise, we'd be able to make a brew before you set off.'

'Never mind – I'll manage without.' Grace was fully dressed except for her coat and hat. When she saw Una, she invited her to come close to the hearth where the last embers still glimmered in the before-dawn light. 'Come and sit down. How's your head?'

'Much better, ta.' The comfort of her voice consoled Una. 'Why are you leaving so early? Won't the roads still be blocked?'

'That's what I told her.' Joyce drew back the red velvet curtains. 'You see? It'll be an hour before day breaks.'

'I'll take a torch,' Grace promised. 'And I'll be able to skirt the worst snow drifts.' There were two reasons for leaving early. One was that she was anxious to see how Edgar was coping with his newly sworn abstinence and the second was that she felt she needed some time to herself to iron out her feelings about Bill and Brenda. 'There's been no snow overnight. I'm sure I'll get through. By the way, Una – this might sound a bit peculiar, but can you describe the knife that Frank was carrying?'

'You're darned right, it's odd.' Joyce looked warily at Una to see if the question had upset her. 'You don't have to answer right this minute.'

'It's fine.' Una knew that Grace must have a good reason to ask. 'As far as I remember, it had a rough horn handle and a long, thin blade.'

'I thought so. That's probably the knife that went missing from the forge. Dad mentioned it on the phone but I didn't take much notice.'

'That means that Frank must have broken in there as well.' First, Beckwith Camp; secondly, the Blacksmith's Arms; and now the hostel. Una thought she saw the motive. 'He breaks into places where he can keep warm at night and maybe find something to eat.'

'It's possible,' Grace agreed. 'He'd obviously been raiding the kitchen shelves before you disturbed him.'

'But that might not be his only reason.' For the time being Joyce inclined towards Kathleen's more sinister motive. 'You've known Frank the longest, Grace. Do you think he's a real danger to women?'

Grace took a deep breath then shrugged. 'I honestly don't know. He does frighten people with his odd behaviour, that's all I can say.'

'And he did try to throttle you and he came at me with a knife,' Joyce reminded Una. 'Which is another reason why I don't think you should set off until it gets light.' She turned to Grace. 'Frank might still be lurking nearby.'

Though Grace thought it was unlikely, she did see that Joyce had a point. 'All right, you win. I'll stay here until eight then I'll definitely have to get a move on.'

'Will that be an extra person for breakfast?' Elsie had poked her head around the door. 'Ma C can't use the kitchen, so it'll be whatever she can rustle up from the larder – a slice of ham or cheese or what have you.'

'Count me in,' Grace agreed, putting down her coat and hat while Joyce and Una nipped back upstairs to get dressed. She was too restless to sit down so she moved around the room, picking up a magazine then looking at the titles of the books on the bookshelf. The door opened again and Brenda came in.

'I heard you talking with Joyce and Una,' Brenda began quietly.

Grace overcame her first inclination to turn her back then delivered a stiff response. 'Yes. They persuaded me to stay for breakfast.'

'Do you mind me coming to find you? I'll go away again if you do.'

She relented a little. 'No – come in. Close the door after you.'

Brenda approached the bookcase. 'I've had a chance to think things through.'

'You're not the only one.' In spite of the break-in, there'd been too much time overnight for Grace to remember what she'd learned. A kiss that she hadn't known about. An embrace that had deepened Bill's lies.

'I didn't know . . .' Brenda faltered. Red patches on her neck were clearly visible beneath her open-necked shirt. 'Honestly – I had no idea.'

'About the engagement? No – Bill and I did a good job of hiding it.'

'If I'd have known, I wouldn't have—'

'Stop, don't go on. I only wish I could have come clean.'

'You didn't need to say it outright – just given me a clue that he was spoken for. I'd have taken the hint, honestly I would.'

Would nothing break this mounting awkwardness? Grace patted the books on the shelf into a tidy row then took a deep breath. 'It doesn't matter now. The engagement is off. Nothing matters.'

Brenda studied her face and saw the effort that it took for Grace to remain cool and calm and not to let her feelings spill out. They were exact opposites, she realized. *I act on my feelings. Everything is on the surface with me. Things run much deeper with Grace.* 'I know you blame Bill at present, but you might not once I've told you exactly what happened.'

'I *know* what happened. There's no need.'

'Listen to me anyway. I set my cap at Bill – you know that. If it hadn't been him, it would have been Jack Hudson or Thomas Lund. It could be Flight Lieutenant Mackenzie, Lorenzo – anyone who captured my fancy. The point is I made the first move – no, moves. I did it more than once.'

Grace walked to the window and saw their two reflections against the dark sky: her own face pale and serious, with Brenda standing by the bookcase, twisting her fingers together and shifting her weight from one foot to the other.

'I'm not even sure that he knew what I was up to. I asked him to fix Old Sloper, knowing full well it was just an excuse. I flirted with him, Grace, and offered to buy him a drink. He brushed me off. But you know what I'm like – I saw that as a challenge. So I went at it again – in the pub, whenever I got the chance. And, as luck would have it, everyone had gone home and I was by myself in the Institute when he came to mend the boiler with his spanners and spare washers and hose – all very romantic, eh?'

Grace turned to look at her, her face impassive.

'I'm sorry. That's me and my two left feet, trying to make light of a bad situation. As I say, I went outside to see what was up and I found Bill busy in the boiler house. I said I'd help. He didn't encourage me but I went ahead and held his torch. I was as close as this to him.' Brenda demonstrated the distance with her thumb and forefinger. 'It was a tiny space. Clumsy me, I managed to fall over – that part wasn't planned, I swear. He helped me up. I snatched a kiss. It was that way round. Bill didn't kiss me. I kissed him. And then you came across the road with the key.'

Grace's brow creased into a deep frown. 'I see.'

Brenda put her hands behind her back then crossed her fingers. 'Do you really? I can't tell you how awful this makes me feel.'

Grace still didn't relent. 'Awful in what way exactly?'

'Firstly because I realize what a chump I've made of myself. And secondly I can see how much I've hurt you.'

'Not you – him,' Grace insisted. 'Bill is the one who let me down. I want to respect the man I love and the moment he tried to push the blame onto you . . .'

'Which he was quite right to do,' Brenda pointed out.

'Even so, he wasn't a gentleman and I was disappointed. He went down in my estimation.'

'But you love him anyway.'

'Who says so?'

'You did. You said you wanted to respect the man you love, so that proves it.' Brenda had got everything to do with Bill off her chest but she still had something important to say so she joined Grace at the window. 'You're not to take umbrage at this next bit, all right? We're chalk and cheese, you and me. I'm all la-la-la and happy-go-lucky. You're buttoned up and serious – sometimes a bit too serious, in my opinion.'

Grace blinked then gave a small shake of her head. 'Even if it's true, I can't help the way I am.'

'Ah but, can't you, though? Think of it this way – it's not the worst thing in the world for your fiancé to keep a few things to himself. I mean, what would have been the point of him running to tell you every last detail about what had happened in that boiler room? No, he probably knew how much it would bother you so that's why he kept quiet.'

'To save my feelings?'

'It could be.' Brenda had regained some of her confidence. She thrust her hands in her breeches pockets and rocked back on her heels. 'And what would be wrong with that, given that it was *me* who led *him* on? In any case, one kiss is nothing. That's the way I would look at it if I were you.'

Grace shot her an astonished look. 'Nothing?' she echoed.

'Not in the grand scheme of things – no. Not when most of the men we love are being shot at and torpedoed and bombed.'

Not in comparison with what Edgar has been through. It was as if the sun was slowly starting to rise on the dark landscape inside Grace's head.

Brenda saw that she had hit the mark. 'And the rest of them who are still at home come downstairs

234

every morning expecting to see their call-up papers land on the mat. Now that's really something to worry about, isn't it?'

Grace's frown eased and she gave a deep sigh. 'It's not you who's been the chump – it's me.'

'You and me both,' Brenda insisted. 'And Bill, too – let's not forget him. We've all made mistakes.'

'But I've still got the ring!' Grace's sudden exclamation came as Joyce and Una returned with a breakfast of ham sandwiches and cold milk. 'It's in its box in my dressing-table drawer.'

'Do you hear that?' a triumphant Brenda said to the others. 'A ring is a binding promise. Grace is still engaged to Bill after all!'

'Forget about the blinking tree!' Kathleen's mind was fixed on getting everyone into the village for their afternoon dress rehearsal. She made them set off in good time and led the way on foot past Peggy Russell's farm, following wide tyre tracks in the snow made by Arnold White's tractor. 'Let's concentrate on the show, for goodness' sake.'

'But we've only got tomorrow and the day after,' Joyce pointed out. It bothered her that they'd set off early for the Institute and had to leave the tree behind. 'That's not much time to lug it down to the village, put it in a tub, decorate it and stick a fairy on the top.'

'I know, but it would have held us up if we'd tried to carry it through the snow. We have to get this rehearsal underway – that's far more important.'

Kathleen had spent the morning chivvying her

fellow performers. She'd reminded them to bring the dresses and shoes they intended to wear and insisted they must all be word perfect. Even the arrival of a middle-aged, moustachioed police constable riding out from the village on the back of Arnold's tractor hadn't diverted her from her main goal. He'd poked around in the kitchen, asked Una, Kathleen and Joyce a few questions, jotted down their answers then gone away again.

'A fat lot of good he was,' Ivy had commented to Jean and Dorothy who had come to the conclusion that what they needed was a Miss Marple on the job.

'A woman makes a far better detective than a man,' Jean had insisted. 'She knows more about how a criminal thinks, what drives him to do what he does.'

Kathleen had given the constable's plodding questions scant attention – yes, she had recognized the intruder, yes, he was carrying a knife, no, she had no idea where he went afterwards. 'Now, if you don't mind, I have lots to do,' she'd told him, returning to the common room to round up the troops ready for the snowy trudge into the village.

So here they were – a gang of twenty Land Girls in overcoats and wellington boots – crunching through a winter wonderland between stone walls, past Peggy's farm where the dog barked and strained at his chain, past barns and over bridges until they came within sight of Burnside.

Brenda had kept a careful eye on Una at the rear of the group and even now wanted to offer her the choice of turning back. 'If you're not up to it, I'm sure Kathleen would understand,' she told her.

'No – I'm feeling better, ta.' In fact, the fresh air and stiff exercise had cleared her head and when she spotted the familiar sight of the POW lorry parked outside the Institute, her heart leaped.

'Aha!' Brenda followed her gaze. 'We still have the decorators in, I see.'

Without saying a word, Una rushed to the front of the group – a small figure in a large, brown coat with a bright red tartan scarf tied around her head. She was the first to reach the junction, where she mounted the bank of soiled snow that had been dumped at the roadside by a plough, then jumped nimbly into the road to run and skid the final hundred yards.

Brenda advanced more slowly, threading between Jean and Dorothy and ignoring their comments about Una making a show of herself.

'Someone's keen,' Joyce remarked as Brenda came between her and Kathleen.

Una had already reached the parked lorry and without waiting for the others, she disappeared into the yard.

Brenda supplied the reason for Una's haste. 'She's waiting for a letter. It's kept her awake at night. But the question is: is Angelo as keen as she is?'

'He says he is.' Joyce didn't sound sure. 'He has all the right words, but when it comes to action, who can tell?'

'The gift of the gab, eh?' Like Joyce, Brenda felt that she should look out for Una. 'What is it about her?' she wondered aloud.

'What do you mean?' Joyce stepped up onto the snow bank then jumped down onto the main road.

'Why do we cluck around her like a pair of mother hens?'

'Do we?' She was surprised then thought about it for a while. 'Yes, I suppose it's because we both know how much Angelo could hurt her.' Heartbreak and loss – Joyce was an expert in both.

Brenda unbuttoned her coat as they approached the Institute. 'Stand by to pick up the pieces,' she warned. 'These Italians have a reputation for loving us and leaving us, don't you know.'

In the main hall of the Institute a gang of prisoners were hard at work under the watchful eye of a solitary guard. Three walls had been given a fresh coat of whitewash and they were underway with the fourth when Una arrived.

'Aye, aye!' Albert recognized her straight away. 'If it isn't our little spud-picker.'

She looked eagerly around the big room. There was a prisoner up a ladder and another stirring pots of paint. Two were on their knees, putting the finishing touches to the skirting boards. So far there was no sign of either Lorenzo or Angelo.

Albert looked at his watch. 'You're a good hour early,' he told her, taking in her rosy cheeks and her beautiful hazel eyes and deciding that she was a welcome break to the monotony of his morning. 'As a matter of fact, I'm surprised you got here at all.'

'Oh no, it takes more than a couple of inches of snow to put us off.' *Where is he? Please let him be here!* Una looked from one prisoner to the next until she finally spotted Lorenzo emerging from the kitchen – a Roman god in paint-spattered overalls, absurdly out of place in the shabby hall. 'Can I go and have a quick word?' she asked the smirking guard.

'Go right ahead.' Seeing the chance of a further small drama being played out in front of him, he took out a cigarette and lit it. *These girls are all the same,* he thought. *They fall over themselves to play Juliet to these Romeos, Lorenzos, Lotharios . . . whatever they call themselves.*

Una hurried towards Lorenzo, her heart beating so hard and fast that it hammered at her ribs. 'Where is he? Is he here?'

Lorenzo gestured with a tilt of his handsome, dark head that Angelo was in the kitchen.

Faster still and harder, her heart practically jumped through her ribcage. She pushed open the door and there he was, washing paintbrushes at the big stone sink. No one else was in the room.

His eyes lit up when he saw her. Putting down the brushes, he reached for a towel to dry his hands. She didn't wait for him to finish, simply rushed to him and threw her arms around his neck. He put his arms around her waist, scooped her up and kissed her on the mouth.

'My Una,' he murmured as he hugged her and kissed her again.

She leaned her head back and felt his lips on her neck. 'Did you get my letter? Did Neville bring it?'

Angelo released her and patted his shirt pocket. 'It is here, close to my heart. You love me now and for ever. I know.'

'Even if you have to go away,' she murmured as she breathed out.

Perhaps he didn't hear. 'Neville, he gives letter to Lorenzo. They put me in room, lock the door.'

Una freed herself so that she could see his face more clearly and work out what he was telling her. 'Who did – the guards? When?'

'Four days ago. I hear motor bike. I know it is you. I try to come.'

'But they caught you and locked you up?' She remembered catching a glimpse of him between two soldiers, being marched towards a brick building.

'Today they open the door. Lorenzo shows me letter and read for me. I am happy.'

Her heart was so full of love that tears shone in her eyes. He was the most precious thing in the world to her, with his deep, faltering words, his soft caresses. 'I've longed to see you so much. I can't believe you're actually here, that we're together in the same room.'

'Believe,' he whispered. 'Every night I dream. One day, I am free. We are together.'

She put her hand up to stroke his cheek and his neck. His skin was warm and smooth. She put her fingertips on the gold cross nestling at his throat.

'You like?' he said, reaching to unfasten it. 'You have.'

She put her hand out to stop him. 'No, you must wear it to keep you safe. I don't need any more gifts, just so long as I know you love me.'

Women's voices reached them from inside the hall – Kathleen's first and then the buzz and chatter of many more. Angelo frowned.

240

Una held his face between her hands. 'Yes, I know we don't have much time. The whole gang is here for our final rehearsal. Soon you'll have to pack up your paint things and leave.'

He drew her close and rested his cheek against her head until the burning question tumbled from her lips.

'Is it true, Angelo – are they going to close the camp?'

Albert's voice rose above the rest, issuing orders to prisoners and girls alike. 'Watch that wet paint. Move that ladder out of the way.'

'I think yes,' Angelo whispered into the soft shininess of her hair.

Her head was against his chest and she felt the solid beating of his heart. 'You think or you know?'

'I know. Yes, we go.'

There was a judge with a black cap, delivering his death sentence, announcing the end. Una gasped and clung tightly to Angelo.

The kitchen door opened and Joyce burst in. 'Albert said I'd find you here,' she began.

Una and Angelo broke apart. Their small world had been invaded and they stared at Joyce with mistrust.

'Don't look at me like that – I've had an idea. I saw the lorry parked outside. We have one empty lorry here and one Christmas tree stuck in the stable at Fieldhead.'

Una was slow to see where this was leading. To her it only seemed as if Joyce had robbed her and Angelo of some precious moments together.

'I mentioned it to Albert and Kathleen and they're both happy to spare us for half an hour. Albert needs thirty minutes for his prisoners to clear up and neither you nor I has anything to rehearse until we get to The Skaters' Waltz at the start of the second half.'

'And what do you want us to do?' Una asked, holding tight to Angelo's hand.

'We three have been given permission to drive back to the hostel to pick up the tree.' Joyce flung the lorry's ignition key across the table and Angelo caught it. 'It's too good a chance to miss. Come on, you two – full speed ahead.'

CHAPTER FOURTEEN

Angelo was already in the cab and Una sitting next to him when Grace called for Joyce from the pub yard.

Joyce picked up an unusual stridency in her voice. 'Hang on a tick,' she told the others before running across the road to see what Grace wanted.

'Be quick,' Una urged. She smiled at Angelo sitting proudly behind the wheel, the collar of his grey jacket turned up and the white scarf setting off his olive complexion. *Smitten,* she thought as she drank in the sight of him. *Smitten, bowled over, swept off my feet* – they were exactly the right words to describe how she felt.

'What is it?' Joyce asked Grace, who seemed to be on the verge of tears. She stood in the cold without her coat, in only the sweater and slacks she'd been wearing the day before. 'Kathleen's wondering where you've got to.'

'It's Edgar. His bed hadn't been slept in when I got back.'

'Not again!' Joyce had hoped and prayed that, once he'd started to talk about what had happened to him, Edgar would begin to emerge from his deep, dark pit of silence and suffering. 'He hasn't wandered off onto the moor again, has he?'

Grace shook her head. 'I didn't know where he'd gone. I searched high and low as soon as I got back – his coat was on the hook so I knew he couldn't have gone far. Dad was still in bed, having a lie-in. He said he hadn't seen Edgar since teatime yesterday.'

'I bet he was in the forge.' Joyce remembered the last talk she'd had with him, sitting in the darkness next to the warm embers of the furnace.

'You're right – he was.' Grace's lip trembled. 'I found him on the floor, dead drunk.'

'Not again,' Joyce murmured for a second time. She felt a thud of disappointment, which she tried her best to disguise. 'Never mind – he's bound to slip off the wagon every now and then. It's not the end of the world.'

'He won't let me near him – I've tried three times. He's hanging onto a bottle of whisky and I can't get it off him.'

Joyce thought quickly. 'Let me have a go. I'll tell Angelo and Una to go ahead without me. You pop into the hall and keep Kathleen happy. Give me half an hour to sort Edgar out.'

She ran back to the lorry and explained her change of plan. 'That gives you two love birds thirty minutes to yourselves.' She slapped the bonnet to send them on their way then beckoned Grace. 'Keep your chin up,' she told her. 'Let me see what I can do.'

Grace hesitated, looking over her shoulder at the entrance to the smithy.

'Go!' Joyce insisted, giving her a small shove in the direction of the Institute. Then she went to try the handle on the wide arched doorway. It didn't turn so she went around the side and found the back door standing open. 'Edgar?' she called as she went inside.

There was no reply so she ventured further in, past rakes, hoes and spades stacked against the wall awaiting repair. She glanced up at the dark rafters, inhaling the smell of smoke and dust then across at the hefty anvil next to the cold, empty furnace. 'Edgar?'

He heard his name through a haze of alcohol. He lay face down by the double doors, oblivious to the icy draught blowing through the gaps, his fingers wrapped around the neck of a bottle. He had no notion of where he was or of how long he'd been lying there, and only a faint awareness that his body was stiff with cold. Light filtered in under the door so it must be daytime. There was his name again, but to hell with that – he was too weary even to turn his head.

'There you are,' Joyce said, stooping over him. He wasn't wearing a jacket so she took off her coat and covered him. 'It's me – Joyce. You'll catch your death at this rate.'

The words drifted over him. He felt the weight of her coat on his back. He hung onto the bottle.

It was pitiful to see him sprawled in the dust. She was moved almost beyond words. 'Sit up,' she whispered as she rolled him gently onto his back.

His limbs were being moved and rearranged; hands touched his face. He opened his eyes.

'Sit up,' she said again, leaning over him and succeeding in raising him. She resettled the coat around his shoulders then rested back on her haunches and waited.

There was someone moving him and speaking to him – a woman. He saw the gleam of the anvil, the maw of the empty furnace. He lifted the bottle to his lips but let it fall without taking a drink.

'That's right – after a while it doesn't deaden the pain. The bottle is empty but the hurt is still there.'

He tried to focus on her face. She was young, her skin was smooth and her voice was soft.

'The same thing happened to my father,' she told him. 'When Dad realized he was losing the family farm, he drank himself silly every single night. It didn't help – he lost it all anyway. But at least he's stopped drinking now.'

Soft and lilting, like a tune inside his head. He closed his eyes again and drifted.

Joyce sat beside him on the stone floor. 'I have to admit I was tempted myself, after Walter went missing in action. I don't mention him much but that doesn't mean I'll ever forget him. I did think for a while about following in Dad's footsteps and reaching for the bottle. I didn't know at the time what stopped me.'

The tune stopped. He turned his head and looked at her again. 'Joyce?'

'Yes, it's me. How do you feel?'

'Bad.' Tremors ran through him, his mind had

cracked and fallen apart into a thousand pieces but the face that kept on coming up through the scattered fragments was Billy's.

She put her hand over the hand that held the bottle. 'I realized recently that the reason I didn't take up drinking had nothing to do with the pull-yourself-together stuff that teetotallers like to bang on about. I was deaf to all of that. No – the reason was fear, pure and simple. I was scared of losing my last little bit of self-control.'

Without knowing it, he released his hold on the bottle. *Talk. Let me hear the tune. Stay with me.*

She took the whisky away then sighed as she looked at his unfocused gaze. 'You're not listening to a word I say.'

'I am,' he said through cracked lips. 'You were frightened.'

'Tempted and scared in equal measure. So what did I do? I ran away – from the farm, from Dad, from Stratford, from having lost Walter. I volunteered for the Land Army and came here. And it was the best thing I ever did.' Suddenly, out of the blue, Joyce started to cry. 'The best thing I ever did' turned to helpless sobbing. Months of managing her feelings evaporated – a year of hiding her grief turned into tears as she sat in the forge with Edgar.

Angelo drove along the snow-covered roads with Una by his side. They sat high in the cab with clear views of the fells to either side of the deep white valley, its frozen streams, its patchwork of walls and stunted trees.

247

'I am king!' he declared as they rode between stone walls, following the road out to Fieldhead.

'King of the world!' Una basked in the freedom of this drive. They were together and might be driving into their uninterrupted, rosy future for all Peggy Russell's noisy dog or the crows in the bare elms at the back of the hostel knew.

They arrived at the deserted manor house and pulled into the yard at the back. Una led Angelo to the outhouse where the Christmas tree was stored. Snow had drifted two feet deep against the stable door. 'It's jammed shut,' she said with a frown.

Angelo laughed and without hesitating he vaulted over it. He stood inside and offered his hand to help pull her after him.

'I can do it by myself,' she insisted. She saw the tree leaning against the far wall and him waiting for her to come a cropper, laughing at her as she swung one leg over the door only to find herself stuck astride it, feet dangling a foot from the ground. 'Oh dear – my legs are too short!'

So he helped her over anyway and they tumbled together against the prickly tree then fell onto the bed of old straw lining the stable floor. They were still laughing when they picked themselves up. Then they weren't laughing, they were kissing and clinging together with nothing in the world except themselves and the love and longing they felt.

Angelo's arms were around her waist, hers were around his neck. She tilted her head back to kiss his lips, feeling her whole body melt against him – his wide shoulders and broad chest, their hips pressing together, him holding her and wanting her. Every inch of her was soft and yielding as she swooned in his arms.

His lips touched her neck and then her throat and she was possessed by strong desire – an uncharted thing that she didn't want to control because it was new and thrilling and she longed to give herself to the moment, not to think or draw back, only to go on kissing Angelo and loving him.

He unbuttoned her coat and slipped his hand inside her sweater to feel the warmth of her body through the soft, smooth material of her blouse. He felt her tremble and leaned away from her. 'Yes?' he whispered.

'Yes.' She loosened the back of his shirt to feel his skin – the way his spine curved in the small of his back, his heat, his hard, solid muscle. They'd crossed an unknown threshold and were driven on, kissing and touching, kissing again.

'Yes?' Angelo paused a second time as his hand cupped her breast.

She held his hand there and sighed. There was wonder and amazement beyond anything she could have imagined.

He laid her on the bed of straw. She was small and delicate, white skin glimmering in the dim light, eyes wide open with desire. She was fragile, even though her body arched towards him. He loved her and would be gentle.

Joyce and Grace agreed between them that they would keep a careful eye on Edgar.

'One of us can pop over the road every fifteen minutes or so,' Joyce suggested after she cornered Grace in the hall porch while Albert allowed the Italians to take their time removing their ladders and clearing away their paint and brushes. She described how she'd walked Edgar from the forge into the kitchen and sat him down beside the fire. Standing at the table, Cliff had watched her settle him in the chair without comment then carried on mending the soles of his boots with a hammer and some tacks. 'Your father's there too.'

Grace breathed a sigh of relief. 'Thank you. But are you all right? You look as if you've been crying.'

'Don't worry about me.' Joyce had once more locked the door on her grief and was ready for action. 'I was sad to see Edgar in such a state, that's all.'

'Thank you again.' Grace squeezed her hand then turned to a snippet of gossip. 'Guess what – Brenda's having a barney with Kathleen over where "We'll Meet Again" should come in the programme. She's threatened to walk out if Kathleen doesn't stop ordering everyone around. It's turning into a proper fisticuffs.'

'Poor Una – I wouldn't fancy sharing a room with those two if they're still at loggerheads when we get back to the hostel.'

'Me neither. Where is Una, by the way?'

'Gone with Angelo to fetch the Christmas tree. I wangled permission for them to drive the lorry out to Fieldhead.'

'Just the two of them?'

'Yes. They should be back any time.' Joyce looked

at her watch. 'In fact, they're taking a bit longer than they should have. Albert will be wondering where they've got to.' Just then there was the sound of an engine drawing up outside. 'Talk of the devil,' she added as she strode back into the hall. 'Relax, Albert. Relax, everyone. The wanderers have returned.'

' "We'll Meet Again" stays where it is, right at the end of the second half.' Kathleen announced her triumph over Brenda with a clap of her slim hands. The prisoners had cleared the hall and loaded everything into the lorry with a team of willing Land Girl helpers to lend a hand.

'Let me and Grace fold those dust sheets for you,' Elsie had offered. 'Stand back and watch the experts – we've had a lifetime's practice with bed sheets.'

Lorenzo and a jolly-looking pal had pretended to approve their sheet-folding technique while in reality they admired the girls' shapely hips and lithe movements, all done up as they were in their best dresses and high heels, ready to go onstage.

Some others had accepted help to clean their brushes at the sink. 'Not like that,' Jean had criticized as she shoved a tall, thin prisoner out of the way. 'If a job's worth doing, it's worth doing properly.' There'd been much splashing and drenching and even Jean had cracked a smile.

So by the time Una had stolen a last kiss from Angelo and rejoined her group, the Christmas tree had been carried in, goodbyes had been said and the prisoners were on the move.

Joyce sat down at the piano and lifted the lid. She

smiled as always as she discussed tempos with Elsie then agreed with Kathleen to play an extra chorus for the Vera Lynn song that was to round everything off. But the talk with Edgar had drained her and she had to make a conscious effort to sit up straight and strike the first chords for the introduction to the Judy Garland song.

'Quiet, everyone!' Kathleen called them to order. It was one o'clock and time was short.

While Joyce played and Brenda sang, Grace and Una busied themselves by finding a suitable container for the Christmas tree. They looked in the kitchen and came across a brass jam pot that wasn't big enough and a bread-making bowl that was cracked across its base. They were about to give up when Una thought of the empty beer barrels stacked in Grace's cellar.

'That's a good idea.' Grace realized she could kill two birds with one stone so they nipped across the road and while Una went into the cellar to select an empty barrel, she went into the kitchen to check on Edgar. She opened the door to see her father hammering rhythmically at his last tack and her brother sitting quietly by the fire.

'You can take that coat off him now.' Cliff gestured towards Joyce's Land Army coat still slung around Edgar's shoulders. 'Give it back to the lass who talked some sense into him. She'll need it for her walk home.'

'You mean Joyce.' Grace removed the coat without a fuss. 'Ta, Edgar. No, you stay where you are. No need to move.'

The flicker of a smile crossed his features. Joyce was the one with the beautiful voice who'd talked then cried. That was a real memory, not something he'd imagined.

'I'll see you later,' Grace told Cliff and Edgar as she went to help Una with the barrel.

'Just right!' was the response when they carried it into the hall and stood the tree in it. It was the right size and shape. Now all they had to do was find a way to make it stand upright.

'We can anchor it between a couple of bricks then add some sand,' Dorothy suggested. 'There's a pile of sandbags outside Maurice Baxendale's workshop. He won't mind lending us a few.'

'Can we have some hush over there?' Kathleen was putting the finishing touches to Brenda's song. 'When you sing "Why, oh why can't I?" you have to clasp your hands under your chin and look upwards as if you're pleading – like this.'

Sitting at the piano close to the stage, Joyce had a good view of the main door, so she was the first to see Edith Mostyn come in with two women who at first she couldn't put a name to. They were both tall and expensively dressed in cashmere jumpers and tweed skirts, with identical upright postures and a sense of the Lady Bountiful about them as they followed Edith into the centre of the hall. Ah yes – the older of the two was Alice Foster from Hawkshead Manor and the younger must be her daughter Shirley.

Brenda stopped singing and Joyce stopped playing. Kathleen swallowed back her irritation.

Edith put down the cardboard box she'd been carrying then apologized for the interruption. 'I'm sorry to put you off your stride, girls. We've brought the decorations for the hall. Mrs Foster has been kind enough to donate them to the Institute.'

Grace emerged from behind the tree. She'd been expecting Shirley to come home for Christmas but hadn't anticipated how she would feel when she saw her. Shirley Foster had walked in as if she owned the place, as in a way she did since one of her ancestors had paid for the bricks and mortar. Her lilac sweater picked up the heathery tints in her kick-pleated tweed skirt. Her pale-blonde hair was immaculately waved.

Una went to rummage through the contents of the cardboard box and pulled out rolls of paper streamers together with sprigs of artificial holly, two Chinese lanterns and bundles of silver tinsel.

'Carefully does it,' Shirley advised as she delved into her handbag. 'Those streamers tear easily. Here are some drawing-pins to hang them with.'

Queen Bee rather than Lady Bountiful in her case, Joyce thought with a frown. Shirley was the sort who expected everyone to dance attendance. She noticed that Grace looked flushed and hung back in the corner.

'Don't let us stop your rehearsal.' Edith did her best to cover up the strain of her husband's illness but make-up didn't disguise the dark shadows under her eyes. While Shirley and her mother helped Una to disentangle the decorations, she went to talk with Grace by the tree.

'All right, everyone.' Kathleen needed no second telling. 'Please take your positions onstage for the start of The Skaters' Waltz.'

Una was about to obey when Edith stopped her. 'Mrs Craven told me on the telephone about last night's break-in. I'll report events to County Office first thing tomorrow, but I have the authority to allow you to take time off work if necessary. That would be within HQ guidelines.'

'Oh no, I'd much rather not,' Una assured her before hurrying to join the others.

This left Edith face to face with Grace as she answered Kathleen's call to action.

'How is Mr Mostyn?' Grace managed to ask. Shirley was in her sightline, dishing out orders about where the decorations should hang while her mother inspected the results of the POWs' decorating efforts. The younger woman wore a gold brooch and matching earrings with a patterned silk scarf around her elegant neck and Grace recognized that there was no one in Burnside anywhere near so self-assured or fashionable as Shirley Foster. She glanced down at her home-made dress of rosebud-patterned crêpe de chine and her heart sank into her boots.

'Thank you for asking, Grace. Vincent is expecting to have an operation tomorrow morning. He's in good hands.' Edith's formal reply gave little away. Her expression was guarded.

Oh yes – the twitch of the curtain as Grace had walked Bill up the path. She grew convinced that Edith had seen them and of course hadn't approved.

'As a matter of fact, Bill is due to pick me up and

take me to the hospital as soon as he's driven Shirley and Mrs Foster back to Hawkshead.'

'Please pass on my regards.' Grace managed a sympathetic smile despite a powerful onrush of unpleasant emotions – a spike of jealousy mixed with sore regret.

Edith shot her a knowing look. 'To whom – my husband or my son?'

'To both,' Grace said firmly. She met Edith's gaze with a look that implied, *It's all right – we both know the state of play.*

'Thank you, I will.' Edith arched her eyebrows and made sure she had the last word before Grace hurried away.

'If looks could kill . . .' Una muttered as Grace joined her onstage. 'What have you done to upset Her Ladyship this time?'

CHAPTER FIFTEEN

'Did you see Mrs M give Grace the cold shoulder earlier?' Brenda sat cross-legged on her bed while Una darned a hole in her sock.

The last thing on Una's mind was the behaviour of the local Land Army rep. She was basking in a warm glow of memory, reliving every moment of making love with Angelo, examining each sensation, both as it was happening and what she thought about it now. She felt none of the guilt she might have expected. After all, she'd always considered herself to be a nice girl – one who wouldn't give a man what he wanted before marriage. Only fast girls did that – and once they were found out, their reputations soon became mud. And yet the events of the day had overturned all that she'd observed and held to during her teenaged years. The experience of love had shattered her preconceptions and instead of feeling cheap, she felt the opposite. She was enriched, uplifted and glad.

'What are you smiling at?' Brenda asked. 'And why don't you answer my question – did you see the look Edith Mostyn gave Grace earlier today? Even making allowances for her old man being poorly, I still thought she was very off-hand.'

Una made a neat job of the hole in the heel of her work sock then rolled it together with its companion before putting them in the drawer. 'I did see it,' she confirmed. 'I asked Grace what she'd done to upset her.'

The dress rehearsal hadn't gone well and Kathleen was currently in Joyce's room making last-minute adjustments to the programme order. The girls were nervous about Tuesday night's performance – all except Brenda who was convinced that it would be all right on the night.

'What did she say?'

Hearing the drone of several planes flying over-head, Una went to the window and looked out at the dark sky. 'Not much. And I didn't get a chance to chat with her after we'd finished.'

'Me neither.' An idea occurred to Brenda and her eyes lit up. 'I say – how much do you bet that Bill has told his ma about his engagement to Grace? That would have set the cat among the pigeons, wouldn't it?'

Una thought it through. 'No, now wouldn't be the best time,' she decided. 'Not while his father is in hospital waiting for his operation. According to Grace, that was the whole reason for keeping it secret in the first place – he didn't want to worry them. Not that wanting to marry Grace should upset anyone, in my opinion.'

'Then why else would Mrs M have taken umbrage?'

'Who knows?' The drone of the engines faded and

Una returned to her bed. She kicked off her slippers and slid between the sheets.

'I bet you a shilling,' Brenda insisted.

'Done.' She was worn out. As soon as she closed her eyes she began to drift off to sleep.

'Poor Grace – I wouldn't fancy having Mrs M as my mother-in-law. Mind you, Grace might seem meek and mild but deep down she's made of sterner stuff. If Bill really has made up his mind to set the record straight with the Aged Ps, there might be a baptism of fire for the pair of them to go through but I reckon Grace will emerge unscathed.'

'I'm sure she will.' Una's drowsy agreement did nothing to halt Brenda's chatter.

'You'll have your Angelo and Grace will have her Bill, but what about poor little wallflower me? Where's my knight in shining armour? Who's going to whisk me away?'

Una smiled as she turned onto her side and peered out from under her bed clothes. 'Honestly?'

'Yes, cross my heart. I have no beau within my sights now that I've found out Bill Mostyn's spoken for.'

'Let me think of a list of eligible bachelors for you, then. Oh yes, there's Jack Hudson, Neville Thomson—'

'Nev! Oh, please!'

Una went on rattling off names. 'Squadron Leader Aldridge, Flight Lieutenant Mackenzie, any number of Canadian pilots, Lorenzo—'

'Never in a month of Sundays!' Brenda declared. 'With a man like Lorenzo you'd have to fight your way through all the competition. I don't have time for that.'

'Mac, then?'

'Now, that's more like it.'

'I'm sure he's had a soft spot for you from the moment you hopped off your motor bike in your airman's jacket.'

'Hmm.' Brenda sounded pleased. It would take a little while to forget the frisson that had passed between her and Bill in the smelly old boiler room but snapping up a handsome Canadian might help her along that road. Tuesday was coming up fast and Mac had promised to be there. 'We'll see.'

'Good. Can I go to sleep now?' Una pulled the blankets over her head.

'Sorry – yes. I'll close the curtains and turn off the light.'

Brenda's hand was on the curtain when she heard it – the growl of an aircraft's engines approaching from the north. At first she didn't see anything but there was a dull thud in the distance followed by a flash and then it was repeated – a thud then a second flash. 'Come and take a look,' she told Una. The throaty noise grew louder. The plane seemed to be flying low to the ground but there'd been no more flashes and now she couldn't see anything except the snow-covered hills beyond the copse of elms that stood dark and still against a white background.

Una grumbled as she got out of bed. 'What am I meant to be looking at?' What else besides darkness and a thick ground mist settled amongst the trees – no wind, no movement in the frozen world?

There was a third heavy thud and an almost simultaneous orange flash that illuminated the horizon.

Una and Brenda saw the outline of a single plane as it crested the ridge, listing heavily, one wing almost touching the ground. Then it was dark again.

'Something's up.' Una cut out her own reflection by pressing her face against the window pane. 'The pilot has had to jettison his bombs.'

'That would account for the explosions,' Brenda agreed, her pulse quickening. 'I wonder if it's one of ours.'

It happened a fourth time – a flash lit up the sky and in that instant they made out the Luftwaffe's black cross on the plane's fuselage. It was possibly a mile away, heading straight for the house. The nose was down, the engines choking and grinding before they cut out completely.

Darkness again and now an uncanny silence. A German pilot was gliding earthwards, dropping out of the night sky.

Brenda and Una stood back from the window. Una reached for her coat, Brenda for her leather jacket, and both slid their feet into their wellingtons. They were out of the door and heading along the landing before any of the other girls. They ran down the stairs and out through the kitchen into the yard, sprinting towards the copse.

Within seconds the whole hostel was alive with shocked voices and hasty, jostling movements.

'A plane . . . heading this way . . . German . . . bombs.'

'Are we sure it's Jerry?' Elsie stood on the landing and spoke urgently to Joyce and Kathleen.

'That's what it looked like.' Joyce had caught sight

of the slim, pencil-like shape of the stricken plane and the black-cross emblem. 'It had a twin tail fin. I've seen pictures of Dorniers on Pathé News. I think it's one of them.'

'What if he drops the last of his bombs on us?' Ivy demanded as she came out of her room with Jean and Dorothy. She held her hands to her mouth as if to push back the mounting fear.

'We'll be done for – that's what.' Jean was fully dressed but by no means eager to be first on the scene.

Dorothy was the voice of reason. 'He can't do that, silly. His engines cut out before he got here. He's taken a nose dive onto the fell behind us – that's what's happened to our Jerry friend.'

By this time, Una and Brenda were running through the vegetable garden towards the elms. Snow hampered them and their feet slid from under them.

'I wish we'd brought a torch.' Una fought her way through some undergrowth at the edge of the copse. She caught hold of a low branch and ducked under it. Gradually her eyes got used to the darkness.

'And we'd be better off without this fog.' Brenda too was making slow progress through the thick mist that had gathered in the valley bottom. The muffled silence was an eerie contrast to the earlier guttural roar of the plane's engines. 'I didn't hear it hit the ground – did you?'

'No, I just heard the engines cut out.' A plane without power would make a crash-landing at best. At worst it would plummet from the sky and be smashed to smithereens.

262

'We might easily be on the wrong track.' Brenda paused in a small clearing and stamped her feet for warmth. She strained to hear anything unusual – the slow churning of propellers or the settling of metal fuselage into soft snow – even the sound of a survivor calling for help. But there was nothing.

Una caught her breath. 'We did see it, didn't we? We didn't make it up?'

'Yes, it was a Jerry. We saw his bombs explode. The question is, where exactly did he come down?'

Una gathered herself together by looking up through the fog towards a faint moon. Yes, there was a war on, she realized, but it had never come so close to where she lived and worked until this terrifying moment. Yes, there was rationing and 'V' for Victory, air raids and the Home Guard, but it was what you read in the newspapers and heard on the wireless. The war happened in big cities and vital ports, on the north coast of France, in Hong Kong, in far-flung places – not on your doorstep, not here in Burnside.

'Did you hear that?' Brenda said suddenly.

'What?'

'A sort of cry – ahead and slightly to our right. Listen.'

Una strained to hear. Yes – a faint, reedy cry, but hardly human. 'Is it an animal caught in a trap?'

Brenda shook her head. 'I don't think so. Let's go and find out.'

So they struggled on in the direction of the sound, sinking into snow drifts until, after ten minutes or so, they cleared the fog-bound trees and stood out in the open, looking up the fell towards the ridge where they'd last seen the German plane. The slope was steep and smooth, unmarked except for a large, dark shape resting on the ground to the far side of a low stone wall.

'That must be it.' Una glanced at Brenda and was surprised by the look of uncertainty on her face. 'What else can it be?'

'You're right.' Taking a deep breath to overcome a sudden squeamishness, Brenda struck out up the hillside. 'This could be nasty,' she warned. 'We might find someone still alive. On the other hand . . .'

'We don't know yet.' The thought of helping a survivor spurred Una on. 'If that really was a person calling for help, the sooner we get there the better.'

'I'm still saying, be prepared.' Brenda was talking to herself as much as to Una. She pictured crushed limbs, mangled bodies and who knew how many victims – one or two, maybe more.

Edgar was awake when the plane came down. He heard the distant sound of the engines – Dornier Do 17, night fighter with twin propellers, a *Fliegender Bleistift*, a *Schnellbomber*. There were four thuds in all and then the engines cut out.

Grace heard it too and rushed downstairs. When she didn't find her brother in the house, she went into the forge and saw him pacing the floor.

'Four five hundred and fifty-pound bombs dropped on the hills above Fieldhead,' he told her with dead certainty.

She gasped and held her breath. 'Fieldhead?' she echoed.

'Yes. Within a mile or so. A last-ditch effort to lighten his load, I should say.'

'Fieldhead? Edgar, we have to go and find out what's happened!'

Out on the street, villagers emerged from their houses and congregated in the pub yard. The Baxendale brothers were all for driving out to the scene, along with Jack Hudson. Bill drove his car up the street to join them.

'Maurice reckons the plane came down practically on top of Fieldhead,' Jack reported. 'He had a pair of binoculars handy – saw everything from his attic window.'

'I only heard it, I didn't see it. Let's hope it missed the hostel.' Bill left his car ticking over then ran into the pub to share his information with Grace. He found her and Edgar fully dressed and putting on their coats. 'Come on – I'll give you a lift out,' he offered without preliminaries. Within seconds they'd followed him outside and got into the back seat of his car. He pulled out of the yard into the road ahead of the Baxendales in one car and Grace's father, Roland Thomson and Horace Turnbull in another. The three old men had been holding a late-night cribbage session in the back room of the pub when they'd heard and seen the bombs go off and were determined not to miss the sight of wreckage spread across the hills.

'Edgar knows what type of plane it is,' Grace told Bill. She had to hold on to the seat in front to stop herself from sliding into Edgar as Bill took a bend at speed. 'Tell him,' she urged.

'Dornier Do 17 – built for speed, outruns anything else in the sky, including a Spitfire. Hard to hit. Attack range – four hundred nautical miles. Four men maximum: pilot, bombardier, two gunners.' Edgar spoke as if skimming through a textbook.

'Well, something hit it tonight – that much we know.' Bill put his foot on the accelerator for the straight stretch of road ahead, ignoring patches of freezing mist. 'Or else why would it be limping home alone?'

Edgar didn't speculate. Instead, he stuck to the facts. 'He went out with a couple of others. I heard them fly over.'

'And you think its target might have been Thornley Dam?' The reservoir supplied water to Leeds, Bradford and many of the surrounding towns so a direct hit would have a big effect.

'This isn't the first time they've tried it,' Grace said when Edgar didn't reply. He sat next to her with his fists clenched, staring straight ahead. She fell silent and prayed that the plane had come down before it reached the hostel. Behind them was a lengthening procession of cars and vans, followed by men and boys on bikes, stretching back for half a mile – perhaps thirty people in all.

'Yes and they failed last time.' Bill gripped the wheel. It would be all too easy to skid off the road on an icy stretch. Eyes straight ahead, minutes ticking by, none of them knowing what they would find.

Out at Fieldhead, Hilda Craven took charge.

'I'm warden here and what I say goes,' she insisted

once she'd emerged from her bedroom at the front of the house – a sturdy, large-busted figure in a hand-knitted fawn jumper and brown skirt. 'I don't want heroics or anyone grabbing the limelight.' She looked from Joyce to Elsie to Kathleen as she spoke. 'Remember, we're Land Girls – we drive tractors and clear ditches. In other words, we stand by and let others take centre stage.'

The girls were assembled in the main hallway, some fully dressed and some in nightclothes, all nervously passing comment in undertones and nudging each other as the warden took up position by the main door and gave her speech.

Joyce was the first to object. 'That's all very well, Mrs Craven, but what are we meant to do when a plane comes down on our doorstep – sit here and twiddle our thumbs?'

'A *German* plane,' Jean said pointedly.

'What difference does that make?' Elsie lined up alongside Joyce, who was itching to follow Una and Brenda. 'If the men in that plane are injured, we can't leave them out there to die of frostbite, German or not.'

'Jerry would do it to one of ours without a second thought.' Dorothy's hatred of the enemy was strong. Her brother had died in Eritrea early that year and a cousin had gone down on SS *Anselm*. The U-boat attack had left two hundred and fifty dead.

'Nobody will be freezing to death,' Mrs Craven insisted. 'I'm reliably informed that some men from the village are on their way out here. Their plan is to send out a search party as soon as they arrive.'

'Where did this reliable information come from?' Joyce let her impatience show. 'Honestly, why aren't we forming a search party of our own?'

'Because, as warden here, I am responsible for your welfare.' Hilda stood her ground. 'Please stop and think about it, Joyce – it would be madness for you girls to venture out onto the fell at night-time, in the fog and snow.'

'When is somebody going to tell her that's exactly what Brenda and Una have done?' Elsie whispered in Joyce's ear.

'Not me, for a start.' As the warden held firm, Joyce's frustration mounted. 'Listen – Mrs Craven can't actually stop us from doing what we want – she doesn't have the authority.'

'So what are you going to do?' Elsie guessed the answer from the determined look in Joyce's eye. 'Don't tell me – you're going to chase after the other two.'

'Yes! Are you coming with me?'

Elsie thought it through then shook her head. 'I'm sorry, Joyce, I agree with Ma C when she says "no heroics". You're on your own.'

'Rightio.' Still determined to slip away, Joyce sidled round the edge of the group as the girls continued to comment and fire questions. She reached the kitchen corridor and backed into it, closing the door behind her. Then she broke into a run, down the corridor, through the kitchen and out of the back door. Una and Brenda had a ten-minute start on her – she would pick up their footprints in the snow and follow them at top speed, with or without the warden's say-so.

Una and Brenda struggled through patches of freezing fog up the fell side. They were breathless and their legs threatened to give way as they slogged on towards the wrecked plane.

'That's definitely it,' Una gasped from a distance of two hundred yards. She could make out the distinctive twin tail fin pointed upwards at an angle of forty-five degrees and one of the wings still intact.

'We haven't heard anyone calling out for help lately.' Brenda wondered if they'd imagined it. 'Maybe you were right – it could have been a fox or an owl.' Or else the desperate cry had been made in a dying breath, as life had ebbed away.

They stopped to take air into their aching lungs – two small, dark figures on a white hillside with a fierce wind whipping powdery snow into their faces and tearing at their clothes.

'Ready?' Una was the first to forge ahead but she immediately lurched into a snow drift and fell forward.

Brenda came alongside her and helped her up. As she hauled her to her feet they heard another cry – human but incoherent, ending in a low groan. They looked at each other in alarm then, without saying a word, they hurried on towards the wreckage.

They reached the wall at last and peered over it. The body of the plane was split in two and one wing had been torn off on impact. Roughly fifty feet long, it lay in the snow twenty yards away with its propeller still attached. The thin tail section had come to rest ten yards from the bulkier cockpit, which lay nose-down against the wall. Close by were shards of crumpled metal and shattered Plexiglas. There was a dark trail in the snow of strong-smelling diesel and engine oil.

'Look.' Una pointed to the damaged nose section of the aircraft. 'It must have skidded along the ground and crashed straight into the wall.'

'Yes, and yet someone's still alive in there.' Brenda and Una climbed the wall and approached with dread. There was more light than usual because of the snow, which reflected the moon's rays, so they could make out the shape of the cockpit and a figure slumped against the control panel.

'Pilot,' Una murmured. She was the first to climb onto the wing and edge her way along its length.

The man wore a leather helmet and an oxygen mask that obscured his face but there was not a shadow of a doubt that he was dead – she knew this from his staring, sightless eyes. His torso was grotesquely twisted and from the angle of his head she could tell that his neck was broken.

Brenda joined her. 'We can't do anything for him, at any rate.' She knew there must be others trapped in the belly of the plane but wasn't sure how to reach them so she jumped down from the wing and went round to the rear of the cockpit where she started to pull at pieces of jagged metal.

Una stayed where she was. There was almost room for her to squeeze past the pilot into the section below but first she would have to shift the body a little. She steeled herself and leaned within inches of the dead pilot's face to push him sideways. As she did so, she saw a dark trickle of blood emerge from behind the mask.

'I can't get in from this angle. How are you getting on?' Brenda called.

Brenda's muffled voice re-energized Una. 'I'm small enough to squeeze in, I think. I can't see much, though – it's too dark.'

Brenda rejoined her, scrambling back onto the wing as a lone figure made its way out of the low-lying fog at the bottom of the hill, a torch lighting the way. She stood and waved both arms above her head. 'Help is on its way,' she reported to Una.

The pilot's dead, grey stare and the dark blood made Una shudder. It was a young, unlined face – this was not much more than a boy. She eased the mask away from his mouth as if this would make a difference – it was illogical, but she felt that a man deserved to be fully visible in death. She wiped away the blood then removed the leather helmet to reveal short, fair hair.

'It looks like Joyce is on her way,' Brenda told her. 'Yes, it is her – I can tell.'

Joyce saw Brenda standing on the wing and waving at her. The wreckage was scattered far and wide, which meant there wasn't much hope of rescuing any survivors and if they did find someone alive, how would they get him off the hillside, away from this remote spot? They would have to wait for reinforcements, she decided, as she made her way through snowdrifts. That would be in the shape of the search party that Hilda had told them about. At least she, Joyce, would be of some use, if only to pass on this scrap of information to Una and Brenda.

'All right, I can get down now.' Una's heart bled for the boy pilot but there was more to be done. She eased herself into the belly of the plane, letting her arms take her weight as she dangled her legs in the space below the pilot's seat. Her foot brushed against a soft object. She heard a groan.

Brenda leaned forward and stared into the cockpit. 'Who's that? What's happening in there?'

'Wait a second.' Una's feet touched a solid surface and she slid from sight. She felt her way, running her fingers along a metal shaft with a barrel and a strip of ammunition – a forward-facing machine gun, she guessed – and then some canisters that she thought might be loose oxygen bottles that rolled and made a clinking sound under her feet. 'I can't see!' She panicked and called up to Brenda.

'Throw me your torch,' Brenda told Joyce who had reached the wall.

The narrow beam danced in the darkness as Joyce threw and Brenda caught. She leaned into the cockpit, casting light on the dead pilot before she directed the beam into the belly of the plane. She trained it on Una's head and shoulders.

'Shine it in front of me.'

Brenda slid the beam forwards, directly onto the face of a second man. He lay on his back, arched across the barrel of the machine gun, his lips stretched into a rigid grin. The back of his skull was smashed. There was blood everywhere.

In the confined, bloody space, Una pressed her body against the fuselage and held her breath.

'Come back up!' Brenda's instant reaction was intended to save Una more distress. 'He's dead. We can't help him.'

'No. Shine the torch the other way – towards the tail section.' Una grew certain that this was where the groaning sound had come from and sure enough, when Brenda redirected the beam, she saw a third man curled on his side. He lay next to his machine gun, following her with his eyes.

She had to step over the dead gunner to reach him and hold out her hand. 'Are you hurt? Can you get up?'

He pushed her away and said rapid words that she didn't understand.

'I think his arm is trapped,' she called up to Brenda, who had been joined by Joyce on the wing. 'He's frightened. He won't let me near.'

'I'll tell you what – Joyce and I will have another go at getting in from the back,' Brenda decided. 'There's a big sheet of buckled metal blocking the way but with two of us we might be able to wrench it free.'

'Leave me the torch!' Staying in the dark belly with the injured man was unthinkable – Una needed light.

'Catch!' Brenda dropped the torch into Una's outstretched hands then slid down from the wing.

'Don't worry – I won't hurt you,' Una promised the German gunner. 'I'm here to help.'

'*Helfen*,' he echoed faintly.

'Yes, that's right.' This man was older than the pilot – perhaps thirty – strongly built and with very short, dark hair. His free hand had been hit by shrapnel, opening up a wide gash from which blood flowed. 'We're going to get you out of here.'

He muttered something then struggled to free the arm that was trapped between the gun mounting and the crushed fuselage.

Una winced. 'Don't – it's best not to move in case something's broken.'

He grimaced and kept on talking under his breath as he managed to twist his body into a kneeling position, with his head hanging and his torso bent forward. From this position he could use the weight of his body to press against the bent mounting. It shifted a fraction of an inch – just enough to release his arm. Once free and still kneeling, he turned towards Una and with a sudden swipe of his hand he knocked the torch from her grasp.

'What was that noise?' Joyce called from outside. She and Brenda worked furiously to open up the back section of the fuselage, striking at it with heavy stones from the demolished wall to create an opening.

The torch rolled against the body of the lifeless gunner. Una darted forward to pick it up and shine it in the injured man's eyes. 'That was me dropping the torch. He's broken free. What should I do?'

'Keep calm. Tell him there's not enough room to haul him out through the cockpit,' Brenda answered. 'We're nearly through. Ask him to stay where he is.'

'He won't understand what I'm saying.' She held

the torch with both hands, kept the beam trained on his face and tried anyway. 'Wait,' she murmured. 'No one's going to hurt you. It's just me and my two friends. We'll get you out.'

Her soft tone confused him. Her double-breasted coat seemed to be part of a uniform, which would make her the enemy, but her voice said something different. She was a slight woman – easy enough to overpower, and yet he hesitated. He glanced down at the blood on his hand, trying to ignore searing pains in his shoulder and leg.

Brenda and Joyce kept on hammering at the broken fuselage. The strong smell of spilt fuel bothered them and they realized that a small spark as stone struck metal might blow the whole thing up so they quickly threw the stones aside.

The gunner nodded and shouted to them about *Feuer*.

'That's right – fire.' It was Joyce who replied. 'Sit tight while we prise this open.'

'Like a tin of sardines.' Brenda's gallows humour only made them try harder. The buckled metal had been weakened by the impact – they used all their strength to fold it back and create enough space for Una and the gunner to crawl through. 'Hang on!' she called through the opening. 'We're almost there.'

'Only a few more minutes,' Una told him as he became aware of his dead comrade sprawled across his gun. He crawled to him and tried to raise him but recoiled when he saw the smashed skull then scrambled back towards Una. He gestured towards the upper part of the cockpit with a questioning look.

Una shook her head. 'I'm sorry – your pilot's dead too.'

'*Tot*,' he breathed. He sagged forward and almost keeled over. She put out her hand to steady him. He tilted his head back and closed his eyes, moving his lips as if in prayer.

It was Brenda who eased herself through the new opening and took in the scene – one man dead and one injured – though not too badly, by the look of him. 'Follow me,' she urged. 'We'll go down on our bellies and slither out.'

'He won't . . . he doesn't . . .' Una tried to explain. Seeing Brenda's face had flooded her with such relief that she lost the ability to speak clearly.

'Come,' Brenda said again as her feet touched the ground and she reached out for him. '*Komm*.'

Nursing his injured shoulder with his blood-covered hand, the man went down on his belly and wriggled towards her.

'It's a miracle how you managed to survive this lot.' Brenda surveyed the mangled metal and the body of the dead gunner. 'I suppose your pilot made some sort of crash-landing before he hit the wall.'

He groaned and inched forward towards the cold air. Una lit his way, anxious not to be left alone in the belly of the plane and preparing to follow him through the gap as quickly as possible. Brenda and Joyce waited until his head and shoulders had emerged then took his weight.

'That's right – give him a shove from behind,' Joyce told Una.

With a yelp of pain he tumbled out onto the ground where he lay on his back clutching his shoulder.

As Una wriggled through the gap, she handed the torch to Brenda. Then she landed in the snow beside the gunner and gulped in the air. Joyce pulled her to her feet and together they stared down at the man they'd rescued.

'What's wrong with him, do we know?' Joyce asked. The man didn't cut a sympathetic figure. There was something in his face that suggested brutality – the set of his jaw, the curl of his upper lip perhaps. And of course the uniform didn't help. 'He's hurt his hand and his shoulder – anything else?'

'He can't speak a word of English, so I'm not sure.' Una exhaled loudly as Brenda brushed the compacted snow from her back.

'No broken bones, by the look of it.' Joyce watched him warily as he sat up and took in his surroundings. 'With a bit of luck, we'll be able to walk him down to the hostel – if he cooperates, that is. We'll probably meet the search party on their way up. One's been organized, according to Mrs Craven.'

Una looked down the hillside into the valley bottom but the foggy darkness hid all signs of activity. 'I suppose he'll be treated as a prisoner of war from now on.'

'I expect so.' Brenda wasn't eager to hand him over to the villagers. She felt he was their prisoner, not the search party's. 'Look, there's a leak from the fuel tank on the wing. Let's move him away from the plane to be on the safe side.' As she spoke, she crouched down beside the man, pointed towards the leak and tried to explain. 'Move, all right? In case of fire – *feuer*.' She sniffed loudly then made an exaggerated boom noise and gave a gesture to show an explosion.

He nodded, got to his feet, then had to accept their support until they'd reached a safe distance.

'I see now why he's limping.' Una pointed to a patch of blood on his trouser leg, just below the knee.

'He's in a bad way, poor chap.' Joyce overcame her earlier judgement. He was bound to be suspicious of them and must be in a state of shock after seeing his comrades killed. She took off the scarf that she wore around her neck then pointed to his leg. 'Bandage,' she explained.

He shook his head and scowled.

'Too proud, eh?' As she rewound the scarf round her neck, she began to understand how he might feel humiliated to have been taken prisoner by three young women.

'Proud or not, we have to escort him off this hill.' Brenda gestured for him to follow as she directed the torch onto the ground. She picked up the tracks they'd made on their way up and made her way carefully. 'Take your time,' she told him. 'There's no rush.'

He hesitated and when he looked back at the plane where his dead friends lay, his pale face was drained and his body shook.

'Poor chap,' Joyce said again. 'It doesn't matter whose side he's on – you have to feel sorry for him.'

Una urged him to continue by touching his shoulder. 'Please come.'

He raised his hand in salute then turned away from the plane. '*Ich komme.*' He mumbled ceaselessly as he followed the three women down the steep slope – a stream of guttural words interspersed with two staccato names that they recognized – Deiter and Conrad – repeated often as he glanced back and seemed to make promises, tapping his fist against his chest and limping on.

They went on like this for several minutes, drawing closer to the elm trees that had been planted long ago to shelter Fieldhead from the worst of the northerly winds.

'This battery's jiggered.' Brenda shook the torch but found that the beam had grown so dim that she could hardly see three feet in front of her.

Their airman stumbled and fell sideways into a snowdrift. Blood from his hand stained the pure white surface. He lay helpless until Joyce and Una pulled him back onto his feet. 'It's not far now,' Una promised.

They were perhaps fifteen minutes from safety when they heard the search party.

'Which way now?' an angry voice yelled. 'Maurice, can you hear me?'

'I'm over here, stuck in a bloody drift!'

'What the hell . . . ? Jack, come over here!' Bob Baxendale was forced to call for help.

A short way up the hill, Brenda came to a sudden halt. The German gunner stumbled into her and pushed her face down into the snow. There were grunts and a flurry of clumsy movements as Una and Joyce picked them both up.

'Just let me get my hands on Jerry.' It was Horace Turnbull's grating, reedy voice – over to the left, deadened by the fog. 'I'll give him what for!'

'If we ever find our way out of here.' Cliff was as lost as the rest, waving his torch wildly at the trees that surrounded him. 'Who knows the bloody way? Where's Roland? I thought he was meant to be leading us.'

Brenda was back on her feet but now the torch battery had failed completely. They were in the dark when the airman broke away from them.

Hearing angry voices in the fog-bound woods below, he seized the moment and started to stagger back the way they'd come.

Una gasped. 'No – stay here!' She was the first to give chase. His injured leg slowed him down and she soon gained on him. 'Stop!' she cried. A glance over her shoulder told her that Brenda and Joyce were already lost in the mist.

He gritted his teeth and pushed on through the snow. The voices belonged to a group of angry men. The enemy was hard on his heels but he wouldn't make it easy for them. Rather than be captured, he would run and run until his lungs burst and he breathed his last breath.

'Wait,' Una pleaded. Should she follow him or let him go? She lost vital seconds as she tried to make up her mind – he'd reached a wall and was intent on clambering over it, but he lost his balance and fell with the high, wailing cry that she'd heard when he'd been trapped in the shattered fuselage. She made her decision and went on alone.

CHAPTER SIXTEEN

Down in the valley there was confusion. No one took the lead so the Burnside men split off in different directions, blaming the darkness and the fog for their lack of progress.

Jack Hudson stayed with the Baxendales and convinced them that they should stick close to the hostel and search the grounds for survivors of the crash. 'If Jerry had any sense, he'd come straight down off the fell and head for the nearest shelter.'

'I agree with that.' Maurice had his own reason for staying within the grounds – he was keen to keep an eye on the Land Girls and make sure that they stayed inside the building while they conducted their search. He and his brother readily fell in with Jack's plan, taking young Neville Thomson and a couple of other lads with them.

Meanwhile, Cliff, Roland and Horace blundered on through the wood.

'Hold your horses – I can't see a flipping thing.' The owner of Winsill Edge had come without a torch and relied on the dim light from a paraffin lamp that Cliff had hurriedly picked up on his way out of the pub.

Cliff held the lamp high over his head. The trees seemed to crowd in on them through the fog and it seemed impossible to find a way through. 'This is a dead loss. I vote that we head home and try again when it gets light.'

Their grumbling voices drew two other men from the village who gathered to discuss the pros and cons of turning back. One of them pointed out that the delay would give the enemy a chance to get clean away. Then again, what hope was there of anyone surviving the crash in the first place?

'Not if it flew slap-bang into the hillside,' Horace agreed with disturbing relish. 'There'd be bits of plane and dead bodies everywhere.'

'If it was me in that plane, I'd have used my ejection seat.' Roland made a point that no one else had thought of. 'Once I knew the game was up – that's what I'd have done.'

'In that case, Jerry and his parachute could have touched down anywhere between Thornley and here.' That was it – Cliff had definitely decided to give up. He swung the lamp in the direction of the hostel but before he and his group had taken more than a few steps, they bumped into Grace, Edgar and Bill.

'You're going the wrong way, Dad.' Grace had kept her bearings in spite of the fog. Arriving to find that the hostel hadn't taken a direct hit had been a great relief but when she'd learned from Elsie that Joyce, Una and Brenda had all disobeyed orders and were out on the fell searching for survivors, she'd grown anxious once more. She spoke quickly and urgently to her father. 'Come with us. They think the plane came down about a mile to the north.'

Cliff resented being told what to do. 'Is that so? Well, you young ones can stay out here and catch your deaths – it's up to you.'

'Why – where are you going?'

'Home,' he snapped. 'And so would you, Edgar, if you had any sense.'

Grace glanced questioningly at her brother who had remained silent ever since he'd identified the plane for Bill. His pale face was partly hidden behind the turned-up collar of his greatcoat.

'I'll stay,' he told her through gritted teeth.

'Aye, well, if you find Jerry, give him a good hiding from me,' was Horace's parting shot as he and the others followed in Cliff's footsteps.

Their ugly mood set Bill's teeth on edge. 'Perhaps it's just as well they're heading back. At times like this we can't let our feelings get the better of us.'

Grace gave a faint smile – typical Bill to keep his emotions in check. But he was right, of course. 'We still outnumber Jerry, probably by ten or fifteen to one.' She pulled herself up over the use of the jingo-istic term. 'Sorry – I sound like Horace.'

Bill smiled encouragingly. 'No – take it from me, you don't.'

'What I mean is – there's no guarantee that everyone in this search party will be able to keep a cool head.'

They didn't notice Edgar slipping away as they

talked, walking on between the trees, leaving a trail of footprints in the snow.

'Edgar?' Grace's muffled call drew no response so she and Bill attempted to follow his tracks. 'He doesn't have a torch,' she realized with a flicker of panic. 'Edgar, wait for us. Where are you going? Come back.'

Two hundred yards away, just clear of the trees, Joyce and Brenda were still searching for Una and the runaway gunner in the icy blackness of the early hours. They'd set off after them and reached the wall where he'd lost his balance. The trampled, flattened snow showed them that an incident had taken place and they were able to pick up the trail again on the far side – two sets of prints skirting the wood instead of heading back up the hill to where the plane had come down.

'What was she thinking, going off without us?' Brenda's fears for Una's safety mounted.

'That's just it – she wasn't thinking.' Joyce realized that their fellow Land Girl had acted on the spur of the moment. 'The scene inside that cockpit was bad enough to addle anyone's brain.'

'All the more reason for us to catch up with them.' Brenda felt a knot tighten in the pit of her stomach as the trail disappeared down a steep gulley with a stream at the bottom. She slid down on her haunches, catching hold of bushes to slow her descent and glad to be wearing wellingtons when her feet landed in the water with a splash.

Joyce stayed at the top of the bank and cupped her hands around her mouth. 'Una!' she yelled.

Brenda waded across the stream. 'There's blood in the snow here,' she called back to Joyce as she reached the far side and bent over to examine the ground.

'Wait there – I'm on my way.'

'Hurry up. Let's hope it's his blood, not hers.'

The sight spurred them on. Now the trail led them back towards the wood, weaving between trees but staying close to the edge, skirting the hostel grounds.

Brenda paused and tried to visualize the way ahead. 'This leads towards the road. If I'm right, it should come out close to Peggy Russell's farm.'

'How would the gunner know that, though?' Was his gut instinct at work here as well as Una's?

'Maybe he forced Una to show him the way.'

They shuddered as they thought how easily power could shift – how Una the rescuer could turn into Una the enemy in the German's eyes. After all, he was a powerfully built, desperate man fighting for his freedom. Who knew how quickly the tables might have turned?

Gripped by this new notion, they hesitated uncertainly as a solitary figure materialized through the fog. He walked straight towards them from the centre of the wood without speaking.

'Edgar, is that you?' Recognizing him by his RAF coat, Joyce ran to meet him. 'Are you part of the search party? Where have the others got to?'

He ground his teeth and clicked his jaw before he spoke. 'The plane – did you find it?'

'Yes – a mile up the hill, split into two halves.'

'How many dead?'

'Two – the pilot and one of the gunners.' She saw in his eyes that he was back in the moments when his own plane had crashed. His eyelids flickered as he looked up at the branches over their heads. 'The other gunner made it out alive.'

A volcanic explosion of anger made Edgar form a fist and punch a nearby tree – once, twice, three times. Overhanging branches released their burden of snow, which thudded softly onto the ground. He gazed at his bleeding, trembling hand.

Joyce made up her mind then spoke quietly to Brenda. 'You'll have to go on without me while I take him back to the hostel.'

Brenda saw that it was necessary. 'If you come across any of the others – Jack or the Baxendales – tell them where I'm headed and why.'

'I'll come back with them as soon as I know Edgar is in safe hands.'

Brenda doubted that Joyce would find her way through the wood. 'Why not bring him this way with me? Once we're on the road, you can walk him straight back to Fieldhead.'

'Yes – that's a better idea.' As Joyce took off her scarf for a second time and used it to bandage Edgar's hand, she explained the new plan. 'The best thing is to get you properly seen to at the hostel. I'll telephone Grace to let her know what's up.'

'Grace is here.' He felt pain and stared at the new bandage.

'Where – here in the wood?'

'With Bill Mostyn. I drove out with them.'

She took in Edgar's new information. 'They'll be wondering where you've got to. Come on – let's go down to the road with Brenda. Grace and Bill have probably gone back to the hostel looking for you.'

Edgar didn't seem to care where he went. As they followed Una and the gunner's trail, he rattled off more information about the Dornier. 'Machine guns to front and rear. Double-drum magazines. Self-sealing fuel tanks to lessen risk of fire.' He halted on the word 'fire' to relive his own escape. Bright orange flames consumed the cockpit. Green trees caught alight, smoke spiralled into the blue sky. He left Billy behind while armed soldiers swarmed up the hillside towards him.

The gunner clutched Una's arm. He dragged her along, skirting the dense wood and just able to make out some features of the landscape through the fog – a gully below them with an icy stream running through it, then a slight rise, beyond which there was a large house with outbuildings. This meant there must be a road close by. He spoke a few harsh words and forced her on.

Una looked down at the water. His grip was strong and he forced her down the rough banking, only letting go when they overbalanced and rolled helplessly into the stream, cracking the ice at its borders and getting a drenching from head to toe. The cold water made her gasp and flail her arms. Before she knew it, he was on his feet and grabbing her arm with his bloodstained hand, pulling her upright.

She struggled and kicked at his shins without

effect. He swung her round so that she was in front of him then hooked his arm around her neck. He spoke again and thrust her up the far bank ahead of him. The girl who had saved him was a hostage now and he must keep her with him, even if she continued to fight. He put pressure on her throat and guided her away from the house.

Everything had changed so fast. One moment Una had been running after him across the dark hillside, hoping to bring him back to safety. He'd overbalanced as he'd climbed the wall. She'd offered him her hand to help him up. Then suddenly he'd tightened his grip and wouldn't let go. The cruel look on his face had told her that he was no longer the hunted.

And now she was alone with him – a prisoner – choking, trying to prise his arm away and ease the pressure on her throat. He glanced over his shoulder as he thrust her towards the wall that bordered the road. There was no help for it – she had to climb over then go wherever he ordered. With the hostel a safe distance behind them, he held her by the wrist and they set off in the direction of Burnside.

Una was dragged along the packed, white surface. After a few yards they slid off the smooth road into the ditch and climbed out again, this time using the soft verges to avoid the ice and pick up speed. There was a barn ahead and a hundred yards beyond that, Peggy Russell's farm. And thank God – Peggy's dog had heard them! He sprang from his kennel, breaking the silence of the night with his furious barking.

The gunner stopped and looked over his shoulder.

Through the patchy fog he saw that half a dozen vehicles were parked outside the big house. Men were still there searching for him so it was useless to go back. The dog was out in the road, straining at his chain. They would never get past. Even if they tried, the farmer would see them and alert the search party – he had no notion that the old woman who lived there was without telephone or any means of transport. Now several men with torches walked onto the road outside the big house and were paying attention to the barking dog. One man climbed into a van and switched on its headlights. Once the driver had turned his vehicle in the narrow road, he and the girl would be caught in their beams.

It was time to lie low. He dragged Una towards the barn and shoved at the door. The wooden frame was rotten so the bolt didn't hold. He pushed her inside then closed the door behind him.

She crouched on her hands and knees, soaked to the skin and breathing in the sharp smell of old sheep droppings mixed with fusty straw. There were slits in the walls to let in air and a ladder leading up to a hayloft with a single narrow opening letting in the dim moonlight. The only sound was the man's breathing and from outside, the fading barks of Peggy's dog.

'I can't see or hear a thing.' As Grace tried to take stock of where she and Bill were, a sense of hopelessness settled on her.

They'd only been able to follow Edgar's footprints a short distance before they'd lost the trail and now they'd found themselves at the edge of the wood and didn't know which way to go.

'Don't worry – he's probably worked out how to get back to the hostel.' Bill was more concerned about Grace than Edgar. She hadn't changed out of the dress that she'd worn for the rehearsal and her coat had been hastily thrown over the top. She was hatless and had on a pair of indoor shoes that were caked in snow.

'What if he went up onto the fell by himself?'

He scanned the hillside and noticed that the fog lay low in the valley, leaving the top of the fell clear. 'I don't see any movement up there. But look – there are tracks coming down the hill and skirting the wood – more than one set of prints, by the look of it.'

They crouched to examine the marks in the snow – the thick tread of a man's boots was mixed up with a much smaller, lighter print made by a woman's foot, definitely heading down the hill as Bill had said. He frowned and thought out loud. 'These could belong to anyone for all we know.'

'That's true of the big set of prints, but how many women besides me are out here?' Grace listed the names as she followed the trail down a steep slope. 'Joyce, Una and Brenda – that's all.' She found more sets of prints and areas of the snow that were badly scuffed and trampled, and then across a stream on the far bank a stained area that could be blood. The sight made her clutch at Bill's hand. 'Is that what I think it is?'

He shone his torch on the patch and confirmed her fears. 'That settles it – that's the way we have to go.'

He descended steadily – ahead of Grace who had grown convinced that the smallest prints must belong to Una. Who else had such tiny feet? But why was the trail so scuffed? Could the other prints belong to a German survivor and was he forcing Una to go with him? And the blood on the bank – did this mean there'd been violence? Her heart was in her mouth as Bill steadied her to jump across the stream. He kept her hand in his as they followed the trail towards the road.

Brenda heard the dog barking. She was on the road but had lost the trail and was wondering which direction to take. Behind her was the entrance to Fieldhead with the parked vehicles and the sound of men belonging to the search party coming and going. Ahead, a few hundred yards down the road, was Peggy Russell's farm – a squat, two-storey building with a thin spiral of smoke still rising from its chimney. It was Peggy's dog who had begun to growl and bark frantically. A light had come on in an upstairs window.

Without further hesitation, Brenda set off towards the farm. The dog's bark faded so whatever had disturbed it – an animal, a person, an unidentified noise – had gone away again. The men at the hostel had heard the disturbance and, like her, must have decided to follow it up because she heard an engine splutter into life and a glance over her shoulder told her that the driver of a van had begun a three-point turn in the lane.

She would carry on ahead of them and have a

word with the old farmer's wife. By the time they arrived, she hoped to have found out what had made the dog bark.

Peggy was at her door in nightdress and dressing-gown, trying to quieten the dog who set to barking again at Brenda's arrival. He saw her and sprang out into the lane, teeth bared. Brenda stayed well back.

Peggy shouted at him from the doorway and made him retreat into the small yard where he took up a crouching position. 'It's all right – he won't bite,' she snapped.

Brenda wasn't convinced. Any guard dog worth its salt wouldn't think twice about sinking its fangs into the leg of a night-time intruder. 'I'll stay here, if that's all right with you.'

'What do you want, anyway?' With her hand clutching her dressing-gown tight around her throat and stray locks of grey hair falling over her forehead, Peggy made it clear that she didn't welcome the disruption. 'What's all the comings and goings at this time of night?'

'A plane came down behind the hostel. Didn't you hear it?'

'I don't hear a thing once I've gone off to sleep – not unless the dog wakes me.'

Brenda still kept a wary distance. 'It's a German bomber. One of the crew's made a run for it. There's a search party from the village looking for him. You haven't seen anything unusual, by any chance?'

'No, I was dead to the world, like I said.'

'You're sure?' Peggy's world-weary lack of curiosity bothered Brenda. Then again, if you got to her age and had lived through all the major catastrophes that the century had had to offer, perhaps you just went around in your own little world, scraping a living and enduring, sleeping through it all.

'I've told you twice, haven't I?'

'So you don't know what set your dog off?'

'I have no clue.'

Brenda was getting nowhere fast. She glanced back towards the hostel to see that the van that had been turning in the lane had backed itself into the ditch. A couple of men armed with shovels were trying to dig it out. Nothing was going right, it seemed.

Una was so cold she thought she would die. She hunched forward in the foul-smelling barn as her wet clothes clung to her and her whole body shook. The gunner stood over her, alert to noises outside the building.

The dog barked again; footsteps crunched over the snow towards the roadside farm. In the distance, an engine started then after a while there was the sound of tyres spinning followed by men's angry voices. He pulled Una to her feet and pressed his hand over her mouth. She bit his palm.

The airman snatched his hand away and swore. A second later he'd seized an old sickle that lay in the straw beside a hoe and a pitchfork and come back at her, threatening her with the rusty blade, making her back away until she collided with a wooden stall and slid to the floor. He went down on his haunches and pressed his face into hers, glaring and issuing threats that she didn't understand.

Something clicked in her brain – a sudden switch from hammering fear to uncanny calm. She grew detached, almost separate from what was happening – from the curved blade and the gunner's dark anger, from her own desperate, bone-chilling cold. What would be would be.

He stood up and pressed a finger to his lips, gesturing for her to stay quiet as he went to the door and listened to the sound of two women talking. He could hear the low growl of the dog against the questioning rise of the younger woman's voice and the flat, brief answers of the older one.

Una looked around. She considered climbing the ladder and easing herself through the loft window as a means of escape. She could jump from there into the soft landing provided by the snow.

As if he'd read her mind, the gunner strode back and jabbed at her with the sickle.

'*Stille . . . ruhe!*'

Una put her hands up in surrender. 'I won't make a noise,' she promised as she stood up. 'If you let me go, I won't tell anyone you're here.'

'*Hier?*' he repeated in a rasping voice. He lowered the farm implement and studied her face, all the while picking up sounds from outside. Along the road, the two women had stopped speaking. In the opposite direction, the engine whined and tyres skidded.

'I won't,' she vowed, low but clear. 'Let me go and I'll keep quiet – *stille*. I won't say a word. You can have all the time you need to get away.'

He shook his head. '*Verstehe nicht.*' The girl had pointed towards the door and then at herself – a gesture that she repeated twice before she put a finger to her lips. Did she mean that she wouldn't betray him? He didn't trust her. '*Nein.*' She was too useful. She had to stay.

There was a force in him too strong for her to overcome – a blind will-power projected by his wide stance, broad shoulders and brutally cropped hair, and in the fierce directness of his gaze. Still Una didn't give in. 'We saved you from the crash, remember? We heard you calling out and knew you were alive.'

There was nothing here that he understood, though she pointed towards the hill that rose steeply behind them. Alive – *lebendig* – perhaps that was what she meant. She spoke as if she was not afraid and this surprised him. She *should* be afraid – he was the enemy.

'Let me go,' she said again, as if repetition would make him understand. 'I won't tell anyone you're here. You can stay until everyone has gone home, until it's daylight. Then you'll have more chance of getting away.'

Her words wormed themselves into his firm resolve. Her eyes were deep and clear and she spoke softly, as if murmuring a charm. '*Nein,*' he said again. He recognized how vulnerable he was – injured and bleeding, bruised from the crash, alone in foreign territory, with a search party on his heels. Men like that were not gentle. They were like a pack of hunting dogs chasing a deer – they would tear him apart. '*Nein.*'

*

Grace and Bill climbed the wall into the lane to find the back end of Maurice's van stuck in the ditch. The silence was broken by wheels skidding and men shouting, the dark sky pierced by headlight beams. They ran towards them while Bob and Jack armed themselves with spades and began to dig Maurice out.

Grace made a beeline for Neville, who was lounging nearby. 'Where's Edgar? Have you seen him?'

Neville jerked his thumb towards the house. 'In there with Joyce.'

'And have you seen Una or Brenda?'

He shook his head then answered Jack's call to lend a hand. There were five men altogether, pushing with all their might, but they couldn't shift the van and nothing could get past until they got it out of the way.

'Are you two looking for Brenda?' While the men pushed, Maurice kept his foot on the accelerator and leaned out the window to talk to Bill. 'I spotted her down the road, heading for Peggy Russell's place.'

'When?'

'A few minutes back. She set the dog off.'

'Perhaps she was onto something.' Bill was the one who decided they should go and find out. He and Grace squeezed past the van and hurried on. When they reached the barn, Grace waved and called Brenda's name.

Brenda heard her and said a quick goodbye to a disgruntled Peggy. 'Sorry to wake you up. You should get back inside and keep warm.'

Peggy nodded and closed the door while Brenda ran to meet Grace and Bill. 'Is Una still missing?'

'Yes,' Grace replied. 'We've followed her footprints, along with another set that could belong to one of the Germans.' The seriousness of the situation hung in the air as they glanced up and down the lane.

From inside the barn, Una heard every word they said. They must have stopped directly outside the door, to judge by the clarity of their voices. All she had to do was to let out a single cry for help.

The gunner's expression changed in an instant – no longer glaring but narrow-eyed and furtive. Realizing he was cornered, he lowered the sickle to the ground and glanced up towards the hayloft.

Una knew she should call out, 'He's here!' Then it would all be over.

Out on the road, Grace heard a sound from inside the barn – the clink of metal against stone. She held up a warning hand to the others then pointed to the door.

The gunner's eyes pleaded with Una. She shook her head. He spun away and climbed the ladder to the loft. With an empty feeling in the pit of her stomach, she walked slowly to the door, opened it and found Bill, Brenda and Grace standing there.

Bill reached out to her. She was trembling and her eyes were wide and dark in her pale face. 'Are you all right? Where is he?'

'Go around the back,' she told them in a faint voice.

Grace and Brenda reacted quickly. They climbed a stile in time to see the gunner leap from the high opening into the field. He jumped ten feet into the snow, gritting his teeth and groaning in agony as he landed awkwardly on his injured leg. He clutched his shoulder and got up, staggered three or four paces before they reached him and dragged him down.

Bill and Una ran to join them. The gunner lay in the snow without attempting to resist, a black shape against a white background, legs together, arms spread wide like a crucified Christ.

CHAPTER SEVENTEEN

The injured airman was eventually bundled into Maurice's van and whisked away. He'd put on a show of surly defiance but Bill had put himself in charge of the search party and made sure that the prisoner hadn't been manhandled before they drove him to Beckwith Camp and locked him up in the secure brick building to await instructions from the powers above.

'Your gunner is a POW now,' Joyce told Una when she brought her breakfast in bed. 'His wounds will be patched up and he'll be interrogated.'

'How do you mean – interrogated?' The word sent a shiver down Una's spine in spite of the woollen blanket around her shoulders and the hot-water bottle resting on her stomach.

'They'll ask him a few questions to find out how much he knows about Jerry's military plans, and such like.' Joyce didn't want Una to worry so she kept her explanation brief. 'Then, as soon as he's fit to travel, he'll be sent off to a German POW camp.'

'Bill said they're not keen on keeping them here in this country.' Brenda sat at the end of Una's bed and watched her take the tray from Joyce. 'They prefer to ship Jerry to camps in Canada and, I suppose, America – now that Roosevelt has brought them into the war at last.'

The gunner's face staring out of the back of Maurice's van as it drove away was the last they'd ever see of him, though Una's memories of finding him trapped in the mangled fuselage, of his blunt-featured, brutal face as it spat angry words at her in Peggy Russell's barn would stay with her for ever.

'It's good to see you haven't lost your appetite.' Joyce watched her tuck into her porridge. She and Brenda had an eight o'clock appointment in the warden's office and were already washed and dressed. 'We were worried sick about you. It got worse by the minute – we had a vision of you lost in the snow, rapidly turning into a block of ice.'

'But no,' Brenda said with an encouraging smile. 'The gunner might have taken you hostage but you kept your presence of mind through it all and waited for your chance. You held your nerve, Una.'

'I only did what anyone else would have done.' Inwardly she was badly shaken and confused by the previous night's events, but she chose not to let it show. She would rather hug the details to herself and put on a brave front. 'And I don't know why I have to stay in bed. I'd rather get up and go to work.'

'No!' Brenda stood up and wagged a stern finger. 'You stay where you are. Joyce and I have to pop down to Ma C's office. I expect we'll be sent out to work this morning with a flea in our ears. That doesn't sound quite right. Should it be "with fleas in our ears"?'

Una managed a smile as Joyce told Brenda to stop splitting hairs. She waited until they'd left the room before she put down her spoon. The porridge lay heavy on her stomach and her arms were almost too weak to lift the tray and put it on her bedside table. She rested back on her pillow and turned her head to stare out of the window at the grey clouds sagging low over the elm trees. As the clock ticked on, it was no longer the captured gunner's face that filled her mind, but Angelo's.

'Come in, girls.' The warden still wore her fawn jumper and brown skirt. She sat behind a small desk and tapped the end of her pencil decisively onto her pad of blotting paper. Apart from the chair and desk with its squat black telephone, the plain office contained only a small green filing cabinet on top of which was perched a typewriter. The tall window overlooked the front garden where four girls were shovelling snow from the drive. Mrs Craven paused long enough for Brenda and Joyce to take in their surroundings, treating them to a long, hard look as they did so.

'I think you'll agree that we've had enough excitement to see us through Christmas well into the New Year.'

Joyce used her elbow to give Brenda a warning nudge. *Look meek and mild; keep your mouth firmly shut if you want to come out of this in one piece.* 'We have indeed.'

Unsurprisingly, the warden's normally friendly gaze was cool. 'And Una always seems to be in the eye of the storm.'

Joyce nodded sagely. 'Yes – Frank Kellett and now the German airman, all within the space of forty-eight hours.'

Hilda Craven slid her fingers up and down the green pencil then turned it and tapped it again. 'Luckily she seems none the worse for wear.'

'Una doesn't let anything get her down.' Brenda took pride in her room-mate's resilience. 'She's sitting up in bed and tucking into her breakfast, complaining about not being allowed to go to work.'

'No matter – I want her to take things easy.' Hilda had already telephoned Edith before she left for hospital to discuss how things stood. Understandably, the area rep had left everything in her hands. 'Mrs Mostyn agrees that Una may be in a state of shock without realizing it. It's by far the best thing for her to rest. As for you two . . .'

Joyce and Brenda stood to attention and expected the worse.

'Joyce – you were also at the centre of last night's events. I understand that you took care of Edgar Kershaw and made sure that he got safely back to Burnside.'

'Yes. He went home with Bill and Grace at about three o'clock.' She'd brought him back to the hostel and dabbed disinfectant on his hand then wrapped it in a clean white bandage. He'd been silent throughout, but when it had been time to get into Bill's car he'd made a point of thanking her.

'You're very welcome,' she'd told him on the steps of the main entrance.

He'd nodded briefly then added, 'I'm sorry.' His

coat seemed to swamp him. The new bandage stood out in the gloom.

'There's no need to be.' She'd gone down the steps and smiled gently. 'You look after yourself, do you hear?'

'Your kindness to Edgar goes some way towards making up for disobeying my order to stay inside,' the warden told her now. 'I'll mention that when I send in my report.'

'Thank you.' Things were working out better than expected, so Joyce risked a sideways glance at Brenda who was still waiting anxiously for judgement.

Hilda tapped her pencil again. Ever since Brenda had arrived, she'd proved to be a handful, with her hat always at a jaunty angle, the sheepskin collar of her pilot's jacket permanently turned up. If there was a rule to be broken, Brenda was the type who would break it. Equally, she would meet any challenge thrown at her, whether it was standing knee-deep in mud digging ditches or spending all night out on the fell searching for an enemy aircraft.

'My report will also include the fact that – unlike Joyce – you, Brenda, had actually left the hostel with Una before I issued my order. That means that technically you're in the clear.'

Brenda shot Joyce a look of astonishment. *Thank goodness Ma C is dealing with this and not Mrs M*, was her first thought. The warden's fairness struck her as a rare thing – very rare indeed.

Hilda dropped her pencil on the desk and sat back in her chair, which creaked as she leaned her weight against it. 'Don't look so surprised. And while I'm at it, let me give you a few reminders as to what's involved when you join the Land Army.' She counted the points on her plump fingers. 'For a start, we don't come under the jurisdiction of any of the three Women's Auxiliary Services. That means you can't be shipped from pillar to post as a member of a proper Service unit may be. Secondly, neither Mrs Mostyn nor I have any disciplinary power if you fail to follow orders. Yes, it's true, Brenda. You're not subject to military law. Thirdly, even the enrolment papers that you signed, promising to give your services for the duration of the war, are not legally binding.'

Brenda's eyes almost popped out of her head. 'What are you saying – that we're free to walk away whenever we like?'

'Yes, or to stay and accept a roof over your head and three square meals a day even if you never so much as lift a finger for the war effort.'

'You don't say!' Of course, Brenda had never bothered to read the small print on the enrolment form and by the look of it neither had Joyce. 'Why are you telling us this? Is it a backhanded way of asking us to leave?' The notion made both Joyce and Brenda take a short, sharp breath.

Hilda saw that she'd skewered them good and proper and thrust her weight forward again. 'Is that what you'd like to do?'

'No!' they said as one. It was the worst thing they could imagine – walking away from Fieldhead and the other girls, letting their country down when it needed them most.

'Very good. Because, between you and me, all Mrs

Mostyn and I have to rely on to keep things on the right track are two things: your willingness to work and your good sense. That applies to every single girl at Fieldhead. We can feed you and clothe you and safeguard your welfare by overseeing the work that the local farmers ask you to do, but that's the limit of our powers. I'll say it again: willingness and good sense. That's what we need from you both.'

'You have it from me!' Joyce felt the tension melt from her. She pushed her shoulders back, newly determined to live up to the warden's expectations.

'And from me!' Brenda echoed. ('Ma C is a blinking marvel,' she said later to Elsie and Kathleen. 'She's one in a million.')

'And you have the morning off work from me,' Hilda told them, standing up and coming out from behind her desk to see them out of the room. 'Catch up on some sleep or keep Una company. Think about what I've said.'

Bill sat with his mother in a green-tiled corridor of the Queen Victoria hospital. The hushed atmosphere had the effect of building his anxiety to an uncomfortable, chest-tightening pitch. He imagined that the silent, head-in-the-air nurses in their crisp blue-and-white uniforms were conveying bad news from operating theatre to relatives waiting in other corridors and that the harried, overworked doctors with stethoscopes slung around their necks must often make elementary mistakes through sheer exhaustion.

Of course he hid these thoughts from his mother.

'It won't be long now,' he murmured. 'They'll soon have Dad back on the ward and sitting up in bed.'

Edith gave a thin smile. 'I've seen this coming for a long time. Your father works too hard and he can't help worrying. It's his nature. He's been this way for as long as I've known him.'

Her words bit into Bill's conscience. It was his job to take some of those worries away from his father – especially now.

A nurse stopped beside them, taking in the care-worn yet well-dressed woman's appearance and the dark-haired, handsome son's struggle to remain calm. 'Mrs Wright?' she enquired.

'No.' He answered for his mother so the nurse went on her way. Doors at the end of the corridor swung open then closed behind her. 'I'll shoulder more of the responsibilities from now on,' he promised. 'Dad will have to take it easy, whether he likes it or not.'

Edith patted his hand. She felt weary to the bone, as if she was a non-swimmer drowning in a sea of worries. 'You're a good boy,' she murmured. 'I don't know what we'd do without you.'

It was an incantation that he'd heard for many years – even before he'd left school, when he'd learned from his father how to take Joe Kellett's old Ferguson engine apart with spanners and wrenches, how to drain an oil sump and replace spark plugs, to fit new gaskets and hoses to keep the tractor going for a few more years. A quick learner, these were the occasions when Bill had won rare approval from Vince, and he'd grown determined to prove his worth first as a mechanic then as a dealer in second-hand tractors, making a profit by reconditioning engines and selling them on. By the time he was eighteen, his father's compliments had dried up but he'd become an essential part of the rapidly expanding business.

A different nurse approached them, her shoes squeaking on the shiny brown lino. She was dark haired with a trim figure and when she spoke she had a pronounced Scottish accent. 'Mrs Mostyn?'

'Yes.' Edith struggled to breathe. She reached out to grasp Bill's hand.

'Come this way, Mrs Mostyn. Dr Renshaw wishes to speak with you.'

Una's experience of the last two days had re-shaped her life. All was different. She was no longer who she thought she was and she floated free of her past – of her grey, orphaned upbringing in Wellington Street, of her home life of cleaning and washing, scrubbing and dusting for her brothers. It was work that had kept her from school books and so limited her to finding a job in the mill. Now, free of all those restrictions and in love with Angelo, the world seemed to open up in front of her. The war would finish and Italy would beckon. It would be her picture that was taken in front of the Leaning Tower with Angelo's arm around her waist. There would be sunshine and summer dresses, loving tenderness and the thrill of his touch.

'A penny for them?' Brenda asked as she came into the bedroom. She had just heard from one of the girls who were clearing snow on the drive that six Italian prisoners had been given the job of removing the two dead bodies from the crashed plane. They were up there now, engaged in the grisly task.

'They're not worth it.' Una pushed back her blankets and swung her pale, slim legs out of bed. 'What did Mrs Craven say? Why aren't you at work?'

'Would you credit it – Ma C gave us the morning off.' Through the window Brenda saw that last night's fog had lifted and it was possible to make out the activity on the hillside, though it was too far away to recognize individuals. The bodies would have to be carried down on stretchers, which would take most of the morning. 'She didn't read us the Riot Act after all. In fact, she was very decent. By the way, she said you ought to stay in bed for a while.'

'What for? I'm not poorly.' Una took her washbag out of her drawer and a towel from the rail next to the window. 'What's going on out there?'

'I don't envy them – they're bringing the dead pilot and his gunner down.'

'Who is?' Una looked more closely at the small gang of men. They were wearing grey uniforms, progressing slowly because of their heavy burdens. 'Have they sent POWs to do their dirty work?'

'Yes, but hold your horses.' Brenda saw Una fling down her towel and start to put on her breeches and Aertex shirt. 'We don't know if Angelo is one of them. Honestly, Una – it's cold out there. You should stay in the warmth.'

Una didn't listen. She was dressed and out of the

room, hurrying along the landing without coat or hat until Brenda ran after her and made her put them on.

Joyce heard their voices and came out of the common room. 'What's up now?' She saw that Brenda was trying to reason with Una, who seemed determined to dash out of the front door. 'Una, aren't you supposed to be in bed?'

Angelo! Brenda mouthed at Joyce as Una rushed on.

'I see.' One word explained everything and Joyce joined Brenda on the doorstep in time to see the team of prisoners carry two stretchers covered with tarpaulins into the yard to one of two waiting Land Rovers. Three British guards stood beside one of the vehicles with rifles at the ready. Among the snow clearers on the drive, Ivy had stopped work and leaned on her shovel to watch the prisoners load the stretchers into the first vehicle.

From the top step Una recognized Angelo at once. He had his back turned to her and was sliding the second stretcher out of sight. She longed to run to him.

Joyce came up beside her and put a restraining hand on her arm. She shook her head.

It wouldn't be right, Una realized. The dead pilot and gunner had to be respected at all costs. She took a deep breath and stayed where she was.

Angelo and another prisoner closed the back door of the Land Rover. One of the guards spoke and handed something to him. He turned and came towards the house. When he saw Una he broke into a run and took the steps two at a time.

A look passed between them. His dark eyes widened and shone. She caught her breath.

He opened the palm of his right hand and showed her a small, shiny object. 'We find in plane.'

It was a green and gold Land Army badge. Una reached up to touch her hat band. The badge was missing. It must have come unclipped when she struggled through the fuselage to reach the gunner.

Angelo handed her the enamelled badge, bright as a jewel in the daylight. He closed her fingers over it. '*I* find,' he told her.

'Thank you.'

Her smile was like a burst of sunshine and he basked in its glow.

The guards were calling; Ivy and the others watched with eagle eyes. Joyce's steady hand still rested on Una's arm.

'I go now,' Angelo murmured. His heart swelled as he gazed at her. He knew *her* heart and the yielding sweetness of her body. He would carry her with him wherever he went.

Una held her badge. There was everything to say and no time in which to say it. Critical eyes were watching. Death stamped its presence.

He smiled at her then turned away, walked down the steps, across the yard and into the Land Rover containing the bodies.

'Good for you,' Brenda whispered to Una as the two vehicles pulled away.

'Yes – well done.' Joyce had seen the look of love and pitied them both. 'You'll see him again tomorrow. There'll be a little more time to talk.'

*

As the new week got underway, the crash-landing of the Dornier stayed at the forefront of everyone's minds. It took the place of Christmas as the main topic of conversation in farmhouses up and down the dale and the men who had made up the search party naturally heightened the importance of their role in capturing the surviving crewman. On his way to the Canadian Air Force base with a consignment of eggs, Horace intended to stop off at Home Farm, bearing tales for the Kelletts about his and Roland's contribution. He offered a lift to Jean and Dorothy on Cragg Hill and they arrived to find Joe giving Grace instructions about hosing down the dairy after she'd finished milking.

'I want it doing properly,' he snapped as he and his dog drove six of his cows across the yard. 'That floor has to be clean enough to eat your dinner off. And after you've finished in there, I want you to muck out the cowshed and lay fresh bedding.'

Jean and Dorothy piled out of Horace's van to hear Grace objecting that it was too much work for one Land Girl on her own to get through. 'You're not on your own,' Dorothy contradicted with an air of taking charge. 'Good morning, Joe. Good morning, Emily. No news of Frank, I don't suppose?'

'No, nothing.' There had been no sign of him since he'd broken into the hostel and Emily had almost given up hope of having him back before Christmas. She'd stopped mentioning him to Joe to avoid the stream of foul-mouthed invective that flowed from his lips every time she spoke their son's name and there was no one in the village with whom she could share her worries. So Frank remained at large, unlooked for and unmissed except by her.

Grace wasn't thrilled to discover that Dorothy and Jean were to be her fellow dairy maids for the day. One was bossy and the other notoriously work-shy. Besides, she would miss having Una and Brenda working alongside her.

'Where's the little one who uses plenty of elbow grease?' Joe cast a critical eye over the two new arrivals.

'You mean Una?' Jean spoke with quiet relish as she took her time to cross the yard. 'They're making her and Brenda stay at the hostel until they've got to the bottom of what went on last night.'

Grace frowned and was further irritated when Dorothy gave her a signal to show that for now their lips were sealed.

Horace hobbled up on his bandy legs and thrust a wooden crate containing half a dozen week-old chicks into Emily's arms. 'Keep 'em warm and well fed,' he instructed. 'And don't say I never give you anything.'

She thanked him for the chickens and carried them into the house.

'We missed you last night,' Horace told Joe before launching into a full account. 'It turned out that we needed all the help we could get. There was me and Roland, together with Cliff. Roland's lad Neville rounded up a few of the younger lads to join the search, but it was like looking for a needle in a haystack out on that fell.'

'It'd take more than that to get me out of bed in

the middle of the night.' The fact that the pilot had ditched his bombs without a thought for who or what they might hit had kept Joe snug and warm in his bed with a clear conscience. 'I take it Jerry was trying to limp back home to Germany?'

'Right first time.' Horace savoured every moment of the retelling. 'He just missed Fieldhead, didn't he, girls? Hilda kept them indoors and out of harm's way, quite rightly if you ask me. Of course, there's always one or two determined to take things into their own hands.' A glance in Grace's direction brought him up short. 'Present company excepted. You were there to keep an eye on Edgar.'

Grace's frown deepened as Jean took up the reins of gossip. 'Joyce and Brenda nearly gave Mrs Craven a heart attack. The poor old thing was running around like a headless chicken, counting and recounting who was or wasn't where they were supposed to be. As for Una Sharpe – well!' Jean's usually pale, apathetic expression grew flushed. 'I shouldn't really say this, Mr Kellett, but everyone knows that there'll have to be an investigation. Una was out on the fell longer than anyone. No one knows exactly what she got up to, but people are saying that the injured gunner was likely to have got clean away if it hadn't been for Grace here, together with Brenda and Bill—'

'None of that is true.' Grace cut across Jean's last sentence. 'Don't listen to them, Joe. It's Una we have to thank for bringing the prisoner in safely.'

'How do you know that?' Dorothy strong-armed her way into the developing argument. Her mid-brown

314

hair was pinned back severely from her forehead and her sturdy, curvaceous figure filled out both jacket and breeches. 'By my reckoning, there's a full hour or more when Una's movements are unaccounted for. It needs investigating, as Jean says.'

'Is this just you two having a go at Una?' Grace could hardly believe her ears. 'Or are the others of the same mind?'

'A lot of the girls agree with Jean and me – Ivy, for one.'

'Elsie? Kathleen?'

'I don't know about them – I haven't asked.' Dorothy folded her arms and outstared Grace. 'What I do know for certain is that Una hasn't been allowed to come to work today – that must tell you something, surely.'

Grace's voice rose to an indignant pitch. 'Yes – that she's exhausted from being outdoors for most of the night!'

'Or else she's under the shadow of suspicion,' Jean said in an aside that Horace caught.

'Yes – you never know with some of these Land Army girls.' He'd had a few bad experiences himself so knew what he was talking about. 'I've had flighty ones who would run away with half the village football team given the chance. And new arrivals who burst into tears at the drop of a hat. Some of them don't know one end of a hen or a cow from the other – you know that yourself, Joe.'

'I'm not listening to another word.' Angrier than she'd ever been in her life, Grace stalked off into the dairy to milk the final batch of cows.

Jean and Dorothy lingered to hear the last trickle of venom from the old men's mouths. 'Una Sharpe is the girl who accused Frank of attacking her,' Joe reminded Horace. 'She seems to be a right little troublemaker. I wouldn't be surprised if she *did* intend to help Jerry escape.'

'Well, that's disgusting.' Horace's short stature and bow legs gave him the air of Walt Disney's bad-tempered dwarf, ill matched to his tone of tub-thumping oratory. Neglecting to mention his early departure from the scene, he piled on the blame. 'We all have to pull together to get through this war. We can't have some silly slip of a girl feeling sorry for the enemy just because she rescues one of Hitler's blue-eyed *Übermenschen*. Where would we have ended up last night if our search party hadn't been on hand? Up the creek without a paddle – that's where.'

Dorothy leaned in towards Jean, winked at her then spoke in a whisper. 'Best not to bring up Una's Italian liaison, eh?'

'Best not.' Jean was taken aback by the strength of feeling behind Horace's rant. It made her uneasy to see how, from one little spark, wild rumours flared, and how close to the surface resentment towards Land Army girls ran amongst some old men in the village. She set off ahead of Dorothy towards the dairy, secretly alarmed by what had been set in motion.

CHAPTER EIGHTEEN

Ivy mulled over the various theories concerning Una's role during the previous night as she and Kathleen carried the snow-clearing shovels into an outhouse next to the row of disused stables at the back of the hostel. The ex-shorthand typist enjoyed giving her suspicions free rein as a juicier alternative to more run-of-the-mill preoccupations – how she would stretch her clothing coupons to cover three yards of pale-green jersey-knit to make a new dress for spring or how to alter the rota to avoid being sent to Winsill Edge the next day.

'Who wants to be plucking hundreds of chickens two days before Christmas?' she grumbled as they entered the brick shed. 'Winsill is way off the beaten track. Without a lift out there and back again, it'll be a miracle if I get back in time for the show.'

Kathleen gave her a dark look. 'You'd better not be late.'

'How can I help it if Mr Turnbull yacks on about his corns and his bunions? You know what he's like.'

You'll have to talk to him nicely – tell him we leave

here at half past five on the dot. The Canadians are sending a lorry to take us into Burnside.'

'Oh yes, we *like* the Canadians,' Ivy said with a sly smile as she leaned the spades against the wall. There was a jumble of apparatus from the old school stacked up in one corner: broken desks, two blackboard easels and a number of metal chairs, one of which Ivy made use of for a quick sit-down.

'We especially like Flight Lieutenant Mackenzie, according to your room-mate.'

Kathleen re-tied the blue-and-white striped scarf that she wore around her head. 'Oh no, Una's not interested in Mac,' she said casually. 'She has other fish to fry.'

'I meant Brenda.' Ivy had heard her over breakfast, wangling her way into being sent to the Penny Lane base after work that day. 'She claims she's happy to pick up tablecloths and serviettes for tomorrow's buffet, but we all know that's just a cover for flirting with the flight lieutenant. By the way, talking of other fish—'

'Wait.' Kathleen heard footsteps cross the yard. She poked her head around the door to see Joyce carrying a dish of cold rice pudding to the end stable where Tibbs, the hostel cat and chief rat-catcher, had taken up residence. 'It's all right – carry on.'

'Other fish and Una.' Ivy was determined to have her say. 'Did you see her and Angelo carrying on earlier?'

'I saw him give her something – yes.' Kathleen wasn't sure that this constituted 'carrying on' but she was content to snatch a few minutes in the outhouse before being allocated her next task – probably in the vegetable garden, digging leeks out of the frozen ground, if she knew her luck.

'She didn't even try to hide how she feels about him,' Ivy complained. 'If I were you, Kathleen, I'd have a word with her.'

'What about?'

'I'd remind her about Eunice, for a start. Tell her that's what happens if you don't keep up your guard against our Italian friends.'

Kathleen didn't like the way the conversation was going. As a matter of fact, she wasn't particularly keen on Ivy, who was thick as thieves with Jean and Dorothy, neither of whom had contributed much to the Christmas show. All three seemed to share a similar, sour outlook on life. 'Una knows how to look after herself, ta. Besides, it doesn't do to jump to conclusions.'

'I don't know why you're sticking up for her, especially after last night.' Ivy picked up a red tartan scarf that was draped over one of the easels and flicked it in Kathleen's direction. 'You know what everyone's calling her, don't you?'

'No, but I'm sure you're going to tell me.'

'Sly little turncoat – that's what.' Ivy rolled the words around her tongue as she idly wound the scarf around her neck. 'That's what you get for disappearing for hours on end with enemy POWs and airmen.'

'Oh, for heaven's sake!' Lost for words, Kathleen stormed out of the outhouse and bumped into Joyce who had been attracted by the sound of raised voices. She nodded towards the shed. 'Ivy's in there, saying nasty things about Una fraternizing with the enemy. Why don't you see if you can knock some sense into her?'

'Leave it to me.' Joyce pushed open the door to find Ivy tying a knot in the scarf and tucking the ends inside her coat. 'What are you doing with Una's scarf?' she demanded.

'Oh, it's hers, is it?' Ivy decided in a flash that attack was the best means of defence. 'So this is where she and Jerry disappeared to last night! They weren't out roaming the fell side – they were hidden away in here for part of the time, having a cosy little chinwag.'

Joyce rushed at Ivy, seized the scarf and tightened it around her throat. 'You take that back! You hear me? I won't have Una's name being dragged through the mud.'

Though Ivy was strong, Joyce was stronger. It was impossible to throw her off and she was in danger of being throttled. 'All right,' she gasped.

'Take it back?' Joyce slowly released her, keeping hold of one end of the scarf as she did so before shoving Ivy back against the easel, which clattered to the floor.

'All right, all right – keep your hair on.' Ivy too landed on the ground. She picked herself up and quickly made her way to the door where she tried to regain some ground. 'I'm only saying what everyone else is saying – Una took an age to hand the enemy gunner over to the search party last night. Then Grace and Brenda found her alone with him in Peggy Russell's barn. That surely has to make you stop and think.'

'Ivy McNamara, you make me sick!' Joyce strode to the door and slammed it after her. It clattered shut and she was left in the dark, clutching Una's scarf with a trembling hand. It was ten whole minutes before she felt calm enough to go back to the house. Meanwhile, she set the easel upright and picked up an overturned chair. She stacked the shovels more neatly then emerged from the outhouse and stared up at the first floor of the big house – at the room occupied by Una, Kathleen and Brenda. There was a figure at the window. The person saw her looking and moved quickly away. An unexpected shiver of doubt passed through Joyce as she pocketed Una's scarf and slowly crossed the yard.

It was mid afternoon when Edith drove herself out to Fieldhead. Bill had offered to take her but she'd refused.

'There's the matter of the Christmas rota to sort out,' she'd told him. 'And final arrangements to be made for tomorrow night's show. Then Hilda will want to discuss her report about last night's events before she sends it off to Area HQ. It could take until teatime.'

'I don't mind – let me drive you anyway.'

'No thank you, dear. You have too much to do as it is.' She'd insisted and he'd given in. They went their separate ways.

Edith tried hard to keep her mind fixed on her Land Army responsibilities, hardly noticing landmarks on her way. Driving gave her a measure of control – her gloved hands on the wheel, frequent glances in her overhead mirror, using her indicator, depressing the clutch every time she wanted to change gear. She concentrated on calculating wages and overtime due to each girl, on average hours and final arrangements for Christmas leave. She didn't think about the hospital.

'Stand by your beds,' Brenda remarked to Una when she saw Edith's car turn into the drive. They sat together in the common room, doing nothing much, hardly talking, each lost in a world of her own. 'Here comes trouble.'

Edith drew up in front of the main entrance. She noticed that the drive had been cleared and the slowly melting snow was neatly and evenly banked to either side. Hilda had spotted the car from her office window and was at the door to welcome her.

'How's Vince?' Hilda asked straight out. There was no telling from Edith's blank expression what the answer would be.

'Weak. Tired. He was sleeping when we left.' The staccato reply disguised an almost unbearable pressure that wasn't relieved by the answer she gave. Vince had survived the operation but he wasn't yet out of the woods, Dr Renshaw had explained. Recovery would be slow.

'Of course. Come into the office.' Hilda led the way across the hall. She sat Edith down then went to the common room to ask Brenda to make them both a cup of tea.

Weak. Not so much sleeping as drifting in and out of consciousness. Left alone, Edith admitted the truth to herself. Vince had lain with his eyes sunken into their sockets, wearing the pallor of a dead man, the rise and fall of his chest scarcely visible beneath the thin green blanket.

The heart surgeon was a small, bald man with steel-rimmed glasses and a quiet, calm voice that conveyed no emotion. 'The operation took a little longer than expected due to certain complications, which fortunately we were able to overcome. The effects of the anaesthetic won't wear off for several hours. I recommend that the patient has uninterrupted rest – in other words, no visitors until morning. Meanwhile, you should go home and wait for further news.'

Weak, tired, sleeping. Alive.

Bill had led her down the corridor out into the car park. The cold had cut through her. She'd been unable to speak all the way back to Burnside.

'Tea.' Hilda accepted the tray from Brenda who delivered it meekly and left straight away. She put in three teaspoons of sugar and stirred vigorously before positioning the cup in front of the troubled rep. 'Are you all right, Edith? Are you sure you shouldn't be at home resting?'

'Yes, thank you – I'm sure. Now, do you have a list of girls wishing to go home over Christmas?'

Hilda took the list out of a drawer. 'Only five have put their names down. Many live too far away. Some of the others – like Una, for instance – feel it's their duty to stay . . .'

'Yes, farm work doesn't grind to a complete halt just because it happens to be Christmas.' Edith studied the short list then sighed. 'I'm sorry I wasn't here to help you keep an eye on everyone last night. You had your hands full, I expect.'

'Yes, but Bill made it through the fog with Grace and Edgar.' Hilda wasn't sure how much Edith had heard so she trod carefully. 'He's probably given you an idea of what went on. Two airmen died but one survived the crash and was missing for a while. Bill had a hand in capturing him, so all's well that ends well, as they say.'

'He mentioned that three of our girls went out onto the fell and played their part in the rescue.'

'Together with Grace,' Hilda added.

Edith passed no comment on Grace's involvement. 'Brenda, Joyce and Una – am I right? I'm assuming they disregarded orders to the contrary?'

Edith's doggedness put Hilda on the defensive. A mottled flush crept up her neck. 'Joyce did. Brenda and Una took things into their own hands and left before I had a chance to issue the order. In any case, I dealt with them first thing this morning. I reminded them of their responsibilities as Land Girls and left it at that.'

'But this is a serious matter.' Edith was worried that the girls' disobedience would be bad for morale. 'You don't see it as a reason for possible referral to HQ?'

'Far from it. They're all much too valuable to us to pursue this any further. Take Joyce, for instance – she's been with us for over a year and she's one of the steadiest, most willing workers I've come across.'

'Joyce, maybe. But you can't say the same for Brenda and Una.' Unwilling to let the matter drop, Edith pushed her teacup and saucer to one side. 'Let me be frank, Hilda. Take Brenda, for a start – she may be a hard worker but she's not the most biddable of our girls.'

'She's spirited, I admit.'

'Quite so. And I've noticed that Una, by way of contrast, is a little naive.'

Hilda cocked her head enquiringly to one side.

'By which I mean that she doesn't quite know how to – shall we say – keep her distance from the Italian POWs.' It was Edith's turn to blush and look awkward. 'It came to my attention at Sunday's dress rehearsal.'

'Liaisons between our girls and the prisoners are not forbidden and I'm not even sure that it's our business,' Hilda said quickly. 'And I don't see how we can stop it either, unless we introduce a new rule that the Land Army can no longer send recruits to work alongside POWs.'

'No – we can't do that.' Edith thought for a while. 'But if Una's lack of worldliness has led her into an unsuitable friendship I do think that it behoves me as the local Land Army representative to have a word with her.'

Much as she wanted to resist Edith's stiff puritanism, Hilda could see her point. 'We don't want a repetition of what happened to Eunice – that's true. But I've given Una the day off to recover from her ordeal. Perhaps you would let me talk to her tomorrow morning, especially bearing in mind what else you have on your plate at the moment?'

Edith considered this as a way forward then nodded. 'Yes, by all means. I'll leave it to you.'

'Good.'

'Meanwhile, Hilda, please make sure that morale in the hostel doesn't suffer.'

'I'll do my best.' The warden's terseness signalled an end to this part of the conversation.

Edith took a red notebook from her handbag and opened it. 'Let's move on to the next item, shall we? I've had a complaint from Ivy that she hasn't been paid her overtime in full. Her hours don't tally with Horace Turnbull's. She has three extra hours at Winsill Edge for the week beginning Monday the eighth of December. Horace has two. Now, who's in the right, I wonder?'

Joyce shook the momentary doubt about Una from her mind as a dog shakes water from its back. What had she been thinking, to consider even for a second that Ivy's suspicions might be justified? She carried the red scarf straight up to Una's room and knocked on the door.

'Come in.' Feeling that she ought to be obeying orders, Una had come upstairs to rest soon after Hilda had taken Edith into her office. She'd been looking out of the bedroom window when Joyce had crossed the yard so wasn't surprised by her visit. 'This is nice. Come and sit on the bed. Is that my scarf you've got there?'

'Yes. Ivy found it in one of the outhouses.' Joyce handed it to her then sat uneasily at the end of the bed.

'I wondered where this had gone.' The scarf had been last year's Christmas present from Tom and she'd been sorry to have mislaid it. 'Where did you say Ivy found it?'

'In the outhouse where we store old school desks and such like – you know the one?'

'No, I don't think I do.'

'That's odd, then.' Odd, but a relief for Joyce to hear that Ivy's vicious suspicions were so easily proved wrong. 'Someone else must have found it lying around then forgotten to give it back to you. They must have left it there by mistake.'

'No harm done.' Una folded the soft woollen scarf then put it on her bedside cabinet. Noticing the edge of her precious carved box poking out from under her pillow, she blushed and was about to surreptitiously push it out of sight when she checked herself and drew it out into full view instead. 'It's where I keep Angelo's letters,' she confessed with touching openness. 'I read them every night – over and over again.'

Joyce let out a small sigh. 'Aah – young love!'

Stung by the amused tone, Una regretted showing Joyce the box and tucked it away under the pillow. 'Are you making fun of me?'

'I'm sorry. I didn't mean to.'

The sudden desire to stand up for herself and tell Joyce the whole truth carried Una forward in a breathless rush. 'It's all right. I know everyone thinks I'm daft – including you, it seems. But Angelo and I are truly in love and I don't care who knows it.'

'I don't think you're daft.'

'I've never felt like this – it's . . . I can't explain. It's wonderful. My heart almost bursts every time I see him. I think about him when I wake up and every minute of the day until I lay my head down at night. My dreams are full of him. Do you know what that's like?'

'Yes.'

'To love someone so much that every single thing he says and does makes you love him more. Every glance, every touch.'

'I do know.' Joyce's own heart ached for Una as well as for her own loss – and for all love that was threatened by this dreadful war.

'Every touch,' Una repeated as she hugged herself and rocked backwards and forwards.

'You mean?' There was a joyous, dreamy look on Una's face that to Joyce could only suggest one thing. 'Oh, Una!'

'It was . . . Angelo is . . .'

'What can I say?'

Suddenly Una broke free from the gossamer web of recent memory into the stark present. 'You won't tell anyone, will you?'

'Of course not.'

'I'm not ashamed of it. I just want to keep it to myself, that's all. Some of the girls already have it in for me and Angelo.'

'I know they do, but ignore them.' Joyce's advice was trotted out hard on the heels of Una's last remark, as if it had been rehearsed.

Una realized this and was on her guard. She stood up and walked across the room. 'Why, what are they saying about me? Tell me, Joyce – I want to know.'

Honest, plain-speaking Joyce had been brought to

the point where anything except the blunt truth would be unfair. 'If Ivy is anything to go by, it's not only talk of you and Angelo that you need to worry about. It's ridiculous, of course, but questions are also being asked about you and the German gunner.'

Una felt the fresh accusation like a hard blow to the stomach. She bent forward and struggled for breath.

Joyce put a hand on her back. 'I thought you ought to know.'

'Oh!' Una gasped then she pushed Joyce away with her elbow. 'Go away – please.'

'Hang on – there's no need to shoot the messenger. You've had a shock; let me stay until I'm sure you're all right.'

Una pulled herself upright then rushed to the door. 'Leave me alone!'

Joyce was left with no choice but still she hesitated. 'I'll find Brenda and send her up.'

'No, no one.' Una waited until Joyce was through the door then she slammed it hard. She took a jagged breath and staggered towards her bed, sank down on it. The ache in her stomach grew sharper, making her curl into a ball. *Questions about me and the gunner.* The desperate man who had stared death in the face. *Me and the gunner.* Free of the mangled wreckage, lost on the fell. *The gunner and me.* His face close to hers, her voice promising that she would let him escape and tell no one where he was. *Him crouched in the dark barn. Me hesitating and pitying him, not crying out for help.* Guilty as charged.

*

Brenda had made sure not to set off for Penny Lane until after Edith had left the hostel. 'I didn't want Mrs M to know about this little errand of mine,' she'd confided in Ivy and Kathleen as she'd zipped up her jacket and jammed her hat onto her head. There was an unusual air of aimlessness about the place, with the snow-clearing team sticking close to the house and no one interested in rehearsing for tomorrow's show despite Kathleen's urging. 'She'd only have tried to stop me.'

'Why – where are you off to?' Ivy was at the front door waiting for Dorothy and Jean to come back from work.

'To Penny Lane.' Brenda put on her gauntlets, ready for the off.

'At this hour?' It was already dark outside. Ivy guessed that Brenda was up to no good.

'Yes – to collect table linen for the trestle tables for tomorrow's buffet. I'll be there and back in an hour.'

'Table linen?' Ivy gave a knowing wink, which Kathleen and Brenda both ignored.

Brenda breezed outside and kick-started her bike. There was an adventure to be had in riding the Sloper down the lonely lane with its one headlight carving a path through the thick darkness, a thrill in negotiating the snow-altered landscape, slowing down for icy bends, leaning into them then pulling the bike upright again for the straight stretches – past Peggy's farm, on towards the village then taking a sharp turn up towards Swinsty Edge, over the white moor top to Penny Lane and the glinting yellow lights of the Canadian base.

She drove up to the gate and dismounted. 'My name's Miss Brenda Appleby,' she announced to a sentry she'd never seen before. 'I've come to see Flight Lieutenant Mackenzie. Please let him know I'm here.'

The guard spoke on the phone and within a minute a smiling Mac strode towards the gate. He was in uniform but without his hat, and his tie was loosened, the top button of his shirt undone. 'Come with me, Miss Appleby. Let's get you in out of the cold.'

'I can't stop long,' she told him as they walked towards the temporary canteen building attached to the back of the original Victorian house. It was a Nissen hut with a corrugated iron roof and a row of tables and chairs running down each side. At the far end was a pot-bellied stove radiating heat throughout the room and beyond that a smaller storeroom for cutlery, dishes and tablecloths. Food from the kitchens in the old house was wheeled on trolleys along a narrow connecting ramp.

'Long enough for a drink, I hope!' Mac grinned as they reached the storeroom and he lifted a whisky bottle and two glasses down from a shelf.

Brenda blinked in surprise then grinned back.

'Sit down.' There were two chairs and a folding card table in a corner of the room. He set down the glasses with a loud clink then poured two drinks. 'No ice, I'm afraid.'

'That's all right. I'm not keen on whisky so a few sips will do me.' *Oh, Brenda!* Silently she mocked her own naivety then raised her glass. The whisky hit the back of her throat and burned its way down.

Mac sat down opposite, his sturdy legs straddling the flimsy table legs. He studied her small, cute nose, full lips and big brown eyes with undisguised admiration. 'So, Miss Appleby . . .'

'So, Flight Lieutenant Mackenzie?' *What's so funny?* He was pretty darned good-looking, staring at her from under heavy eyelids, with a cleft in his clean-shaven, square chin and sporting the typical Canadian crew cut. But it felt odd for them to be squashed in a corner of a storeroom – not much more than a cupboard – with two glasses and a bottle of whisky.

'Are we all ready for the big event?' His hand rested loosely around the glass but he didn't drink.

'Oh – you mean the show? Yes, almost ready.' She drank again without thinking. Once more there was a burning sensation and this time she couldn't help coughing.

He didn't hide his amusement. 'I can't wait to see you doing a star turn. I guess you'll be in costume?'

She raised an eyebrow and told him that he would have to wait and see. 'About those tablecloths . . .'

He shrugged then leaned across the table to murmur words that at first she didn't pick up. 'You're my dream girl – you know that?'

The phrase sank in slowly. 'You're not so bad yourself,' she countered gamely. Events were moving fast and definitely in the right direction. *But keep your feet on the ground*, she reminded herself. *Don't let him think that a few sweet words are all it takes.*

'What I mean is – you're beautiful and you're fun too. I'm a sucker for that combination.'

'About the tablecloths,' she said again, but in a way that let him know she was flattered.

'You're my kind of girl, Brenda. I knew that the first time I saw you.' Mac stood up and raised her to her feet. He put his arms around her waist and moved in for a kiss. 'And you didn't really come for table linen, did you?'

She leaned the top half of her body away and put a finger against his puckered lips. The space around them seemed to have contracted, as if the walls were closing in. Or maybe it was the whisky that had already gone to her head. 'Steady on.'

He laughed and held her tighter. 'What am I – a horse? Gee-up, Neddy. Steady on!'

Before she knew it, he was kissing her long and hard on the mouth.

She pulled back and looked at him in astonishment. The kiss had taken her aback but now that it had happened she realized that she'd enjoyed it. 'You're a fast mover, Flight Lieutenant – I'll say that for you.'

Yeah, Miss Appleby, you know what they say – "Seize the day".' He leaned in and snatched a second kiss – a quick touch on her mouth before he moved his lips to her cheek and then her neck.

The soft, nibbling sensation made her almost coo with pleasure, but when one of his hands moved up her back and round to her front, she drew the line. 'I really can't stay long,' she insisted. He didn't release his hold so her only way out was to duck down and dodge sideways – not very dignified but an effective end to the petting that she'd been in danger of enjoying too much.

Mac frowned. 'Come on – you like it, I can tell.'

'I like *you*.' The difference between 'it' and 'you' mattered to Brenda. 'I'd like to get to know you better.'

'Then come on, what are we waiting for?' he wheedled, making another grab for her.

Brenda backed out of the storeroom. She came up against the hot stove and had to dodge again as Mac pursued her. 'That's not what I mean and you know it.'

At the far end of the room, Squadron Leader Aldridge came down the ramp connecting the Nissen hut to the main building. He took in the scene without comment. 'Mac, the kitchen needs to see the roll-call for the guys who got in earlier today – name, rank and number.'

'You bet,' he said with a last lingering look at Brenda.

'Right away.' Aldridge kept his eye on him as he walked the length of the room then switched his attention to the visitor. 'And how can we help you, young lady?'

Brenda cleared her throat and hoped that she wasn't blushing too fiercely. 'Table linen,' she said in a clear voice. 'For the buffet at the Institute tomorrow night – that's the reason I came.'

CHAPTER NINETEEN

Bill couldn't remember when he'd felt more tired. His limbs ached, his head felt heavy and he was shaking with cold. 'It's not even as if I've done a hard day's work,' he told Edgar when he encountered him in the pub yard. 'All I've done is drive my mother to the hospital and back then catch up with some paperwork.'

The two men stood in the cold night – one in a trilby hat, sports jacket and slacks with a woollen scarf tied high around his neck, the other bare-headed in his heavy RAF greatcoat – both tall and looking older than their years. In Bill's case it was his face that showed the strain of recent events – his posture was still upright, his shoulders broad and strong. But he frowned deeply and there were shadows under his eyes. Edgar, however, was thin and stooped. His limbs moved stiffly as he delved into his pocket, drew out a packet of cigarettes, tapped the bottom then pulled one out with his lips. He struck a match and the light flared to show his gaunt face and unshaven chin.

'It must be something to do with the late night we

had last night.' Bill struggled to make conversation. 'How's your hand, by the way? I see you've still got it strapped up.'

'What will they do with the Dornier?' Edgar's non sequitur came between deep drags on his cigarette. 'Will they leave it where it is?'

Bill nodded. 'It's not worth anyone's while trying to move it. It'll rust away to nothing soon enough.'

'What about the pilot and his gunner? What will they do with them?'

There was a glittering intensity in Edgar's eyes that Bill thought it best to ignore. 'Don't worry – a bunch of POWs saw to that.'

'And the one that got out?'

'He'll live. They're holding him at Beckwith Camp for the time being.'

Edgar had almost finished his cigarette before he spoke again. 'His problems aren't over yet.'

'No? Surely he's the lucky one?' Bill saw Edgar's lips stretch in a thin, humourless smile and quickly understood what lay behind it. 'I'm sorry – I wasn't thinking.'

'Jerry won't forget. I don't. No one does.' His throat constricted and his voice croaked with emotion.

'In time, maybe?'

Edgar blew out the last cloud of smoke then ground the butt under his foot. He looked at Bill, nodded briefly then walked off towards the forge.

Weary, overburdened and unsure, Bill was on the verge of turning around. It seemed he couldn't get anything right. He'd just upset his mother. She'd said he should stay in and get an early night. He'd snapped back that he wasn't a kid and would go to bed when he liked. He'd stormed out of the house and left her in tears.

To hell with it, he thought – a drink would do him good. There was also a glimmer of hope that he could spend time with the woman he loved, who might, in her most secret heart, still have feelings for him.

So he went into the bar, into a warm fug of tobacco smoke and the hum of voices, to the dull glint of pewter tankards displayed on a shelf behind the bar and to Grace, neatly dressed in a white blouse and grey skirt, serving pints to Jack and the Baxendales.

'Now then, Bill – what'll you have?' Maurice had been in the middle of praising Grace for keeping calm in the face of the enemy. Now he generously included Bill in the scenario that had led to the capture of the gunner. 'I didn't know you were a rugby fullback. That was some tackle you made last night. I saw it all from a safe distance – Jerry jumping out of the barn in a last-ditch bid for freedom and you bringing him down with a wallop.'

'I'll have a pint of bitter, please.' Bill smiled a nervous hello at Grace then watched the amber liquid foam and froth into the dimpled glass. They hadn't spoken since he'd dropped her and Edgar off in the early hours so he quietly answered her questions about his father then mentioned that he'd just had a short talk with Edgar.

Grace nodded hopefully. 'What did he say?'

'Not much. I put my foot in it, though. I said Una's

gunner was lucky to get out alive. He soon put me in my place.'

'He wasn't Una's gunner,' Grace said with a frown.

'You know what I mean.'

'I do, but others might not.' Signalling to her father that she was taking a short breather, she came out from behind the bar and went with Bill to the ingle-nook seat by the fire. 'I've overheard some nasty rumours,' she told him. 'Two of the girls I was working with seem convinced that, far from helping to capture that gunner, Una was trying to help him escape.'

'Come again?' Bill rolled his eyes and held his glass midway between the table and his mouth. Her physical closeness was all he wanted – to be able to breathe her in and to listen to her soft, rich voice.

'Just so – it's ridiculous. But Dorothy and Jean aren't the sort to let the truth get in the way of a good story. Horace and Joe were as bad. If we're not careful, Una will be taking the blame for something she didn't do – *guilty* until proved innocent.'

He put down his glass without drinking. 'It'll soon blow over. Tomorrow night's show will take every-one's mind off it.'

'Let's hope so.' Grace studied his face in the flickering glow of the coal fire. 'You're tired,' she said quietly. 'You've got other things on your mind.'

'You could say that.' He gave a wry smile. 'As you well know, most of my problems are of my own mak-ing. I'm talking about you and me, Grace. I've been a fool as far as that goes. That's why I went to the hostel to clear the air with Brenda.'

'Let's not go through it all again.' It didn't seem the time or the place to delve deep into emotions – something that neither of them was good at, in any case. Bob and Maurice had just found a seat at a nearby table and newcomers were trickling into the pub every few minutes. Before long, Grace would have to start serving again.

'I think Mum knows about us,' Bill said in a sudden, confessional rush.

Grace's eyes widened. 'Why?'

'She must have seen us through the curtain – when we walked up the path together.'

'I thought as much. What did she say?'

'That we looked very "friendly". She didn't even seem surprised – she just shook her head and then went up to bed.'

'And nothing since?' Grace remembered Edith's frostiness towards her at the Institute, when she'd dropped by with the two Foster women and the box of decorations.

'No. We haven't had a chance to talk about it.' Bill's weariness was partly to do with the hospital business, but also the result of the growing realization that, despite his visit to the hostel and despite the hours he and Grace had spent together searching for the missing gunner, he might after all have left it too late to mend things with Grace. It brought with it a crushing mixture of guilt and self-loathing, combined with a yearning to go back to what they had once been.

Grace thought she read defeat in his eyes. It unnerved her. Why was he so ready to give up after the efforts he'd made to put things right?

'I'm sorry, Grace. I can't seem to help letting you down.'

She didn't demur and instead made a confession of her own. 'I still can't rid myself of the notion that you felt something for Brenda. Did you?'

He shook his head then frowned. 'Something, I suppose. I'm not sure what.'

'But something?' Her heart fluttered then began to pound. This was a strange sort of self-punishment to subject herself to but she couldn't help it.

'A spark, I suppose. It was there and then it was gone. I'm sorry.'

'Please will you stop saying that?'

'I'm telling you the truth. Yes, Brenda made an impression, but no, I didn't want to follow it up. I was engaged to you.'

In her present mood, Grace read this not as a victory, but as another defeat. She had a vision of him drifting away from her, out to sea, and she lacked the strength or the certainty to pull him back. 'There's something I've been meaning to do,' she murmured. Quietly she asked him to come into the empty forge with her. He followed with a sense of dread, breathing in the ashes of the day's fire, the lingering smell of red-hot metal and a thread of cigarette smoke curling out of the shadows.

Grace dipped her hand into her pocket and drew out the small box containing her ruby and emerald ring. 'I've been meaning to return this as soon as I got the chance.'

A sharp pain shot through him – through his

heart, his spirit, the centre of his being. 'Keep it,' he pleaded. 'Maybe we can still work things out.'

'I can't keep it, Bill – not with things as they are.' She forced him to take it and make an ending, feeling her bruised heart break. 'I can't be sure of anything any more. It wouldn't be right for me to hang onto the ring.'

Their whispered words rose into the dark rafters. Grace turned and quietly left the forge.

Watching from the door that led out onto the back field, Edgar saw Bill bow his head – a strong man brought low.

After dinner that evening, Dorothy and Ivy collared Jean in the common room. 'Did you notice – you could've cut the atmosphere in there with a knife,' Dorothy began as Ivy made sure that there was no one else in the vicinity then shut the door for a private chat. 'Everyone sat as far away from Una as possible – well, everyone except Joyce and Brenda. They were the only ones prepared to risk sitting near her.'

'Yes, no one wants to get tarred with the same brush as Una.' Ivy's nostrils flared in disdain. She was a narrow girl in figure and in mind, with a long, pale face and a down-turned mouth. 'Even Kathleen went and sat at Elsie's end of the table. Oh, and by the way, I've made a complaint to Mrs C.'

'About Una?' Jean was taken by surprise. 'Weren't we supposed to do that altogether – all three of us, once we'd worked out what we were going to say?'

'Not about Una, silly.' Ivy picked up the poker and gave the fire a stir before carelessly chucking on more coal from the scuttle. 'I complained about Joyce and what she did to me in the outhouse – coming at me the way she did.'

'What did Mrs C say?' Jean felt queasy as she got a clear picture of the way things were lining up – her, Ivy and Dorothy versus Joyce, Brenda and Grace – three of the most popular Land Girls in the area. They would have to tread carefully if they wanted to get other Fieldhead girls on their side.

'She made a note of everything then she had the cheek to ask me what I'd said to make Joyce snap.'

'I hope you didn't tell her.' Dorothy's face was flushed from sitting too close to the newly stoked fire as she smirked at Jean. 'Mrs C doesn't need to know the full details, eh?'

'Do you take me for a simpleton? No – I steered well away from our theory about what Una and Jerry got up to in that barn and stuck to the part about me finding Una's scarf in the outhouse and Joyce threatening me and trying to choke me to death.'

'That's the ticket. In the end, it's just your word against Joyce.'

'And Kathleen,' Jean reminded them. 'Didn't you say she was there as well?'

Ivy frowned then jabbed the poker into the fire again. 'Yes, but she was long gone before Joyce muscled her way in. Dorothy's right – it's my word against Joyce's.'

'We all know what'll happen now.' Jean's all too apparent cautiousness irritated Ivy. 'Mrs C will have to report the incident to Mrs M and Joyce will be dealt with. Meanwhile, we'll keep on sending Una to Coventry and if anyone asks us why we're doing it, we'll tell them outright – Una is far too friendly with the enemy. Girls of her sort can't be trusted.'

Dorothy agreed. 'It's not just us who are thinking it. Jean, you've heard what they're saying in the village. There must be something in it for Joe and Horace to pin the same label on her.'

'I know, I know.' Why then was Jean still feeling uneasy?

'It's our duty to keep an eye on Una,' Ivy asserted. 'For King and country, and all that.'

'Yes.' Jean's long sigh was the sign that she'd brushed away her doubts. 'You're both right. Goodness knows, we ought not to trust Una Sharpe or, for that matter, anyone else who fails to do their utmost to bring Jerry to his knees.'

'Would you like me to cheer you both up?' Brenda asked her glum room-mates.

Kathleen had fretted her evening away by putting the final touches to tomorrow's programme while Una had written what might be her last letter to Angelo before Beckwith Camp was cleared of prisoners. Her hope was that they would be able to spend a few minutes together during the interval and that she would be able to hand the letter to him then.

'Come on – let me tell you about my latest amorous adventure.' Brenda sat cross-legged on her bed with her newly washed hair tucked behind her ears, her skin glowing and scented from her recent soak

343

in the bath. 'It involves our Canadian friend, Flight Lieutenant Mackenzie, who, it turns out, has quite a way with the ladies.'

'Oh, Brenda – what have you done now?' With an exaggerated, exasperated sigh, Kathleen looked up from the closing speech she was writing for the show. It was almost eleven and by rights all three of them should be fast asleep.

Una broke out of her latest reverie about Angelo. 'Have you been over to Penny Lane?'

'I certainly have. And who took me under his wing when I got there, but Mr Wonderful himself!'

'Oh, dearie, dearie me!' Kathleen put her speech to one side and steeled herself to hear the details. 'Are you ready for this, Una?'

'Yes, hold onto your hat,' Una said with a slow smile. There was no stopping Brenda when she was in this mood.

'Picture this. There's me in my dungarees and leather jacket and there's the handsome John Mackenzie, off duty with his shirt collar open and a smile as broad as you like, leading me into a titchy little store-room and before you know it, he's handing me a glass of whisky and telling me I'm his dream girl. Five seconds later I'm swooning in his arms and he's kissing me like I've never been kissed before. Cross my heart, he—'

'Hold on a second.' Kathleen tilted her head to one side. 'He said you were his dream girl?'

'Yes. What's wrong with that?'

'Nothing. I just thought—Oh, never mind. Carry on.' Kathleen picked up her speech to show that she was no longer interested in Brenda's romantic escapades.

'As I say, I was swept off my feet,' Brenda told Una. 'I was a little bit woozy from the whisky but I did manage to draw the line when Mac's hands began to . . . er . . . wander, shall we say?'

'Oh, please!' Una put her hands over her ears. 'Spare us.'

Laughing, Brenda reached for her hairbrush and ran it through her wet hair. 'Just wait until he gets an eyeful of me tomorrow night in all my glory – in my yellow dress with the white daisy pattern, my white sling-back sandals, with a touch of rouge and lipstick to finish the effect. You watch – he won't be able to keep his hands off me . . . again!'

'Are you sure that's what you want?' Una sensed a strain behind Brenda's gaiety – a flicker of uncertainty in her eyes.

'Yes, why not? No more playing the wallflower for me. I'll be the envy of the Jeans and Dorothys of this world when they see me cavorting with Mac.'

'But . . . ?' Una prompted, while Kathleen made an impatient display of picking up her washbag and towel then heading for the bathroom.

'But nothing,' Brenda insisted, putting down her brush and going to sit on Una's bed. 'Ignore me – I was only trying to cheer us all up.'

'I know.'

'I seem to have nettled Kathleen – I'm not sure why.' Brenda felt her own mood plummet. 'Then again, everyone's been down in the mouth today, which shouldn't come as any surprise after last night.

How are you bearing up, Una? Have you got over the shock?'

Una ran her fingers along the edge of her sheet and avoided looking at Brenda. 'Did Joyce mention what some of the others are saying about me?'

'That you were secretly on the gunner's side? She didn't have to – Jean and her cronies made it obvious. But you know what I think? I'm absolutely, one hundred per cent certain that the best way to deal with this situation is to ignore them. Keep in mind what really happened – that you were the one who kept your head while the rest of us were running around from pillar to post, not getting anywhere. Without you, he'd have got clean away.'

Una felt hot tears well up. She began to concertina the sheet between her fingers.

'What is it?' Brenda asked gently.

'The trouble is there might be a grain of truth in what they're saying.' The tears spilled over and cooled on her cheeks. 'I didn't feel towards him the way we're meant to. We're all supposed to hate the enemy, aren't we? And I didn't.'

Brenda sat quietly, waiting for her to go on.

'He'd watched two of his friends die a nasty death and he nearly died himself. And do you know something? He might have been a big, strong chap but his eyes were frightened – when I found him inside the plane and afterwards when he found his way down to the road, when he made me go with him into Peggy's barn. He was scared to death. And I felt sorry for him. There, I've said it.'

'It's only natural. That doesn't turn you into a traitor, if that's what you're afraid of.'

'But I could have called out to Grace and you earlier if I'd wanted.' Seconds had ticked by as the gunner had crouched in the barn – sickle in hand – when she, Una, had teetered on the brink. Had she committed treachery in those moments when she'd been caught between pity and duty and had failed to act?

Brenda took her hands in hers and spoke softly. 'Listen to me: you're no more a traitor than the rest of us. I won't have you thinking this way. Of course you felt sorry for the poor soul – who wouldn't? But you were the brave one who crawled into that plane without knowing what you were going to find. You were the one who stayed in there when any moment the whole thing might have gone up in flames. Without you, we'd never have got him out. You saved a man's life – do you hear me?'

Una nodded. 'I'm mixed up. It's all a jumble inside my head.'

'Because you were bang in the middle of it – that's why. It'll take a while for you to see straight again, but when you do you'll find that I'm right. I'll say it again – feeling sorry for someone is not the same as helping them to escape. You have nothing to blame yourself for.'

'And Angelo?' Una needed one last reassurance.

Brenda squeezed her hands and smiled. 'You love him. How can that be wrong?'

'I do love him.' It was one certainty in a shifting, dangerous world. Una squeezed back. 'And he loves me.'

*

For the first time since she'd arrived at Fieldhead, Joyce spent the night wishing she was elsewhere. While her room-mates slept and the clock crept towards six o'clock, she stood at the window, looking out on the bleak woodland scene and thinking of the rolling hills of Warwickshire, of apple orchards frothy with pink blossom, of timbered cottages with thatched roofs, of sedate swans sailing along the tranquil river and of sheep grazing the pastures of her father's farm. She was aware that it was all seen through the rosy, hopeless glow of nostalgia – nevertheless, the pictures and sounds filled her mind. She heard her father's excited voice calling up the stairs to her when she was a child. *Joyce, get dressed. Come down and see our first lambs – two sets of twins.* It was still dark and the barn was lit by paraffin lamps. Four newborn lambs nestled in the yellow straw. Later, much later, the unmistakable sound of Walter's early-morning footsteps crossing the empty farmyard – long strides before he flung open the door and found her struggling with her father who lay slumped over the kitchen table, dead to the world. 'Leave him to me,' he said, kicking away the bottles that rolled under his feet. 'Go on outside, Joyce. I'll sort him out.' But it was too late. One week after that, everything had gone: the farm to creditors, her father to drink and despair and Walter back to the navy.

I'm better off up here in Yorkshire, she decided. Here where memories of home flitted into her consciousness only occasionally, where she could at least feel she was working hard and doing some good.

I'll be glad to get Christmas over. With a bit of luck all the fuss surrounding Una and the Dornier will have died down and we'll be back to normal. Just ditch digging and egg collecting, milking and mucking out, and looking forward to spring and the uplifting work of turning the dark soil with the keen steel blade of the plough, ready for new growth.

A movement caught her attention in the yard below – a door swinging open, a long shadow on the stone flags. Or had she imagined it? A glance at her watch told her that it was still two hours before dawn. The movement of the door had been no more than the wind blowing, the shadow cast by the moon through tree branches. And yet she wasn't convinced. She looked more closely to see that the open door belonged to the outhouse where Ivy had found Una's scarf. That did it – Joyce would get dressed and then go down and take a look, not knowing what to expect, only wanting to make sure that she hadn't been imagining things after all.

She tiptoed downstairs carrying her shoes and a torch. The house was still asleep. There were no lights in the corridor leading to the kitchen, no sign of Hilda or any of the other girls. Outside in the yard, Tibbs the cat stalked towards her, green eyes glaring. 'I'm sorry, Puss, I haven't got any food for you,' she murmured. The cat flicked her tail and walked on.

Of course – it must have been Tibbs casting long shadows, weaving in and out of the row of outhouses. Joyce was on the point of turning back but one small niggle prevented her. Yesterday, amid the jumble of desks and chairs, Una's bright red tartan scarf had stood out, instantly recognizable in the gloom. The fiery argument with Ivy had happened in a flash, but in the split second before that, Joyce had seen something else out of the corner of her eye that she'd meant to follow up. Afterwards it had completely slipped her mind until this moment when she stood at the open door.

It was worth a look now, she decided. She directed her torch until its beam fell on the upturned desks, entering the musty space but making sure that she propped open the door with the nearest chair. The last thing she wanted to do was somehow to get trapped inside and have to call for help. She looked again at the easels and desks and spotted something white tucked between them and the wall. She reached for it and pulled out a small handkerchief with a lace edging and pale-blue embroidered flowers in one corner. When she felt in the crevice a second time, she found something even more surprising – a neatly rolled nylon stocking, soft and silky to the touch.

Joyce shone the torch on the objects that she held in the palm of her hand. Though she couldn't prove it, she felt convinced that both belonged to Una. The thought made the hairs at the back of her neck stand on end. What on earth were Una's scarf, handkerchief and stocking doing here in the disused outhouse? She shook off an encroaching shudder then dragged the chair away from the door, catching it before it closed. She swung the torch around the yard, shrugging off the idea that someone was watching her and making her way back towards the house. She entered through the back door into the kitchen, to come face to face with Hilda.

'Gracious, you frightened the life out of me!' Hilda stood in her slippers and flowered overall with rolling pin raised, ready to strike. She had a big pan of porridge on the stove behind her and rows of bowls set out on the table.

Joyce stared at her without speaking.

'For goodness' sake, Joyce, come in and close that door. Turn off your torch – don't waste the battery. Where have you been?'

'I found these in the outhouse.' Joyce handed over the gauzy stocking and the handkerchief. 'I think they're Una's.'

'What were they . . . ? What were you . . . ?' Confusion puckered Hilda's lips and creased her forehead.

'I haven't the faintest idea what they were doing there – or her scarf, either.' Finding Hilda in the kitchen had tipped Joyce further off balance and the words tumbled out. 'I thought I saw someone in the yard so I came downstairs to check.'

'Stop right there.' Hearing the word 'scarf' reminded the warden of the previous day's incident with Ivy. 'What do you mean by throttling a fellow Land Girl with Una's scarf?'

Joyce felt the blood rush to her cold cheeks. 'I'm sorry but Ivy said some rotten things about Una.'

'And you stood up for her?' Though Hilda couldn't afford to show partiality, she found it easy to imagine Joyce sticking up for her friends and equally easy to picture Ivy being mean spirited. 'Let's get one thing

351

straight – if you have a dispute with a fellow worker, you must always come to me.'

'I know that. I'm sorry.' Joyce's thoughts whirled chaotically and then suddenly fell into place. 'Frank Kellett!'

Hilda shot her a quizzical look.

'Don't you see? These three things – Una's scarf, the stocking, the lace handkerchief – they mean that Frank has been back. He's been here, in this building without anyone knowing. He's most likely been up to her room!'

'But why?' There was no rhyme or reason that Hilda could work out. She stared at the flimsy objects draped over her palm.

Joyce spoke loudly and with conviction. 'Because, in his odd way, Frank is in love with Una.'

The truth of this and the trouble that it brought with it struck Hilda so hard that she had to sit down.

'He can't say it in words so he shows it by following her around. Then, after he's been beaten senseless by his father . . .'

'Yes, what did Frank do to deserve that?'

'Maybe Una isn't the first one. Some of the girls here say that Frank followed Eunice around too.'

'So perhaps Joe knew the signs and wanted to stop it happening again.' Hilda closed her eyes and sighed. 'Yes – more than likely.'

'Frank was punished and ran off – we know that much.' Joyce followed her train of thought to its conclusion. 'So he grows desperate. He follows Una to where she lives. She finds him in the kitchen and doesn't understand what he's doing there. He still can't get through to her and she falls over and hits her head. Then he pulls out the knife and threatens us, you call the police and so it goes on, out of Frank's control. It's only after things have calmed down that he dares to come back. He finds that the closest he can get to Una is through bits of clothing that belong to her.' Joyce took back the stocking and dangled it in front of Hilda. 'So he breaks into the hostel and steals whatever he can lay his hands on.'

'We must call the police again,' Hilda decided. 'We must warn Una. We mustn't let her out of our sight.'

'*If* I'm right,' Joyce agreed. 'First we have to make sure that these things do belong to her – without worrying her, I mean.'

'Yes, it wouldn't do to upset her without good reason. How will you find out?'

'I'll wait until she comes down for breakfast then I'll take a look in her drawer. There may be other hankies the same as this one.'

'Yes and report straight back to me.' Beset by fresh worries heaped onto her lap two days before Christmas, the warden agreed to Joyce's plan perhaps too readily. What with dead Germans on the fell, a madman on the loose and loud grumblings in the ranks, Hilda didn't know which way to turn.

CHAPTER TWENTY

It didn't take Joyce long to prove her theory. While everyone was at breakfast, she slipped into Una's room and went through her things, lifting the neatly folded jumpers and blouses, the silky underwear and headscarves until, at the back of the drawer, she came to small items such as handkerchiefs, socks and stockings. Her hand hovered over them as a ripple of guilt ran through her. These things were highly personal and it felt wrong to be rummaging in someone else's drawer. Worse still, it placed Joyce in Frank Kellett's surreptitious shoes.

There were faint voices in the hallway followed by the opening and closing of the front door. It meant that breakfast was coming to an end.

If Joyce was right, Frank had done exactly this – waiting for his moment before creeping upstairs and along the corridor, coming into the room and searching the chest of drawers until he found out which one belonged to Una. Deaf Frank in his worn-down boots and threadbare jacket, with his sunken eyes and hangdog look, rummaging through her white petticoats, fingering her brassiere and suspender belt,

354

lifting up one of her stockings. He would have had to rely on vibrations on the stairs to warn him of interruptions. What if Brenda or Kathleen had approached the room – what then? Joyce glanced at the sash window and imagined him sliding it open and squatting on the stone sill, reaching for a nearby drainpipe to shimmy down, then away across the yard with his nylon trophy. She shuddered then lifted out a small pile of lace handkerchiefs – one, two, three, four small linen squares edged with lace and decorated with pale-blue embroidered flowers.

'How's Una?' Grace asked Brenda and Joyce when they came knocking at the door of the Blackmith's Arms at nine o'clock that morning. They were armed with snow-clearing shovels, wrapped in coats and scarves, with their slouch hats tilted low over their foreheads to protect them from light flurries of snowflakes blowing in on a northerly wind.

'She still has her heart set on staying here over Christmas,' Brenda explained.

'Is that out of a sense of duty, or does a certain Angelo have something to do with it?'

'A bit of both, I expect. Anyway, Ma C's kept her on light duties for the day,' Brenda explained. 'Some of the farmers are winding down so there's not as much call for Land Army labour until after Christmas. That's why we've been sent to clear the Institute yard, ready for tonight. You're to join us for a morning's work snow shifting.'

'Says who?' According to Grace's rota she was due at Brigg Farm.

'Says Ma C.' Brenda looked up at the sky and wondered if there was any point starting work while the snow continued to fall. 'Mrs M has handed everything over to her while Mr M is in hospital. Our orders are to work here until midday then do half a day out at Brigg Farm.'

While Grace went to fetch her coat and hat, Joyce followed Brenda's gaze. 'What's the weather forecast for today?'

'Snow at first then blue skies later. I reckon we should hold off until it stops snowing. We could get the Institute key off Bob Baxendale and start setting out chairs for tonight's performance instead.'

'Good idea.' Joyce was distracted by the snow dancing through the air before settling and melting on her face. She was fretting about leaving Una under Hilda's watchful eye.

'Couldn't she come to Burnside with Brenda and me?' she'd asked the warden after she'd gone to the office and reported her latest findings about Frank.

Mother-hen Hilda had been adamant. 'No, it's best for her to stay here. I'll find some housework for her to do.'

'We'd look after her . . .' Joyce had tried to insist but Hilda had shooed her out of the office. 'Will you telephone the police?' she'd asked before the door was shut in her face.

No answer. And when Joyce had tutted and muttered a futile protest, she'd seen Jean, Ivy and Dorothy hugger-mugger in a corner, casting dark looks in her direction.

'What's up?' Ivy had called across the hallway. 'You've got a face like thunder.'

'Mind your own business,' Joyce had retorted before rushing off.

'What's up with you?' Brenda unconsciously echoed Ivy as Grace rejoined them. They crossed the road together and went to rouse the caretaker who lived in the end of terrace house next door to the Institute.

'Nothing. I'm concerned about Una, that's all.'

'We all are,' Brenda agreed. There was a pause while Bob answered their knock then produced the large iron key from his pocket.

'You can save me a job by sweeping the floor while you're at it,' he said slyly.

'As long as you promise to help us set out buffet tables in the kitchen before our audience arrives,' Brenda shot back.

The deal was done and Brenda, Grace and Joyce set about their morning's work. They used wide, soft brooms to sweep up dust, old sweet wrappers and cigarette ends from under cast-iron radiators and generally make the hall ready.

'The Christmas tree looks a bit bare,' Joyce remarked as she swept behind it. 'It needs more baubles.'

Grace stood back and examined it. 'We've used everything in Alice Foster's box, but I've forgotten to bring the silver pine cones that you brought.'

'Never mind the baubles, what about Una?' Joyce brought them back to their original topic. 'I'm worried about what Jean and Co. are up to behind her back.'

The others agreed. 'Jean never took to Una from the start,' Brenda pointed out.

'Well, I did,' Grace said firmly. 'I'd stick up for her any day.'

'You might have to.' Joyce rested her broom against the wall and gathered them into the corner close to the tree. 'This mustn't go any further until I know what Mrs C intends to do about it, but I've found out that Frank Kellett is still pestering Una – well, worse than that, he's broken into the hostel again and started stealing her things.'

There was a shocked intake of breath and a stunned silence.

'Are you sure?' Grace asked after she'd gathered her thoughts. So much had happened lately that Frank seemed to have slipped from everyone's thoughts. Even Emily and Joe rarely mentioned him.

Joyce recounted the evidence to more shocked gasps. 'Think about it – who else but Frank would do something like that?'

'You're right.' Brenda kept her voice down because of an uneasy sensation that someone might be eavesdropping. She glanced quickly around the empty hall to convince herself that this wasn't true. 'How did Una react?'

'I don't know if Mrs C has told her yet.' This was the crux of what was making Joyce so uneasy – surely Una had the right to know that Frank was back in the picture and in the worst possible way. 'Perhaps that's why she's kept her at Fieldhead – so she can take her to one side to put her in the picture then explain what action she's going to take.'

'Let's hope so.' Like Brenda, Grace was rattled by the news. 'In the meantime, there must be something we can do.'

'You mean you, me and Joyce?' Brenda brightened at the idea. 'You're right – it can't be too hard to track down Frank Kellett once we set our minds to it. Between us, we know every inch of these hills and dales – better than Policeman Plod, at any rate. You know how long the boys in blue take to organize themselves.'

'Especially coming up to Christmas.' In Joyce's mind, the only obstacle was tonight's performance, which was taking up most of their spare time. But then, when she thought about it, perhaps the show was a good opportunity to pass the word around. 'There'll be more than sixty people in this hall later,' she realized. 'Each with a sharp pair of eyes. We'll let them know who we're looking for and pick up any information we can – who might have seen Frank lately, whether or not he's been back to Beckwith Camp for food, and so on. Then, if anyone happens to spot him, they can nab him and turn him in.'

'That's a tip-top idea,' Brenda agreed. 'And after tonight's over and done with, we can ask for an extra day off and spend the whole of tomorrow scouring the countryside for him.'

The plan made them feel better so Grace turned her mind back to the silver pine cones stored at home in a box under the kitchen sink. 'I won't be long,' she promised Brenda and Joyce before she slipped across the road to fetch them.

The door to the forge was open and lanky,

lackadaisical Neville stood in the arched entrance with old Major while Cliff was hard at work fashioning an outsize metal shoe. Grace's father was dressed in his leather apron over some faded blue overalls, sleeves rolled up and his bald head covered by a worn flat cap.

He pulled a red-hot shoe from the furnace with a long pair of tongs, placed it on the anvil and, with sparks flying in every direction, began to beat it into shape.

'Flippin' horse has lost another shoe,' Neville complained over the clang of the hammer when he saw Grace.

She smiled briefly and hurried on. Inside the house, she found Edgar sitting by the kitchen fire, leafing through her sketchbook. He looked up at her with new interest. He'd made the effort to shave and get dressed in shirt and dark trousers held up by braces, but hadn't bothered about a collar and tie. He still wore the bandage that Joyce had tied around his left hand. 'Who drew these?'

'Me,' she said simply before blushing and trying to snatch the book away.

He moved it out of reach and held it open at a page containing a pencil drawing of his own face in profile, hair flopping forward, mouth open and eyes closed. 'When did you do this?'

'A few days ago; while you were nodding off by the fire.'

Edgar studied the sketch. 'I look like an old man – bags under my eyes, lines on my forehead, the whole lot.'

'You're not old,' she told him as she took the book away then searched under the sink for the cones. There was a smell of shaving foam on his warm skin and she picked up the faintest hint of the old, slightly vain Edgar in the way he complained about how she'd drawn him. She smiled to herself. 'By the way, you don't happen to have seen Frank lately, do you?'

Edgar stood up and put his uninjured hand in his trouser pocket. 'Why, what's he done now?'

She pulled the box out then stood up to face him. 'I can't tell you – it's not common knowledge yet. But if you do spot him, will you let me know?'

'Actually, I have seen him and he was looking like death warmed up,' Edgar said slowly.

'When?'

'Twice.' He rattled the change in his pocket. 'He was hanging around in the back field last night, after the pub had shut. I bumped into him when I went for a walk.'

'You should've told someone,' Grace said with a frown. 'You know the police are after him for breaking into the hostel.' She resisted asking him why he'd been walking alone in the field at midnight.

'I didn't have the heart,' Edgar admitted. 'The poor bugger scarpered as soon as he saw me. Anyway, he's harmless, if you ask me.'

'I don't.' Her angry retort surprised them both. 'Ask you, that is. And if you must know, Frank has been making even more of a nuisance of himself since the first break-in. You say you've seen him twice. When was the first time?'

'The night before that – Sunday, when the Dornier

came down.' It came as another surprise that he could say these words out loud without stammering or shaking. Staring at his injured hand, he slowly began to untie the bandage. 'Frank was heading for one of the outhouses at the back of the hostel. I spotted him through the sick-room window, while Joyce was seeing to this hand. I reckoned it was the only place he could find to keep warm.' Edgar unwound the white gauze, took away the iodine-stained lint pad then laid it on the draining board. He flexed his fingers and examined the scabs. 'Starting to heal nicely,' he murmured. Then, before Grace could hurry back to tell Brenda and Joyce what she'd just learned, he went to the door and blocked her exit.

He looked at her fair and square. 'I was there last night when you gave Bill his engagement ring back.'

'In the forge?' Edgar's eyes and voice were clear – that's what she noticed more than anything else. He wasn't miles away in a world of burning planes and dying comrades. He was there in the room with her.

He nodded. 'You didn't see me but I saw you.'

'Edgar, I'm busy. I don't want to talk about it.' Try as she might, she couldn't get past him with her box of decorations.

'It didn't make sense to me – giving the ring back. Not when you love him and he loves you.'

When Brenda returned the Institute key to Bob Baxendale at midday, she went back to Joyce and Grace with the news that several POWs were being sent over to Burnside early with supplies for the interval buffet table.

362

'Bob couldn't name names but I'd say there was a fair chance of Angelo being amongst them as usual,' she predicted with a gleam in her eye. 'What do you say to me cycling back to Fieldhead and letting Una know? Wouldn't she just love to be here when he arrives?'

'You'll have to snatch her from under Mrs C's wing first,' Joyce warned.

They were sitting eating sausage rolls in the pub porch, looking out at an inch of fresh snow cover and clearing skies.

'But it would mean the world to Una.' Grace approved of Brenda's plan. 'Joyce and I will go on ahead while you pass on the message. We'll see you up at Brigg Farm later.'

So Joyce and Grace finished their packed lunches and cycled off, passing Neville riding bareback as they neared their journey's end. The grey carthorse plodded steadily up Cragg Hill, hooves sliding over packed snow, tossing his tangled mane and breathing out vast clouds of steam through his wide nostrils. Neville's legs dangled to either side of his round flanks, heels down and toes up, whistling as he went.

'Give us a tow,' he called out as the women overtook him.

'Huh, it'd take a Cruiser tank to pull you up this hill.' Joyce was breathing hard and her legs ached.

Grace had no breath to spare so she cycled silently on, grateful to turn up the rough, ice-bound lane then walk her bike the final few hundred yards until they came to the spread of low farm buildings on the brow of the hill.

Roland greeted them from the hayloft above Major's stable. 'Have you seen any sign of that half-baked son of mine?' he shouted to Joyce as she propped her bike against a wall.

'Neville's on his way.' Joyce saw Ivy emerge from the stable with a barrow load of soiled straw. She managed a civil greeting then waited with Grace for instructions from Roland.

Ivy returned the greeting then wheeled the barrow around the back of the stable. Soon afterwards the farmer descended the stone steps from the loft. He dusted hay from his jacket and sneezed loudly. 'Now that you two have decided to put in an appearance, you might as well load turnips onto the cart, ready to feed the sheep in the bottom field,' he said grudgingly. 'You'll need that wheelbarrow when Ivy's finished with it. Don't stand around doing nothing – make a ramp for it with those two planks of wood.'

The work was well underway when Major plodded into the yard with his passenger aboard. Neville hopped off the horse's back and opened the stable door. As he passed close to the half-loaded cart, he stopped to tap his top pocket and whisper in Grace's ear. 'I've got a letter for your friend from a certain person. Shall I give it to you for you to pass on? I'd need a nice shiny sixpence for my trouble, mind you.'

'You've already been paid, you cheeky thing!' Grace watched him pull out the letter but had to stand aside when Ivy came out of the stable and sidled past Major who stamped his feet impatiently. The horse dwarfed them all with his high withers, broad back and enormous head.

'You three – get out of the road!' Roland yelled from the farmhouse door.

They shuffled to one side to let Major enter his stable then Neville closed and bolted the door.

As he did this, Ivy snatched the letter out of his hand. It was written in pencil on a piece of lined paper taken from a cheap notebook. 'What's this?' she said as she began to read its contents out loud. *'My Oona, my love. I dream of holding you. Always I dream . . .'*

She stopped and laughed, waving Angelo's letter under Grace's nose. 'Don't tell me – this is from the Italian gigolo!'

'Give it to me.' Grace fixed Ivy with a stone-cold stare.

'I think of you always, every moment . . .'

'I said, give it to me.' To have Una and Angelo exposed to Ivy's ridicule was more than Grace could bear. With a rapid flick of her hand, she tried to take the letter from her. The thin paper tore in half, leaving Ivy with Angelo's signature and a row of kisses.

Ivy laughed again. Joyce put aside the wheelbarrow and strode across the yard to join them.

If Ivy felt outnumbered and intimidated, she didn't show it. 'If it's not bad enough for Una to fraternize with the enemy whenever she gets half a chance, you two have to encourage her,' she mocked.

'What do you mean by that?' Grace had regained her self-control. She held her head high and didn't budge as Ivy attempted to push past.

'You're always sticking up for her, aren't you? You

and Kathleen, and Brenda as well. In fact, Brenda's the worst of the lot.'

'We don't have to stick up for Una – she can hold her own against you and your pals.' Joyce used the last word disparagingly to show just how little she thought of Ivy, Jean and Dorothy.

'Girls, girls!' Neville came between Joyce and Ivy and pushed them apart. 'Simmer down.'

Ivy pushed back, shoving the scrap of paper at him. 'You're as bad!' she said furiously. 'Carrying messages and sneaking about. What have you got to say about that, Mr Thomson?'

Roland strode towards them. 'What's going on? Why aren't you loading the cart?'

Ivy ran to meet him. She was a match in height for the wiry, grey-haired farmer and gesticulated wildly as she spoke. 'Did you know that Neville is in cahoots with a girl from our hostel? He takes silly love letters from Una Sharpe to an Italian at the camp and vice versa.'

'Does he now?' Roland narrowed his eyes then made a beeline for his son. 'Is that right?'

Neville stuffed the torn note into his pocket. 'What if I do? There's no law against me making a bit of pocket money on the side.'

Ashamed to be a part of the unseemly squabble, Grace held the other half of the note in her shaking hand. Joyce sighed and fumed inwardly.

Ivy pointed to the scrap of paper. 'There's the evidence. And, would you believe it, these two don't see anything wrong in it.'

Slowly Roland made sense of what was going on.

'Is Una Sharpe the lass who pulled the Jerry gunner out of the plane wreck?' he asked Grace.

A furious energy pushed Ivy to jump in with an answer. 'That's the very one. And, if you remember, she went AWOL with him for a couple of hours afterwards. No one knows where they went or what they got up to.'

Roland looked from Ivy to Neville then to Grace and Joyce. 'Una Sharpe?' he repeated with a perplexed shake of his head.

'Yes. We've got a turncoat among us.' Ivy's sense of self-importance made her puff out her chest like an angry robin. 'I'm not afraid to call a spade a spade, Mr Thomson. Una's only been at Fieldhead for a few weeks but ever since she came, her antics have turned the whole place upside down.'

While Grace shook and Joyce fumed, Neville took an uncoordinated, angular step forward. 'Don't listen to her, Dad. She's talking a load of old codswallop.'

Roland couldn't have been more surprised if Neville had told him that Major had won the Grand National. 'Why are you sticking your oar in?' he grunted.

'Because it's not fair, that's why.' Neville's shoulders went back and his chin came forward as he squared up to Ivy. 'When has Una ever put a foot wrong? Give her a job and she does it. She's never late and she works twice as hard as some I could mention.'

'Yes, all right, Neville.' At this rate, it would be too late to hitch Major up to the cart and take the turnips down to the sheep in the bottom field. Roland turned on his heel and went to fetch a halter from the hook by the stable door.

Neville followed him. 'I mean it, Dad. Una doesn't deserve to have her name dragged through the mud.'

'A fat lot you care,' his father retorted as he got ready to unbolt the stable door. 'All you mind about is losing your precious pocket money.'

Major appeared at the door. He kicked it with a front hoof the size of a dinner plate and the low boom echoed around the yard.

'Here – give me that.' Neville took the halter and buckled it around Major's head then let him out. 'You're wrong,' he told his father as he steered Major a few inches too close to where Ivy stood, forcing her to take a quick step back. Before she could protest, he muttered a few words under his breath, to the slow rhythm of his horse's clopping hooves – one short syllable at a time so there could be no mistake. 'You leave Una alone, or else.'

'The tide is starting to turn in Una's favour,' Grace told Brenda when she turned up on her motor bike late in the afternoon. Joyce had ridden on the cart with Neville and Ivy to feed the sheep, leaving Grace to tidy up the yard. 'Neville put Ivy in her place good and proper.'

'Oh, I wish I'd been here to see that.' Brenda leaned on the wall overlooking the Thomsons' land. In the valley bottom she saw a hundred sheep running from all directions towards the turnip-laden horse and cart. They looked grey against the white hillside. 'Good for Neville, at any rate.'

'I know. He really meant what he said. How is Una, by the way?'

'How do you think?' Brenda had cycled back to Fieldhead as planned. She'd found Una moping in their room, fresh from an interview with Mrs Craven, who'd informed her about the latest developments. 'I could see that she was shaken up by the news of Frank stealing her things and about the police being involved again. By the way, she said there should've been a set of six hankies in that drawer. I went down and told Ma C it would do Una good to ride with me into the village. Keeping busy in the Institute would help take her mind off the nasty business with Frank. She could take everything she needed for the show – her dress and shoes, et cetera, then there'd be no need for her to go back to the hostel.'

'And she agreed?'

'After a few honeyed words from me – yes. On the way in I let Una know there was a fair chance that Angelo would get to the hall early. Her face lit up at that, I can tell you.'

'And did he?'

Brenda shrugged. 'There was no sign of anyone from the camp when we got there. I offered to stick around with her but she said no, she'd be fine on her own.'

Grace gave a quiet tut.

'What?' Brenda retorted. 'I can't help it if she didn't want me to stay, can I? Anyway, the POWs were due any time.'

'I suppose you're right.' Grace bent to pick up stray turnips that had fallen from the cart. She tossed them into the nearby wheelbarrow and they landed with a clunk. The Christmas show was due to start in less than three hours. She glanced down at her frayed woollen mittens and felt her damp scarf flap against her cheek. Her feet were frozen solid despite three pairs of socks. 'Not long now until show time,' she said with a hollow laugh.

It came as the best Christmas present imaginable when Angelo found Una alone in the hall, putting the finishing touches to the Christmas tree. Coloured streamers looped down from the ceiling and at the far end of the room shabby green velvet curtains were drawn across the stage where the Land Girls were due to perform.

She sensed his presence before he spoke and her heart lifted. She turned with a smile.

He saw her framed by the green tree. Lights reflected in the delicate glass baubles. A white angel was perched on the top.

'You are here.' He opened his arms wide.

'I am.' There was nothing more natural than going to him and feeling his arms close around her, than tilting her head back and sinking into his kiss.

'I came. I did not hope to find you,' he murmured, his lips against her cheek.

Everything melted away when she looked into his eyes – the cold hours on the fell side, the sound of bombs thudding to the ground, the grip of death.

'I wrote my love for you.' He stroked her cheeks with his thumbs, cradling her head in his hands. In his eyes there was no woman more perfect, with her silky skin so smooth and soft and her eyes the colour of dark honey, flecked with gold.

'I wrote too.' The letter was in her coat pocket, slung over the back of a chair. Now it seemed not to matter what she'd written because everything she'd said was held here in this moment, needing no words. Here, in the village hall with red and green streamers, fresh white walls and a pine tree glittering silver for Christmas. Gazing at him, knowing that she was loved in body, heart and soul.

Lorenzo opened the door from the kitchen and saw them together. He closed it quietly and left them in peace.

CHAPTER TWENTY-ONE

Fifteen rows of chairs were set out in the hall and the buffet tables were laid in the kitchen when one by one the Land Girls arrived. Kathleen came early to allocate pegs in the small anteroom overlooking the football pitch where the Burnside team got changed for their Saturday matches. There was a pungent smell of damp plaster mixed with liniment, old sweat and brilliantine. A toilet cubicle in the far corner smelled even worse. Kathleen tried not to breathe in too deeply as she greeted Joyce.

'Pooh, can we open a window? It smells like a farmyard in here.' Joyce held her nose as she hung up her coat. As piano player for the evening, she'd decided to dress conservatively in a plum-coloured, jersey-knit dress with long sleeves and a sweetheart neckline and to keep her thick brown hair up in an elegant chignon, leaving it to those onstage to dazzle with their bright summer silks and cottons. She sat down to take off her Land Army brogues and slip on a pair of grey leather court shoes with a small heel.

'Elsie, you can take peg number three,' Kathleen

told the next arrival, who had shown up in her uniform so as not to spoil her evening attire during the ride into the village in the back of the CRAF lorry.

She took her peg and quickly slipped out of breeches and jumper and into a peach-coloured silk dress overlaid with cream lace. Then she used the mottled mirror above the mantelpiece to put on rouge and lipstick.

After this, the dancers and singers arrived thick and fast. Jean came in a bright green, tight-fitting dress with wide shoulder pads – a hangover from the days before clothing coupons came in. She claimed to have lost her voice and croaked out a protest that she wasn't fit to sing but that she was happy to stay in the kitchen preparing refreshments for the interval.

Knowing that this was no great loss, Kathleen agreed. 'We'll need you for The Skaters' Waltz straight afterwards,' she reminded her fretfully.

Joyce saw that nerves were getting the better of Kathleen. She'd already snapped at Dorothy when she took the wrong peg then panicked when she thought she'd forgotten her copy of the running order.

'I've looked everywhere,' she wailed, her usually perfect blonde hair messed up and two top buttons of her royal-blue dress undone.

Joyce produced her own version for her to look at. 'Everything's in hand. Nothing is going to go wrong.' However, she didn't feel as calm as she sounded. It wasn't butterflies fluttering in her stomach so much as a herd of baby elephants. She looked around the room, glad to see that Grace was there and looking lovely in a knee-length lilac dress trimmed with white and white shoes to match. And here was Brenda, breezing into the room in a sleeveless yellow frock printed all over with white daisies as if it was the middle of summer. There was a big white bow to finish off the daring, asymmetric neckline and a white silk camellia pinned in her dark hair.

Kathleen ticked names off on a list. 'Dorothy – here. Ivy – here. Una . . . Where's Una?'

'Here I am.' Una had waited until the last possible moment to say goodbye to Angelo, making herself useful in the kitchen where he and Lorenzo were setting out the buffet with two Canadians. Hilda had been there too, cutting up sandwiches and arranging Victoria sponges that she'd baked herself. Meanwhile, inside the hall, the full contingent of prisoners and Air Force men had begun to file in and take their seats.

But here she was, present and correct in a pale-blue summer dress that fitted her perfectly, her dark-auburn hair shining, her cheeks glowing.

'Five minutes to curtain up,' Joyce warned. She took up her sheets of music, ready to make her entrance into the hall and sit at the piano. 'When you hear me play the opening bars of "Back to the Land", that's your cue to take your places for the first number.'

'Curtain up!' Kathleen echoed faintly. 'Oh, Lord – who's going to do that?'

There was a flurry of skirts and the clicking of shoes as, nerves tingling, twenty girls climbed three wooden steps onto the stage.

'I will,' Brenda said with a wink. 'Then I'll enter stage right!'

Quietly Joyce parted the green curtains and slid into view of the audience who immediately started to clap and stamp their feet. The POWs took up the first five rows, dressed in their uniform of grey trousers and jackets, all smiling and whistling as, clutching her sheet music, she made her way down the steps then settled herself on the piano stool. The Canadian airmen occupied six or seven rows behind them, looking relaxed and eager in their civvies – mostly open-necked shirts, slacks and sports jackets. Mac was there, Joyce noticed, but not Jim Aldridge, the senior officer at the base. She busily arranged her music then glanced again at the audience and was surprised to see that several locals had shuffled in and occupied standing room at the back of the hall – Bob and Maurice Baxendale, for a start, with Neville hoping not to be noticed in the corner by the tree. Finally, hovering in the doorway, she spotted Bill. *No one's invited them, but who cares?* she thought. *The more the merrier.* Taking a deep breath, she struck the first chords of the Land Army song.

Brenda tugged at the rope attached to the pulley that raised the curtain. It jerked and moved slowly at first so she pulled harder and whisked it up.

'Back to the land, we must all lend a hand!' Twenty voices sang as one. The Land Girls stood shoulder to shoulder under the spotlights in bright summer dresses of every colour of the rainbow, voices raised in praise of their work, air filling their lungs to tell of hoeing and ploughing, going back to the land to grow barley and wheat to feed the nation and do their bit to help win the war.

Brenda waited in the wings ahead of Una and Elsie as Kathleen pranced her way through 'Anything Goes'. All sign of nerves had disappeared as she twirled and winked, cooed and looked coyly over her shoulder at her appreciative audience. 'Glimpse of stocking' she sang, and an accompanying action raised a raucous round of applause and filled the hall with wolf whistles, as did her pert march towards the front of the stage, inviting the audience to join in the last chorus of her Cole Porter song.

Brenda pulled a face at Una. 'Blimey – I have to follow that!'

Una quaked in her high-heeled shoes. 'Good luck,' she whispered as the applause for Kathleen died away and Brenda took her place onstage for her solo from *The Wizard of Oz*.

The footlights glared up at her, dust motes dancing in their bright beams. She found her spotlight and waited for Joyce to play the introduction. It was worse than facing a firing squad. Her knees shook, her palms were moist with sweat. *Help! So much for breezy, couldn't-care-less me! I was an idiot to agree to this.* Fearing complete disaster and total humiliation, she opened her mouth to begin.

She sang with her gaze fixed wistfully on the battery of spotlights overhead – floating over the rainbow to a sunny dream world filled with happy bluebirds. 'Why-oh-why?' sang the lonely, sad girl, looking for hope in the skies beyond. The slow song held the audience of homesick men in its gentle grasp. They swayed and began to hum the chorus then to join in with the words. Back home on Italian shores and in the Canadian mountains and forests there was someone, somewhere who every man missed – a mother, a girlfriend, a daughter for whom his heart yearned.

The song ended and Brenda clasped her hands in front of her and gave a solemn bow.

The hall erupted into applause. At the piano, Joyce saw Lorenzo get to his feet, followed by Angelo beside him and then the rest of the front row. Soon everyone in the hall was standing and clapping. Mac put his fingers to his mouth and whistled. More men from the village had joined Bill in the doorway – too late to hear Brenda's soulful rendition. Joyce registered with a small start that the newcomers included Edgar. She smiled to herself then quietly and carefully arranged the next piece of music on the stand.

Brenda bowed again. Elated as she skipped from the stage, she whispered good luck to Una and Elsie.

After 'Over the Rainbow', the jaunty feel of 'I Get a Kick out of You' went down a treat. The girls matched the words to a carefully rehearsed routine of dance steps and cheeky actions, perfectly in time to the music – especially the kick with the right foot that coincided with every repetition of the title line. 'I get a kick – kick – kick out of you!' they concluded, with pointed feet, two neatly turned ankles and the brightest of smiles.

Angelo and Lorenzo were on their feet again,

calling for more. The airmen stamped their feet and whistled. Maurice told his brother Bob that Elsie was the girl he'd had his eye on for some time – he liked the look of her curly bob and her impish smile. 'I'm going to go up to her and talk to her during the interval,' he bragged.

'What about the other one – the one in the blue dress?' Bob asked.

'Una Sharpe? Too late, mate – she's been snapped up by an Eye-tie,' Maurice told him as the curtain came down for the interval.

After that there was a scrum for refreshments – everybody jostling to get first choice of sandwiches and cakes in the kitchen. Standing at a trestle table in front of two arched, leaded windows, Jean poured tea from a giant brown teapot, her voice miraculously back to normal. She even smiled at Jack Hudson as she handed him a cup, but once a gaggle of performers had joined the queue, she was back to her dour self.

Joyce stood by the door and surveyed the noisy scene – voices raised above the chink of cups, the tinkle of cutlery and the hiss of steam from the Ascot boiler in the corner. She spotted Neville, his plate piled high with food and Bill standing back, waiting for others to be served – but where was Edgar? He was nowhere to be seen. Never mind – he'd come to see at least part of the show and that was better than nothing.

'Hello, Joyce.' He came up behind her and spoke quietly.

'Edgar.' Her heart skipped a beat. He was at her

shoulder, not looking at her but frowning at the bun fight in front of them, smartly dressed in a blazer and slacks.

'Are we going to hear you sing later on?'

'No. I'll stick to playing the piano.'

'That's a pity.' He did look at her then, with a self-conscious glance. He smiled then he was gone.

Voices babbled in Italian. Lorenzo reached the head of the queue but with a gentlemanly gesture stood to one side for Brenda who claimed she was dying of thirst. Mac stepped in to praise her for the 'Rainbow' song and said no, he had never seen Judy Garland in the film. She looked and sounded wonderful, he said. Then they were away, chatting ten to the dozen, with the gas jets behind the counter bursting into flame and steam hissing from the top of the boiler.

Lost in the bustle, Una tried to find Angelo. Where was he? Every minute was precious. She wove between Dorothy and a Canadian airman, her heart beating rapidly until she saw him stepping up onto the low stone windowsill to look for her. She waved. He smiled then jumped down. Five seconds later he was with her and they were slipping away, fingers entwined, out through a side door into the cold, silent night.

Then, looking up at the stars, it hit her that this might be the last time they would be together – the last time before they moved him to Scotland in a crowded lorry to work in a munitions factory or on a shipyard building battleships. The thought made her shiver then tighten her fingers around his.

He looked at her and understood, folded his arms around her and let her rest her head against his chest.

'I give you this,' he said softly – a piece of paper with an address written on it.

She read the words – 'Angelo Bachetti' then the number 36, followed by '*Via*' meaning 'road', she thought, then an unfamiliar word: '*Torrione*'. Underneath this line came his home town – 'Pisa'.

He handed her a pencil and a blank piece of paper. 'You write your *casa*, your house.'

She printed her name and address with a shaking hand. 'Una Sharpe, 15 Wellington Street, Millwood.'

He took the paper from her and folded it carefully.

Two separate worlds. Two lives colliding. Two lovers entwined.

'This fight is not for ever.' He enfolded her in his arms again.

War would end in great men talking and signing papers, in counting the dead and drawing new lines on the world map – in Africa and the Far East, in Poland, Russia and Germany.

'After, I come to this place.' He patted the paper with her address. 'I find you.'

She believed him and hoped for it with all her heart. 'When do you leave the camp?'

'Two days more,' he said as he stroked her hair and looked deep into her eyes. 'On Christ's day.'

No one forgot the words to their song; no one fell over in the middle of The Skaters' Waltz. By popular demand, they followed up the original Vera Lynn finale with another rendition of 'Back to the Land', wearing their slouch hats and marching and waving from stage left to stage right then back again.

The whole ensemble did two choruses then Kathleen thanked everyone for coming. Still there were cries for more, so they marched one last time then flung their hats into the air during a final rousing burst of the Land Army song. The boards creaked under their feet and off they went, with Brenda at the helm as the curtain fell and the girls disappeared down into the damp annexe.

From there they heard the scrape of chairs as their audience stood up, ready to leave. The POWs filed out of the hall into their waiting lorry, followed by the Canadians, all except four men who had been assigned by Mac the job of clearing away the chairs and packing up the leftover food from the buffet.

'Well done, Kathleen – that was a topping show.'

'We couldn't have done it without you to knock us into shape.'

'Thank you, Joyce. And Happy Christmas, everyone!'

Satisfied comments filled the annexe as girls changed out of their dresses, back into trousers and pullovers.

Anticlimax soon followed elation, however.

'I'm worn out,' Elsie said with a sigh as she buttoned up her coat.

'Is that it? Is it really all over?' Jean was the first to leave, soon followed by Dorothy and Ivy, who stuck together like glue. Others drifted out after them, leaving an almost empty room.

'Put a big pan of hot chocolate on the stove if you get back before us,' Brenda called after Elsie. She was still in her yellow dress, helping Una check underneath benches to make sure that nothing had been left behind.

Elsie left the door open and cold air rushed in.

'Brrr. I'm going to be the last out of here at this rate.' She closed the door then looked at Joyce, who had just come out of the toilet, and Una, already in their outdoor clothes.

'We've got a lift back with Mrs C. We'll ask her to wait for you if you like,' Una offered.

'No ta, I'm on Old Sloper.' Brenda thought that Una looked sad so she gave her a sympathetic smile. 'I'll see you back at the hostel and we'll have a good natter.'

Left alone, she swiftly started to get changed. She kicked off her shoes and was out of her dress, standing in her petticoat when she heard someone walk across the stage and come down the three wooden steps.

'Good – you're still here.' It was Mac.

With one swift movement Brenda took her leather jacket from its hook and held it up in front of her. 'Hey, a girl needs some privacy here.'

Instead of retreating, he sat down on the steps and watched her closely. It was the same way of sitting as before, in the storeroom – legs akimbo, one hand thrust deep into his trouser pocket. For a while he didn't move – simply lapping up the sight of her in her underclothes, hiding behind her jacket.

'Mac, you can't come in here,' she said. 'This room is for ladies only.'

'You don't say.' He sniffed the liniment in the air then contradicted her by jerking his head towards the framed photographs of Burnside football teams that hung on the far wall.

'I mean it – you shouldn't be here.' Brenda listened out in vain for other sounds in the building. 'Don't you have to be somewhere else, with your men?'

'They went on ahead. I'm the only one left, so I guess it's just you and me.' He stood up slowly and advanced towards her.

Quickly she flung her fleece-lined jacket around her shoulders then slipped her arms into the sleeves. She held it tight across her chest, shaking her head as he drew close.

He reached out and put his arm around her waist. 'Lucky, huh? Just me and you, alone together.'

She twisted out of his grasp then backed away. She felt grit beneath her feet on the cold stone floor, heard the low hiss of the toilet cistern as it slowly refilled. There were two ways out – up the wooden steps onto the stage or out of the back door into the football field.

Guessing what she was thinking, Mac lunged at her and took hold of her wrist. 'Come on, little Miss Judy Garland – no one's going to know.'

Brenda swung her free hand and smacked him hard on the cheek.

He tightened his grip and backed her towards the open door of the toilet. 'We can make it nice and easy or we can make it hard – either way suits me.'

His lazy drawl frightened her more than anything

else – more than the strength of his grip or the mocking look in his eye. This was obviously something he'd done before. Raising her right foot, she aimed and kneed him hard in the crotch, felt him let go of her wrist and saw him double up in pain then recover quickly enough to catch her again before she could reach the door. This time, breathing hard and swearing, he used his full weight to push her down on the floor.

She lay face-down on the doormat, her legs splayed. He put his foot on the small of her back.

Brenda smelled mud and rot, felt the cold wind on her face as it whistled under the door. The weight of his boot on her back told her he was not going to change his mind.

Then, out of the corner of her eye she saw a woman's legs on the wooden steps, heard her name, felt Mac lift his foot and spin around.

Kathleen jumped down the steps and ran at him and beat him with her fists – pounding his chest, his face – anywhere she could reach. She screamed at him and told Brenda to get up. She screamed a second time for Mac to get out, to leave and not come back.

Slowly Brenda picked herself up. Her ribs ached where he'd pressed with his boot, breath came short but she staggered towards Kathleen, who caught her and held her up as Mac sprang up the steps and disappeared.

CHAPTER TWENTY-TWO

Once Brenda had struggled into her trousers and sweater, Kathleen led her out of the changing room into the main hall. She left her sitting on the edge of the stage while she went to check in the kitchen.

'It's all right – he's cleared off,' she told Brenda when she came back. 'I heard a car engine and looked through the window in time to see him drive away.'

Brenda stared straight ahead at the Christmas tree at the far end of the hall. She felt dazed and hollowed out, unable to make sense of what had just happened.

Kathleen hoisted herself onto the stage and sat next to her, her legs swinging, hands folded in her lap. 'I've had my eye on Mac all night. I don't trust him. That's why I came back to see if you were all right, and I'm glad I did.'

Brenda didn't reply. Her thoughts whirled inside her head, unable to find expression.

'Don't worry – we'll report him to his squadron leader. This time he won't get away with it.'

Brenda took a shuddering breath then turned her head towards Kathleen. 'This time?'

Biting her lip as if unsure how to go on, she hesitated.

'Has he tried it on with you?'

'Not me – no.'

'Who, then?' Their voices echoed in the empty hall. The piano lid was down, the chairs stacked to one side – silent reminders of the evening's lively entertainment. 'Come on, Kathleen, what are you trying to say?'

'It was something you said yesterday – late last night, as a matter of fact, when you were telling Una and me about you and Mac.'

Brenda remembered with a flash of shame how she'd sat on her bed and crowed about her visit to the Penny Lane base – laughing about how she'd gone into the storeroom and lapped up his whisky and compliments. 'I gave him the wrong idea,' she muttered. 'Is that what you mean?'

'No.' Kathleen's reply was loud and firm and she rearranged Brenda's jacket to make sure that it sat more comfortably around her shoulders. 'It wasn't you who brought this on, Brenda. What bothered me was that Mac told you that you were his dream girl.'

'Yes – that's when you took umbrage.'

'It was those two words that upset me and at first I didn't know why. Then, when I was in the bathroom brushing my teeth, it all fell into place. I've heard the same thing before – only back then it wasn't *you* being thrilled to bits because Mac had called you his dream girl, it was Eunice.'

'He said that to her?'

'The exact same thing. She swore me to secrecy,

and of course she didn't tell who the man was or a single thing about him. She just mentioned that she was walking out with someone – a handsome chap who sweet talked her and called her his dream girl. It's not a phrase you hear every day around these parts – only when you go to the flicks or see a play.'

'I see.' Brenda's heart thudded.

'She seemed over the moon about it so I was surprised when she never mentioned him again. Then I forgot all about it because it was around the same time that Frank Kellett started pestering her. And of course it was only a few weeks afterwards that Eunice . . .'

Brenda took a deep breath to try to calm herself. 'I thought it was Frank's fault that she seemed generally down in the dumps, and later I suspected Lorenzo was the culprit. Eunice struck me as the quiet type – she didn't give much away – but then I had no time to get to know her.'

Though the hall was empty, Kathleen leaned sideways and spoke in a whisper. 'I think we've all suspected Frank and Lorenzo at various times. But, don't you see, this throws a different light on things? Suppose Mac was Eunice's handsome chap and she was his dream girl. Suppose he did to her what he just tried to do to you.'

'Only he got the better of Eunice and . . .'

'And the worst happened. She fell pregnant and didn't feel able to tell a single soul.'

'Because she was ashamed.' Brenda's voice was hardly audible.

'Yes, and especially because of the way she was

brought up. Did you know her father was a Methodist minister – very strict, by all accounts?'

'I didn't know that.' Brenda relived again the moment when she realized what Mac was about to do – the arrogant look in his eye, the smile that turned to a sneer on his lips when she'd grabbed her jacket and used it to shield herself. The sense that this was not the first time he'd planned to do something like this.

'Do you see what I'm saying? I think Mac was the father of Eunice's baby.'

'And not Frank.' Brenda jumped down from the stage and strode the length of the hall, past the piano and stacked chairs, under the festive paper streamers. 'Even if it's true, Mac will never admit it,' she said as she came slowly back.

'But that still doesn't stop you from reporting what happened here tonight.'

Brenda closed her eyes and tilted her head back. She spoke through gritted teeth. 'No – what does stop me is thinking that I'm at least partly to blame. I could have, *should* have behaved better!'

'And what difference would that have made?' Kathleen had never seen Brenda like this – unsure of how to act and crippled by self-doubt. She even seemed to have shrunk inside the big jacket and her face was deathly pale. 'If you can't face going to Penny Lane, you could report it to Mrs Mostyn instead.'

Brenda ignored her and stared down at her hands, still grimy from contact with the muddy doormat. 'I feel dirty. I can't breathe properly.'

'We could do it now,' Kathleen insisted gently. 'Her house is only a little way down the street.'

Brenda sighed and shook her head. 'No, not now.'

'Why not?'

'It's late. She'll be in bed.' Shame and humiliation beckoned. No matter what Kathleen said, Brenda envisaged how this would be bound to work out. John Mackenzie would deny it outright. In the village there would be sideways glances and mutterings – her word against his. And every time she cycled out to work on the farms, she would be known as the Land Army girl who played fast and loose with the Canadian airman and got what she deserved.

Christmas Eve was declared a day off for all the girls at the Fieldhead hostel. The few, including Elsie, who had planned to travel home to spend Christmas with their families, were able to set off a few hours early, while the rest could safely put their feet up in the common room or spend their time wrapping gifts and writing last-minute cards.

Before Elsie left to catch the bus from Burnside, she popped her cheerful face around the door of Una's room. 'I wanted to wish you a happy Christmas and to give you this card.'

'Come in.' Una was half regretting her decision not to go home for Christmas. She was staying out of Ivy, Dorothy and Jean's way and quietly grieving over Angelo's imminent departure.

'We put on a good show last night.' Elsie joined her at the window. 'I'd say the audience got a "kick" out of our little number, wouldn't you?'

'Yes, it went down well.' Looking down on the yard and the row of outhouses brought a chilling reminder of Frank's recent presence, so Una backed away as she opened Elsie's hand-made card. They chatted about how long her journey to her home in the East Riding would take, the unreliability of the weather forecast and the latest news on the wireless about Allied progress in Benghazi.

'Chin up, eh?' Elsie said as she prepared to leave. 'Angelo may be on the move up to Scotland, but he'll still be able to use this address to write to you.'

'Yes. Ta, Elsie.' Following the well-meaning advice, Una decided to try to make the most of her extended Christmas holiday. She went downstairs with Elsie and stood at the front door to wave her off on her bicycle ride into Burnside. 'Happy Christmas!' she called.

'Ta-ta!' Elsie waved back and pedalled off down the lane.

'Well, well.' Ivy came out of the common room as Una closed the front door. She was still in her dressing-gown and slippers. 'I bet you don't have a lot to say for yourself without Brenda, Joyce and Grace to back you up.'

The sight of Ivy with a mug of cocoa in her hand, leaning against the door jamb and sneering at her, set Una's teeth on edge. It was time to have it out with her, she decided. So, instead of retreating to her room, she went up to her without realizing that Dorothy and Jean were lurking in the common room. 'Listen, if you have anything to say to me, say it outright and to my face.'

Ivy raised her eyebrows. 'Did you hear that?' she called to the others, who came up behind her. 'Una wants to know what we think of her. Shall we tell her?'

Dorothy took up the cudgels. 'What – that she's a sly one who looks as if butter wouldn't melt, but that really she doesn't have a loyal bone in her body and if it was left to her she'd let Jerry run circles around not just us but the whole country?'

Their malice took Una's breath away and she stared back at them without speaking.

'Jean, do you know what makes girls like Una tick?' Ivy called for reinforcements. 'Is it just that she can't resist a handsome face – as simple as that? Or is there more to it?'

Jean, not one to relish confrontation, put a restraining hand on Ivy's arm.

'Well?' Dorothy continued to lean on the door post – an insolent posture that indicated how little she thought of her opponent. 'Did you or didn't you?'

'Did I do what?' Una's blood was well and truly up. Drawing herself up to her full height, she barely came to Ivy's shoulder. 'No – don't bother. I won't lower myself to frame an answer. All you need to hear is that I'm as loyal to my country as you are.'

'If not more so,' Joyce added. At the sound of raised voices, she, Brenda and Kathleen had come quietly downstairs, along with three of the other girls.

Una's confidence was boosted by their presence. 'I came to Fieldhead to do my duty and help feed my country instead of letting Hitler starve us all to death. I answered the call, just the same as everyone else in this building and like thousands of other

391

girls across the whole of England and beyond. And I intend to be here for the rest of the war, down on my knees grubbing for turnips or working the threshing machines, hedging, digging ditches, milking, collecting eggs – whatever Mrs Mostyn asks me to do.'

There was another murmur of approval from Joyce and the others. Jean quietly retreated from view while Dorothy pushed past Ivy and continued to sneer. 'The worm turns,' she muttered melodramatically. Then, 'You can work your fingers to the bone for King and country, but it doesn't alter the fact that you fraternize with the enemy and you don't even try to hide it. Can anyone here tell me I'm wrong?'

Brenda would have jumped to Una's defence, but Joyce shook her head. Una was doing just fine.

'Oh yes? And am I passing on secret information about how many sacks of potatoes I've filled or how many yards of ditch I've dug? Does Angelo send on this information via Rome to German high command? No – I don't think so.'

'Ask her about her friend, the gunner,' Ivy muttered. 'Let's see what she has to say about helping Jerry to escape.'

Una jumped in before the question could be posed. The time of doubting herself was behind her, thanks to Brenda. 'He was not my friend. I didn't help him. I did what anyone else would have done to survive those hours out on the fell – the same as you, Dorothy, Jean or anybody.'

Jean heard her name spoken and drifted back into view. Looking past Dorothy and Ivy to the small figure confronting them and then to the group of supporters hovering in the hall, she felt a withering sense of shame and regret.

Una wasn't finished yet. 'And here's the proof: he'll be locked up out of harm's way for the rest of the war. He won't be dropping any more bombs on Thornley Dam – or anywhere else, for that matter.' She felt six inches taller and buoyed up by the power of her reasoning, easily the equal of Dorothy and her pals.

There was a hum of assent behind her and a dawning realization on Dorothy and Ivy's face that they had better back down, however ungraciously.

'When you look at it like that . . .' Ivy conceded.

'You could have told us all this in the first place and set the record straight.' Fury boiled inside Dorothy, scarcely concealed beneath her conciliatory remark. She hated to lose any argument and knew that this one would eat away at her for weeks and weeks.

'You might have taken the trouble to ask me.' Una spoke in a lower, more even tone. She recognized Jean's hangdog look and knew there was little pleasure to be had by rubbing salt into the wound. 'Anyway, let's forget all about it, shall we?'

'Yes – let's.' Jean came forward, nodding eagerly and with new respect for Una, while Ivy and Dorothy still hung back.

Joyce smiled at Brenda and Kathleen, then watched the other girls crowd around Una with more questions – was the Dornier still carrying any of its bombs when it came down, had she known there was anyone left alive before she climbed in, hadn't she been afraid that the whole thing would blow sky-high?

'Good for her,' Brenda murmured. Una had raised her spirits a little after a night spent tossing and turning over John Mackenzie's attack.

'Let's invite Grace to cycle over here then we can all go out for a walk,' Joyce suggested. 'Now that the show's out of the way, we can concentrate on Frank Kellett and plan where to start our search.'

'Frank hasn't vanished into thin air,' Grace told them as they walked through the elm wood. The snow was beginning to melt and patches of black earth had started to show, though there was a cold wind sighing through the branches overhead. 'Edgar told me that he'd spotted him two nights on the trot – once close to Fieldhead on the night the plane came down and then again the following night, outside the pub.'

'Then there's every chance he's still trailing around after Una.' It was clearer than ever to Joyce that they should use the rest of the day to track down Frank. 'I did mention his name and gave his description to a couple of people in the audience last night – Angelo and Lorenzo promised to keep their eyes peeled while they're packing up at the camp and getting ready to leave. Mac said he'd pass the word around, too.'

Brenda didn't manage to hold back a shudder and Una asked her what was wrong. 'Has something happened?'

'No. I'm all right, ta. Let's keep our minds on the job in hand.' She walked on ahead but stumbled into a drift clinging to a hollow on the bank of a small

394

stream. Grace and Joyce pulled her out and helped to brush her down. 'I'm not saying we should change our minds about going after Frank . . .'

'But?' Grace prompted.

'But I have heard something that could make a difference.' Brenda was cagey about the circumstances in case it led to her having to speak about Mac. 'I don't want to go into the whys and wherefores – only that Frank might not be the villain we've been painting him. In other words, he might follow girls around but not actually do anything to harm them.'

'But he stole Una's things,' Joyce pointed out before she turned to Grace. 'We've asked you for your opinion once before – is Frank a danger or not?'

Grace rested against a tall tree trunk then looked down at the trickle of water running between the steep banks. 'We need to hear more, Brenda. What's made you change your mind?'

She took a deep breath before she spoke. 'It turns out he didn't have anything to do with Eunice being pregnant. That's what everyone has been thinking for these past few weeks – that Frank was the father and so he was the reason why Eunice couldn't go on. But he wasn't. It was someone else.'

Joyce wasn't convinced. 'That still doesn't make it all right for him to pester Una. The police don't think so either.'

'I know. I agree. I just don't think we need to worry that he'll harm her unless he's cornered – the way he was that time in the kitchen.'

'Can I say something?' Una had listened to them talking about the problem of Frank as if she weren't there. 'It's crossed my mind before now that he's not as dangerous or as frightening as people might think. It's just that he can't get anyone to understand how he's feeling or what he wants to say. It's been happening to him all his life – wanting to explain something but not being able to.'

'Yes, and he's had Joe treating him worse than one of his dogs.' Grace saw Una's point. 'Of course, Frank has to learn that he can't break into places and steal things, but who besides Emily would take the time and trouble to teach him?'

'And she can't – not while he's wandering about on the moors.' Joyce slowly began to see that the real reason to track Frank down might be to offer him some help rather than to punish him. 'That's if you're right, Brenda.'

They set off again, threading their way between tree trunks and hoping to avoid the wet snow that slid from the branches and landed on the ground with a soft thud. Joyce and Grace led the way while Una stayed behind with Brenda. Before long they came to the edge of the wood and stared up at the fell where the German plane had come to grief. There was a covering of fast-moving cloud on the highest ridge, blowing from west to east.

Una turned to Brenda and was shocked to see that her cheeks were suddenly wet with tears. She said nothing but stayed with her when Joyce and Grace set off again.

'Don't mind me,' Brenda sniffed.

Una linked arms with her. The other two were a little way ahead, discussing where Frank might hide on a day like today – not too cold, with hardly any-one around and most of the farms and their surrounding buildings quiet in the run-up to Christ-mas. 'Who told you that Frank wasn't the father?' she asked.

Brenda pressed the back of her hand to her fore-head. 'Kathleen. Last night. She realized she'd been in the wrong to accuse Frank and explained to me who the real culprit was.'

'Who?' Una had been so wrapped up in thinking about Angelo that she'd pretended to be asleep when Brenda and Kathleen had finally come upstairs to bed. This morning she'd been up before them and hadn't had a chance to talk to Brenda until now.

Brenda made a choking sound, a monosyllable that began as a laugh but ended as a sob. 'Mac.'

Una stood stock still, looking up through the branches at black rooks riding the wind currents. 'I see. But there's more to it than that?'

Brenda's tear-streaked face held no expression. She spoke in a monotone. 'Yes. Last night at the Institute – I wasn't dressed. He attacked me. If Kath-leen hadn't come in when she did, I wouldn't have been able to stop him.'

CHAPTER TWENTY-THREE

None of Brenda's reasons for keeping quiet about the attack held sway with Una, Joyce and Grace. In the cold woods at the back of the hostel they gathered around her like soldiers in battle protecting their fallen comrade.

'Mac will deny it,' she sobbed as they cleared snow from a rocky ledge then sat her down. 'He'll say I've made it all up.'

'But you have Kathleen as a witness,' Grace pointed out. She crouched beside Brenda and held her hand.

'He'll say we're ganging up on him. They'll take his word against ours.'

'"They" – who's "they"?' Joyce felt ready to argue against anyone who labelled Brenda a liar.

'Squadron Leader Aldridge, for a start.' Brenda took a deep breath and swallowed back her tears. 'And if I went to the police, it'd be the same. There'd be a bobby behind a desk writing things down. I'd have to tell him I was only in my underwear. He'd make another note and underline it. He wouldn't have to say anything but he'd look at me and I'd know just what was going through his mind.'

Una was the most adamant of the three that Brenda should report her attacker. 'Never mind that. We'll back you up. In fact, I'll come over to Penny Lane with you – right now, this minute. Whatever you do, you mustn't let Mac get away with this.'

Brenda let their defiant words trickle into her consciousness. They began to dissolve the hard block of shame that had formed inside her overnight.

'Do that,' Grace advised. 'Go with Una to the base. Ask to see the squadron leader.'

'Yes – stand your ground. Don't let them turn you away.' Joyce helped Brenda to her feet then squeezed her hands. 'Explain what happened – when, where, and so on. Don't leave anything out.'

Grace watched Brenda wipe away her tears and set her shoulders back. 'Will you try?'

Brenda pressed her lips together and looked from one to the other as if drawing strength from them. 'I will,' she agreed.

Brenda rode away from Fieldhead with Una riding pillion, leaving Joyce and Grace to begin the search for Frank.

'It's worth checking the outhouses first.' Joyce had decided on their course of action. 'If we don't see any sign of him there, we'll make our way into Burnside and carry on looking.'

Una and Brenda had promised to join them as soon as they got back from Penny Lane.

'Only if Brenda feels up to it,' Joyce had cautioned as they'd set off along the lane.

Now, with a cold wind on her face, but protected by hat, scarf and gauntlets, Brenda steeled herself to find Jim Aldridge and state her case against Mac. She sped along the familiar route, handling her motor bike with ease, listening to the reliable roar of the engine as she opened the throttle and it sailed up the steepest of hills. She was aware of Una behind her, leaning into the bends with her, shifting her weight, hanging on for dear life as Brenda turned sharp right onto the long straight Roman road. She slowed down for the last stretch, trying to compose herself as they approached the entrance to the Canadian base.

Una felt the engine ease. The blurred verges became clear – dark rushes and clumps of flattened grass poked through melting snow. The dark walls lining their route were topped by slabs of flat stone placed on their sides to form a jagged outline. She saw a glimpse of Beckwith Camp in the distance – rows of Nissen huts backed by tall pine trees – and felt a jolt of sadness. Angelo was there for the present, but tomorrow he would be gone.

Brenda turned off the lane and rode up to the sentry box. It was manned by an unfamiliar airman, who leaned out to speak to her.

'Hey,' he said, smiling suddenly as she took off her hat and stuffed it inside her jacket. 'You're the girl in the yellow dress. You sang the "Rainbow" song.'

Still sitting astride the bike and letting the engine idle, Brenda cleared her throat. 'Yes – that was me.'

The thickset man came out of his box. 'It's my wife's favourite. She's seen that movie three times.' He turned his attention to Una, sitting quietly behind. 'Now let me see – don't tell me. Aren't you the song and dance gal, one half of a duo?'

As she stepped off the bike to let Brenda push it to one side and park it, Una nodded and kept him chatting. 'How did you enjoy the show?'

'I liked it a lot,' the sentry said. He was around thirty, with short dark hair, brown eyes partly concealed by puffy eyelids and a wide face. 'All the guys agreed it was a terrific night.'

'Good, because we all had kittens beforehand.'

'Come again?'

'We were really nervous. It wasn't easy to learn all those steps and words in a couple of weeks.' Brenda seemed to be taking a long time so Una glanced in her direction to see her hanging back and looking as though she was about to change her mind. So Una forged ahead. 'We've come to see Squadron Leader Aldridge. Could you make a telephone call to tell him we're here?'

'Sure,' the sentry said, returning swiftly to his box. 'Give me your names.'

While he made the call, Una went to fetch Brenda. 'You'll be all right,' she assured her. 'Once you've got this off your chest, you'll feel a lot better.'

Approaching the barrier and looking up at the tall house, they heard the sentry's voice saying their names – 'Una Sharpe and Brenda Appleby . . . to see the squadron leader . . . OK, I'll tell them.'

He came out of the box with a shrug and a shake

of his head. 'Sorry, you're out of luck. Squadron Leader Aldridge is off base.'

'So who's in charge while he's away?' Una asked, holding tight to Brenda's sleeve in case she bolted.

'That'd be Flight Lieutenant Mackenzie. He's the one I just called. I did my best for you, girls – I asked if you could come in and wait, but no luck, I'm afraid.'

At the mention of Mac's name, Brenda felt her nerve fail. 'Come on – let's go,' she muttered under her breath.

'If it's urgent, you could come back in an hour.' After his talk with his senior officer, the sentry gradually dropped his casual air and he studied them more circumspectly. 'The flight lieutenant gave an order not to let you hang around at the gate.'

They had no choice, but as Brenda wheeled her bike back onto the lane, a dark-grey Land Rover approached. It slowed down and the driver gave a hand signal showing that he wanted to turn into the base. Brenda wheeled her bike out of his way.

As the sentry raised the barrier and the Land Rover eased past, Una recognized the uniformed driver. She ran after the car and tapped on the windscreen. Jim Aldridge opened his door and stepped out.

Joyce and Grace made a thorough search of the outhouses in the hostel yard. They concentrated on the one where Joyce had discovered Una's belongings, lifting the easels and stacking them outside to give themselves room to move the desks and chairs. The only signs of recent occupation were a pile of rat droppings in the darkest corner and cobwebs hanging down from the ceiling.

'I'll tell Mrs C we've got too many rats for Tibbs to deal with,' practically minded Joyce decided as she emerged into the fresh air.

Grace was next door in the outhouse where they'd stored the Christmas tree. 'There's nothing in here,' she reported.

They went along the row and found no evidence that the fugitive had been back then, for good measure, they searched the vegetable plot for footprints and other signs of disturbance. Nothing again.

Stiff from bending and lifting, Joyce put her hands on her hips and eased her back. 'If I put myself in Frank's shoes, this is one of the places I'd keep on coming back to.'

'Regardless of his interest in Una, you mean?'

'Yes. Think about it.' Joyce gestured towards the rows of leeks, cabbages and Brussels sprouts. 'A starving man would eat raw cabbages. Frank's been here often enough to know that he could keep himself going on those vegetables.'

'But there are no footprints or gaps in the rows to show that he's dug anything up.' Grace agreed that they should move on from Fieldhead to other likely places. 'Let's head for the village and ask Bob Baxendale if he's seen anyone lurking round the back of the Institute. And if Edgar's at home, we can talk to him. He seems to have a knack of running into Frank when he's out on one of his long walks.'

It was approaching midday when they were ready

to set off, leaving word with Kathleen not to expect them back before nightfall.

'Everyone's deserting the sinking ship,' she complained as she watched them wheel their bikes around the side of the building. 'I spotted Brenda sailing off with Una earlier. Pity me – at this rate, there'll only be me, Ivy, Dorothy and Jean here for dinner.'

'Brenda's gone to Penny Lane.' Joyce thought it only right to bring Kathleen up to date.

'You managed to persuade her to speak to Aldridge?' Her smile showed that she was surprised but pleased.

'Yes – it was Una mainly. Keep your fingers crossed for her.'

'I will.' Kathleen duly crossed them. 'And let's hope he gives her a good hearing.'

'He'll have to.' Grace believed that truth always floated to the surface and that justice would prevail. 'What Mac did was against the law.'

'So stand by to act as a witness,' Joyce added as they finally mounted their bikes and cycled away.

They didn't talk much on the way – only stopping off at Peggy's to ask her to keep a lookout for Frank.

'What then?' their elderly neighbour asked, while her dog lay in his kennel, quiet for once. 'They say Joe's washed his hands of him. Even if I spot Frank and manage to talk sense into him, where's he going to go if his own father won't have him back?'

'Emily might bring Joe round – you never know.' Grace's heart was heavy as she and Joyce set off again. It was true – there was only more heartache for Frank in the foreseeable future.

They cycled on in silence until they came to the junction where they met Maurice driving his van, with Bob in the passenger seat. Joyce flagged them down.

'Hello, girls.' Bob was the one who wound down his window. 'That was a good show you gave us last night. It put us all in the right frame of mind for turkey and Christmas pud.'

'If you can get hold of a turkey in this day and age.' Maurice leaned across his brother. 'We'll be lucky to get a scrawny pot boiler off Horace this year.'

Joyce seized the opportunity to spread their search. 'Is that where you're going now? If it is, can you be sure to tell Horace we're on the lookout for Frank? And, Bob, can you keep your eyes peeled too, please? The Institute seems to be one of Frank's favourite haunts.'

'Right you are,' they chorused. The Baxendales' promise was made without conviction and they went on their way.

'Next stop – my house.' Grace was in a hurry to find Edgar, while Joyce followed more slowly.

True, she'd had a conversation with Edgar during last night's interval and he'd seemed to be on the mend, but he still wasn't strong or completely at ease with himself and she wasn't sure that asking him to join the search for Frank was wise. So she stopped in the pub yard while Grace went inside.

'Edgar?' Grace looked in the kitchen then upstairs. She came down again and noticed that his coat was gone from the hook.

She heard her father's chesty cough then saw him

through the window, coming out of the forge to talk to Joyce. She ran outside to join them.

'Edgar went off on one of his walks,' Cliff reported. 'Don't ask me where.'

'It's up to you and me, then,' Joyce told Grace with fresh determination.

They said goodbye to Cliff then rode two abreast to the far end of the village, where Bill stood at his gate with Edith, warmly dressed in a neat black hat and a mauve coat with a fox-fur collar. Their two cars were parked in the drive beside the house.

Grace's heart felt squeezed at the sight of him. She was all for saying a quick hello then cycling on, but Joyce braked and came to a halt.

'Hello, Mrs Mostyn. How's Mr Mostyn?'

Edith concentrated on putting on her gloves and gave her stock response. 'He's as well as can be expected, thank you.'

'That's good to hear. Hello, Bill. You haven't seen Edgar, by any chance?'

Bill saw Grace out of the corner of his eye. It wounded him that she kept her distance and let Joyce do the talking. 'Not lately. Why?'

'We were planning to ask him to swell the ranks of our search party. Grace and I are out and about looking for Frank.'

'Frank Kellett?' With a last tug at her glove, Edith switched her attention to Joyce. 'Is that poor man still missing?'

'I'm afraid so. He's been getting himself into trouble at Fieldhead again. Mrs Craven's had to call the police twice now.' From Edith's agitated reaction,

406

Joyce wished she'd given less away. 'Don't worry – if the bobbies don't find him, Grace and I will.'

'Dear me, missing all this time?' Edith looked to Bill in alarm. 'Emily must be at her wits' end. And Frank can have no idea of the trouble he'll find himself in with the police.'

Bill touched her elbow. 'Mum, it's time to go if we want to make the most of visiting time.'

'No, Bill – you stay here to help Joyce and Grace.' Edith raised a hand to wave away any argument. She looked directly at Grace as she made her decision. 'I'll drive myself to the hospital.'

He hesitated. 'Are you sure?'

'Absolutely certain. It will be much better for three people to search for Frank in your car rather than two girls on bicycles.'

The simple observation carried a many-layered significance that everyone picked up but each saw differently. To Joyce it meant that Edith Mostyn's brittle shell hid a deeply ingrained sense of duty to her community and a heart warmer than it seemed. She cared enough about Frank to put him above her own concerns. To Bill it signalled a sudden but unmistakable release from a dutiful past and present. A future where he could be his own man at last hove into view. He would no longer be torn. All in those few short, simple words.

'Grace agrees with me, don't you?' Edith said.

Grace saw that she was accepted at last. The irony brought a bleak smile to her lips. Now that the die had been well and truly cast, Edith had finally undergone a change of heart. She'd let go of her aspiration to climb the social ladder to the level of the Fosters of Hawkshead Manor and riding out with the hounds. In that moment of inviting Grace in, she gave up hopes of displaying copies of *The Lady* on her low coffee table and buying couturier costumes from the best dressmaker in town. Grace's eyelids flickered shut then she opened her eyes and settled her gaze on Bill. 'Yes, I do,' she murmured.

Bill drove Grace and Joyce out as far as Kelsey Crag. The light was already starting to fade when they knocked on Henry Rowson's door and asked him the question that they'd been asking all afternoon. 'Have you seen Frank Kellett in this last couple of days?'

The answer was always no, with a telling phrase tagged on the end – 'No, thank goodness', 'No, poor chap', 'No, God bless him'. Few people were interested enough to ask questions – most closed the door on Grace, Joyce and Bill and returned to their baking of mince pies or their shoe-cleaning, their bed-making without a second thought.

It was when they drove up above the crag, along the top road over into the next dale, that Joyce, sitting in the back seat, saw Edgar walking by the frozen tarn. He was recognizable by his RAF coat even from a distance of quarter of a mile. 'Stop!' she called.

For a moment, Grace and Bill thought she'd spotted Frank. Bill slammed on his brake and the car squealed to a halt. Joyce jumped out of the car and ran across the bare moor.

'Wait a minute – that's Edgar.' Grace was quick to

follow. She soon caught up with Joyce and together they called out his name.

Edgar had walked all day until he was weary. To walk off the nightmares, to walk into a brighter future – that was his intent. He strode by the riverside then up the hill out of the tree-lined valley onto the exposed, boulder-strewn tops. Cold and alone, stripped of memories.

He turned when he heard them shout. He waited. The ice on the lake was crazed and cracked – a jagged piece sank when he tapped it with his toe. 'Look at this,' he said to Joyce, stooping at the black water's edge to pick up a piece of soft white rock. He crumbled it between his fingers. 'It's a piece of tufa – a form of limestone. Quite rare.'

'That's very interesting,' she told him. He looked and sounded as if his ghosts had fled at last. He was clearer, stronger. 'But just now we have more pressing things on our mind.'

'Do you remember that old shooting hide here on Swinsty Edge?' On the way back to Burnside, Edgar leaned forward to tap Bill on the shoulder.

'Which one? I can think of at least three.'

'The one you can see from the road, not far from here. It gives a bit of shelter if you're caught out by a sudden storm.'

'I know the one.' Bill recalled that this was where Edgar had been heading out from when he and his father had spotted him and brought him home. He recognized that Edgar shared a fugitive's instincts with Frank but said nothing to Joyce and Grace.

'Shall we take a look there before the light goes?' Edgar pushed harder for them to take up his suggestion.

'Yes – it's worth a try,' Bill agreed.

Joyce sat quietly beside Edgar, gazing out at the hillsides and mistaking every shadow cast by a hawthorn tree, every humped rock for the missing Frank. Grace was in the front passenger seat, doing the same.

The car swooped into a dip then climbed a hill. The road sign told them that it had a gradient of one in four. They crested it and came to a wide open view of the grouse-shooting moor where the round hides stood – rolling rises and dips unbroken by walls or trees. Bill parked by the stile that gave access to the moor and the four of them climbed it and set off through the snow.

They found straight away that the ice-encrusted surface didn't bear their weight and they sank almost to their knees in soft, wet snow. It made for hard going and there was a fair distance to cover before they came to the hide that Edgar had described.

'Are we going to get there before dark?' Joyce was on the point of turning back, but Edgar urged her on.

'It's not that far. And look, there are footprints.' He pointed to a single, meandering track that led to the hide.

Grace saw that the prints were blurred by a light covering of snow. 'Made before the last snowfall – when was that?'

'Yesterday morning.' Studying the prints, Bill

was worried that they led up towards the hide but didn't come back down. If these turned out to be Frank's, he pictured him taking refuge in the hide then setting out again onto the wild moor top where there would be no sign of habitation for miles on end.

They walked on with their hearts in their mouths, breathing hard and sometimes staggering or slipping as they made their laborious way up the steep hill. The blackened stones of the roofless, circular hide stood out bleakly against the white slope and as they walked higher, the wind buffeted them more strongly. They leaned into it until they came to the low, crudely built structure.

The entrance lay to the leeward side of the prevailing westerly. A feeble hawthorn tree had taken root in the thin soil, its twisted trunk and bare branches leaning with the wind, so Bill, who was the first to reach the hide, had to stoop under it to look inside. He stiffened then put up a warning hand.

Joyce and Edgar came to an uncertain halt but Grace joined him in the entrance. She peered into the circular hide, some four feet high and crumbling after years of neglect. Sheep had nibbled at the surrounding heather and dislodged some of the stones – the weather had done the rest.

Frank lay on his side, curled like a child in the womb. His jacket was stiffened by frost, his bony wrists and bare hands exposed. There was no movement, no breath. His eyes stared into nothingness.

Grace slid past Bill then crouched beside the body. She felt the urge to take off her coat and cover Frank

CHAPTER TWENTY-FOUR

Jim Aldridge was in no hurry. Taking a pair of reading glasses from his pocket, he shuffled paperwork on his desk while Brenda and Una stood in the doorway to his office.

It was a large, bare room furnished with tall, military-style filing cabinets and shelving, with brown lino on the floor, walls painted khaki green and with dark-green roller blinds that were seldom raised to reveal a view of the front drive and the sentry box beyond. The electric light suspended from an elaborate ceiling rose had no light shade, adding to the functional feel.

'I'm sorry to keep you waiting, girls. I've been busy liaising with the guys at Beckwith Camp, ready for tomorrow's take over. If I don't put these lists into the correct files, it'll be mayhem.'

Brenda took shallow, uneven breaths, trying to frame her first sentence once she was given the opportunity to speak. 'I'm sorry I have to break this to you . . .' or 'I'm sorry to bring bad news, but . . .' *No – saying sorry is a bad start. It sets me off on the wrong foot.* 'I've come to make a complaint . . .' *No, not strong enough.* 'I have a serious complaint against Flight Lieutenant Mackenzie.' *Or, better*: 'A very serious complaint . . .'

Una glanced at her with a reassuring smile, unaware that John Mackenzie was hovering in the corridor behind them.

Aldridge was about to pin one of his lists to the noticeboard behind his desk when he looked up and saw him. 'Yes, Mac – what is it?'

Brenda's stomach lurched and every word of her prepared speech fled.

Mac came up behind her until he was so close that she could feel his breath on the back of her neck. 'A request from the kitchen, sir. They want permission to order extra bully beef, potatoes, baked beans et cetera to feed the new arrivals on the twenty-seventh.'

'Come in, Mac – I didn't get all of that.' Aldridge smiled apologetically at Brenda as Mac pushed past her. 'Write it down here so I don't forget.'

Mac had made sure to brush against Brenda. She recoiled from the feel of his hand on her hip. Now she shuddered as she watched him reach over the desk to take the piece of paper that Aldridge slid towards him – broad shoulders, strong, stocky build like a middleweight boxer's.

The squadron leader's genial manner continued. 'Ladies, I hope Mac thanked you properly for inviting us to your Christmas show. It was much appreciated, I'm sure.'

Mac finished writing, put the kitchen's request on a spike then turned to face the visitors with his top lip curled into a sneer that Aldridge couldn't observe. 'I sure did. I stayed behind specially to say my thank-you to Brenda.'

The gorge rose in her throat and she felt the situation slip from her control. Una too was so taken aback that she couldn't speak.

'That's great. We'll have to return the favour,' Aldridge said. 'Next time we put on a dance here at the base we'll make sure to invite the Land Army.'

Mackenzie looked cock-a-hoop as he walked to the door. 'I'll see you then, girls,' he promised. 'I can promise you a four-piece band playing all your favourite songs.'

The door closed behind him. Aldridge finished shuffling papers then gestured towards two canvas chairs. 'OK, come right in and sit down.'

Brenda sank into the chair, her face pale and drained. Una sat beside her.

'Now – to what do I owe the pleasure?'

Mac's interruption, together with Aldridge's affable style, rendered Brenda speechless and she cast a desperate look at Una for her to begin.

'This will come out of the blue, I'm sure.' Una's voice was soft but her head was up and she didn't sound apologetic. 'But something happened last night that you ought to know about.'

Aldridge took a guess. 'Uh-oh, don't tell me – one of my men got a little over enthusiastic. What did he do – climb up onstage and join in?'

Una shook her head. 'Worse than that, I'm afraid.'

'Was he drunk? Did he get out of hand?'

'No. No one interrupted the show. It was afterwards.' She paused and turned to Brenda.

'Afterwards, when I was getting changed.' Her throat was dry and her tongue stuck to the roof of her mouth. But Una had begun and now she felt able to go on. 'Flight Lieutenant Mackenzie came into the changing room.'

'Yes, to thank you – he said.' Aldridge placed both hands flat on his desk and leaned forward, as if realizing that there was worse to come. The overhead light cast shadows across his clean-cut, handsome face.

'No, that was a lie.' Brenda's voice grew stronger. Whatever it cost in dignity, she would get it out. 'He wouldn't go away, even when I told him to. He came up to me and . . .' She faltered then steeled herself to go on. 'Then he tried to kiss me and I slapped him. I couldn't make him stop.'

Aldridge nodded slowly, looking for a way to phrase things delicately. 'Maybe he thought . . . I mean – maybe he misunderstood?'

'No.' She looked directly at him. 'I told him to his face – go away, get out. He ignored me.'

'So he overstepped the mark.' Something in Aldridge's tone suggested that he wasn't surprised but that he would still do his best to play this down. His hands remained flat on the desk as a way of holding steady and following an official line. 'Things may have got a little out of hand, but that happens sometimes. It usually turns out to be nothing.'

'Brenda had to slap him and use her knee against him but then he pushed her onto the floor.' Una leaned towards him. 'I don't call what Flight Lieutenant Mackenzie did to Brenda nothing.'

Aldridge closed his eyes for a moment then

opened them again. 'But he was just here. He came in, cheerful as you like, said hi to both of you – everything completely normal.'

'To throw you off the scent.' Una spoke vehemently. 'He did that on purpose – don't you see?'

Brenda breathed in deeply then stood up to gather every ounce of will-power and speak evenly. 'What Mac did to me was as bad as it gets – him using all his strength to make me do what he wanted me to do. I could make it easy or hard, he didn't care – that's what he said. He treated me like dirt.'

The squadron leader knew with chilling certainty that what she said was true. He'd never felt at ease when he observed his second in command's behaviour around women – had even pulled him up over it occasionally. But he'd turned a blind eye and now the consequences were staring him in the face.

Una gave Brenda a small smile of encouragement.

'And it's not the first time he's done it,' Brenda went on. 'We – that is, Una, Kathleen, Joyce and Grace – have put our heads together and come to the conclusion that he did the same to another Land Girl called Eunice Mason.'

Aldridge's self-control suddenly snapped. His face changed again as he jumped up and strode to the door. 'Wait here,' he told them before he yelled down the corridor. 'Someone, get Mac for me.'

There was a flurry of activity – hurried footsteps, doors opening and closing, voices calling. Within seconds Mackenzie had reappeared. 'Come in and close the door,' Aldridge ordered.

He closed it warily then waited.

Aldridge struggled to control his temper. 'Mac, does the name Eunice Mason mean anything to you? Did you meet her in the pub maybe, or take her to the movies?'

Mac shook his head as if puzzled then slid his eyes angrily towards Brenda.

'Is that a no? I put it to you again, Mac – and take care what you say because if you deny it then I go to the girl and she gives me a different story, you could be in deep trouble.'

'Oh no.' Startled, Una tried to step between them. 'You can't do that.'

'Why not?' Exasperated, Aldridge turned to her.

Suddenly Brenda was the calmest one in the room. She went to within a foot of Mac and looked him in the eye. 'Because Eunice is dead. She was expecting your baby, Mac. You got her pregnant then you dropped her like a ton of bricks. So she killed herself.'

The accusation made him reel backwards against the door. Brenda felt herself pushed to one side and saw Aldridge launch himself and pin Mac back with his forearm. He shoved his head backwards. Brenda and Una heard the thud of bone against wood. 'True or false?' he spat.

With spittle dribbling from the corner of his mouth, Mac thrust him off then straightened his collar. 'So what if it's true?'

'So you forced yourself on two girls – that's what!' Disgust ran through the squadron leader's whole body at Mac the sweet talker and dapper dresser, drinking companion and man about town. 'One's dead because of it.'

Mackenzie wiped his mouth and fought his corner to the last. 'Says who? Says one crazy Land Girl!'

'Not just one,' Una jumped in. 'Kathleen is willing to be Brenda's witness.'

Aldridge shook his head and groaned. Giving up on forcing Mac to admit his guilt, he picked up the telephone and dialled a number to ask for two armed guards who were there within seconds, ready to escort the culprit from the room. Then he sat Una and Brenda back in their chairs.

While Brenda came to terms with the last violent, bitter look that Mac had thrown at her before he was marched away, Una was the first to break the deep, uneasy silence. 'What will happen to him?'

Aldridge sounded weary. 'We'll draw up charges. Flight Lieutenant Mackenzie will have to face a military court. We don't like to lose trained pilots so I can't say for sure that he'll be drummed out of the force even if he's found guilty. I do know he'll be stripped of his rank, though.'

'But he won't stay on here at Penny Lane?' Brenda asked. The surrounding silence weighed heavily on them all. The blinds cast a subdued, green-tinged gloom over their skin.

'No. You'll be asked to give evidence but after that you won't see him again.' It was time for Aldridge to escort them from his office, down the corridor to the main entrance with its red and green stained-glass door. He said nothing more but his face was full of regret as he shook each of them by the hand.

Brenda and Una felt numb as they walked down

the drive. 'Well done – you did it,' Una murmured while the sentry raised the barrier.

'*We* did it,' Brenda corrected her. 'I'm pleased for Eunice's sake that the truth will come out.'

'And I'm pleased for Frank that he won't get the blame.'

Brenda sat astride her bike and stared down the straight road as she waited for Una to mount the pillion seat. The sentry glanced curiously at them from his box. 'Shall we go and give Joyce and Grace the good news?'

They'd fought hard to set in motion justice for Eunice – a good reason to feel satisfied. 'Yes, what are we waiting for?'

The reality of Frank's lonely death wove a cocoon of silence that wasn't broken until Bill and Grace dropped off Joyce and Edgar in the pub yard. During the drive back from Swinsty Edge, they'd each been lost in their own thoughts.

Bill had been working out the practicalities of how to get an ambulance out there to collect the body this late on Christmas Eve. He'd decided to ask Edgar to phone the hospital while he and Grace drove to Home Farm to inform Emily and Joe – that was, as long as Grace was prepared to go with him. It would be better to have her there to break the news as gently as possible. Meanwhile, Edgar had put himself in Frank's position, imagining his final few days of cold wandering, cast out by his father and utterly alone. And why? Because Frank Kellett hadn't fitted in – that was why. Because he'd been a misfit all his life, misunderstood and living in a silent world that he'd never made sense of. *Poor bastard*, Edgar thought over and over. *Poor, bloody bastard.*

If only we'd got to him sooner. Joyce's regrets centred on the fact that they'd left it too late to form their search party. The build-up to Christmas had got in the way – rehearsals for the show, especially. And besides, everyone feared Frank's strangeness and had shied away from him. *I was looking out for Una instead of him – we all were.* She stared out of the car window at the darkening hillsides and saw only her own reflection and Edgar's beside her. His hand closed over hers where it rested on the seat and she left it there.

Grace had stared straight ahead as the car headlights carved a way through the darkness. She would never forget the sight of Frank's emaciated body lying on its side in the snow, curled tight as if to conserve the last, fleeting warmth of his body before ice had entered his veins. She prayed that he hadn't been aware, that death had crept over him like sleep and he'd drifted away without fear, clutching the few fond memories that his harsh life had offered – instances of his mother's dogged, determined care for her broken boy, or perhaps a fleeting picture of Una's lively, laughing eyes.

She said yes right away to Bill's request to drive out to the Kelletts' farm and they left Joyce and Edgar outside the Blacksmith's Arms and drove straight there. Theirs was the only car on the road. The clear sky was studded with a million stars. When

421

they turned into the lane, Joe saw the headlights and came to his door.

Grace got out of the car and walked towards him.

He knew the truth the moment he saw her face in the light from the oil lamp hanging in the porch. 'Emily, you'd better come.'

Frank's mother knew it too without being told. No one visited after dark unless it was an emergency. Besides, she'd been dreading this for days. She came from the kitchen into the porch, carrying a cup and a tea towel, only waiting for Grace to say the words.

'Emily, Joe – I'm very sorry.'

Joe's eyes flickered with a sorrow that quickly faded. 'Where did you find him?'

'Up on Swinsty – in one of the hides. He'd been there a while.'

'*Who* found him?' Emily took in the news without flinching. The waiting and wondering was over. Now she could get on and grieve.

'I did.' Gently Grace steered her indoors and sat her down, prepared herself to answer the questions that never came.

'They'll take him to the hospital morgue,' Bill told Joe, who stayed out in the cold. 'You'll be able to go and see him if you like.'

'It makes no difference to Frank whether we do or we don't.' He jerked his head towards the house. 'She'll want to, though.'

'I am sorry.' Bill shook his head helplessly.

'Aye.' Joe walked away, across the yard into the empty dairy. He sat alone with his thoughts until he heard Bill and Grace drive off.

'Is there anything I can do?' Grace asked Emily, who had put down the cup and silently twisted and wrung the tea towel between her hands. 'Can I fetch someone to stay with you?'

'No.'

'Would you like *me* to stay?'

'No – thank you.' She'd battled for Frank. She'd fed him and clothed him, sent him to school, stood up for him all his life. She'd loved him. 'You get off back to the pub,' she told Grace as she untwisted the cloth then folded it neatly. 'It's Christmas Eve – your father will be run off his feet.'

Joyce and Edgar stood at the forge door after Bill and Grace had driven away. Neither had felt like going into the pub, where a steady flow of early-evening drinkers came and went. They'd preferred to talk.

'Benghazi is under Allied control but it seems likely that Hong Kong will go to the Japs.' Edgar had started to keep up with the news again. The war that he'd crashed out of in his burning plane still raged on – battleships had been sunk in the South China seas, Hitler had made himself Supreme Commander in Chief of the German army.

Joyce had been in no hurry to leave but she'd wanted to steer him away from bombing and killing into calmer, clearer waters. 'What have you got lined up for tomorrow – will you be sitting around the table for the usual Christmas fare?'

'I don't know. I leave that to Grace.'

'Have you bought her a present?'

'Yes. I caught the bus into Northgate and bought her a box of watercolour paints and a new sketch pad.'

'She'll like that.'

'How about you?'

'It's turkey and all the trimmings at the hostel for me and the girls, courtesy of Ma C, as Brenda calls her. She's been saving up coupons for weeks.'

'You could come down here afterwards and have tea,' Edgar had suggested. He'd realized he wanted to see her again, to hear more of her rich, mellifluous voice. 'If you'd like to, that is.'

'Just me? Or does that include Una and Brenda as well?'

'All of you – the more the merrier.' *But especially you in the same room as me, sitting by the fire – me listening, you talking.*

'I would like to,' she'd agreed. 'I'll bring a pack of cards. We can all gather round your kitchen table and play a game of rummy.'

It was settled by the time Bill drove Grace back home. Edgar and Joyce had said goodbye. He'd gone into the house and Joyce had walked down to Bill's house to fetch her bike.

Bill got out of the car in the pub yard then opened Grace's door for her. He held out his hand and she took it. 'You've had a rough day. Are you sure you're all right?'

'I feel for Emily, but otherwise, yes.' Sad and exhausted, with a sharp, unaccustomed awareness that life wasn't always fair after all, Grace felt as if she'd lost her bearings.

424

'I'll stay with you a while,' he said quietly and they went hand in hand towards the field behind the forge. They leaned on the stile and looked out across an expanse of white snow criss-crossed by animal tracks.

'It's getting late. You should go home to your mother.' She remembered the times that they'd walked across this field together – in spring, when the emerald grass was studded with gold, purple and white meadow flowers, or in high summer when brilliant red poppies sang out amongst feathery swathes of hay-ripe grass. Their petals dropped the moment you brushed past them. Blackthorn blossom in the hedges marked the day when Bill had first asked her to walk out with him – the melting look of a young puppy in his brown eyes. Daisies for the times when they'd crowned their love with kisses, wild roses at the edge of the woods when he'd proposed. Now it was stars sparkling in the night sky.

Bill gazed out across the empty field. 'I'd rather stay here,' he insisted. 'I want to stand beside you for ever and never leave.'

Grace turned her head to look at him. He was calm and quiet and her heart stopped then skipped and skittered unevenly.

Staring straight ahead, hands clasped on the top bar of the stile, he went on. 'I'll say how I feel in case I never get another chance. You know me, Grace, better than anyone. You can see what the future looks like for me – all nicely mapped out to take Dad's place in the firm. It'll be comfortable, but never exciting – I'll go to work and play my sports, with no danger of being called up because the tractors are part of the war effort. There'll be no heroics.'

His skin was smooth in the moonlight, his hair almost black, with a lock falling forward over his forehead. She felt him weave a cloak of soft words around her.

'I'm not one for big, romantic gestures – you know that.'

She smiled in recognition. 'Neither am I. We both shy away from that.'

'But you mean the world to me, Grace, and I want us to get back to where we were – before all the silly misunderstandings with Brenda.'

'They happened. I don't think we can pretend they didn't.' Her forehead creased into a thoughtful frown. 'Brenda got the wrong end of the stick – I realized that from the start. But I felt my hands were well and truly tied.'

'That's you and me all over – both giving other people's opinions too much weight. What with me bowing to family pressures and you sticking by what we'd agreed, we got ourselves into a right mess.'

She nodded in agreement. 'Poor Brenda didn't know where to put herself when she found out.'

'I let it go too far – I should have owned up earlier.' He remembered his brief fascination for the girl on the motor bike, riding into Burnside like a breath of fresh air.

Grace picked up his train of thought, recalled the kiss then scraped up the courage to tackle it head on one last time. 'You liked her, though?'

'In a way, yes. But liking is different to loving – it didn't scratch the surface compared with my feelings for you.' He looked down at his clasped hands then turned to face her. 'I was a fool. I hurt you and I'm sorry.'

'Brenda's hard to say no to,' she acknowledged. 'She and I are chalk and cheese. So are the other girls at Fieldhead – all completely different. But when it comes down to it, we have a lot in common. We work and play together and we stand up for each other through thick and thin.'

'I know you do – Herr Hitler had better watch out.' Bill smiled at her earnestness. 'And since we're down to brass tacks, the business between me and Shirley Foster never got beyond Mum's fertile imagination.'

'So I was jealous over nothing.'

'Were you – jealous?'

'A little bit. I was over Brenda, too.' She blushed to remember it. 'Bill, we've grown up together here in the same village and yet sometimes I feel as if we don't really know each other.' With the hum of noise from the pub in the background, she looked out across the field. 'We should have talked more honestly and been more open.'

'That's what we're doing now.' His voice was slow and tender. 'I've watched you this afternoon. I've seen how you were with Emily, and before that, how you acted when we found poor Frank. No one could have done more. You were the caring, gentle Grace that I know – the Grace that I love.'

She felt her lips tremble and her eyes fill with tears. 'Life's not fair. Frank shouldn't have been allowed to die like that. Edgar shouldn't have been shot out of the sky in that plane.'

'It's the war.' Bill put his arms around her and held her close. He felt her lean into him, her head on his shoulder. 'And no, life isn't fair but we have to make the best of it. And that means that you and I should be together. We should get married.'

Grace nodded. 'We should,' she agreed with a quiet, slow smile. Together she and Bill would step out into the world.

CHAPTER TWENTY-FIVE

'Have you seen Saturday's rota?' Joyce laid a run of hearts onto Grace's kitchen table. She, Brenda and Una had spent a jolly Christmas morning at Fieldhead, exchanging presents before tucking into a slap-up dinner of turkey and roast spuds, courtesy of Mrs C who had worked wonders with their meagre ration allowances. The hostel table had groaned under the weight. Rosy Land Girl faces had been wreathed in smiles and absent loved ones remembered with fond sighs.

'What about the rota?' Una asked now.

'All four of us are down for ditch digging at Henry Rowson's.'

'What a treat!' Brenda took a card from the deck. 'Blow me – Queen of Clubs,' she grumbled before discarding it again.

'Yes – it *is* a treat,' Grace insisted. 'You, Joyce, Una and I will be the four musketeers, one for all, all for one!'

Bill stood with his back to the window, blocking what little light there was. 'It's a long way to cycle – all the way out to Kelsey Crag. I can gift you a lift.'

'Ooh, ta, Bill – we'll take you up on that,' Brenda said with a grin. 'But it'll be a squash in your little Austin 7. Una, you might have to sit on my knee.'

It was Una's turn to take a card. She made a set of three aces and laid them down. Christmas morning had been hard for her, knowing that Angelo was still tantalizingly close yet she was helpless to do anything about it. She'd kept his carved box in her pocket and taken out the picture of him and his sister and the piece of paper showing his home address. How long would it be before the war was over, she'd wondered – six months or a year perhaps? Though, truth be told, the Allies were having a hard tussle against the Japanese and Mr Churchill had warned on the wireless that the fight for victory might be long and hard. Two years at the most, then. In the meantime, she would wait each day for letters from Scotland and hang on every word that Angelo wrote.

'Edgar, it's your turn.' Joyce jogged him with her elbow.

He laid off a seven and an eight of hearts on her run of three. She was here, in the warm, cosy kitchen with a fire ablaze in the hearth and the daylight fading. He smiled at her and she smiled back.

'Bill, why don't you join in the next game?' Grace asked. His proposal of the night before lay warm around her heart. Later today, after the card game had finished, they planned to walk down the street and announce their engagement to his mother then they would all drive to the hospital and tell his father. Her cheeks glowed and her grey eyes gleamed with happiness.

Bill looked at the circle of faces around the table. Edgar had come downstairs at the last minute and drawn up his chair next to Joyce's. No one had said anything but all had been glad to see him – Grace especially because it meant that he was slowly but surely getting back to his old self. Joyce had willingly made room for him. Bill wondered idly if she and Edgar would eventually begin a romance. They would make a handsome couple and she would be good for him, he thought. But then there was the small matter of Edgar returning to his squadron to rejoin the war effort to consider, so best not to bank on anything until after the war.

'Bill?' Grace moved her chair to offer him a space.

'Yes, Bill – come and sit down,' Brenda cajoled. 'You're blocking our light.'

All was easy and relaxed in the homely room.

As Bill moved away from the window, Una saw something outside that made her throw down her hand of cards and jump up from the table. Before the others knew it, she'd run into the yard without her coat.

Brenda was the first to follow, in time to see a slow-moving green lorry pull into the pub yard. It was crammed to the gunnels with prisoners from Beckwith Camp, all scrambling over each other to see out of the back. 'Grace, Joyce – come and say goodbye to our Italians!' she called over her shoulder.

Una's heart was in her mouth as she ran towards the lorry. Angelo must be there, she must see him one last time. Faces smiled down at her, voices laughed and hands reached for her, fingers splayed.

'*Arrivederci! Addio!*'

She searched for his face – the only one that mattered.

'Una!' He called her name as Lorenzo shoved him forward and the others made way.

Her heart stopped. She stood on tiptoe and their fingers touched. The wind blew her dark hair across her cheeks and made the hem of her red dress flutter.

He clasped her warm hand, mouthing words that she didn't need to understand to know that he loved her.

'Write to me as soon as you get there,' she whispered back.

'Take!' he said as he slipped something into her hand.

The lorry driver revved his engine. It was Albert and he'd recognized the girl in red from when she'd been working on the potato clamps at Brigg Farm – in fact, who could forget that auburn hair and those big brown eyes? He'd heard Lorenzo shout for him to stop. *Why not?* he'd thought. *What difference will a couple of minutes make?* But he couldn't hold up for too long, or else his sergeant would have a go at him. *Greenock, here we come!*

'I write,' Angelo promised. The lorry eased away but Una kept pace with it. 'Every day, I write.'

'I love you,' she whispered.

Twenty faces smiled and cheered. The POWs waved as the lorry picked up speed.

'*Ti amo, mia cara.*'

It drove away and Brenda, Joyce and Grace came to stand beside Una. They watched Angelo wave one last time as the lorry passed the chapel then disappeared round the bend.

All was silent in the gathering dusk.

'You'll see him again, I bet my life on it,' Brenda murmured.

'I know.' Una's heart beat strong and steadily because Angelo loved her. She opened her hand to see his last gift to her – his precious gold cross and a chain that linked them with an unbreakable promise. She raised it to her lips and kissed it, vowing to carry his love with her until the guns fell silent and the last bomb dropped on the war-torn earth.

Barbara Holmes in her Women's Land Army uniform.

AUTHOR'S NOTE

My mother, Barbara Holmes, joined the Women's Land Army in 1943, aged 19.

I have two black-and-white photographs of her in uniform that were taken in the back garden of her family home in Beckwithshaw village just outside Harrogate, North Yorkshire. In one she stands bare-headed in shirt and tie, knitted sweater, corduroy breeches, long socks and brogues. The other shows her in a short, belted coat and felt hat, complete with Land Army badge. They capture her in character-istic stance – her head tilting shyly forward, but smiling proudly.

Like Grace in the novel, she continued to live at home to help her father run the village pub, with her two older sisters Connie and Sybil, and twins Joan and Myra. Brother Walter was in the RAF and Ernest had joined the army.

Practical by nature and upbringing, she took to Land Army tasks with determination and gusto, working alongside old school friends for neighbour-ing farmers whom she'd known all her life; namely, the landowning Williams family who held an almost feudal status in the village (they owned the Smith's Arms and most of the houses, built the church, vicarage and village institute) and the Wintersgills' hen farm that was close to the now famous RHS Harlow Carr.

There was a certain glamour attached to being a Land Girl – at least to the image of it if not the reality, which meant ploughing, tractor driving, digging, weeding, trimming and labouring in all weathers. After working all day in the fields, Mum would cycle home to join her sisters behind the bar in the Smith's Arms. It was here that she met my father, Jim Lyne, home on leave from the Royal Navy in 1944. The story goes that Connie looked out to see him and his pals crossing the yard. 'Watch out, here comes the Navy!' she warned. Well, the Navy arrived in Mum's life and never left. There was a whirlwind courtship and an engagement soon after; a ruby and emerald ring and long separations while Dad served in the Mediterranean, only returning home on leave on rare occasions.

Meanwhile, disaster! Mum's precious ring was lost while working in the hen huts. She and her Land Girl pals were down on their knees in a frantic search through beds of straw. Triumph; the ring was found and safely restored to Mum's finger in time for Dad's next shore leave.

Like many women of the time, once the war ended, Mum settled into the more traditional roles of housewife and mother. She rarely looked back to her wartime service, except perhaps to mention that the uniform was hard wearing and well made, especially the coat, or that the life was hard but worthwhile. She never boasted about her contribution to the war effort or softened her experience with fond nostalgia. That was not her style.

But I found among her possessions after her death in 2008 a plain, somewhat scuffed cardboard box. I opened this little treasure carefully and folded back the tissue paper to reveal a small green and red enamelled badge, embellished with a wheat sheaf and a royal crown with three words that sang out Mum's unspoken pride. The badge read 'Women's Land Army'.

If you loved The Land Girls at Christmas *don't miss . . .*

The Telephone Girls

1936. George Street, West
Yorkshire, houses a gleaming,
brand-new telephone exchange
where a group of capable girls
works the complicated electrical
switchboards. Among them are
Cynthia, Norma and Millicent,
who relish the busy, efficient
atmosphere and the
independence and friendship
their jobs have given them.

But when Millicent connects a
telephone call for an old friend,
and listens in to the conversation – breaking one of the
telephonists' main rules – she, and then Norma and
Cynthia too, become caught up in a story of scandal,
corruption and murder.

Soon, the jobs of all three girls are on the line.

Norma's romance is in ruins.

And Millicent has entered a world of vice . . .

In tough times, the telephone girls will need to call on
their friends more than ever.

Available now . . .